HORSE TROUBLE

Kristin Varner

First Second
New York

First Second

Published by First Second
First Second is an imprint of Roaring Brook Press,
a division of Holtzbrinck Publishing Holdings Limited Partnership
120 Broadway, New York, NY 10271
firstsecondbooks.com
mackids.com

Library of Congress Control Number: 2021906631

Our books may be purchased in bulk for promotional, educational, or business use.
Please contact your local bookseller or the Macmillan Corporate and Premium Sales Department at (800) 221-7945 ext. 5442 or by email at MacmillanSpecialMarkets@macmillan.com.

FIRST EDITION

First edition, 2021
Edited by Robyn Chapman and Rachel Stark
Cover design by Kirk Benshoff
Interior book design by Kristin Varner and Molly Johanson
Equestrian consultant: Allison Wicks

The artwork for this book was sketched by hand using Staedtler non-photo blue pencils.
Final art was digitally inked and colored in Adobe Photoshop.

Printed in China by RR Donnelley Asia Printing Solutions Ltd., Dongguan City, Guangdong Province

ISBN 978-1-250-22588-7 (paperback)
10 9 8 7 6 5 4 3 2 1

ISBN 978-1-250-22587-0 (hardcover)
10 9 8 7 6 5 4 3 2 1

Don't miss your next favorite book from First Second! For the latest updates go to firstsecondnewsletter.com and sign up for our enewsletter.

BY ART WE LIVE

For Mom and Dad,
who lovingly supported all the horse years

Chapter 1
Saddle Slip

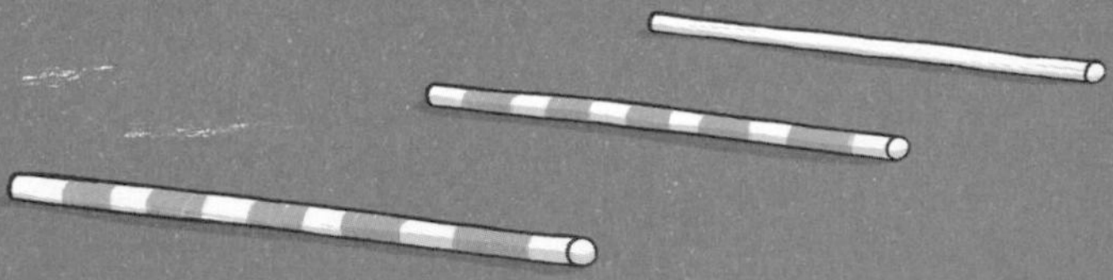

Ground Poles

A basic training tool to help build balance, focus, and coordination in both the horse and rider before jumping fences.

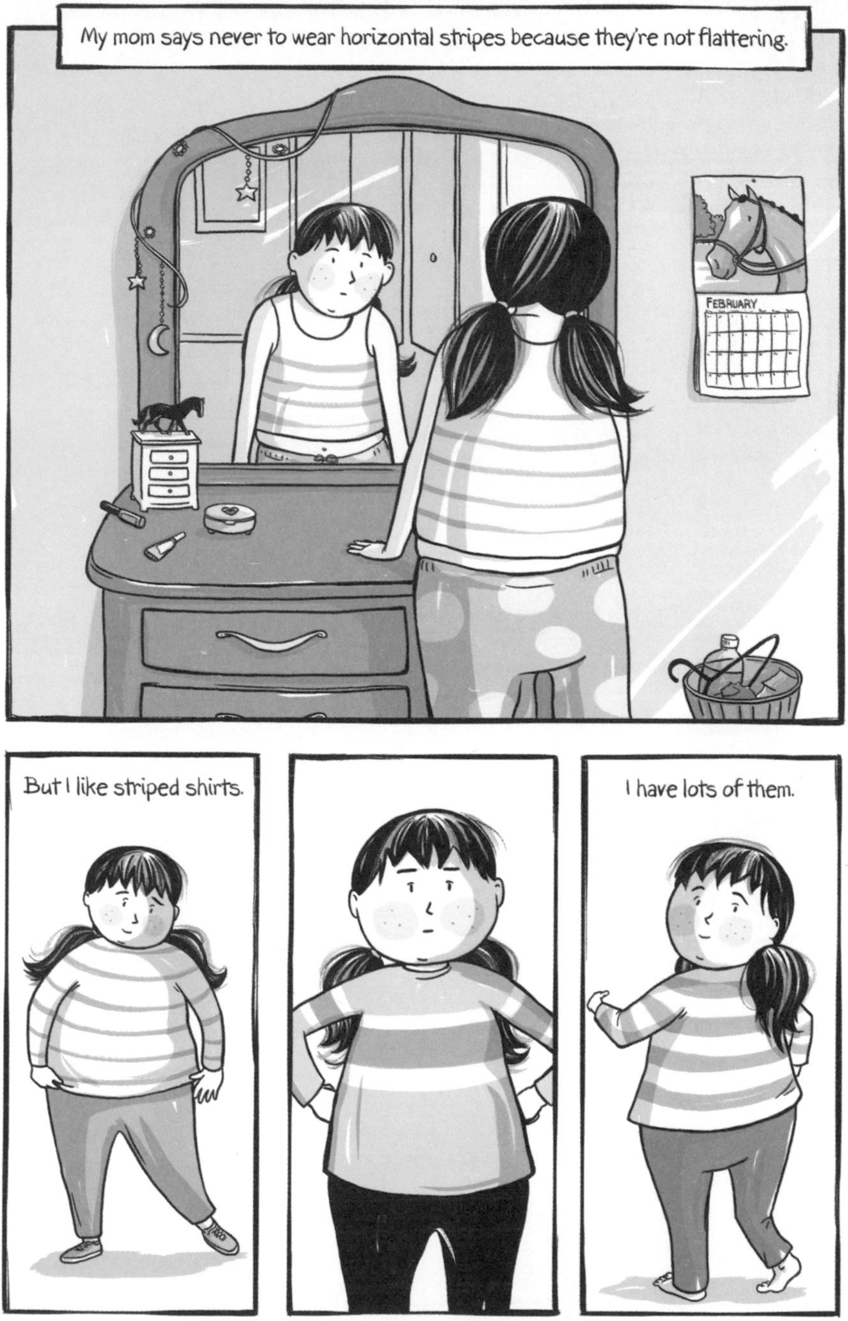
My mom says never to wear horizontal stripes because they're not flattering.
FEBRUARY
But I like striped shirts.
I have lots of them.

My mom means well, she just doesn't get it.
She wasn't chubby as a kid or at any point in her life.

I don't know when I started getting pudgy.

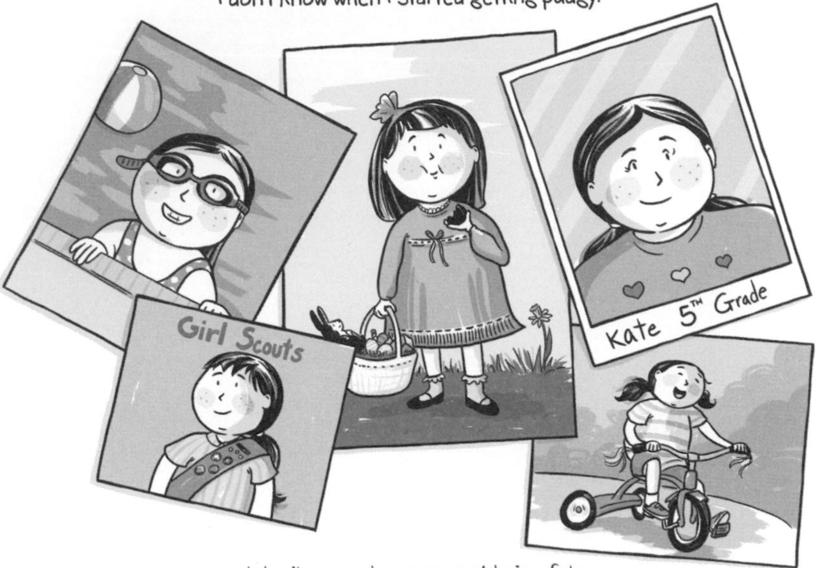
Girl Scouts
Kate 5TH Grade

I don't remember ever **not** being fat.

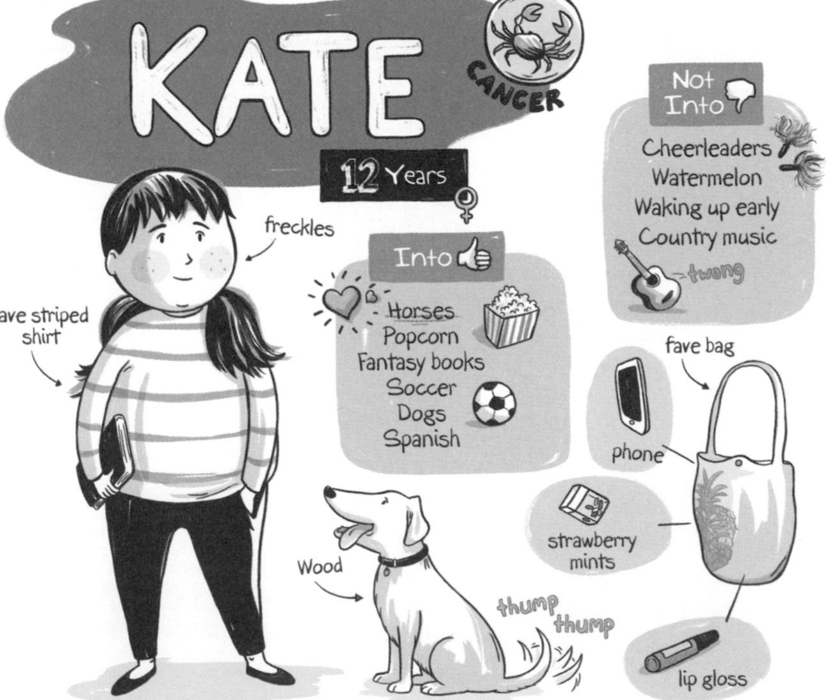
KATE
CANCER
12 Years
freckles
fave striped shirt
Into
~~Horses~~
Popcorn
Fantasy books
Soccer
Dogs
Spanish
Not Into
Cheerleaders
Watermelon
Waking up early
Country music
twang
fave bag
phone
strawberry mints
Wood
thump
thump
lip gloss

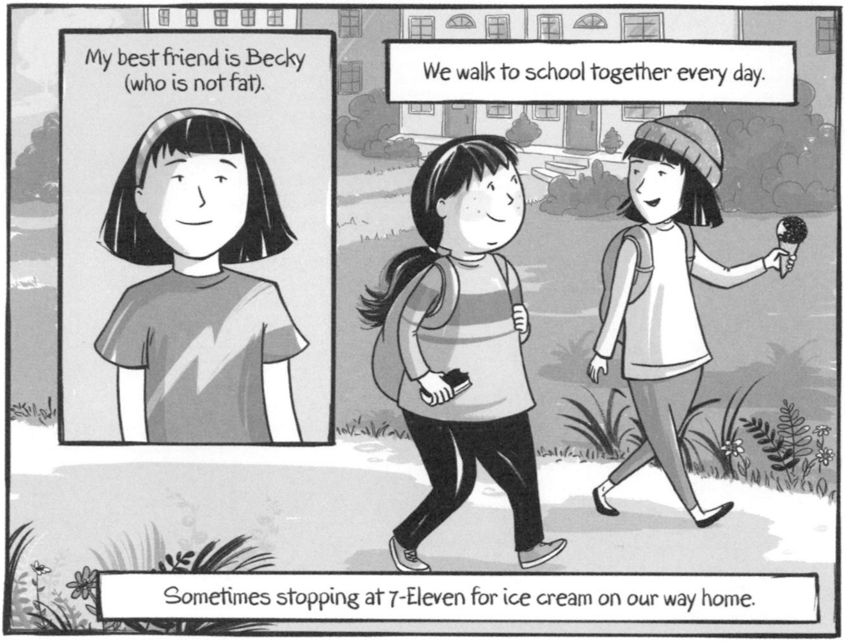
My best friend is Becky (who is not fat).
We walk to school together every day.
Sometimes stopping at 7-Eleven for ice cream on our way home.

Becky and I have been friends since preschool when the Lee family moved in up the street. Our families started hanging out, a lot.

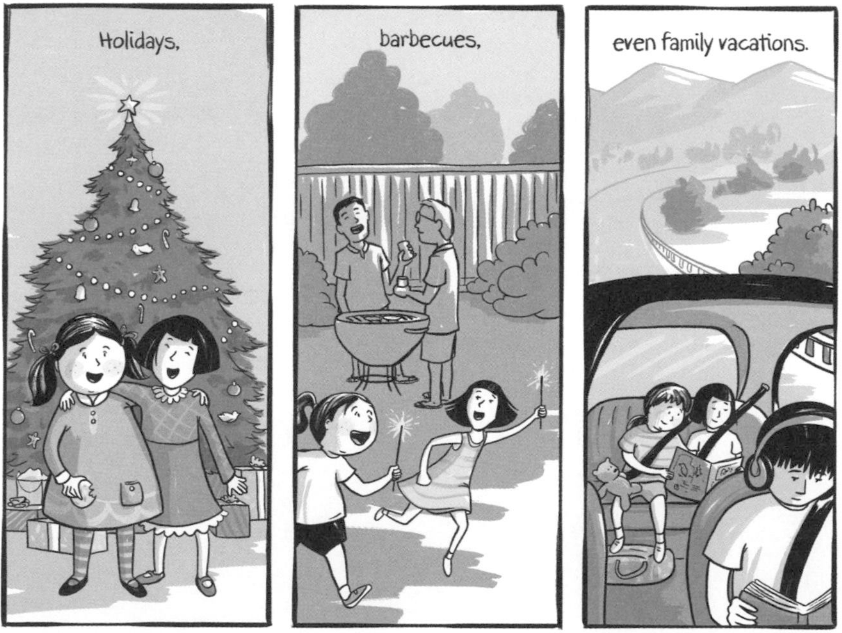
Holidays,
barbecues,
even family vacations.

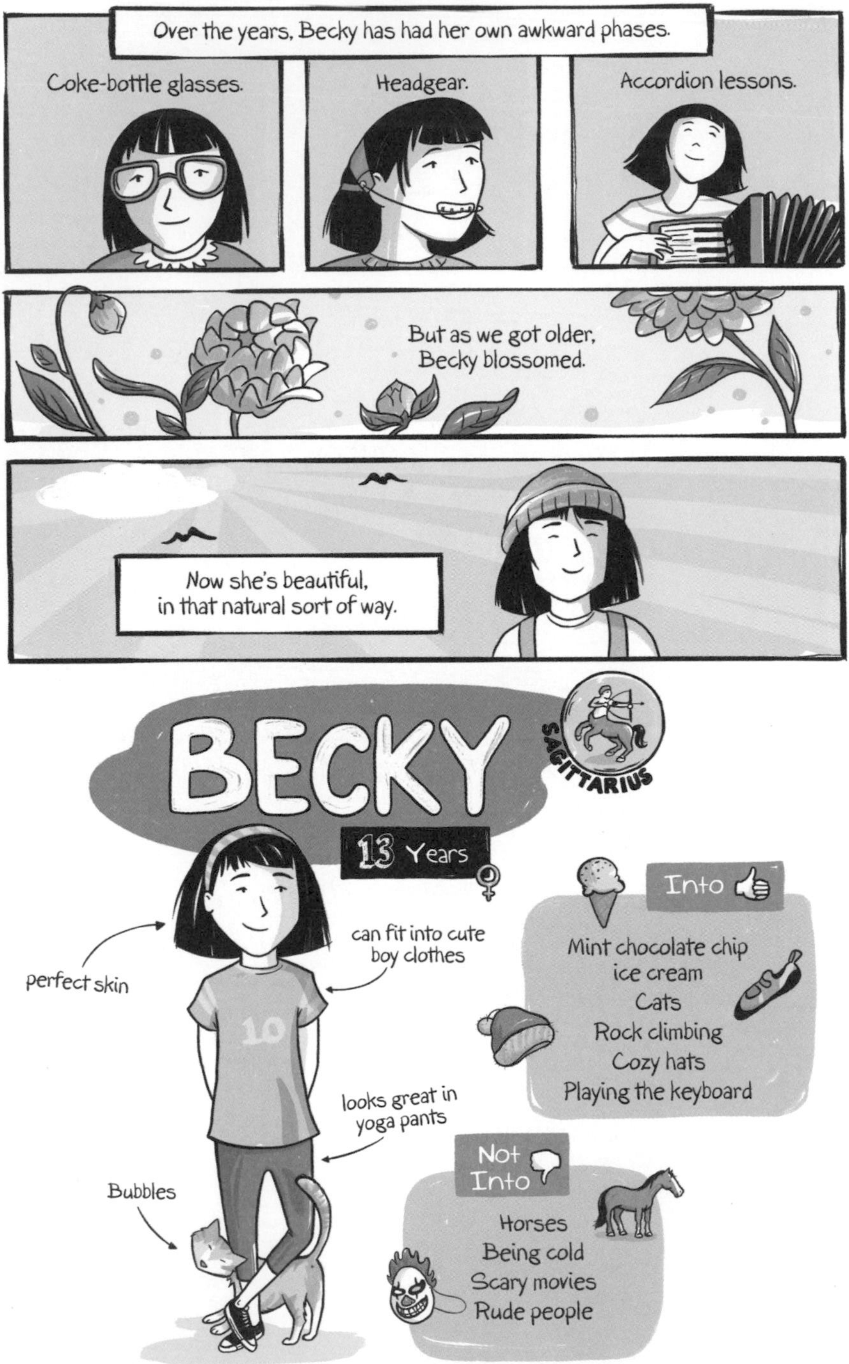
Over the years, Becky has had her own awkward phases.
Coke-bottle glasses.
Headgear.
Accordion lessons.
But as we got older, Becky blossomed.
Now she's beautiful, in that natural sort of way.
BECKY
SAGITTARIUS
13 Years
perfect skin
can fit into cute boy clothes
looks great in yoga pants
Bubbles
Into
Mint chocolate chip ice cream
Cats
Rock climbing
Cozy hats
Playing the keyboard
Not Into
Horses
Being cold
Scary movies
Rude people

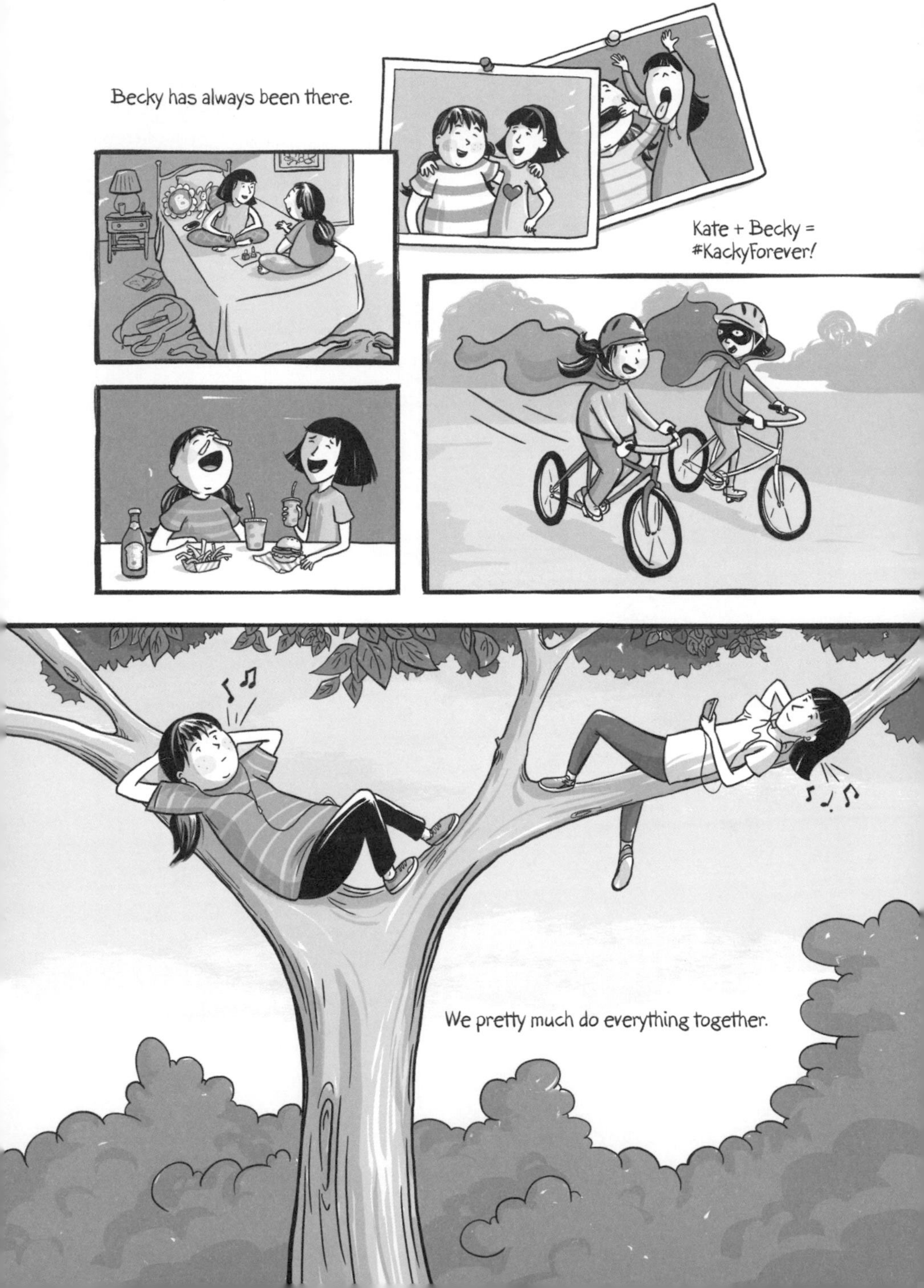

Becky has always been there.
Kate + Becky =
#KackyForever!
We pretty much do everything together.

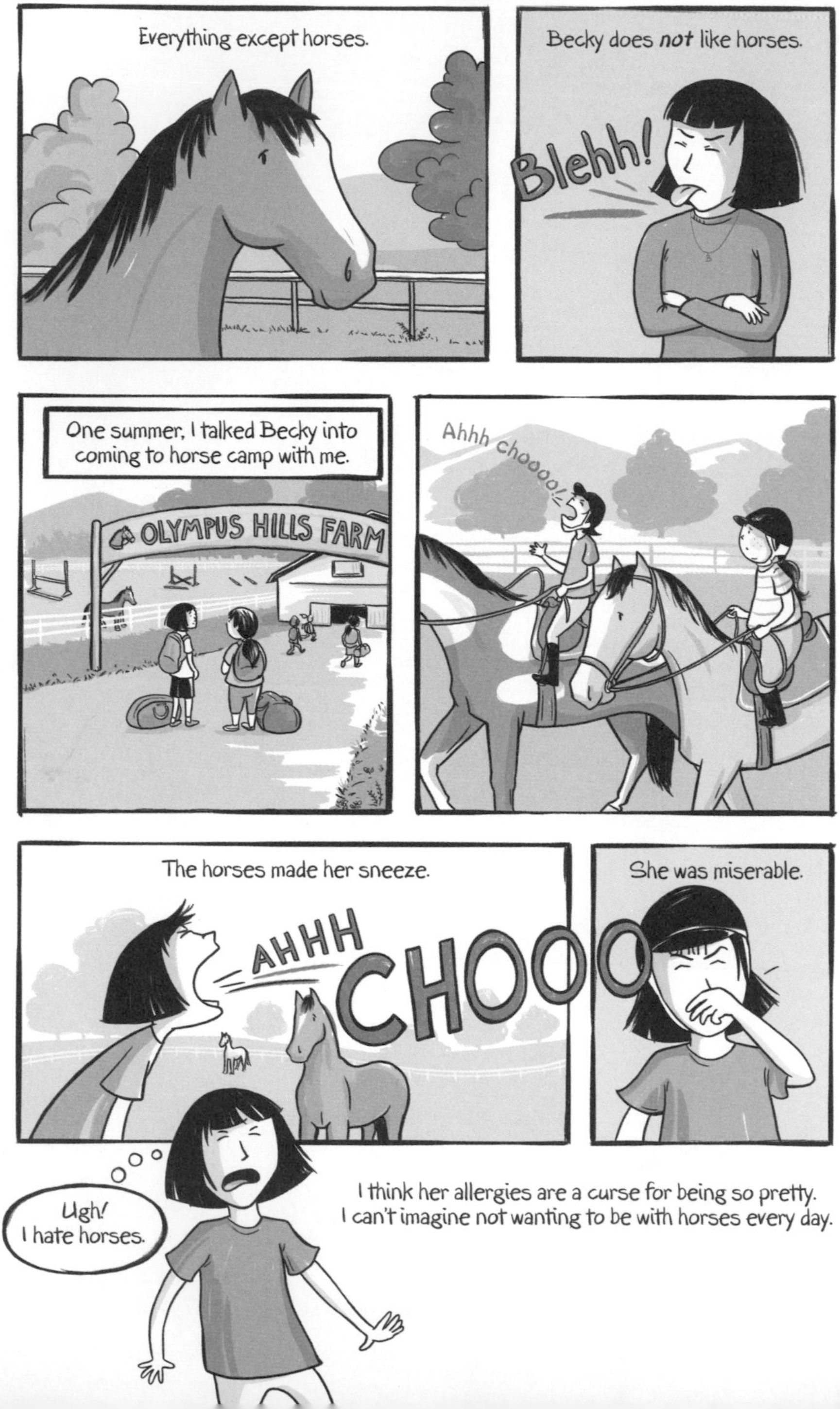
Everything except horses.
Becky does **not** like horses.
Blehh!
One summer, I talked Becky into coming to horse camp with me.
OLYMPUS HILLS FARM
Ahhh chooooo!
The horses made her sneeze.
AHHH CHOOOO
She was miserable.
Ugh! I hate horses.
I think her allergies are a curse for being so pretty.
I can't imagine not wanting to be with horses every day.

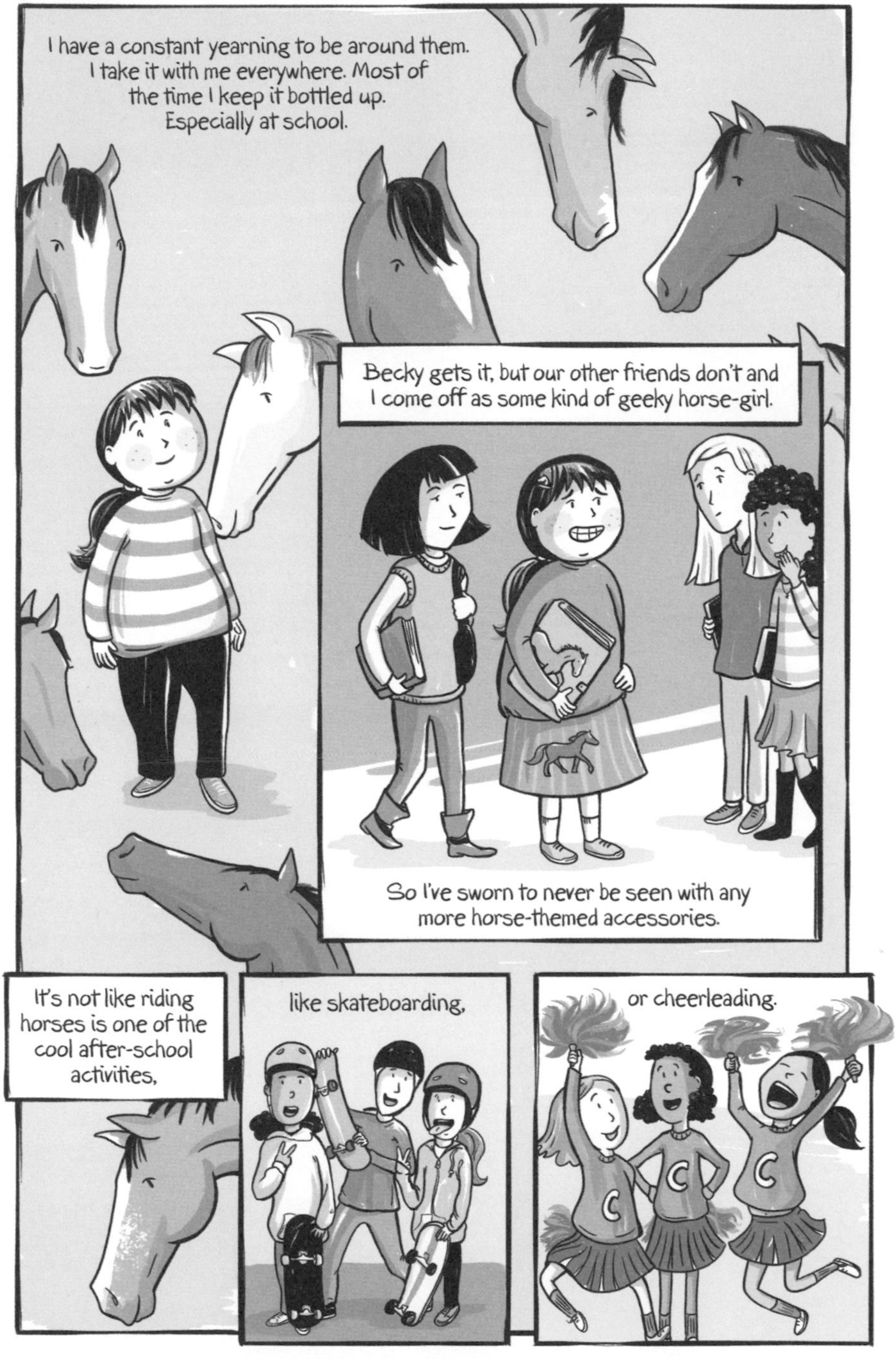
I have a constant yearning to be around them. I take it with me everywhere. Most of the time I keep it bottled up. Especially at school.
Becky gets it, but our other friends don't and I come off as some kind of geeky horse-girl.
So I've sworn to never be seen with any more horse-themed accessories.
It's not like riding horses is one of the cool after-school activities,
like skateboarding,
or cheerleading.

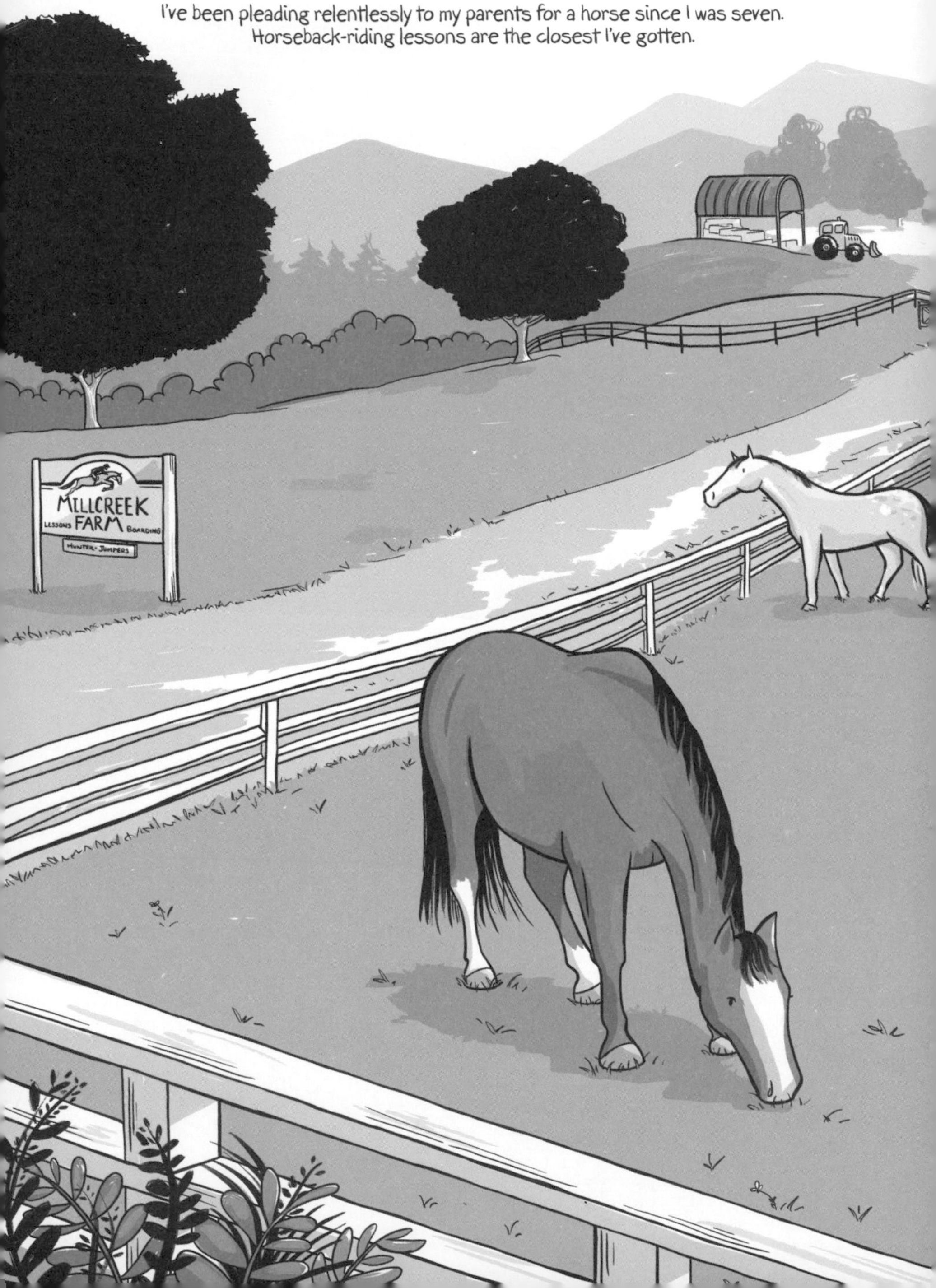
I've been pleading relentlessly to my parents for a horse since I was seven.
Horseback-riding lessons are the closest I've gotten.
MILLCREEK
LESSONS FARM BOARDING
HUNTER-JUMPERS

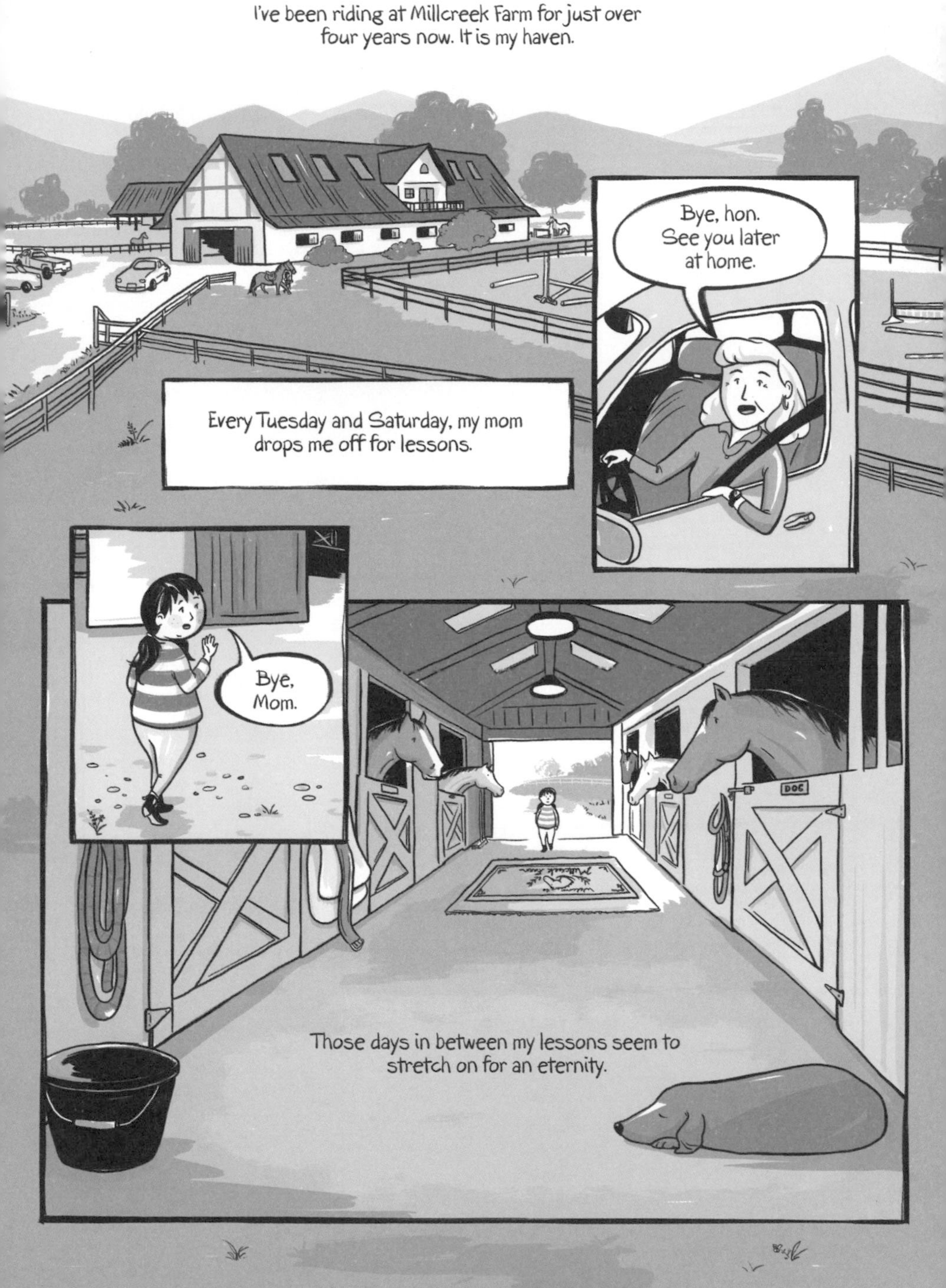
I've been riding at Millcreek Farm for just over four years now. It is my haven.
Bye, hon. See you later at home.
Every Tuesday and Saturday, my mom drops me off for lessons.
Bye, Mom.
DOC
Those days in between my lessons seem to stretch on for an eternity.

I clean stalls and do whatever job is needed around the barn.
It allows me more time with the horses and helps pay off my lessons.

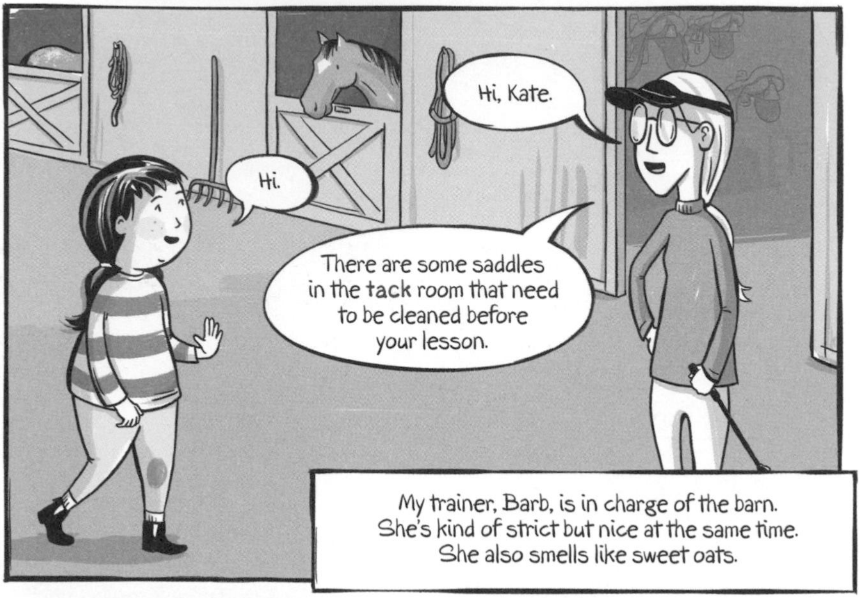
Hi, Kate.
Hi.
There are some saddles in the tack room that need to be cleaned before your lesson.
My trainer, Barb, is in charge of the barn. She's kind of strict but nice at the same time. She also smells like sweet oats.

I love being around Barb
and the horses.

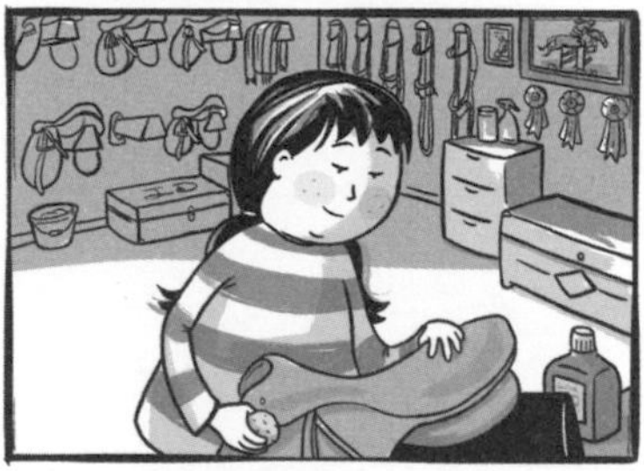

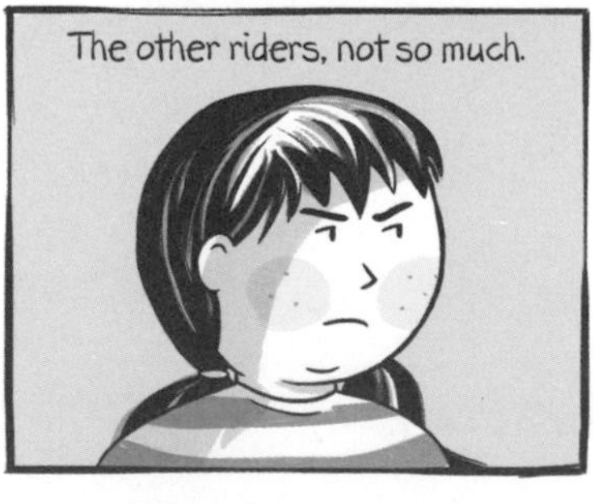
The other riders, not so much.

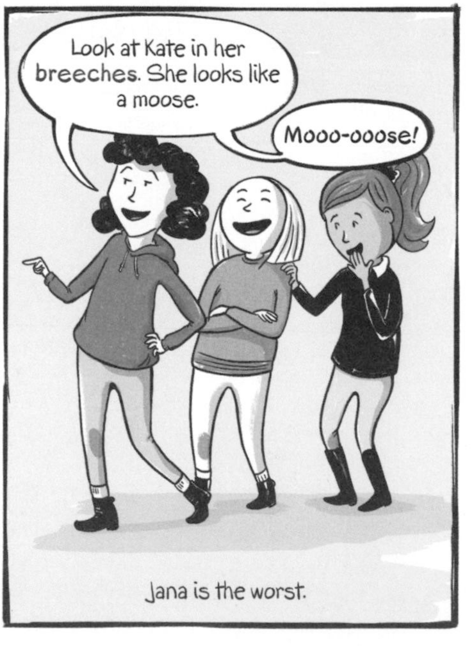
Look at Kate in her **breeches**. She looks like a moose.
Mooo-ooose!
Jana is the worst.

Tack: Gear, such as the saddle and bridle, that is worn by horses to help people ride them.

Breeches: Riding pants

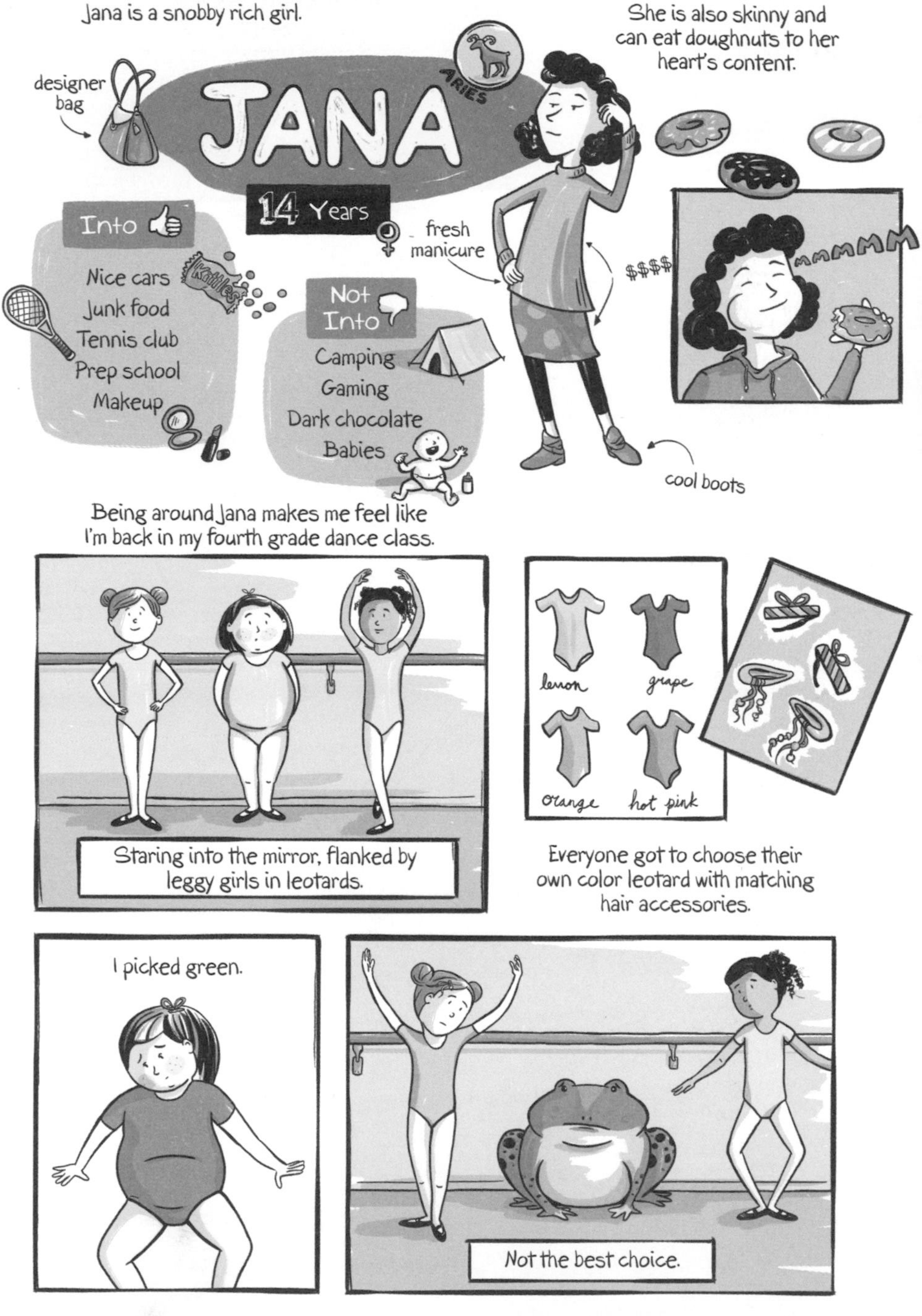
Jana is a snobby rich girl.
designer bag
JANA
ARIES
14 Years
fresh manicure
Into
Nice cars
Junk food
Tennis club
Prep school
Makeup
Kittles
Not Into
Camping
Gaming
Dark chocolate
Babies
She is also skinny and can eat doughnuts to her heart's content.
$$$$
MMMMM
cool boots
Being around Jana makes me feel like I'm back in my fourth grade dance class.
Staring into the mirror, flanked by leggy girls in leotards.
lemon
grape
orange
hot pink
Everyone got to choose their own color leotard with matching hair accessories.
I picked green.
Not the best choice.

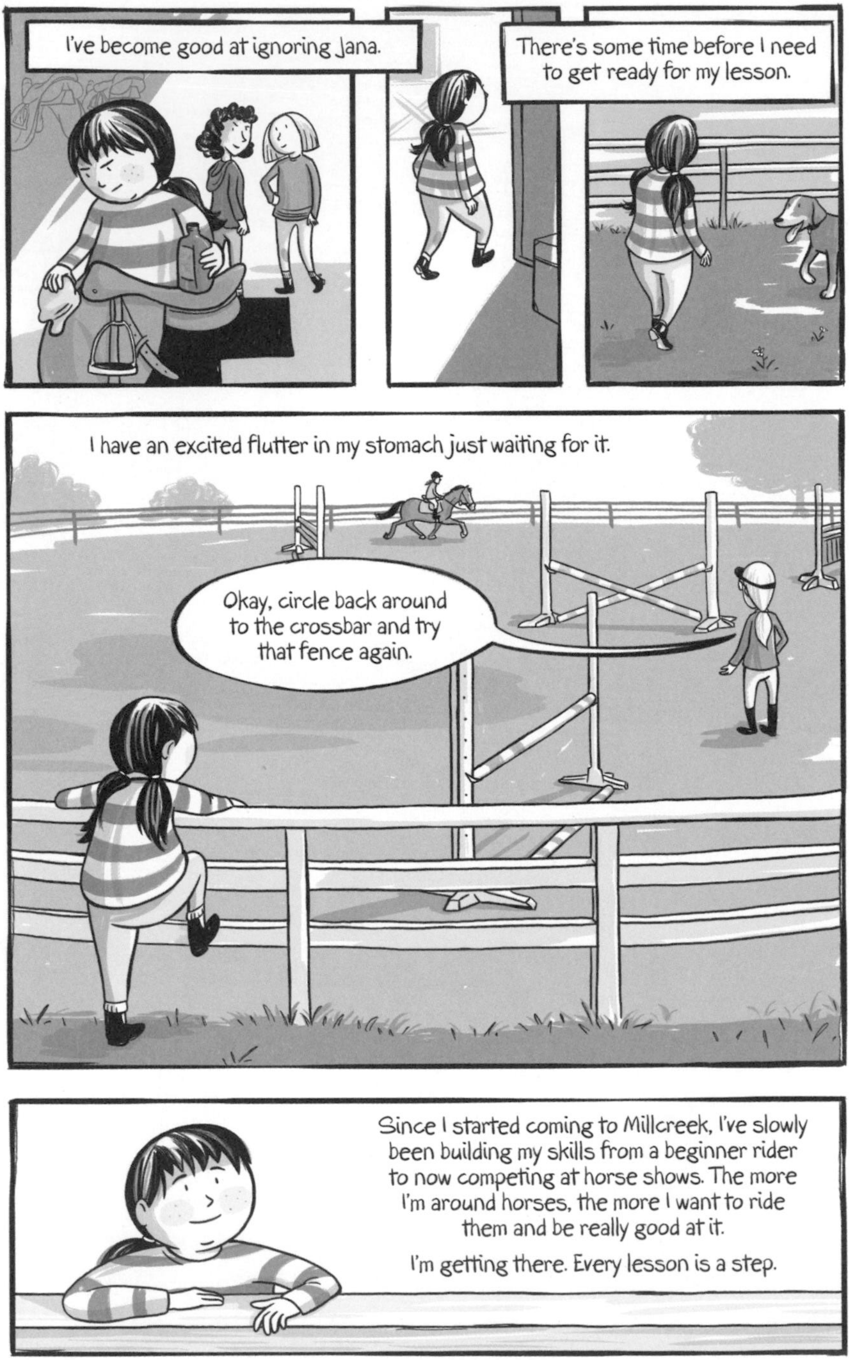
I've become good at ignoring Jana.
There's some time before I need to get ready for my lesson.
I have an excited flutter in my stomach just waiting for it.
Okay, circle back around to the crossbar and try that fence again.
Since I started coming to Millcreek, I've slowly been building my skills from a beginner rider to now competing at horse shows. The more I'm around horses, the more I want to ride them and be really good at it.
I'm getting there. Every lesson is a step.

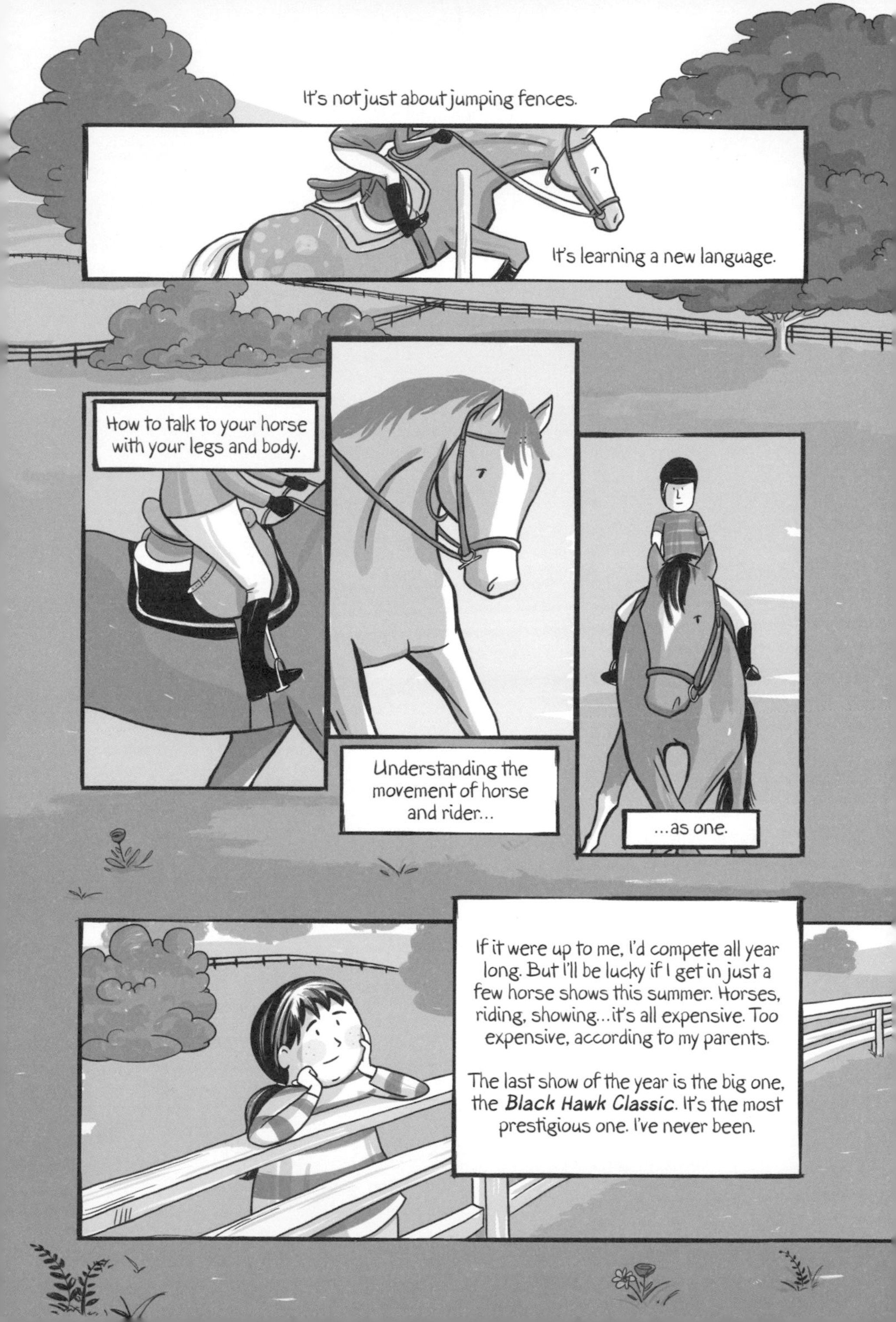
It's not just about jumping fences.
It's learning a new language.
How to talk to your horse with your legs and body.
Understanding the movement of horse and rider...
...as one.
If it were up to me, I'd compete all year long. But I'll be lucky if I get in just a few horse shows this summer. Horses, riding, showing...it's all expensive. Too expensive, according to my parents.
The last show of the year is the big one, the ***Black Hawk Classic***. It's the most prestigious one. I've never been.

When it's almost time for my lesson, I get Felix ready.
He's one of my favorite horses at the barn.

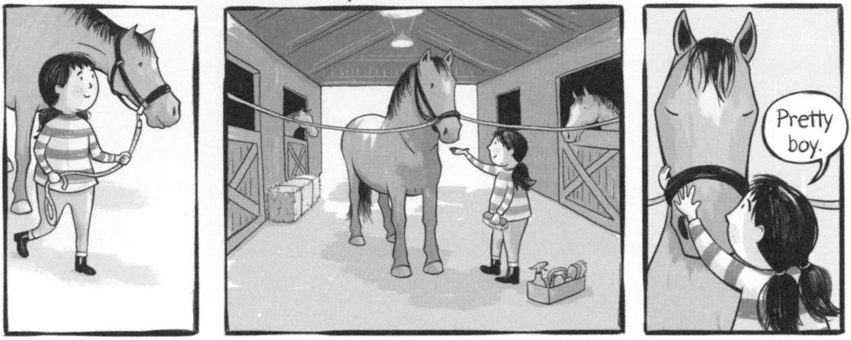
Pretty boy.

Halfway through my ride, my saddle comes loose. It slips all the way over to Felix's side when we take a sharp turn after a jump.

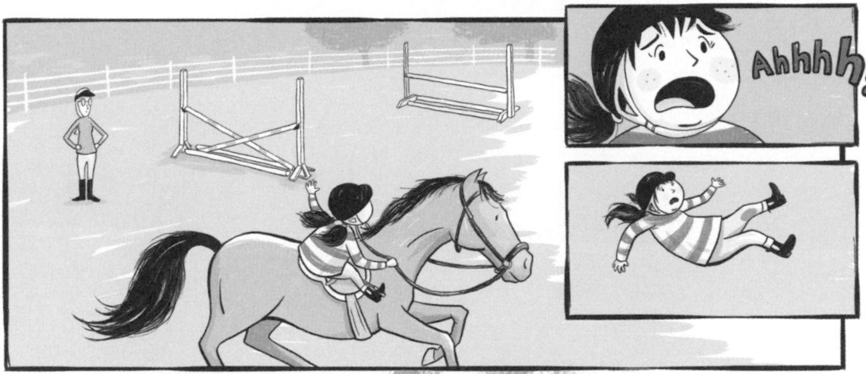
Ahhhh!

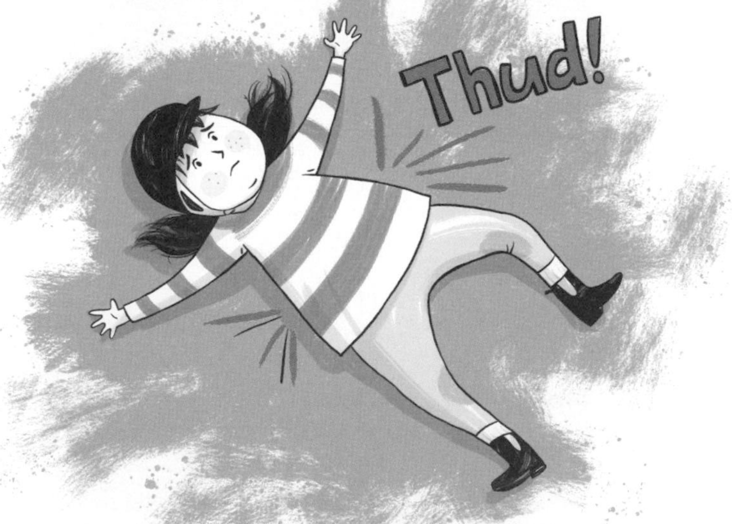
Thud!

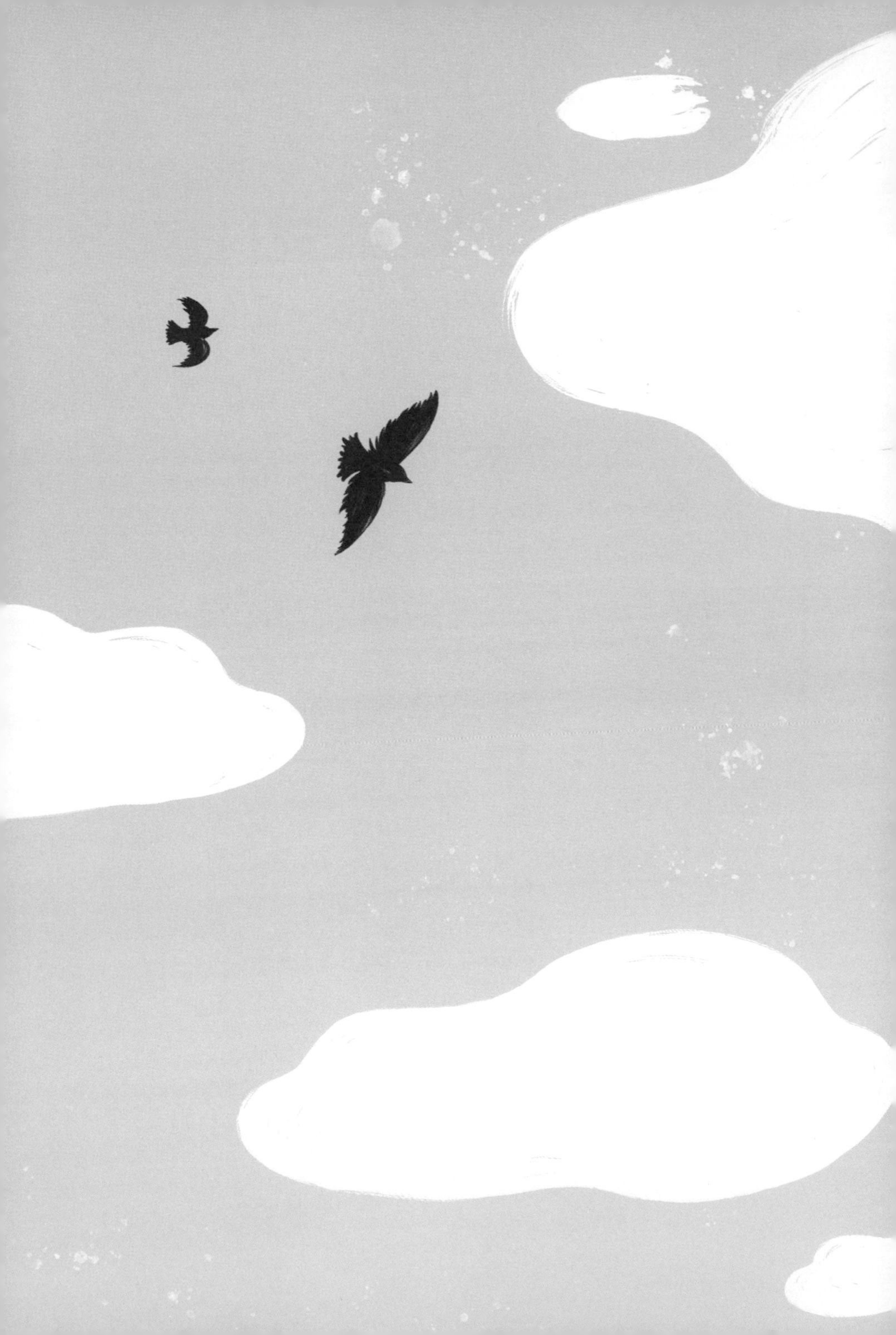

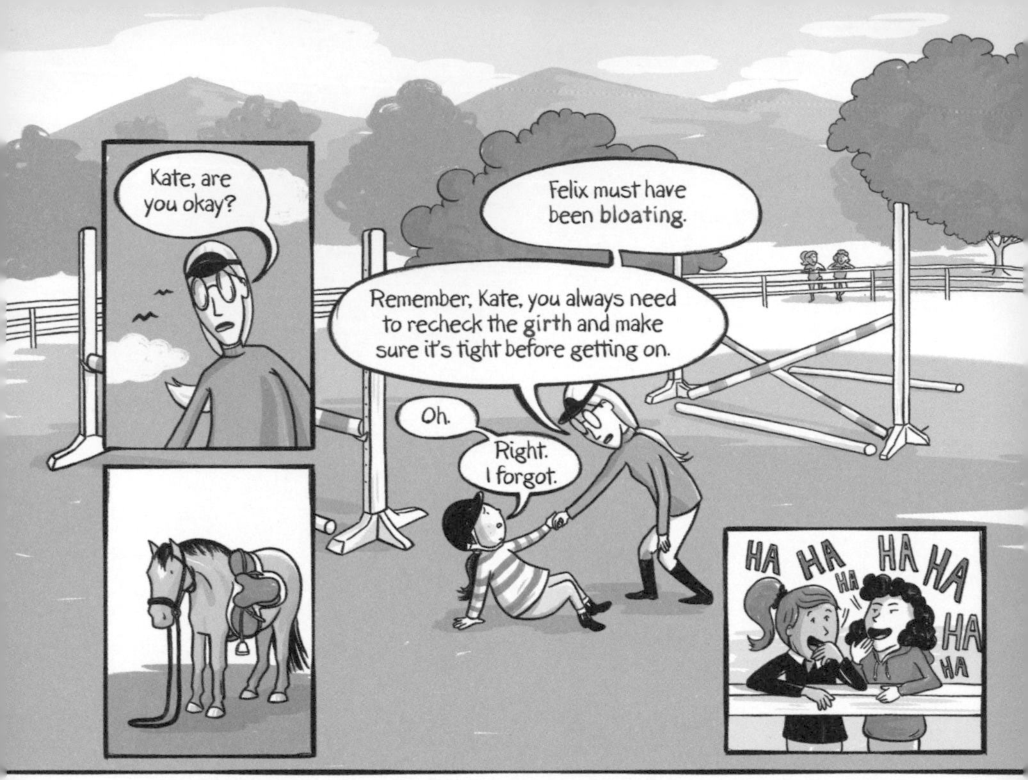
Kate, are you okay?
Felix must have been bloating.
Remember, Kate, you always need to recheck the girth and make sure it's tight before getting on.
Oh.
Right. I forgot.
HA HA HA HA HA HA HA HA HA

How could I be so ***stupid?!***
Rechecking the girth was one of the first things I learned about putting a saddle on.

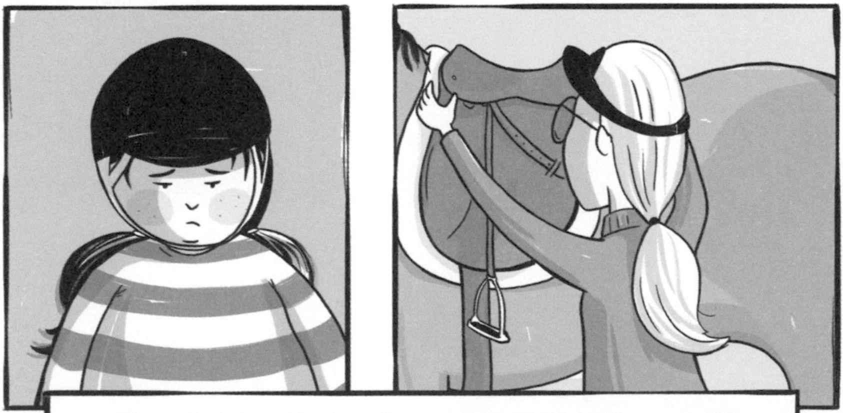
I bite my lip to keep the tears from coming while Barb fixes my saddle.

Bloating: When a horse expands their belly while they are being saddled. Once the horse relaxes their abdominal muscles, the girth loosens, allowing the saddle to slip.

Girth: The band that's attached to the saddle, used to secure it on the horse by fastening around its belly.

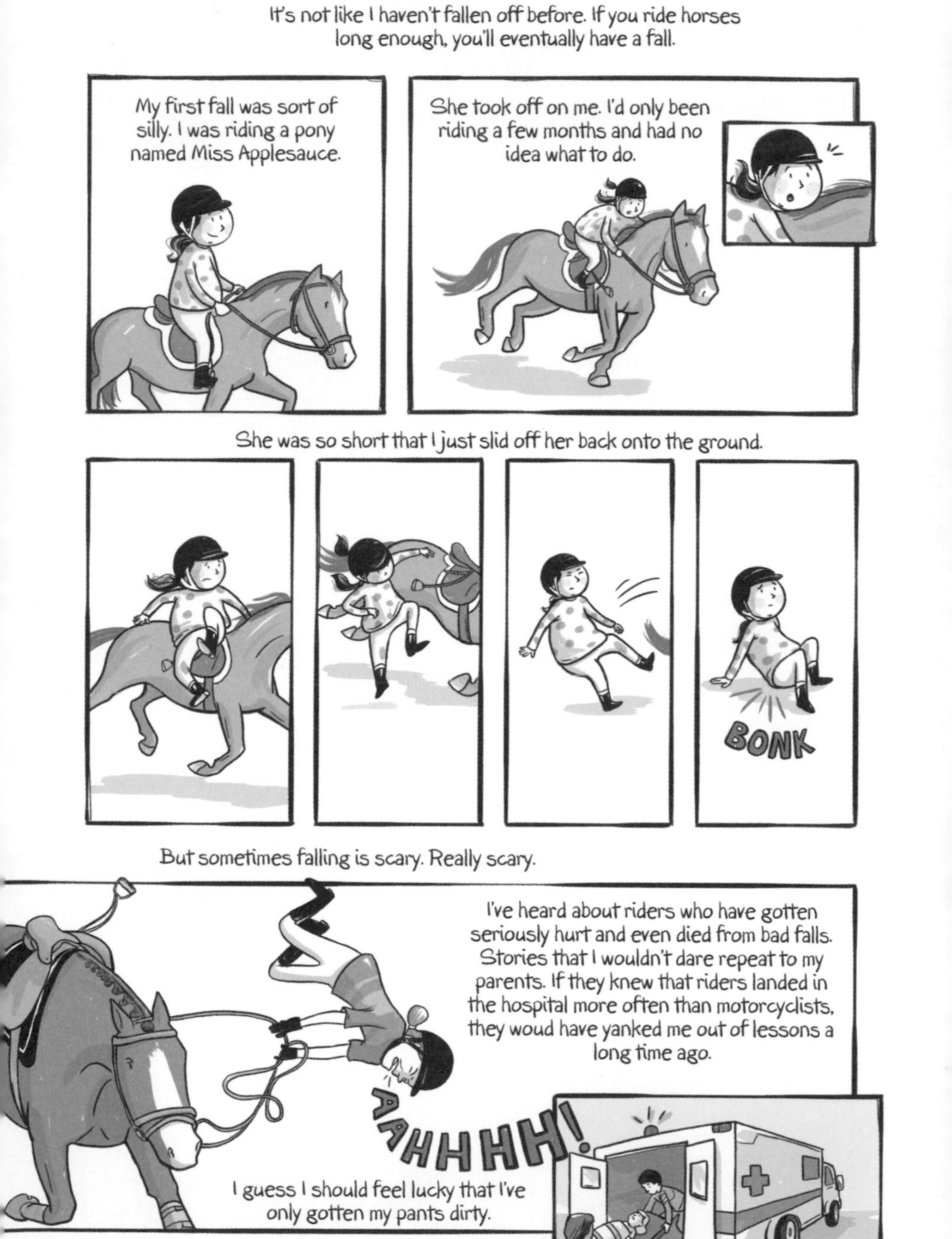
It's not like I haven't fallen off before. If you ride horses long enough, you'll eventually have a fall.
My first fall was sort of silly. I was riding a pony named Miss Applesauce.
She took off on me. I'd only been riding a few months and had no idea what to do.
She was so short that I just slid off her back onto the ground.
BONK
But sometimes falling is scary. Really scary.
AAHHHHH!
I've heard about riders who have gotten seriously hurt and even died from bad falls. Stories that I wouldn't dare repeat to my parents. If they knew that riders landed in the hospital more often than motorcyclists, they woud have yanked me out of lessons a long time ago.
I guess I should feel lucky that I've only gotten my pants dirty.

Barb is waiting for me to get back on.

tremble

tremble

I force myself to breathe.

Barb has me do a few exercises over poles, but we don't jump any more fences.

I spend the rest of the lesson counting the minutes until it's finally over.

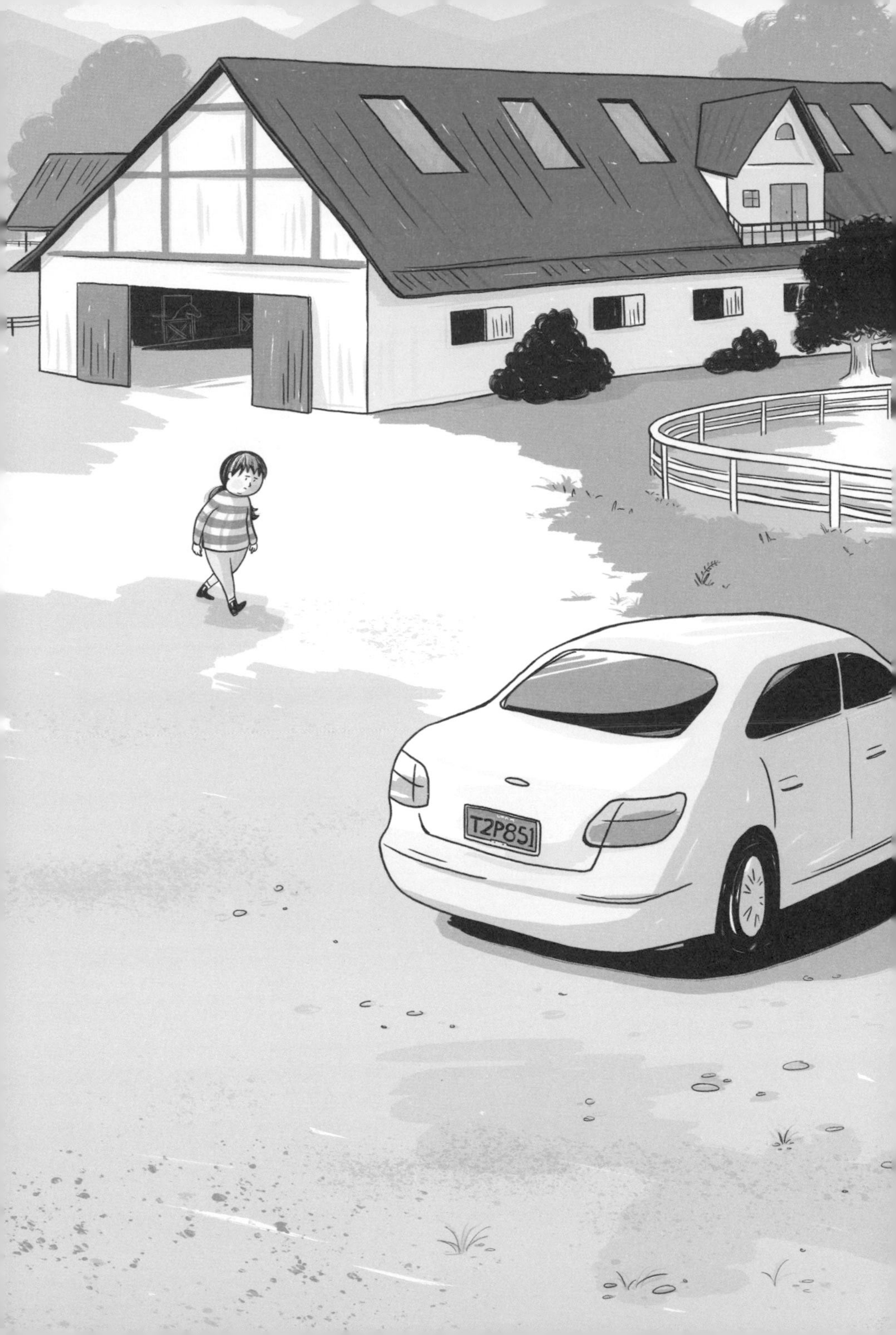
T2P851

To make matters worse, my brother, Ross, has shown up early.

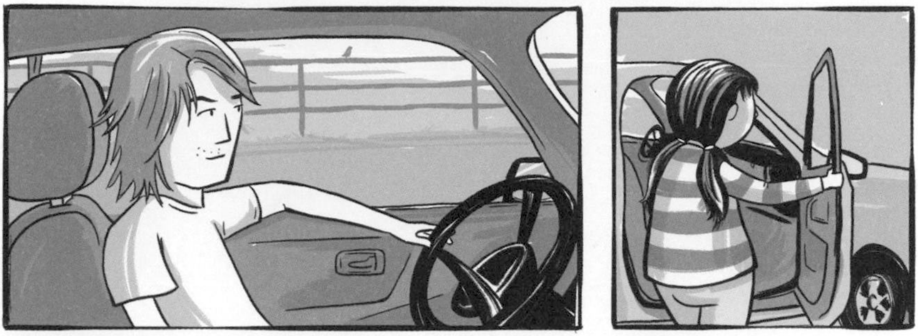

Ross is not a fan of the barn. My mom makes him pick me up every Tuesday on his way home from band practice.

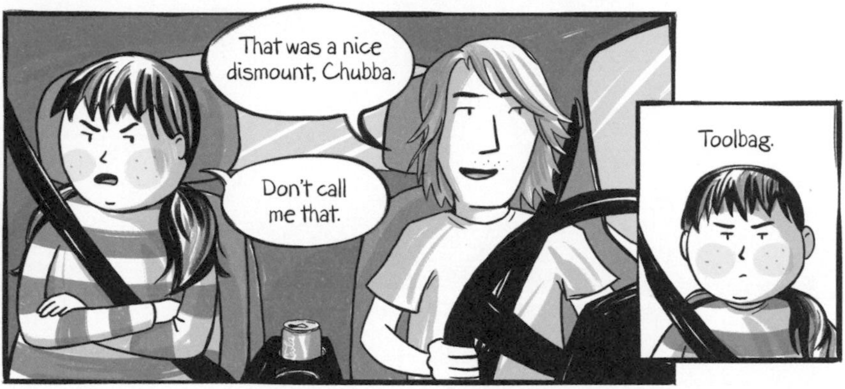
That was a nice dismount, Chubba.
Don't call me that.
Toolbag.

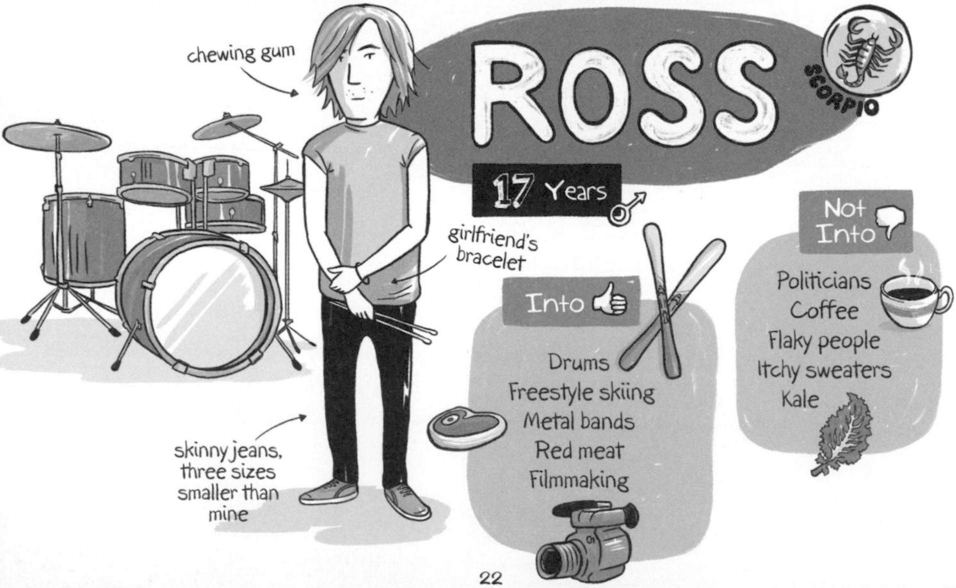
chewing gum
ROSS
SCORPIO
17 Years
girlfriend's bracelet
Into
Drums
Freestyle skiing
Metal bands
Red meat
Filmmaking
Not Into
Politicians
Coffee
Flaky people
Itchy sweaters
Kale
skinny jeans, three sizes smaller than mine

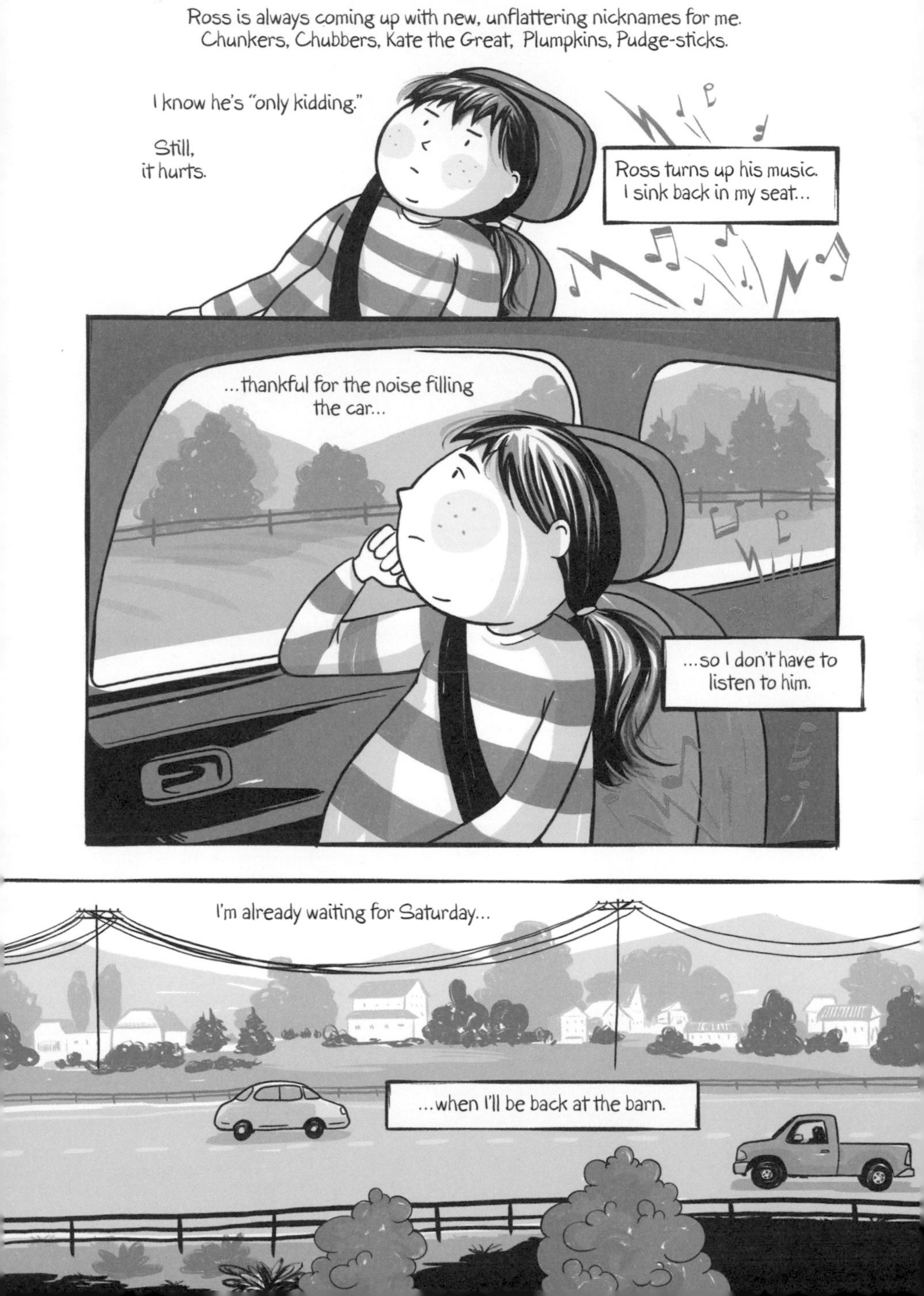

Ross is always coming up with new, unflattering nicknames for me. Chunkers, Chubbers, Kate the Great, Plumpkins, Pudge-sticks.
I know he's "only kidding."
Still, it hurts.
Ross turns up his music. I sink back in my seat...
...thankful for the noise filling the car...
...so I don't have to listen to him.
I'm already waiting for Saturday...
...when I'll be back at the barn.

Chapter 2
Gravel Toss

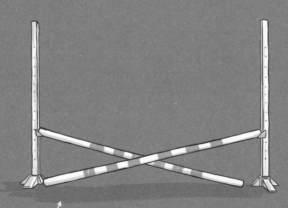

Crossrail

Normally the first kind of fence used for horses and riders just learning how to jump. The center is lower than the sides and encourages the horse to jump the middle of the fence.

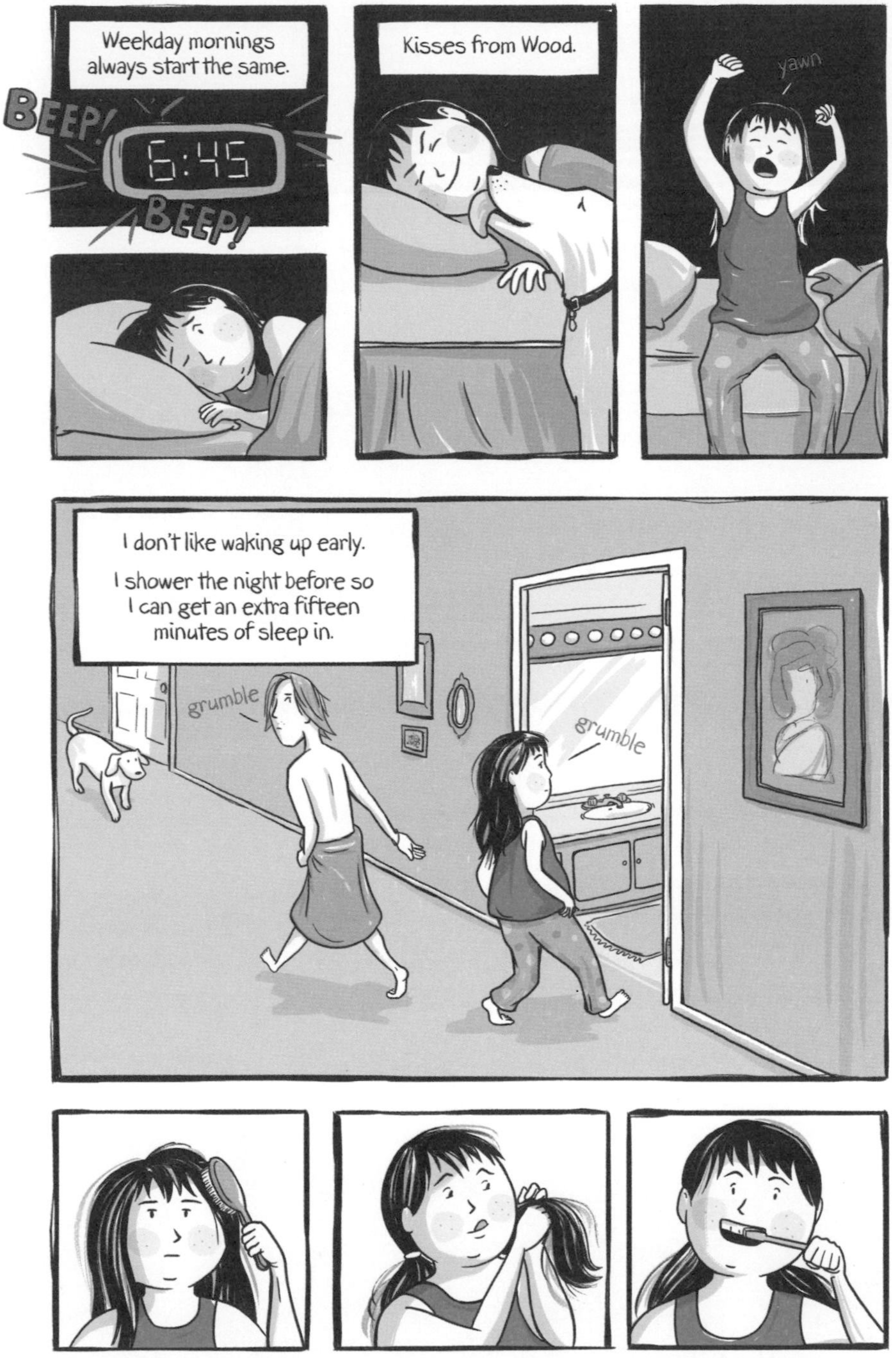
Weekday mornings always start the same.
BEEP!
6:45
BEEP!
Kisses from Wood.
yawn
I don't like waking up early.
I shower the night before so I can get an extra fifteen minutes of sleep in.
grumble
grumble

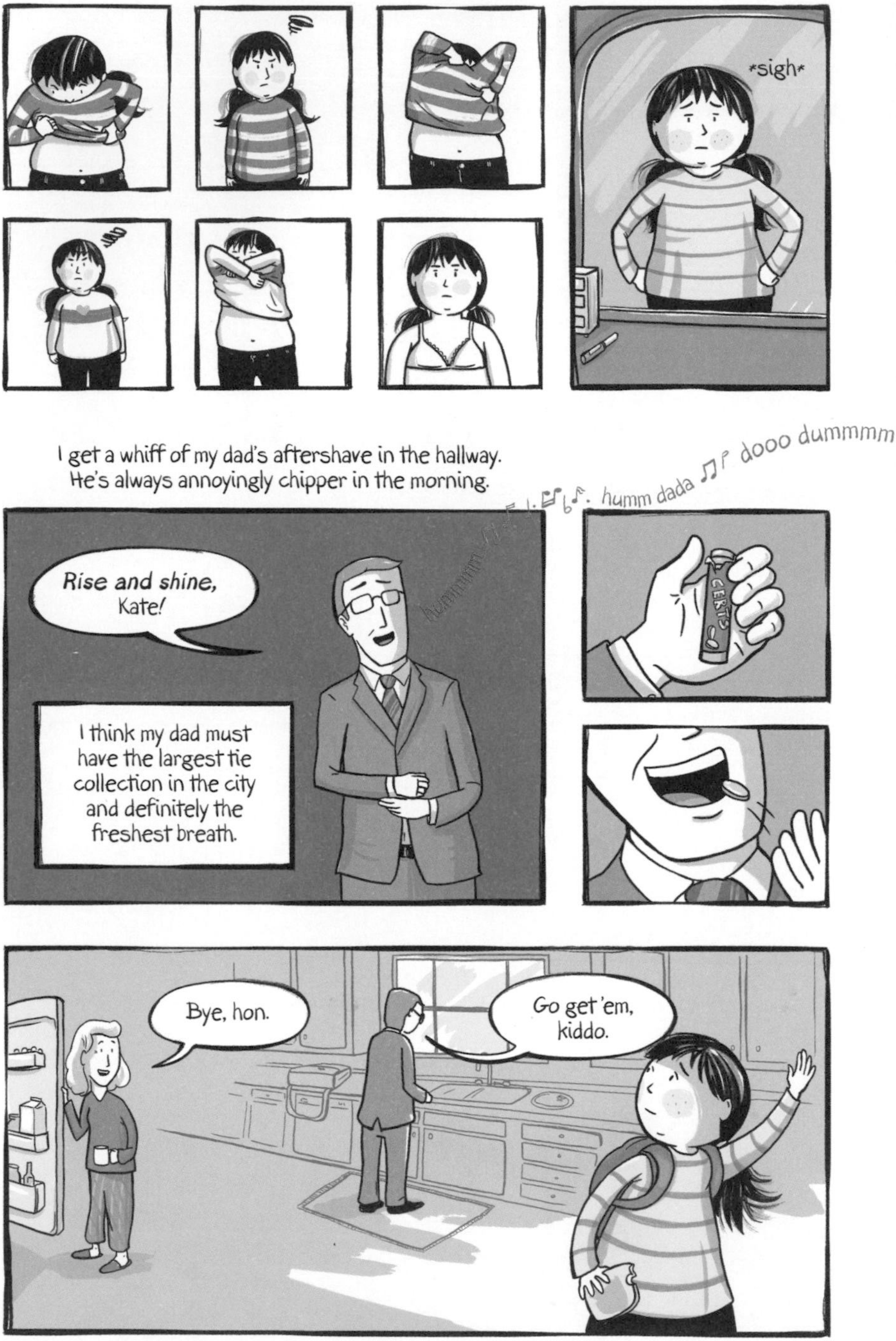
sigh
I get a whiff of my dad's aftershave in the hallway.
He's always annoyingly chipper in the morning.
humm dada
dooo dummmm
Rise and shine, Kate!
I think my dad must have the largest tie collection in the city and definitely the freshest breath.
CERTS
Bye, hon.
Go get 'em, kiddo.

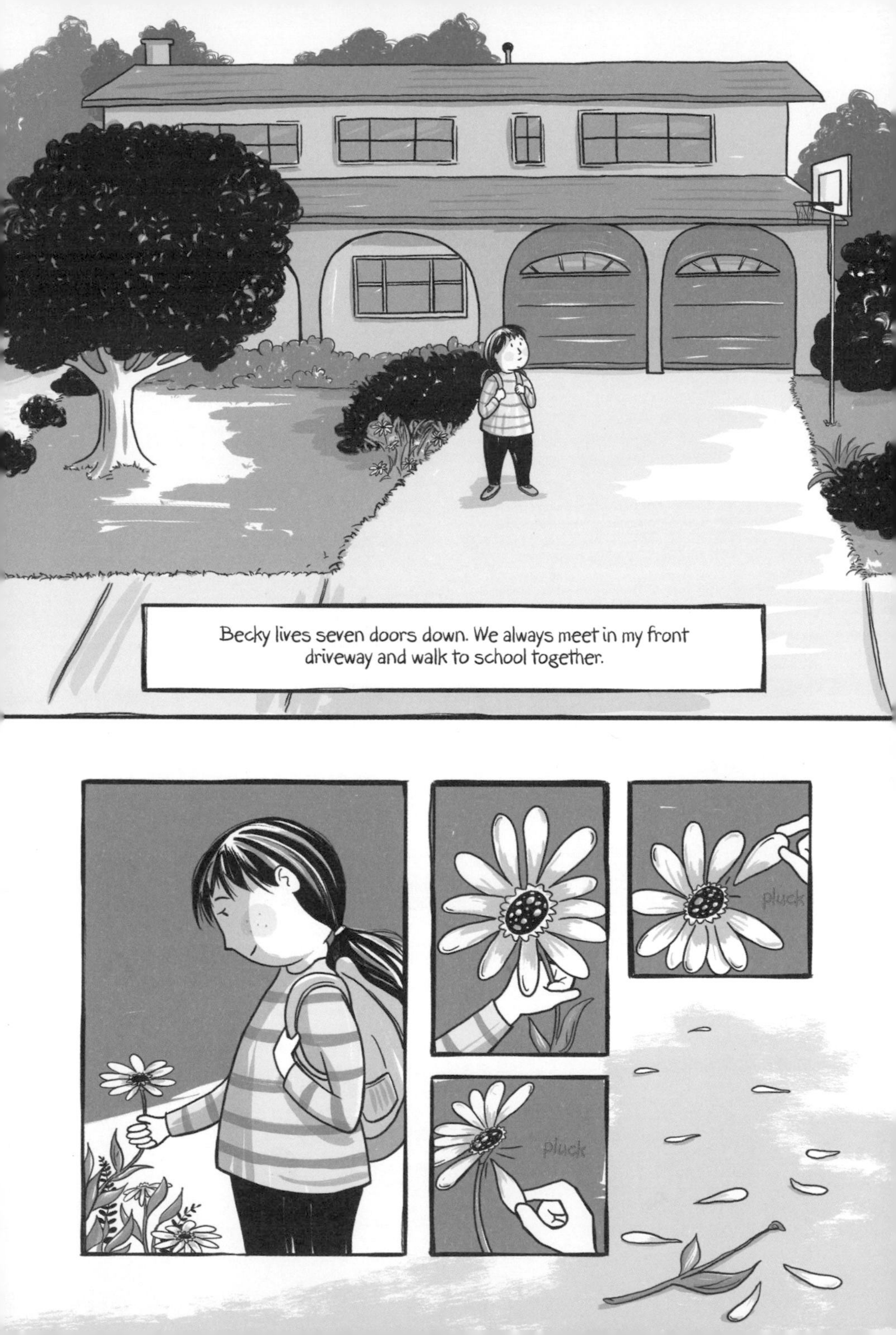
Becky lives seven doors down. We always meet in my front driveway and walk to school together.
pluck
pluck

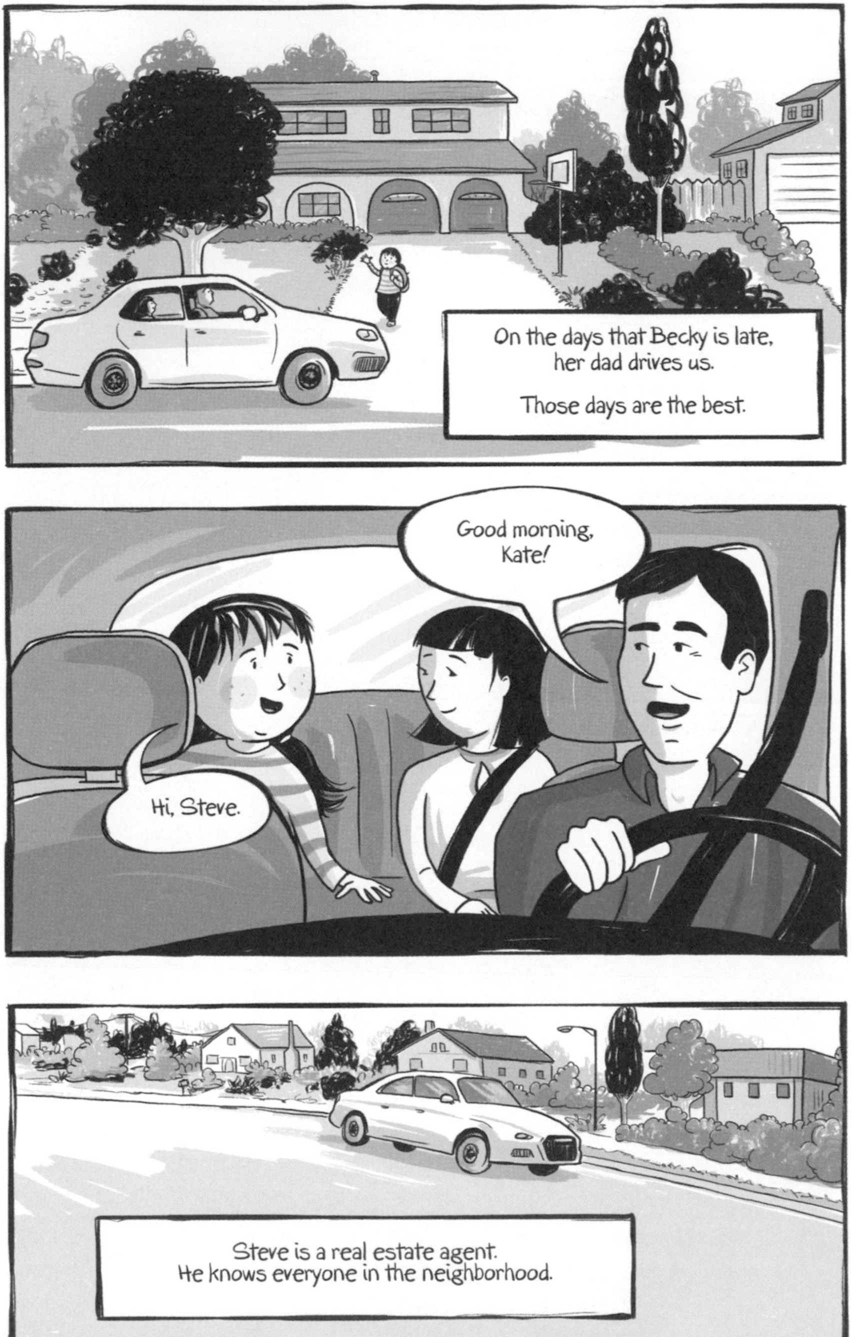
On the days that Becky is late, her dad drives us.
Those days are the best.
Good morning, Kate!
Hi, Steve.
Steve is a real estate agent. He knows everyone in the neighborhood.

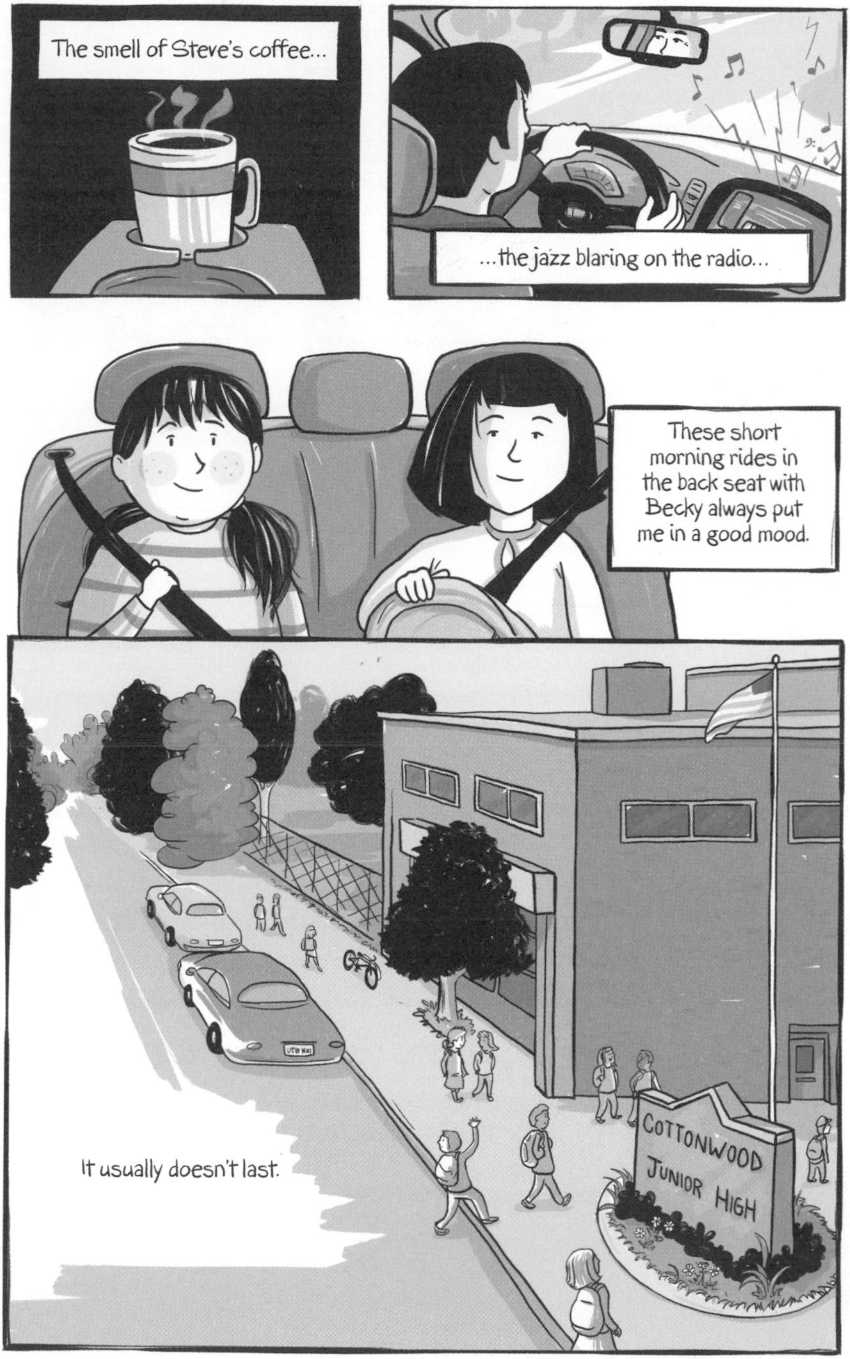
The smell of Steve's coffee...
...the jazz blaring on the radio...
These short morning rides in the back seat with Becky always put me in a good mood.
COTTONWOOD JUNIOR HIGH
It usually doesn't last.

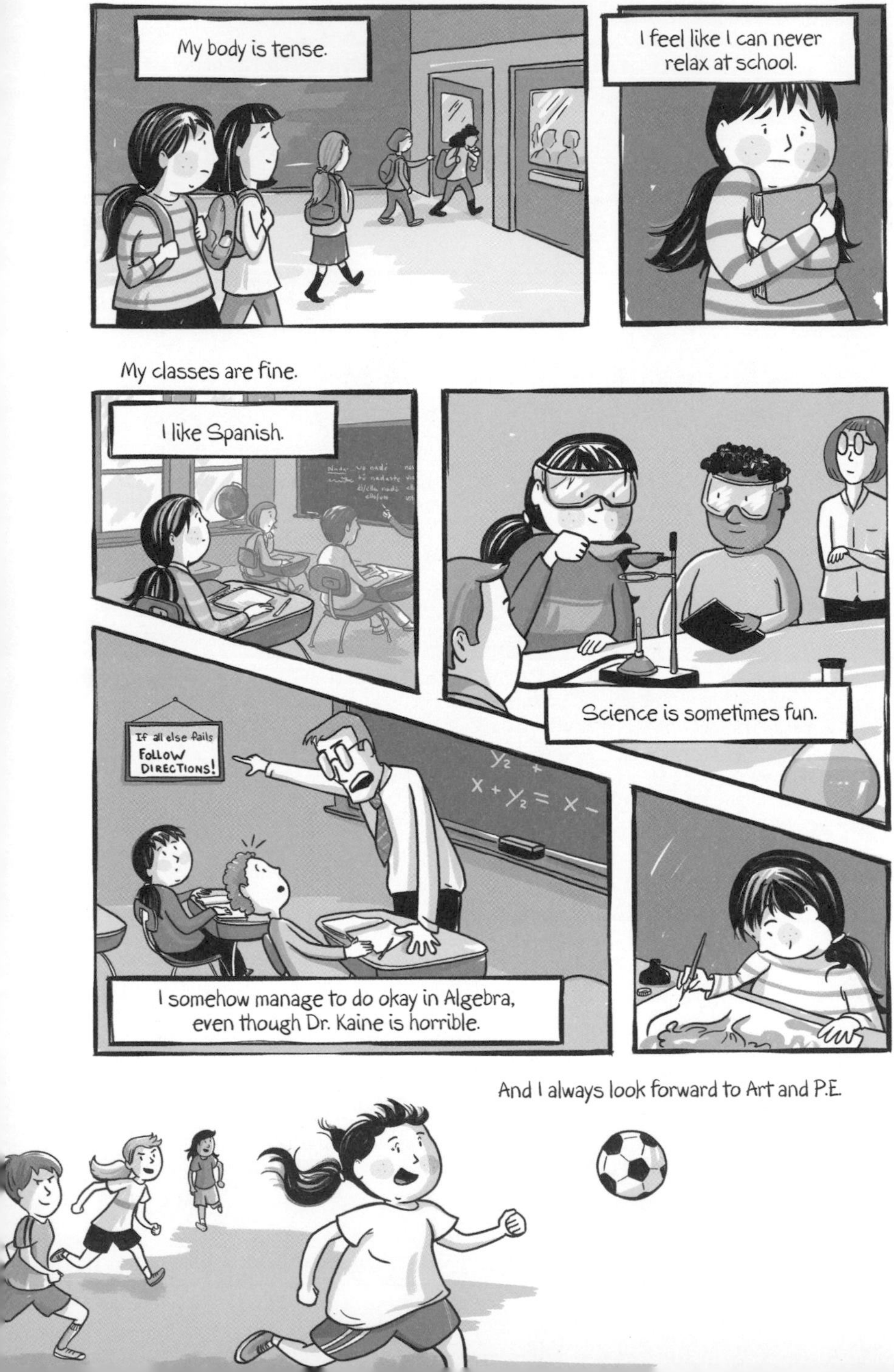
My body is tense.
I feel like I can never relax at school.
My classes are fine.
I like Spanish.
Science is sometimes fun.
If all else fails FOLLOW DIRECTIONS!
I somehow manage to do okay in Algebra, even though Dr. Kaine is horrible.
And I always look forward to Art and P.E.

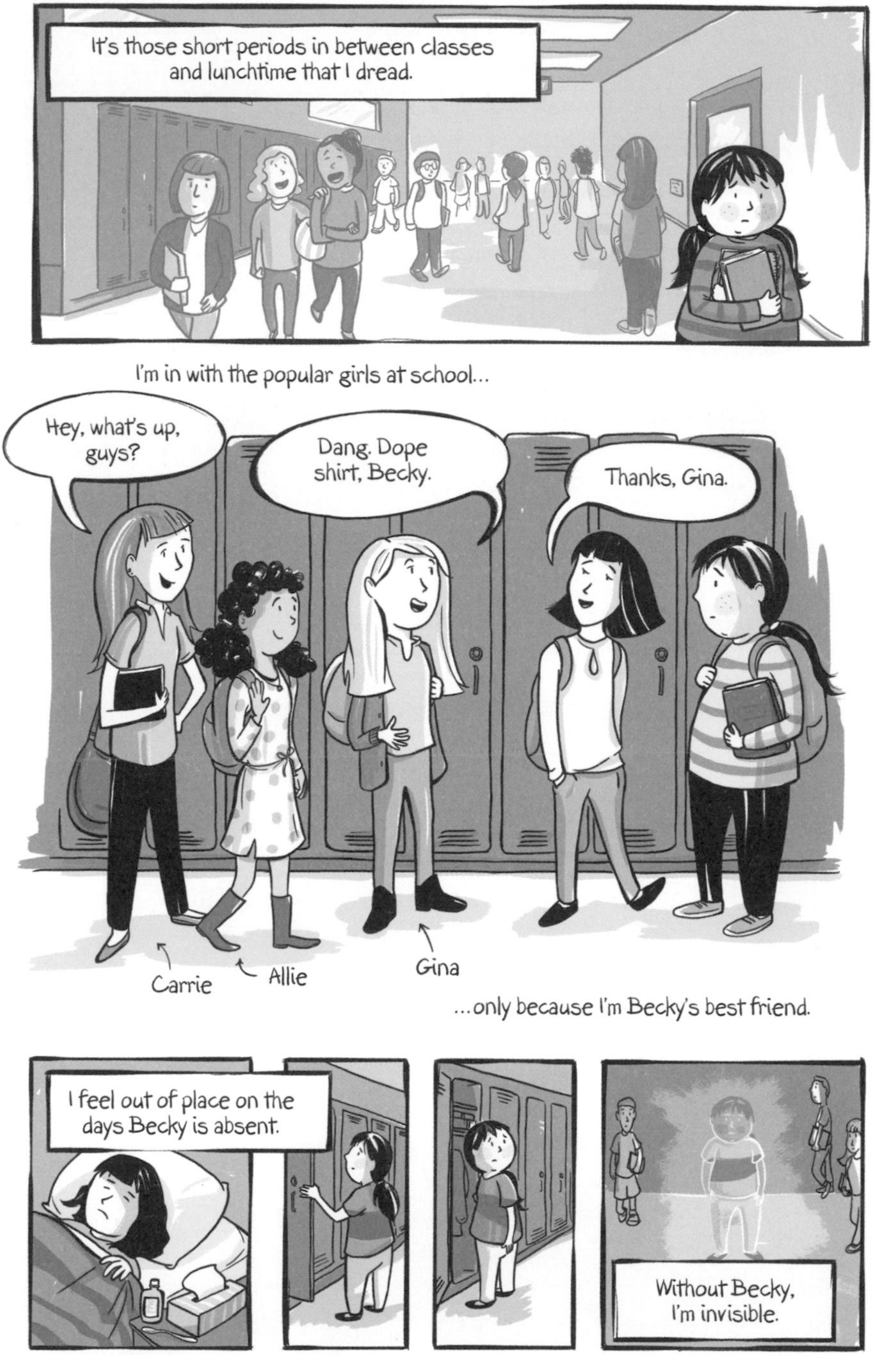
It's those short periods in between classes and lunchtime that I dread.
I'm in with the popular girls at school...
Hey, what's up, guys?
Dang. Dope shirt, Becky.
Thanks, Gina.
Carrie
Allie
Gina
...only because I'm Becky's best friend.
I feel out of place on the days Becky is absent.
Without Becky, I'm invisible.

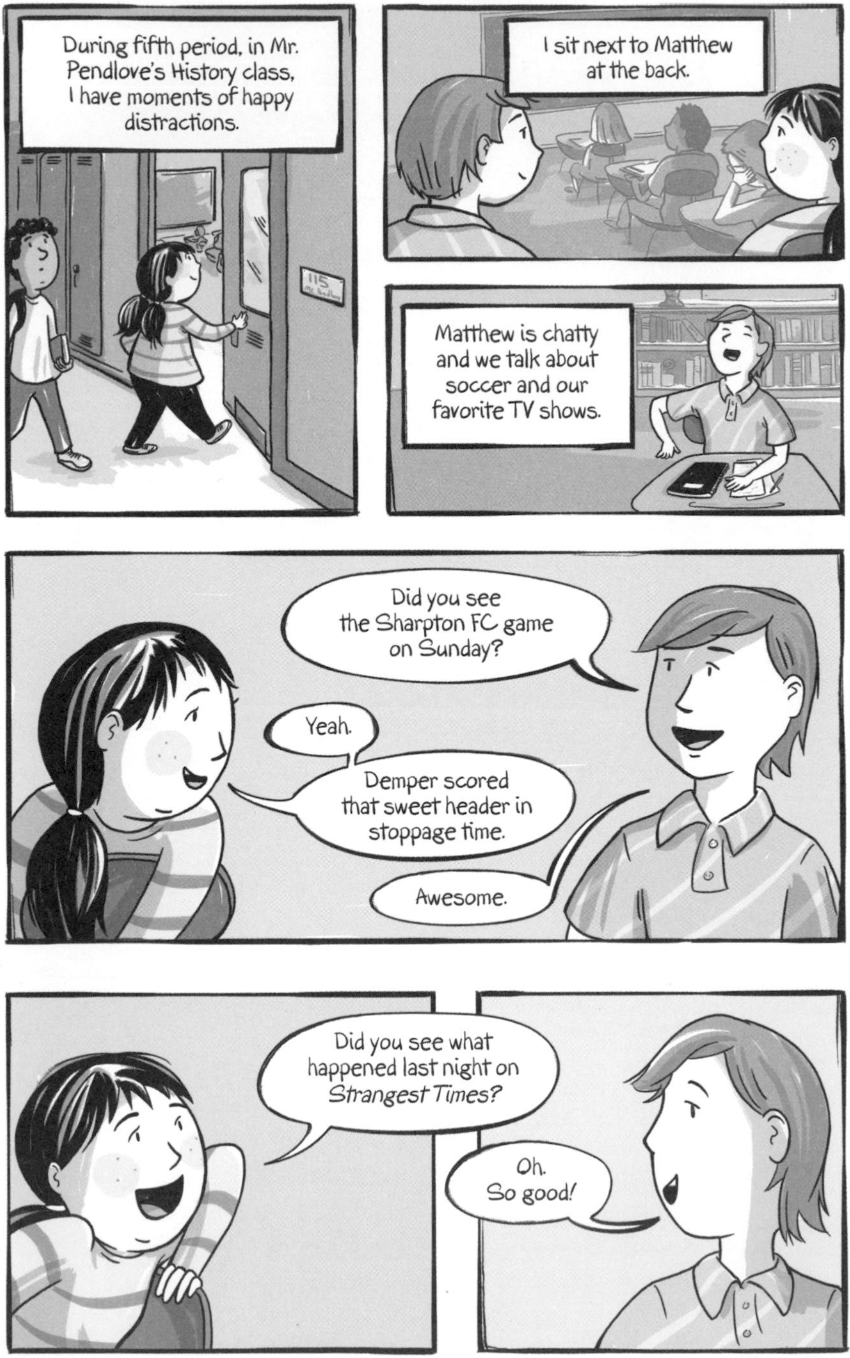
During fifth period, in Mr. Pendlove's History class, I have moments of happy distractions.
I sit next to Matthew at the back.
Matthew is chatty and we talk about soccer and our favorite TV shows.
Did you see the Sharpton FC game on Sunday?
Yeah.
Demper scored that sweet header in stoppage time.
Awesome.
Did you see what happened last night on *Strangest Times*?
Oh. So good!

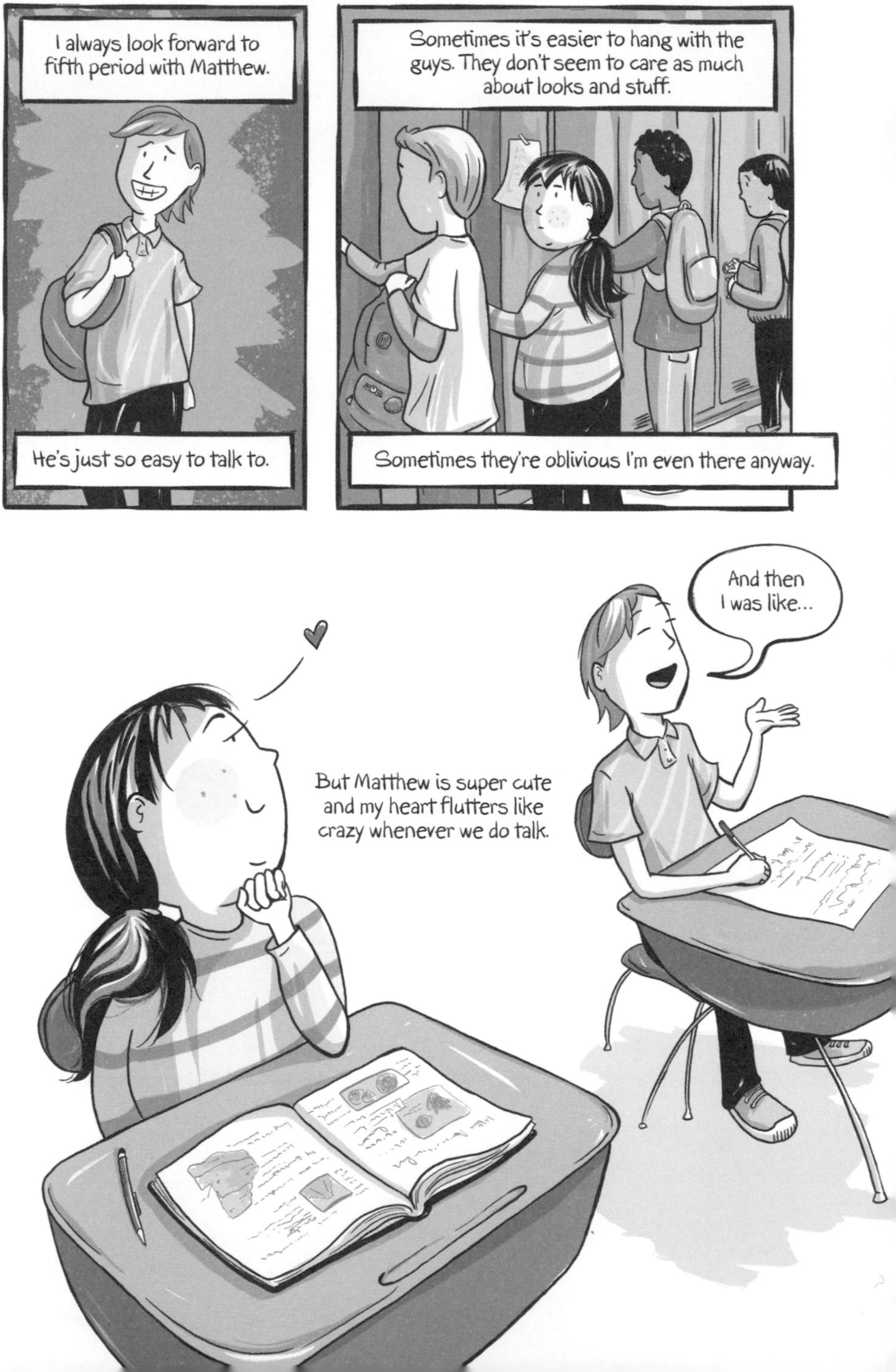
I always look forward to fifth period with Matthew.
He's just so easy to talk to.
Sometimes it's easier to hang with the guys. They don't seem to care as much about looks and stuff.
Sometimes they're oblivious I'm even there anyway.
And then I was like...
But Matthew is super cute and my heart flutters like crazy whenever we do talk.

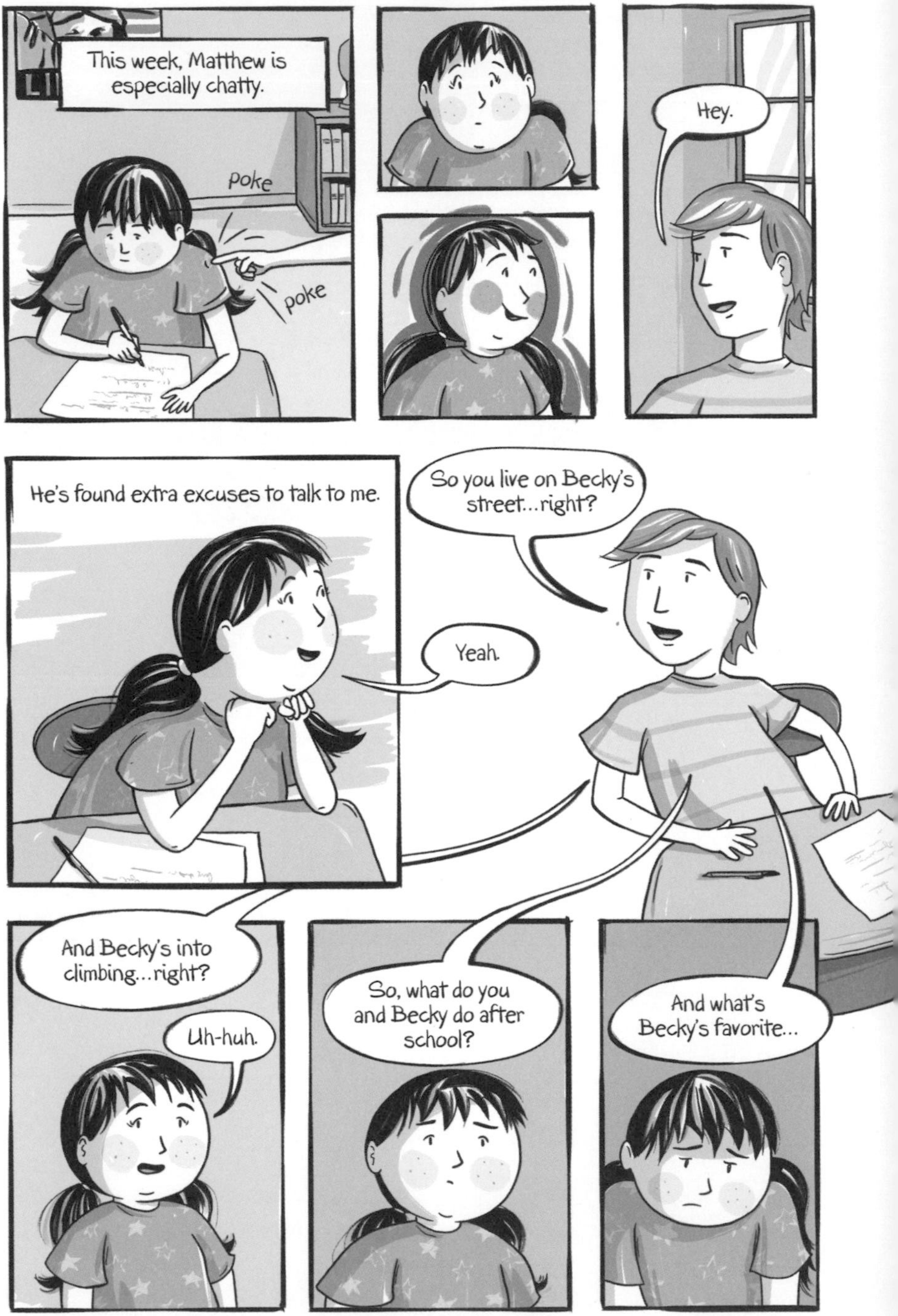
This week, Matthew is especially chatty.
poke
poke
Hey.
He's found extra excuses to talk to me.
So you live on Becky's street...right?
Yeah.
And Becky's into climbing...right?
Uh-huh.
So, what do you and Becky do after school?
And what's Becky's favorite...

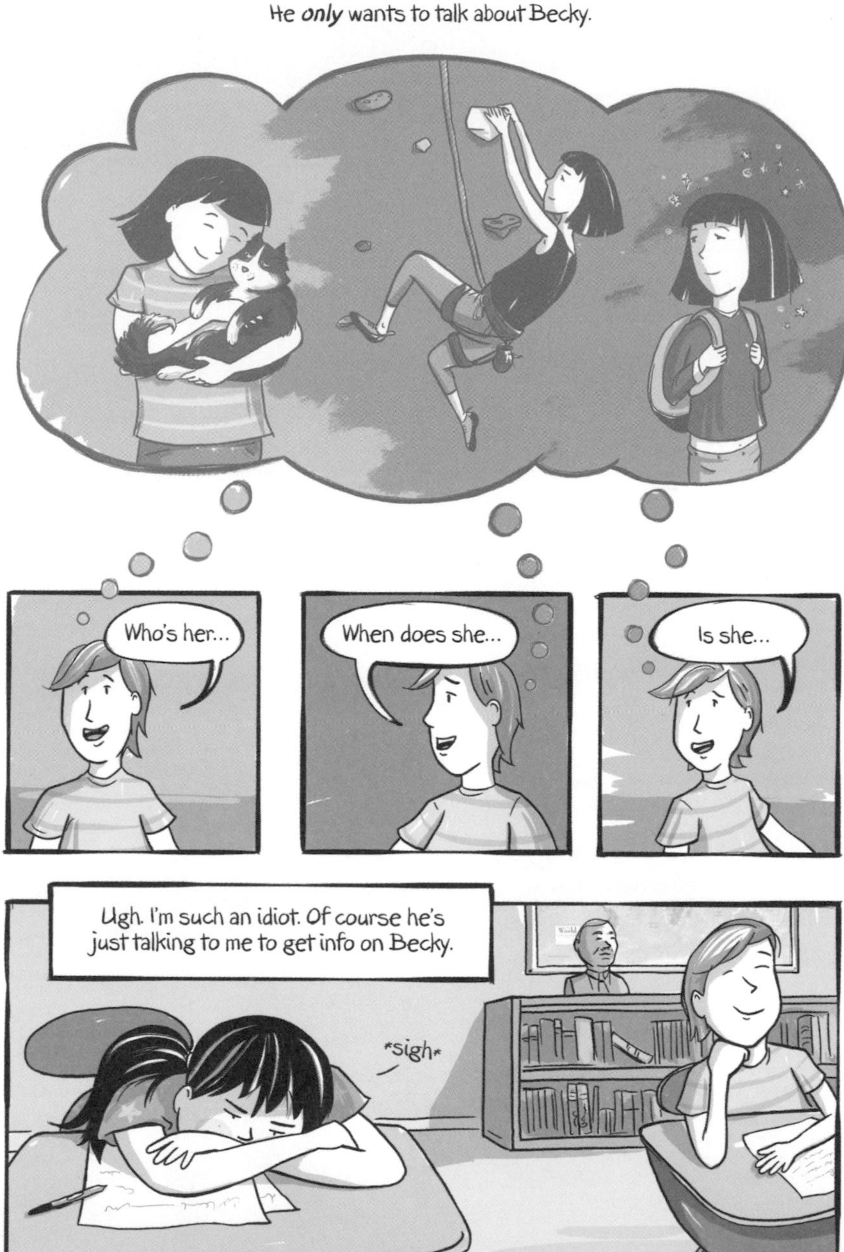
He *only* wants to talk about Becky.
Who's her...
When does she...
Is she...
Ugh. I'm such an idiot. Of course he's just talking to me to get info on Becky.
sigh

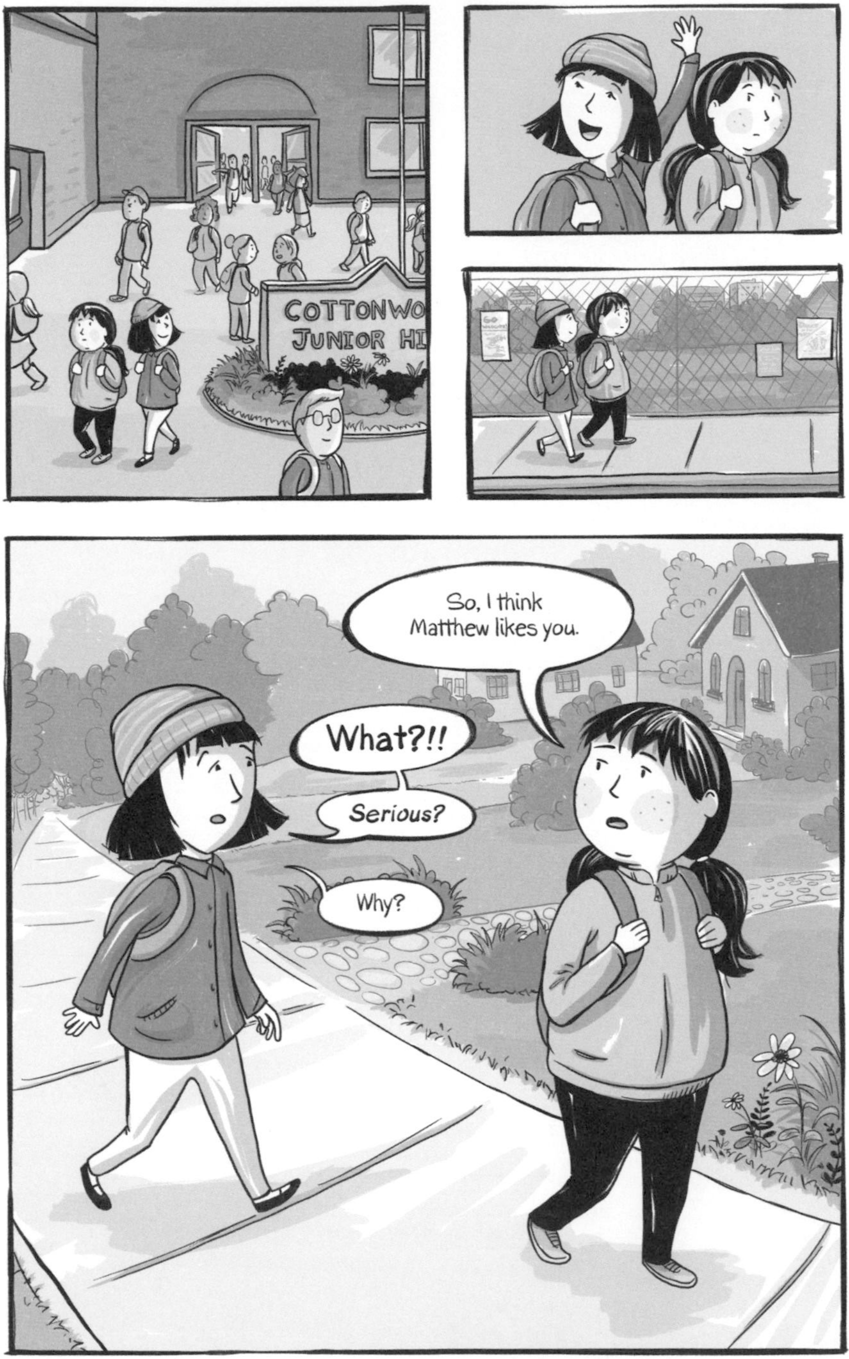
COTTONWO
JUNIOR HI
So, I think Matthew likes you.
What?!!
Serious?
Why?

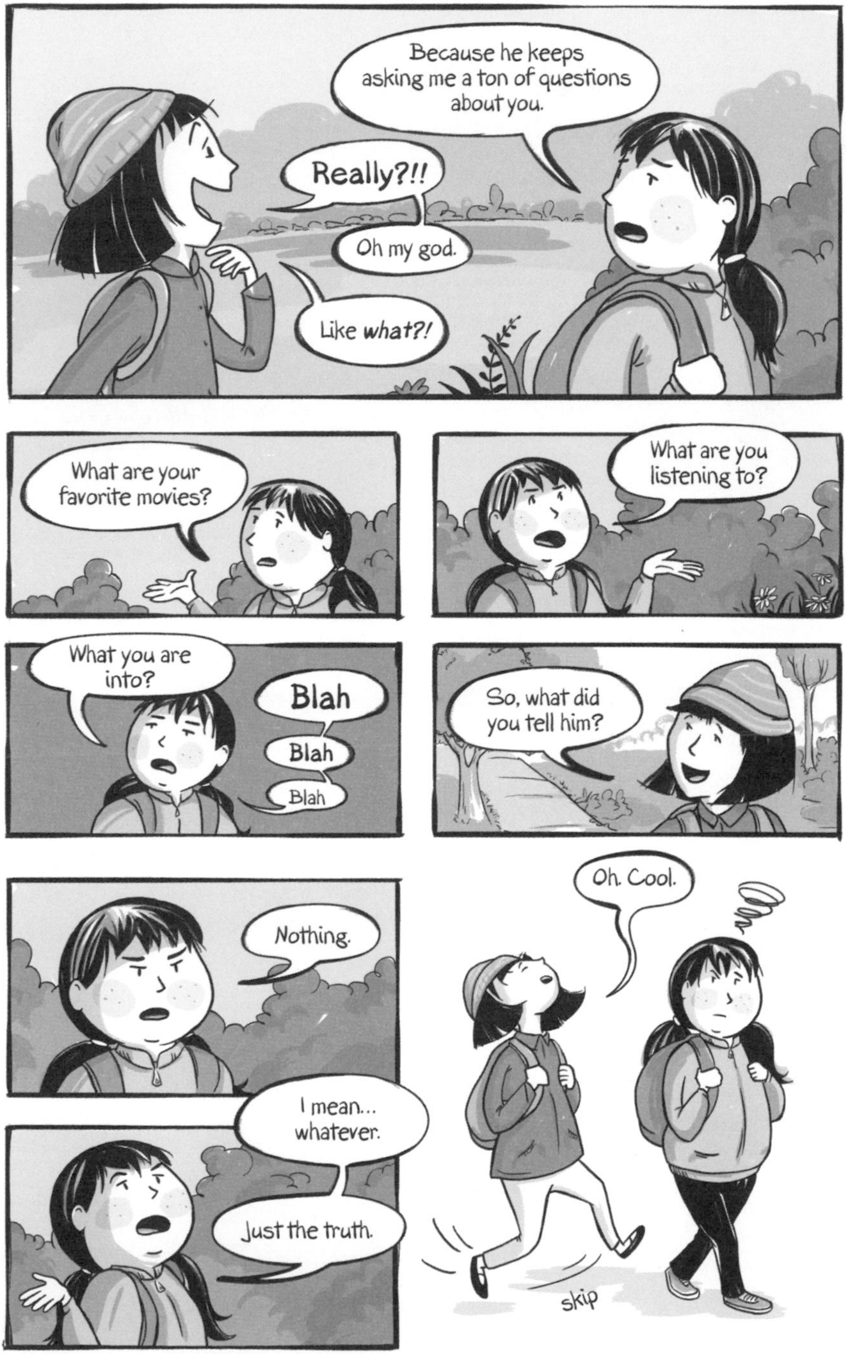
Because he keeps asking me a ton of questions about you.
Really?!!
Oh my god.
Like what?!
What are your favorite movies?
What are you listening to?
What you are into?
Blah
Blah
Blah
So, what did you tell him?
Nothing.
I mean... whatever.
Just the truth.
Oh. Cool.
skip

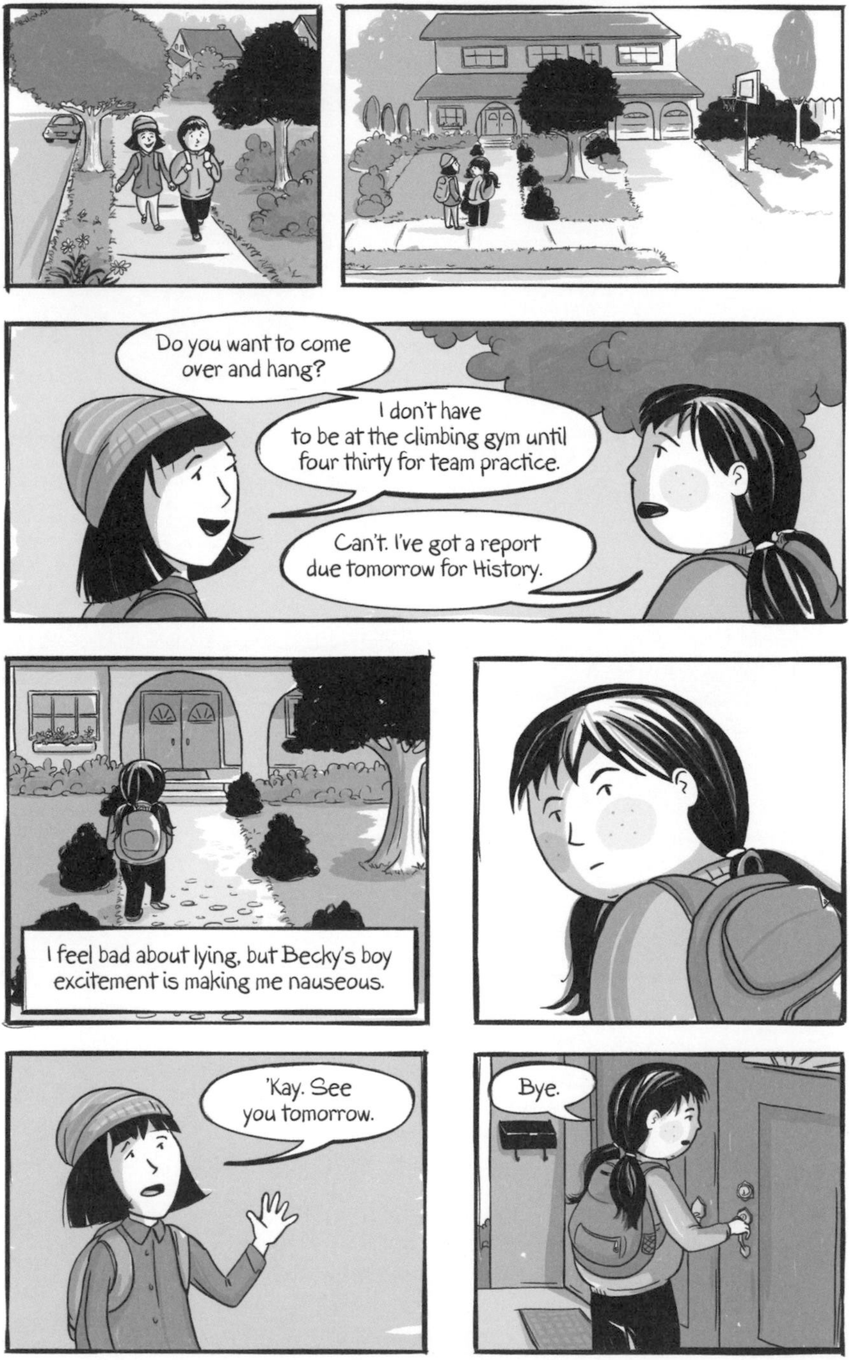
Do you want to come over and hang?
I don't have to be at the climbing gym until four thirty for team practice.
Can't. I've got a report due tomorrow for History.
I feel bad about lying, but Becky's boy excitement is making me nauseous.
'Kay. See you tomorrow.
Bye.

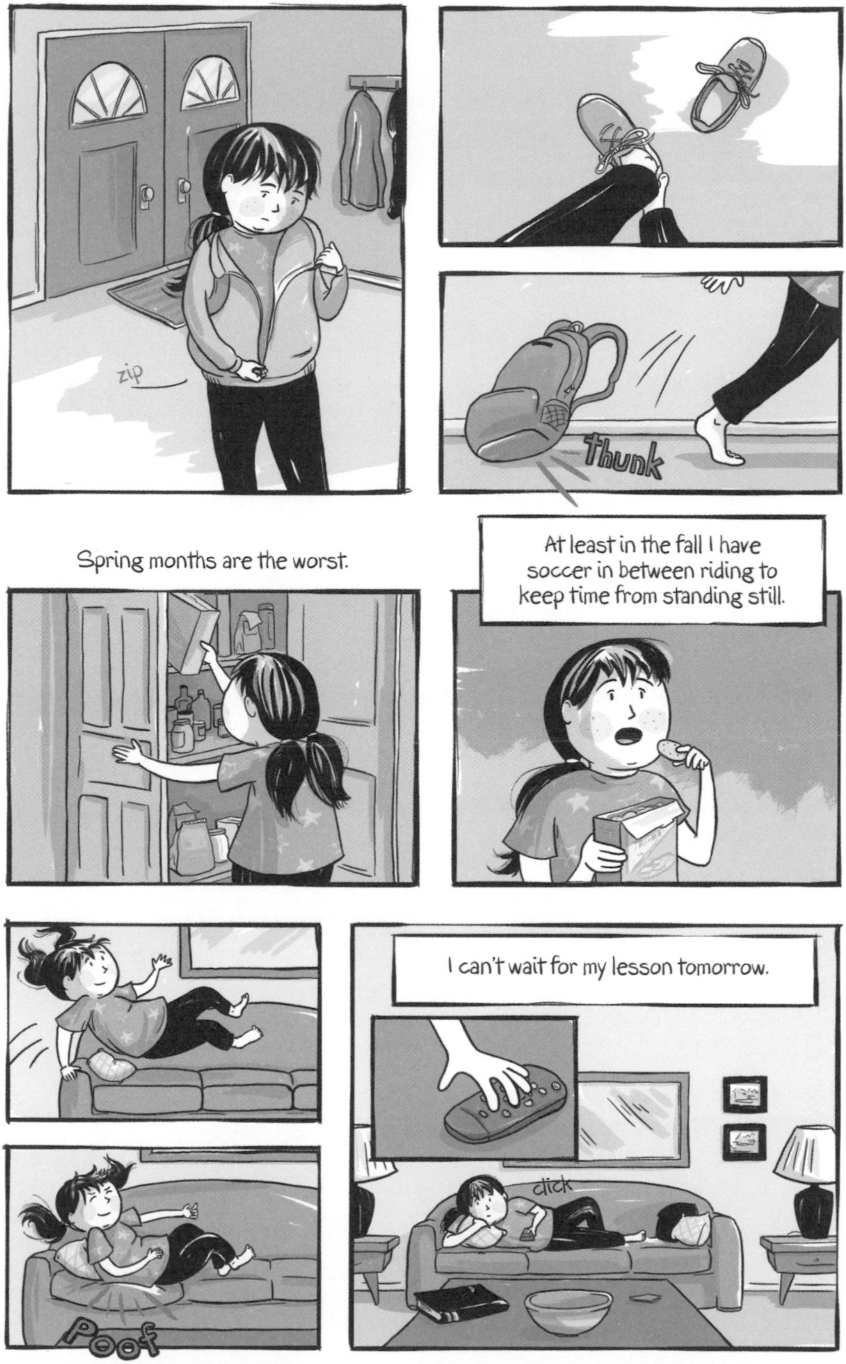
zip
thunk
Spring months are the worst.
At least in the fall I have soccer in between riding to keep time from standing still.
Poof
I can't wait for my lesson tomorrow.
click

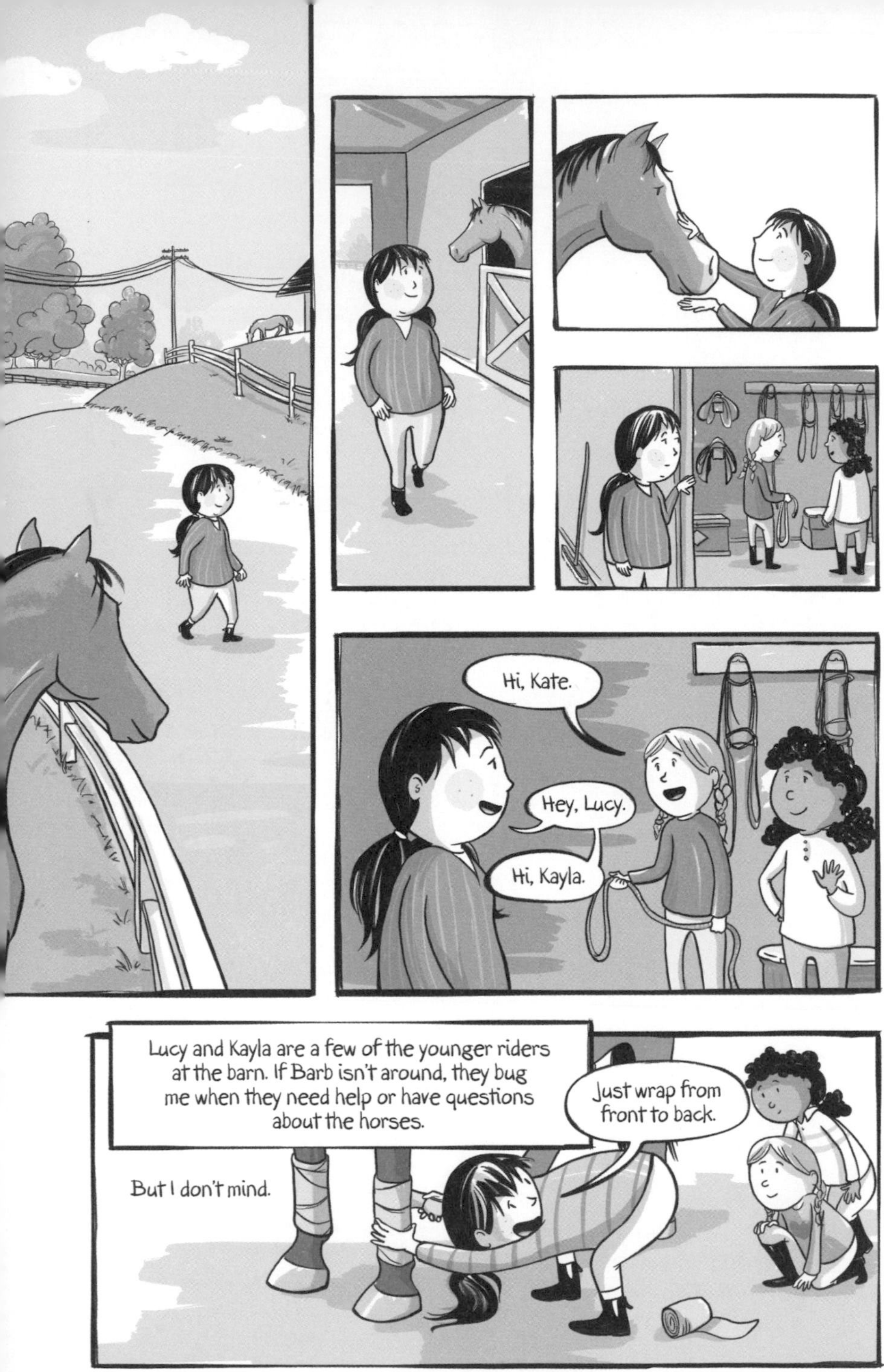
Hi, Kate.
Hey, Lucy.
Hi, Kayla.
Lucy and Kayla are a few of the younger riders at the barn. If Barb isn't around, they bug me when they need help or have questions about the horses.
Just wrap from front to back.
But I don't mind.

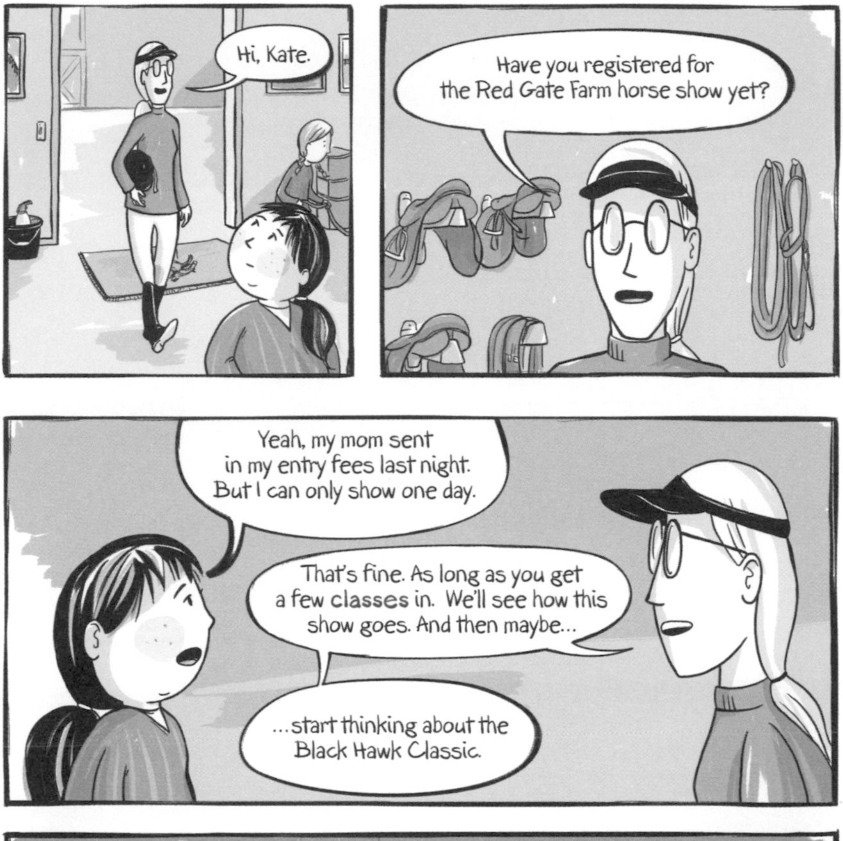
Hi, Kate.
Have you registered for the Red Gate Farm horse show yet?
Yeah, my mom sent in my entry fees last night. But I can only show one day.
That's fine. As long as you get a few **classes** in. We'll see how this show goes. And then maybe...
...start thinking about the Black Hawk Classic.
Really?!! The Black Hawk Classic?
You might be ready for it this year.
The jumps are higher and it's definitely the most competitive show in the state. You've got all summer to keep training.
But you'll need to really push yourself.

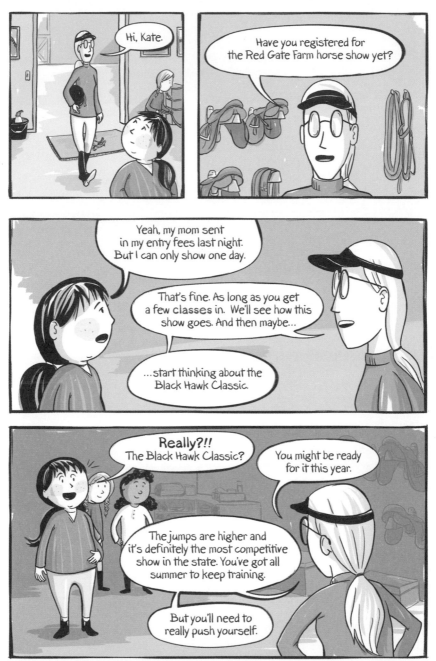

Class: The specific event at the horse show in which the horse and rider are competing. Classes are often divided by ability levels, the rider's age, fence height, etc.

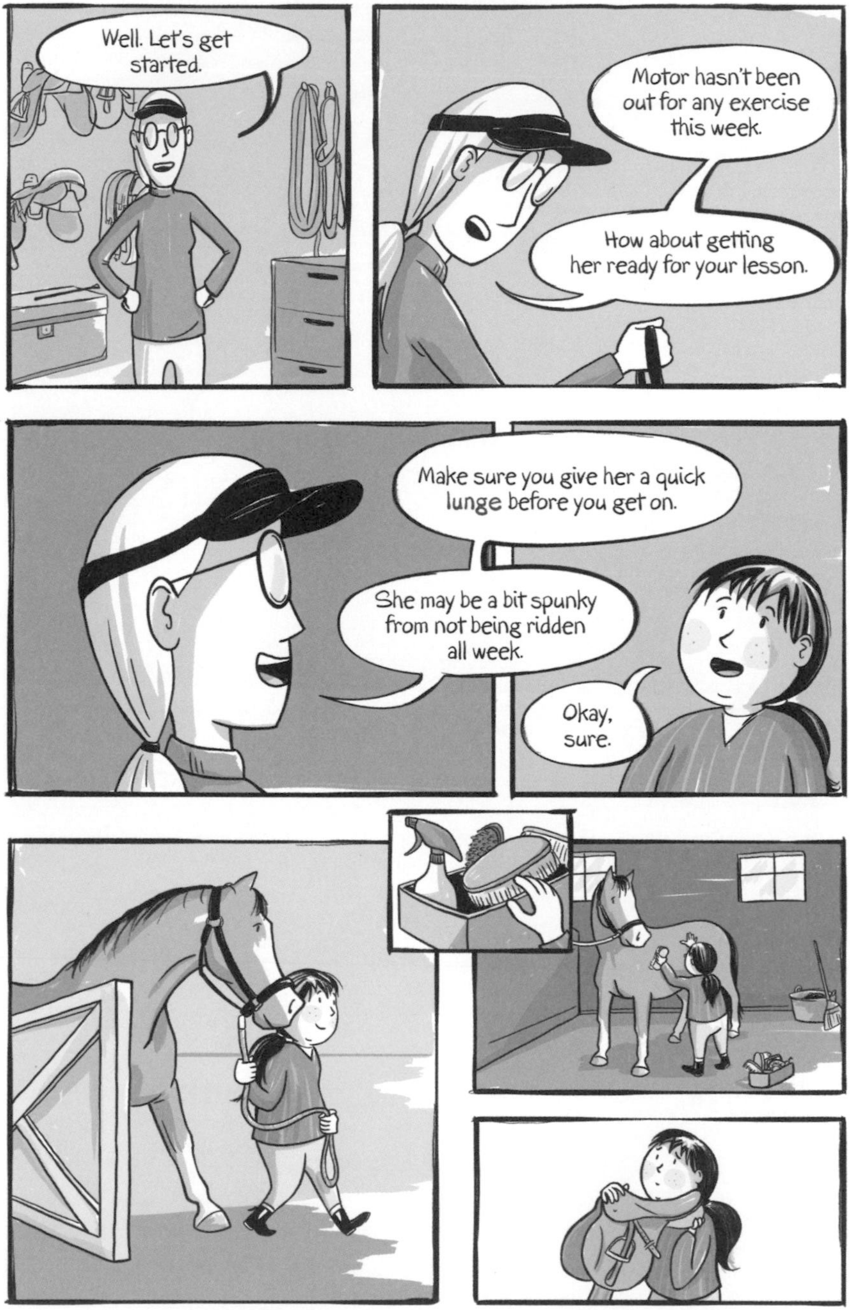

Well. Let's get started.
Motor hasn't been out for any exercise this week.
How about getting her ready for your lesson.
Make sure you give her a quick lunge before you get on.
She may be a bit spunky from not being ridden all week.
Okay, sure.

Lunge: Attaching a line to your horse, then holding the other end and having them exercise around you in a circle.

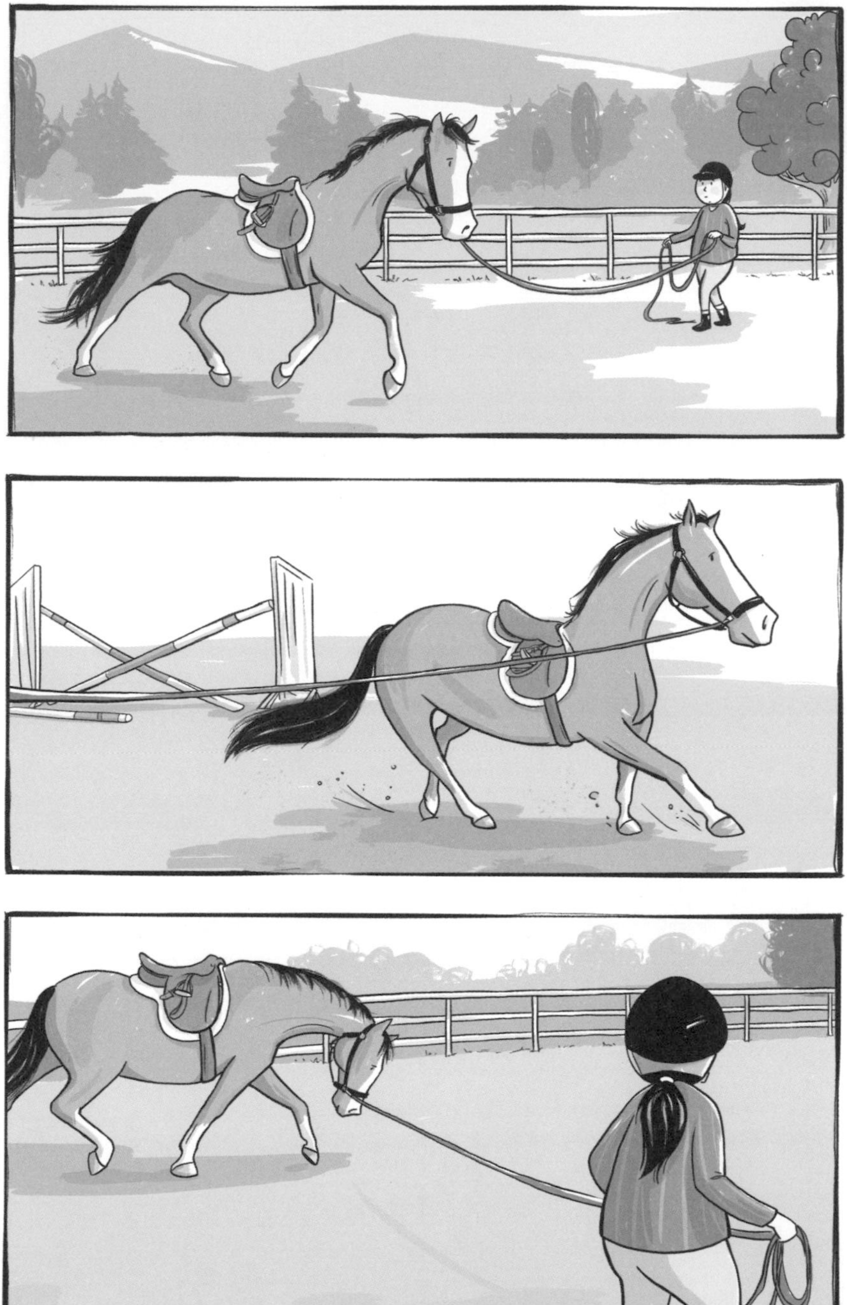

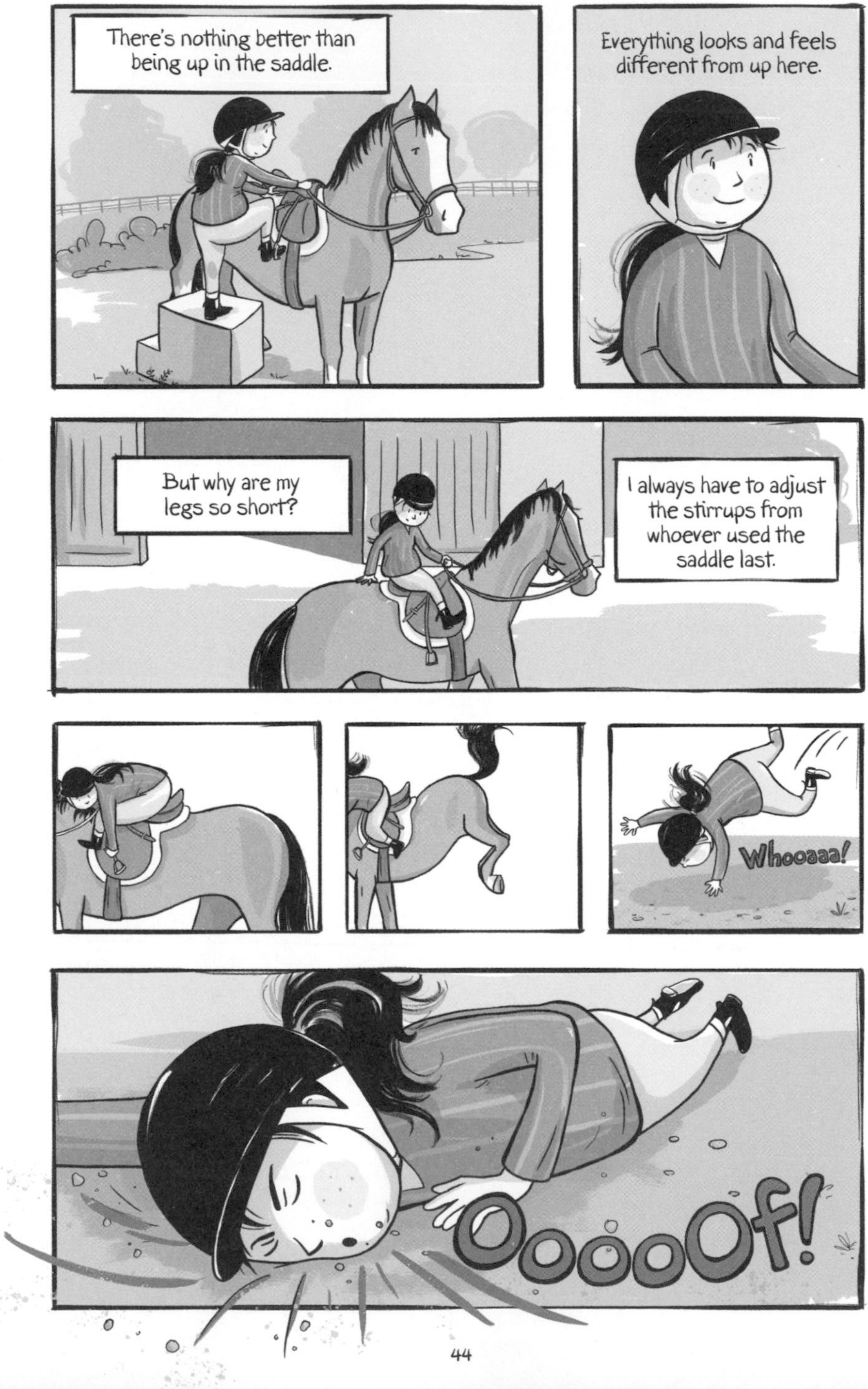
There's nothing better than being up in the saddle.
Everything looks and feels different from up here.
But why are my legs so short?
I always have to adjust the stirrups from whoever used the saddle last.
Whooaaa!
OooooOf!

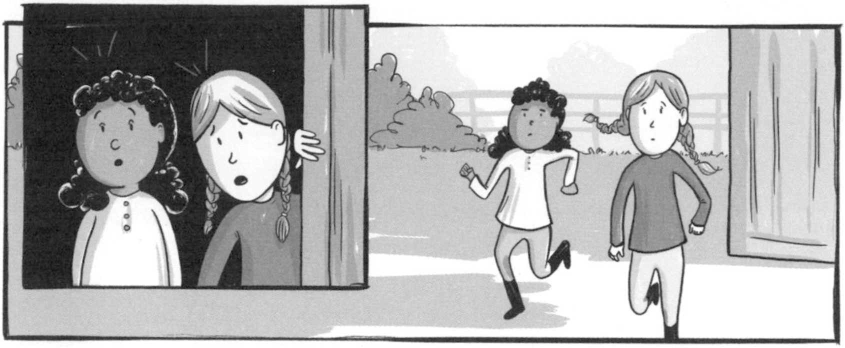

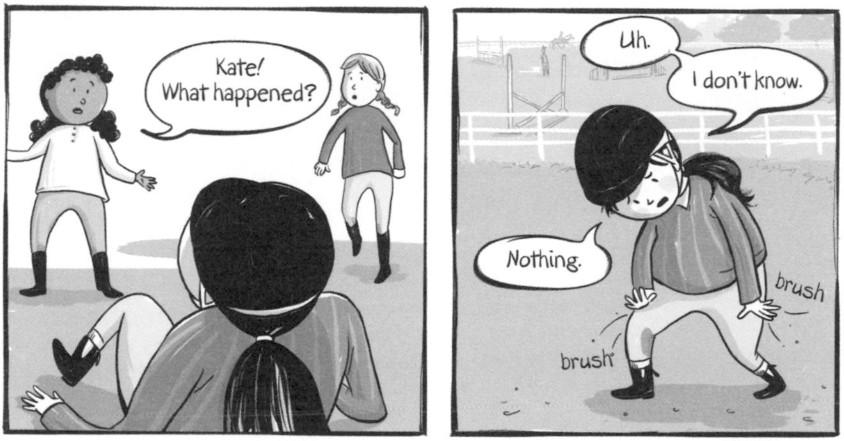
Kate!
What happened?
Uh.
I don't know.
Nothing.
brush
brush

Oh, great! I don't want Barb to think that I didn't lunge Motor first like she asked. If she thinks I can't follow directions—or worse, that I can't stay on my horse—how will she ever think I'm ready for the Black Hawk Classic?!

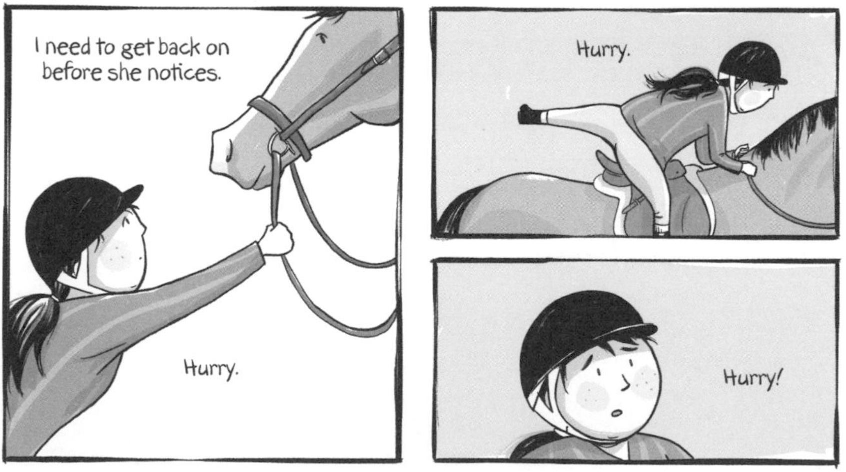
I need to get back on before she notices.
Hurry.
Hurry.
Hurry!

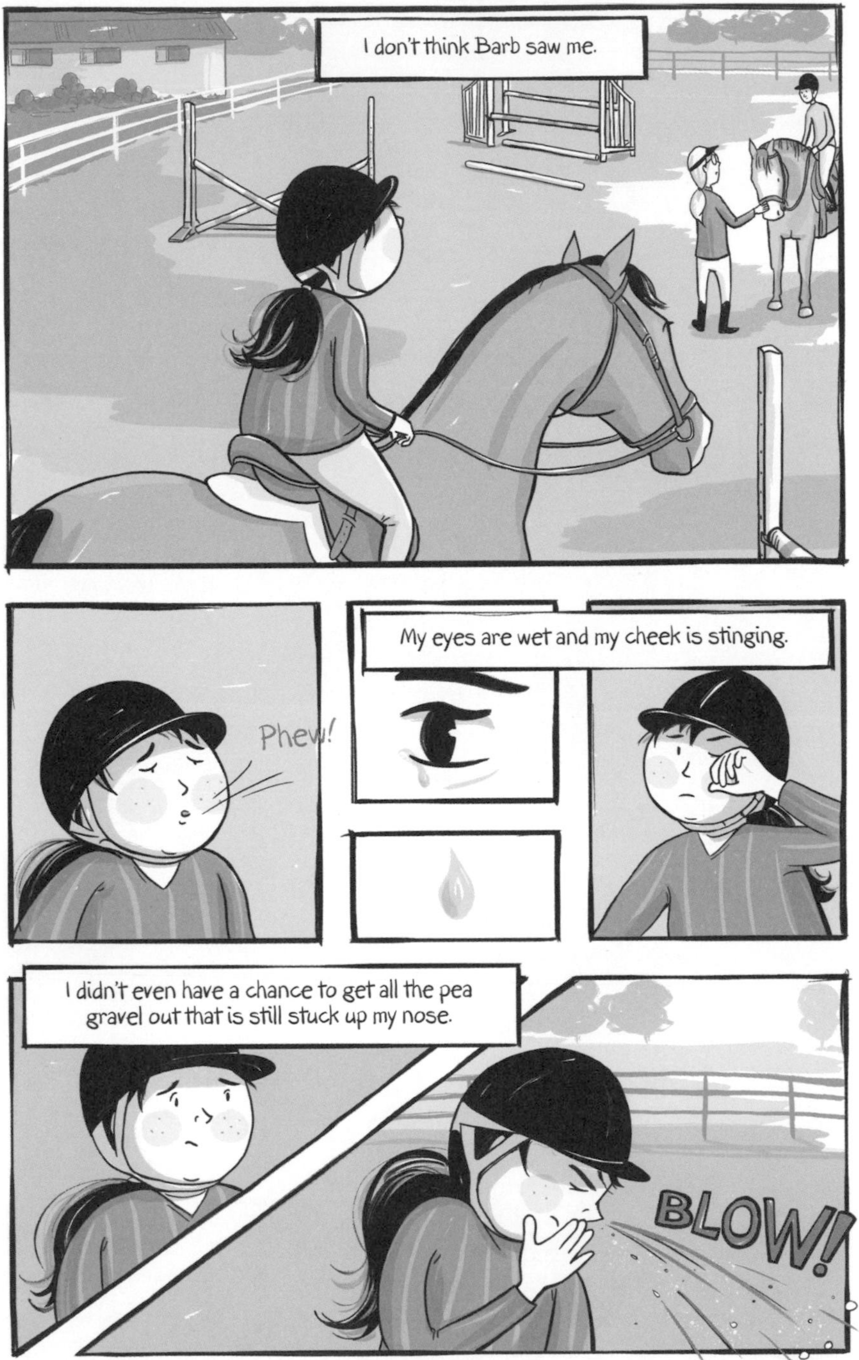
I don't think Barb saw me.
Phew!
My eyes are wet and my cheek is stinging.
I didn't even have a chance to get all the pea gravel out that is still stuck up my nose.
BLOW!

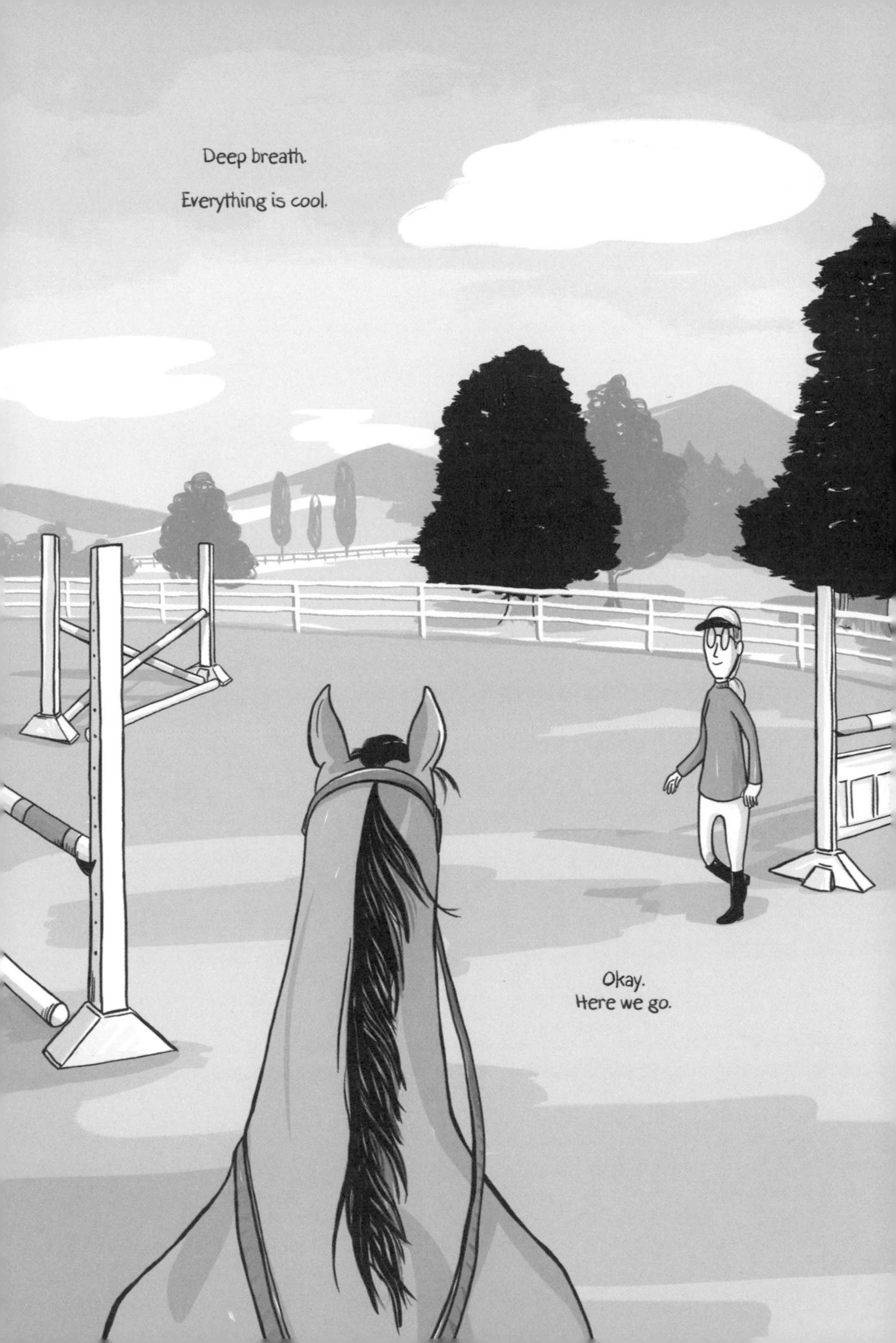
Deep breath.
Everything is cool.
Okay.
Here we go.

Chapter 3
Butt Clench

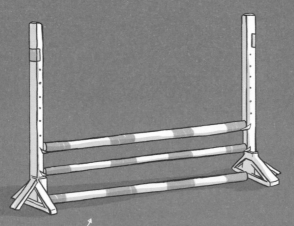

Vertical

A singular fence with poles or planks placed one directly above another.

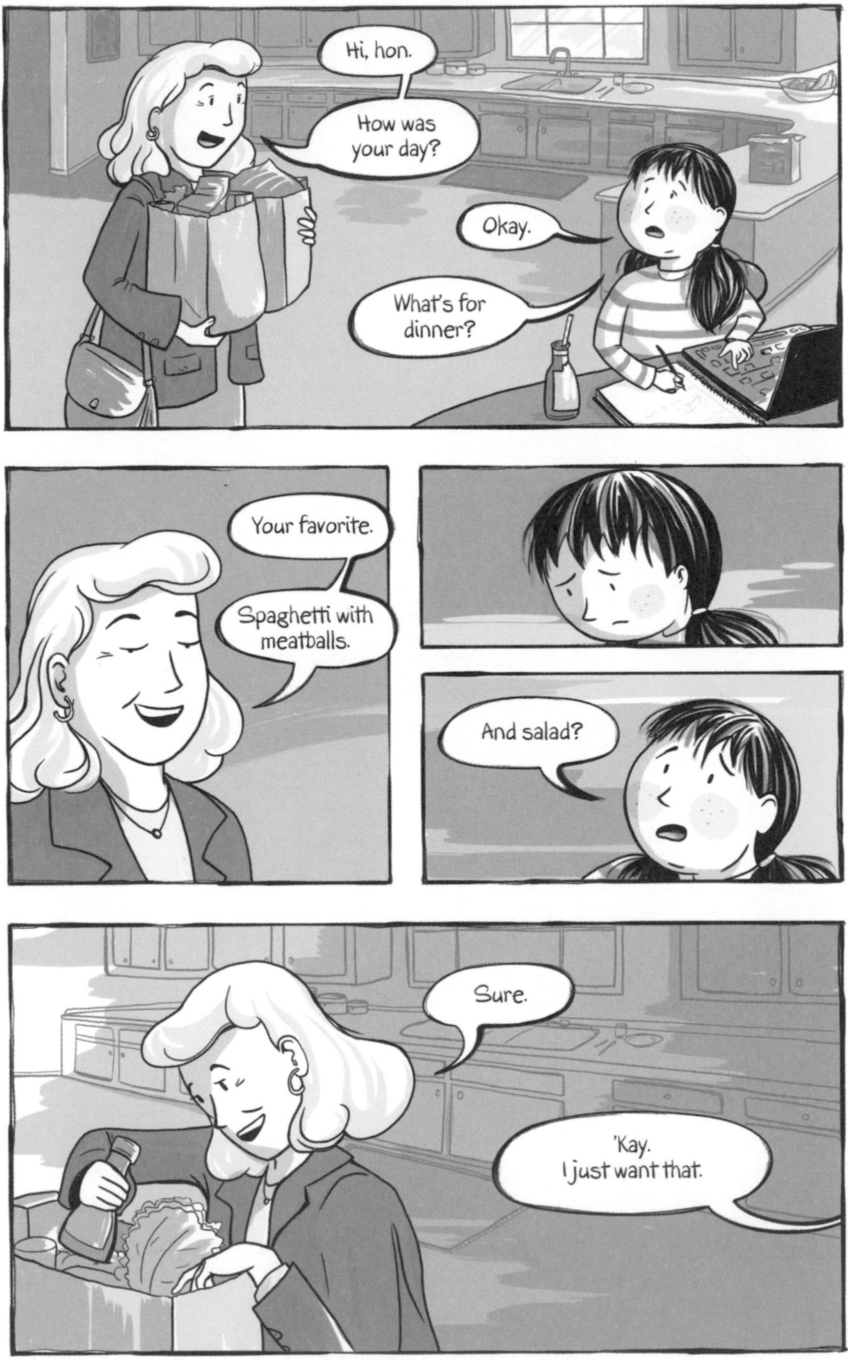
Hi, hon.
How was your day?
Okay.
What's for dinner?
Your favorite.
Spaghetti with meatballs.
And salad?
Sure.
'Kay. I just want that.

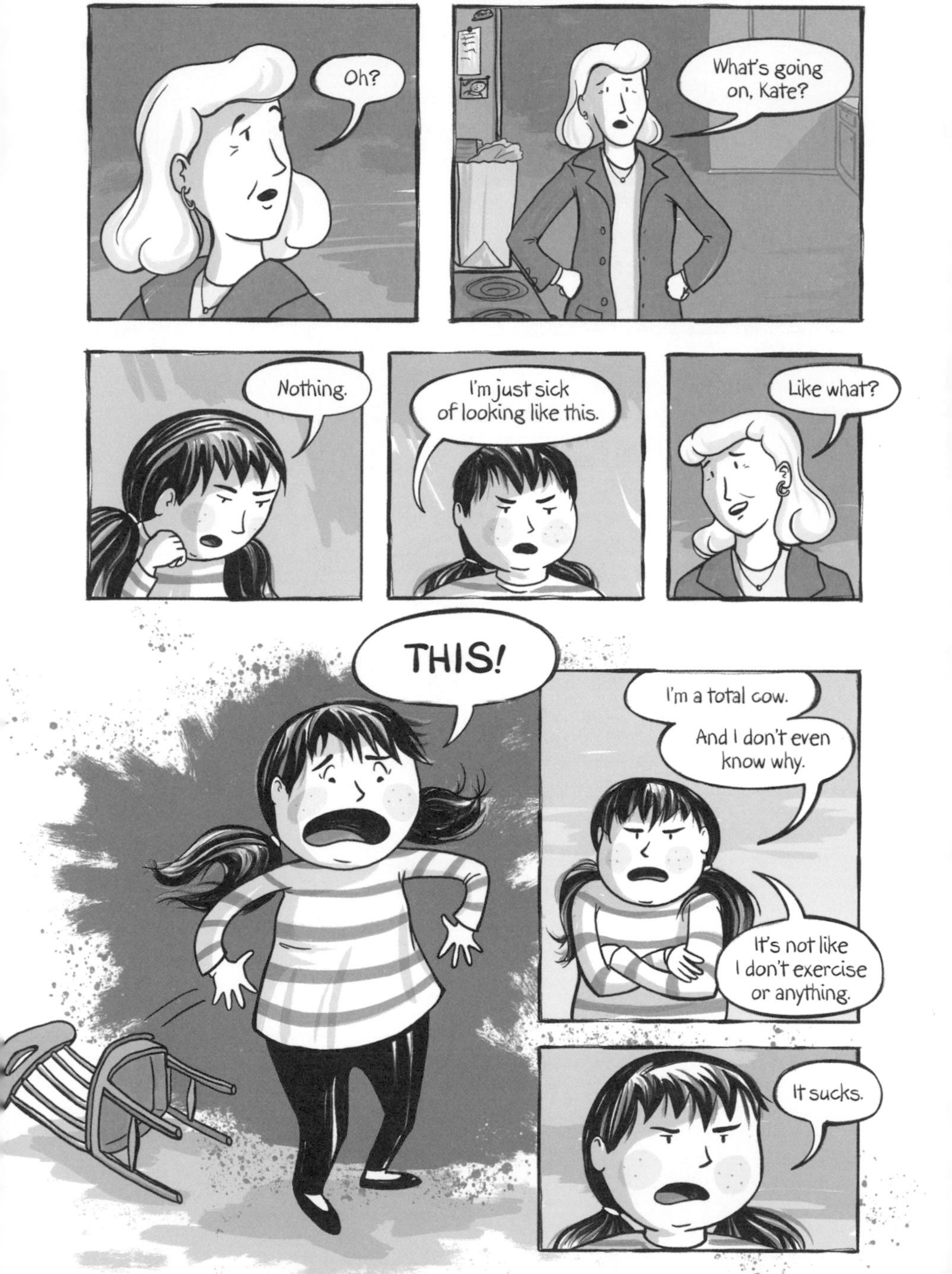
Oh?
What's going on, Kate?
Nothing.
I'm just sick of looking like this.
Like what?
THIS!
I'm a total cow.
And I don't even know why.
It's not like I don't exercise or anything.
It sucks.

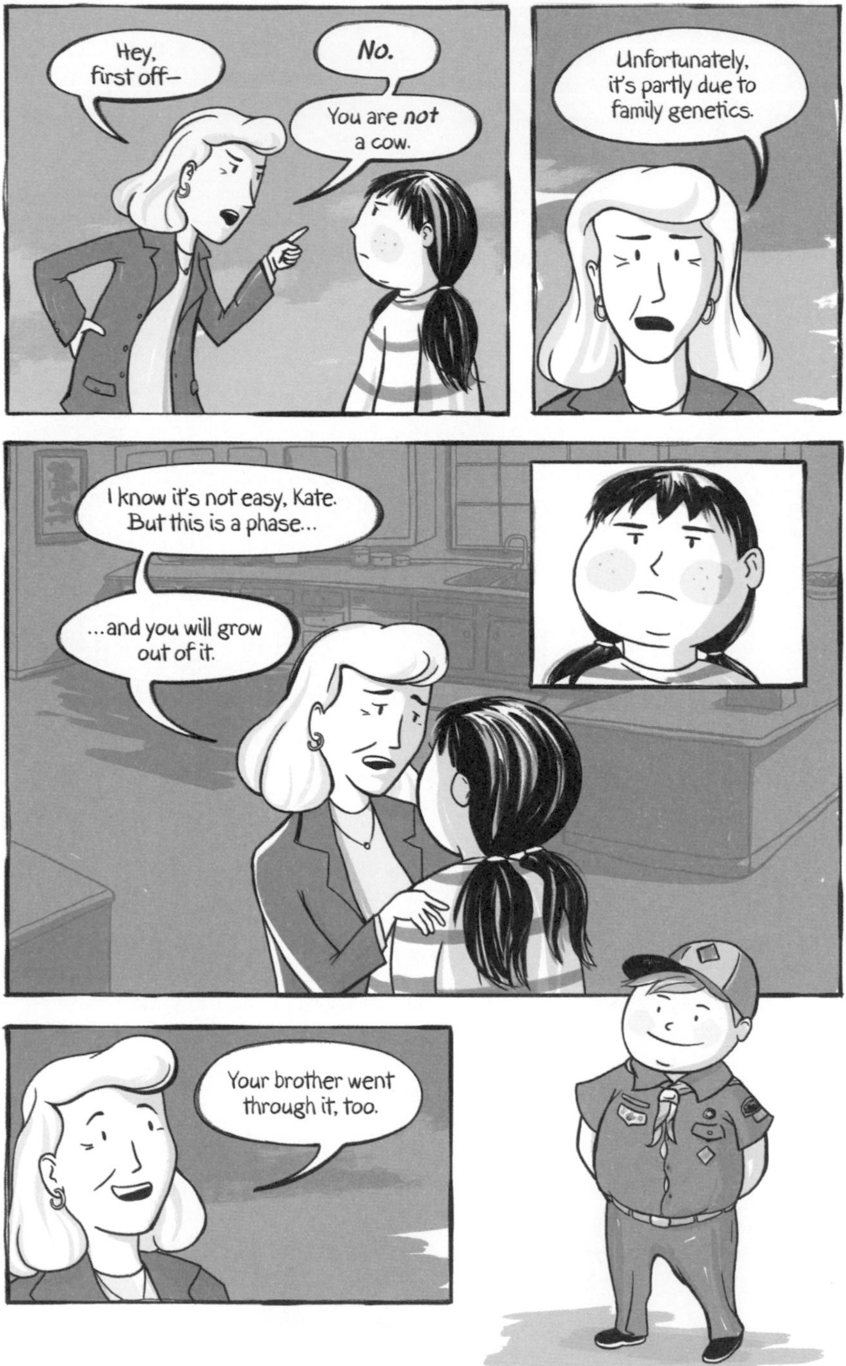

Hey, first off—
No.
You are *not* a cow.
Unfortunately, it's partly due to family genetics.
I know it's not easy, Kate. But this is a phase...
...and you will grow out of it.
Your brother went through it, too.

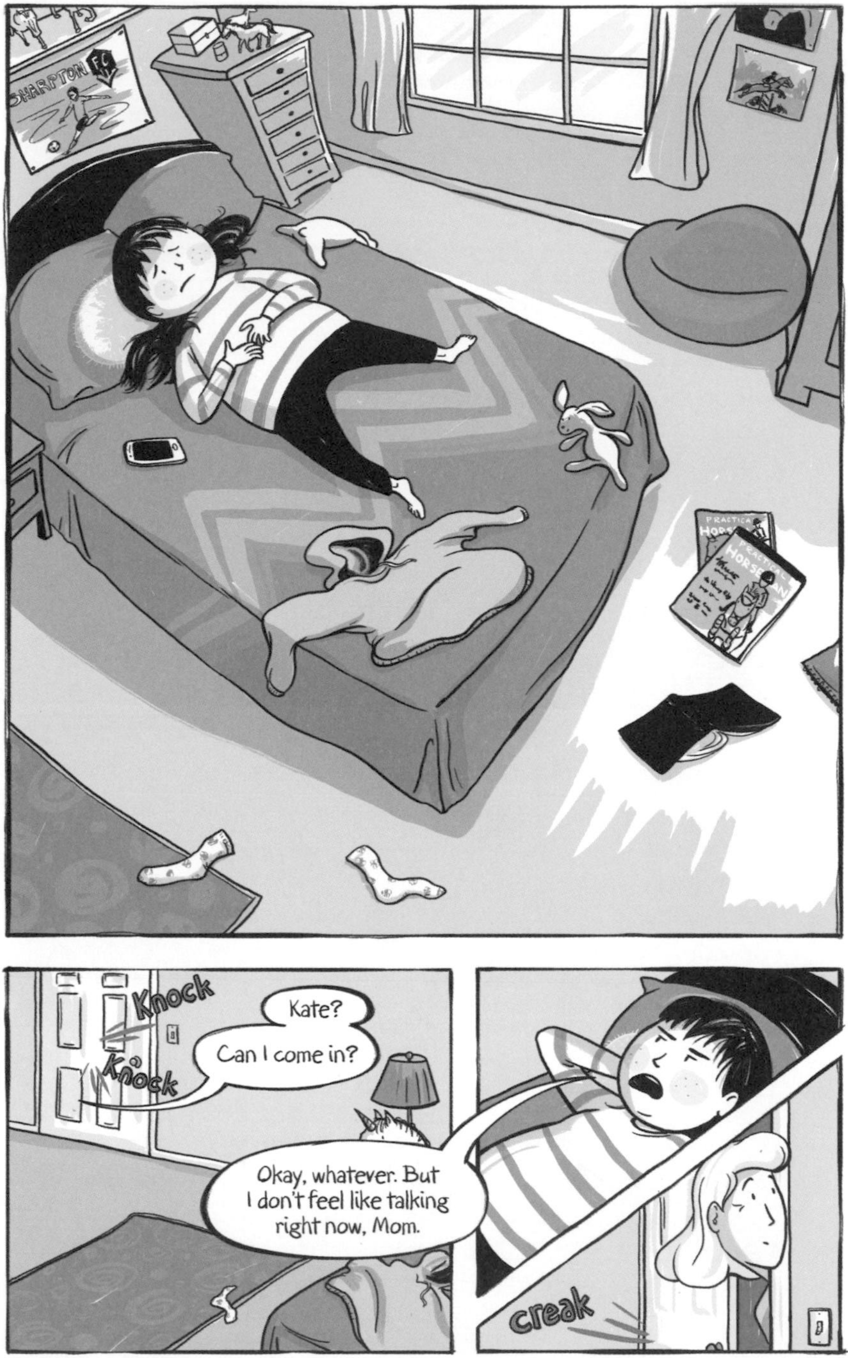
SHARPTON FC
PRACTICAL HORSEMAN
PRACTICAL HORSEMAN
Knock
Knock
Kate?
Can I come in?
Okay, whatever. But I don't feel like talking right now, Mom.
creak

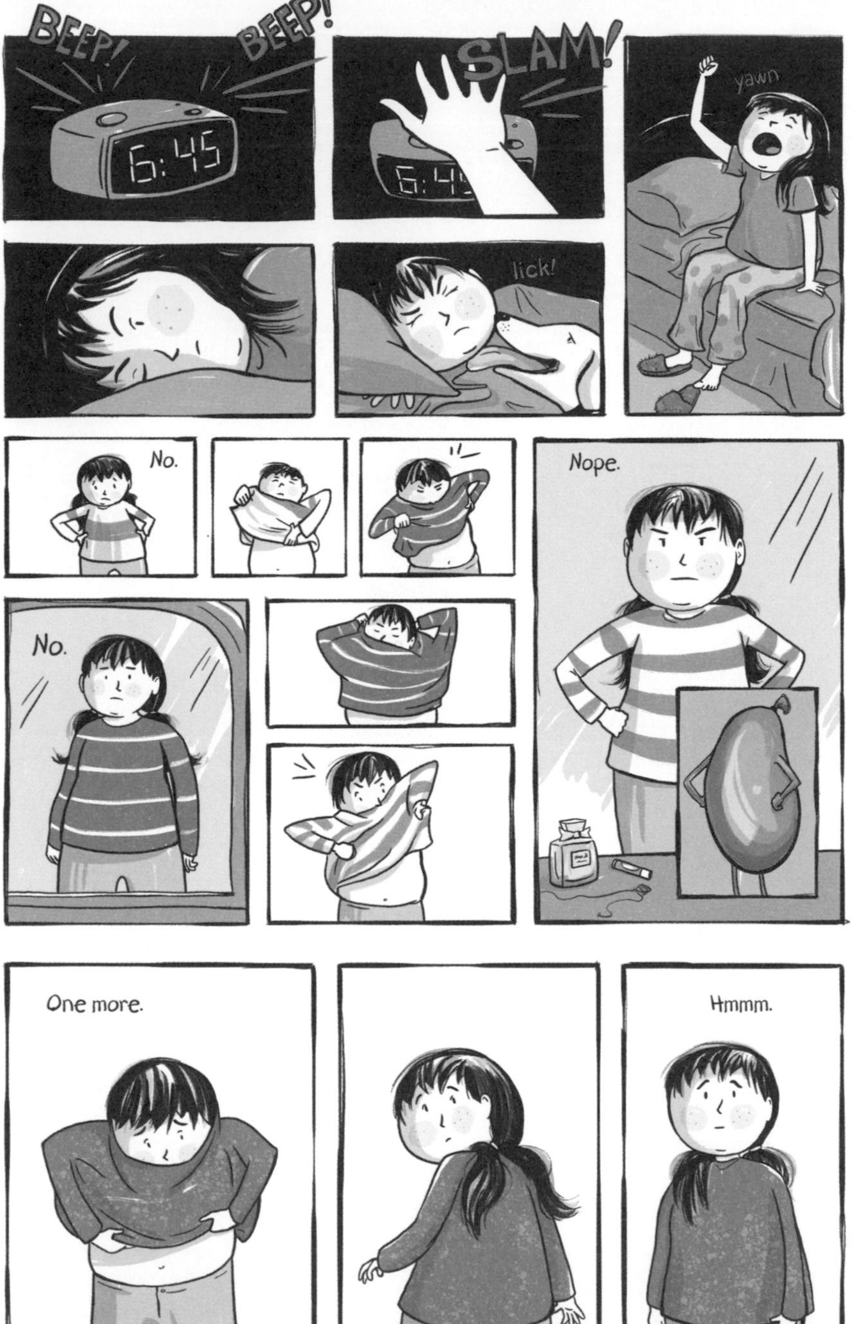
BEEP!
BEEP!
6:45
SLAM!
yawn
lick!
No.
Nope.
No.
One more.
Hmmm.

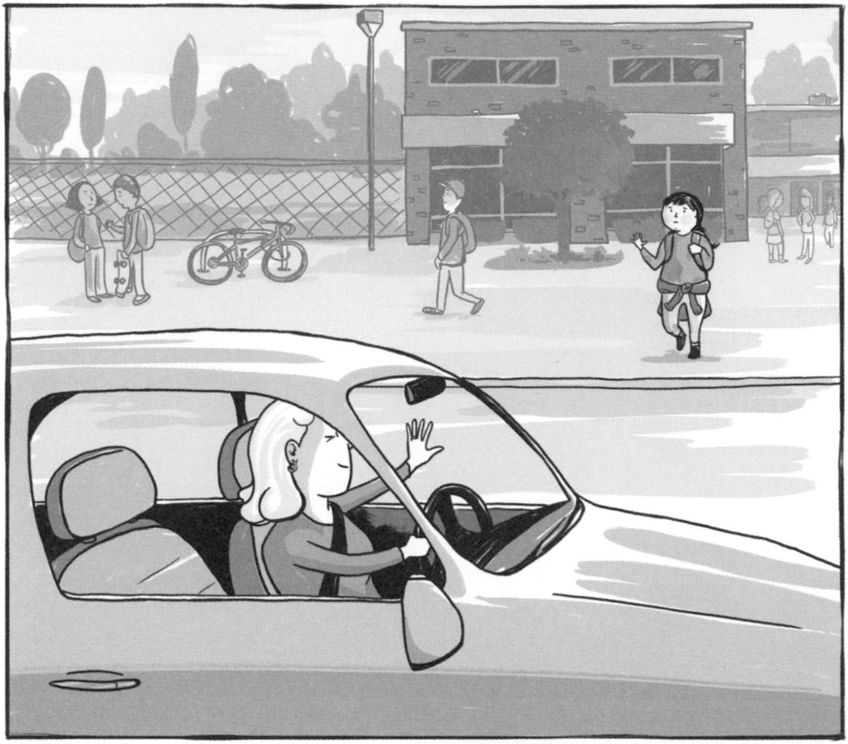

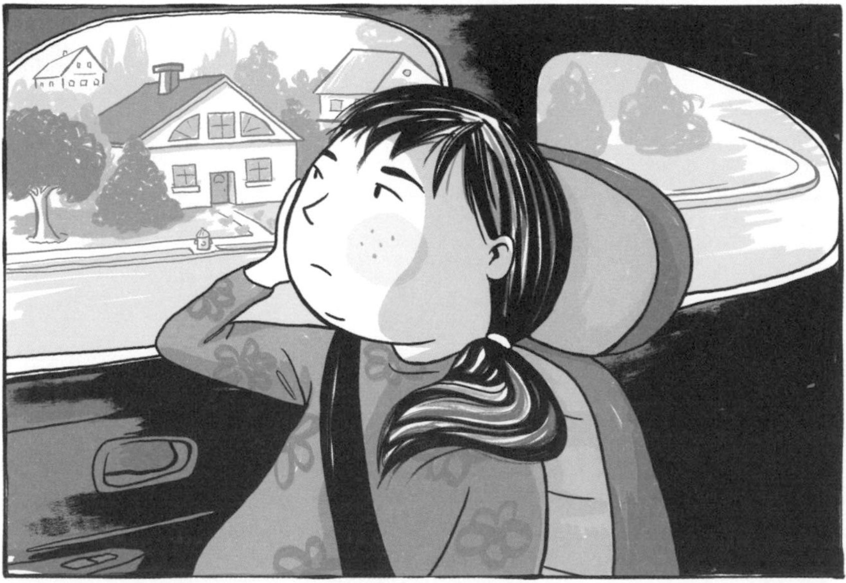

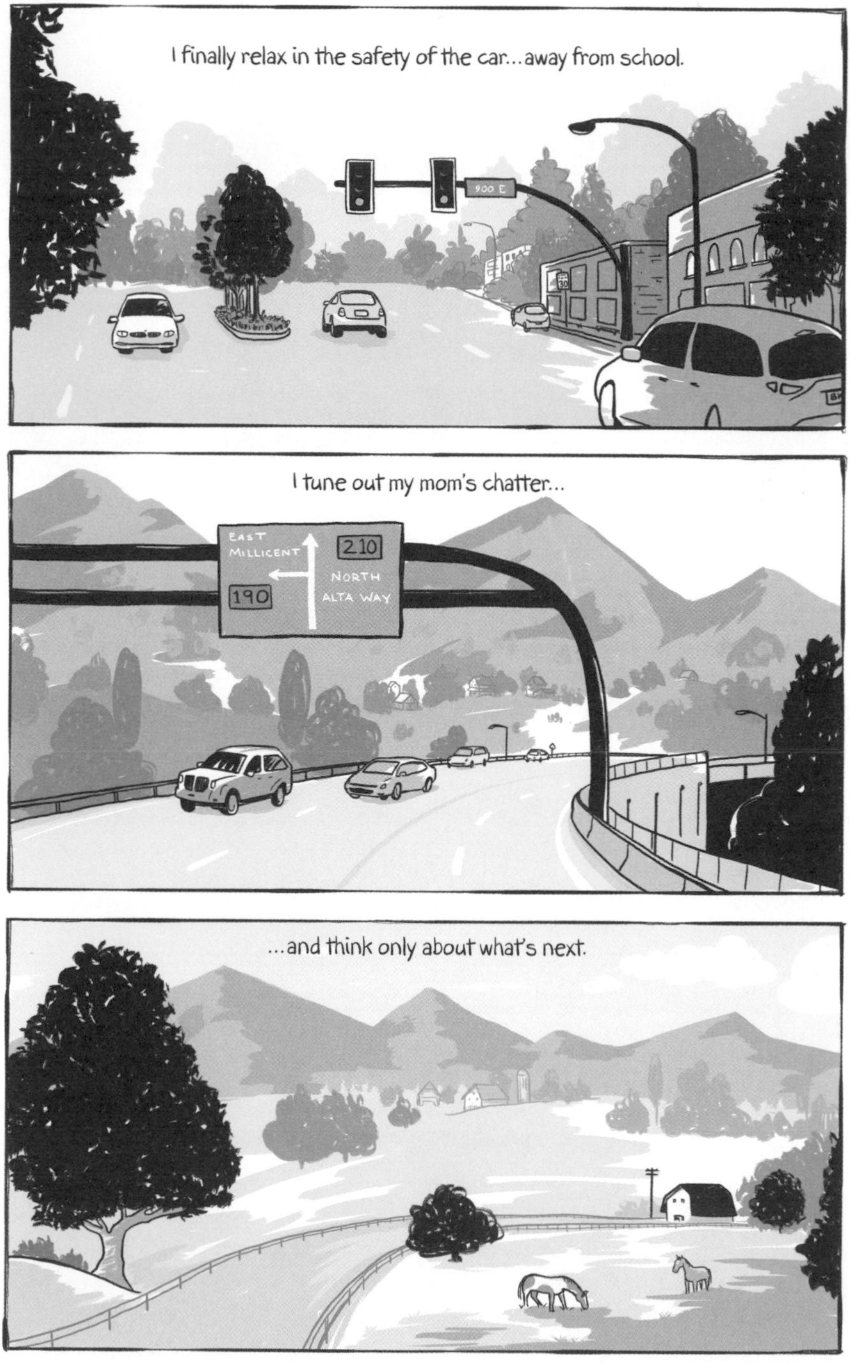
I finally relax in the safety of the car... away from school.
900 E
I tune out my mom's chatter...
EAST MILLICENT
210
NORTH ALTA WAY
190
...and think only about what's next.

Equitation: One of the three main divisions at a horse show (hunter, jumper, and equitation). Equitation is judged solely on the rider's ability and their positioning on the horse.

Appaloosa: A breed of horse best known for their colorful, spotted coat patterns.

Schooling horse: An experienced horse at a barn that is used for lessons, often for beginner riders or riders who do not own their own horse.

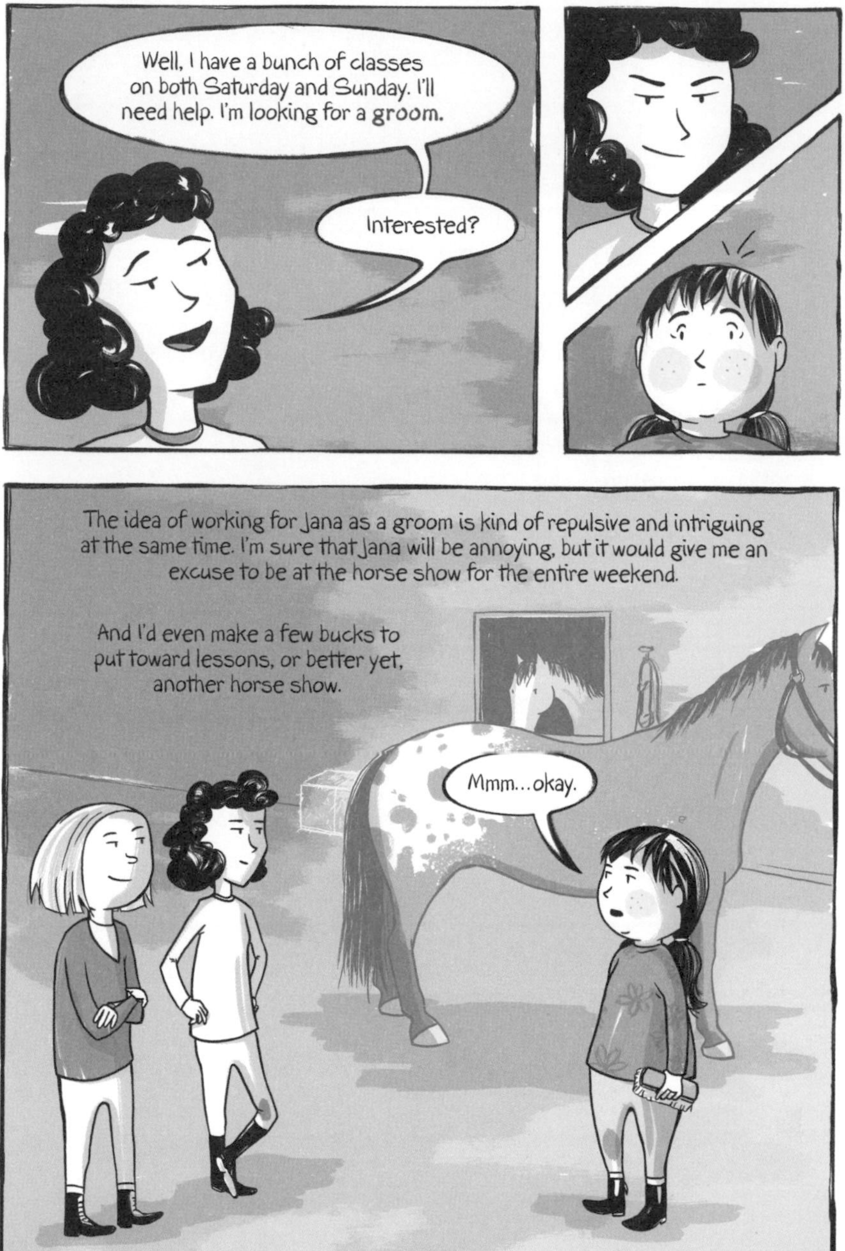
Well, I have a bunch of classes on both Saturday and Sunday. I'll need help. I'm looking for a groom.
Interested?
The idea of working for Jana as a groom is kind of repulsive and intriguing at the same time. I'm sure that Jana will be annoying, but it would give me an excuse to be at the horse show for the entire weekend.
And I'd even make a few bucks to put toward lessons, or better yet, another horse show.
Mmm...okay.

Groom: Someone hired to help clean, braid, and ready a horse for a horse show as well as perform any other jobs that the rider requires.

Seat: Using your body weight, posture, and positioning in the saddle to communicate with your horse.

Ziggy patiently stands in the middle of the arena while I do 360-degree rotations on his back.

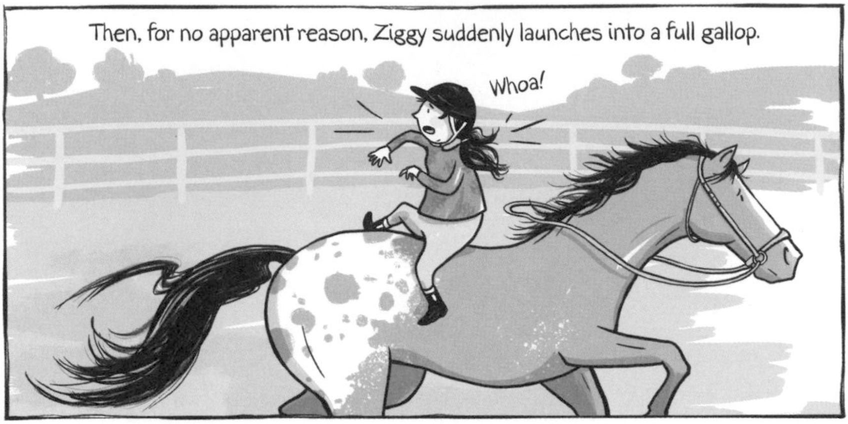
Then, for no apparent reason, Ziggy suddenly launches into a full gallop.
Whoa!

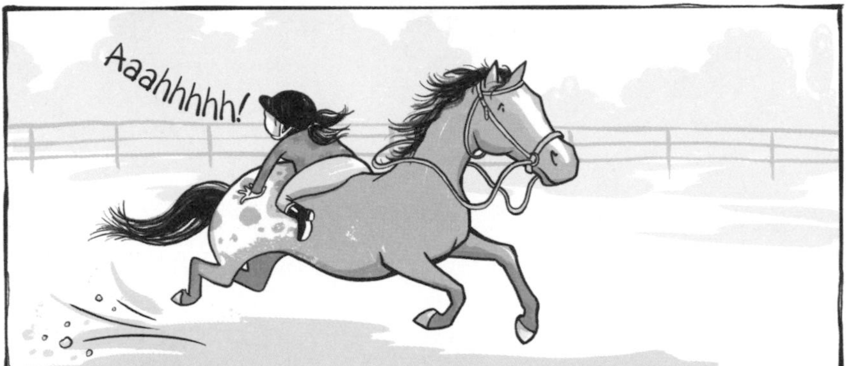
Aaahhhhh!

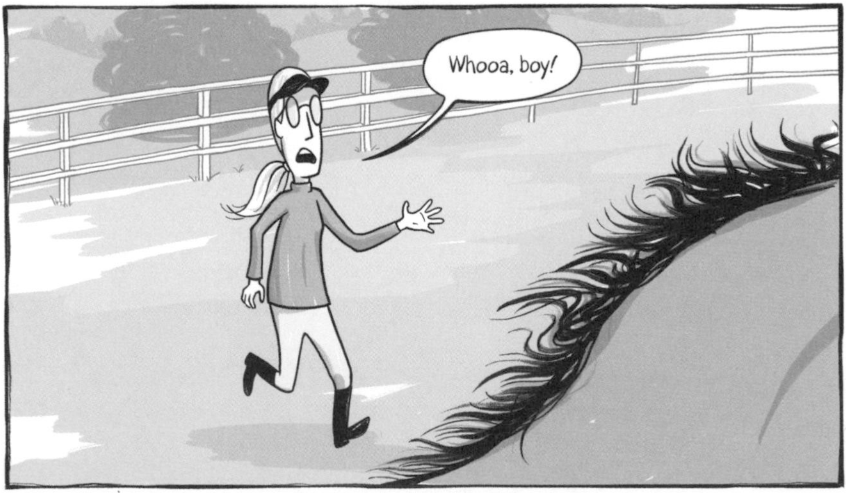
Whooa, boy!

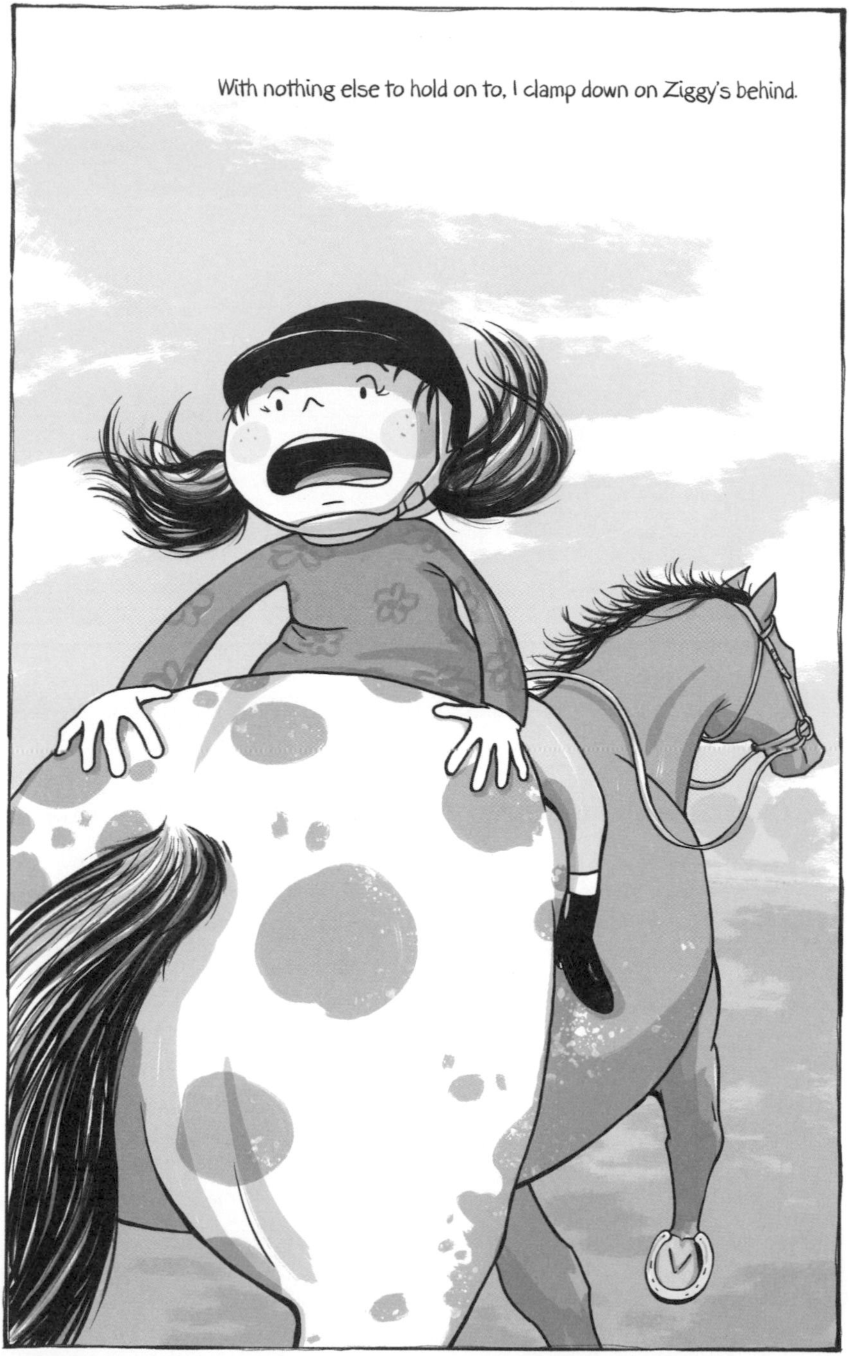
With nothing else to hold on to, I clamp down on Ziggy's behind.

Chapter 4
Shadow Spook

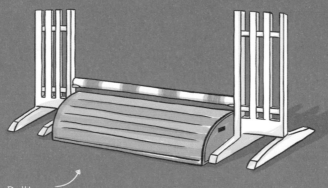

Rolltop

A jump with a rounded, half-barrel appearance.

Western vs. English: Two different types of riding styles, with differing equipment and attire. Western developed from the needs of cowboys who worked cattle from horseback. English riding takes many of its traditions and equipment from European mounted military styles.

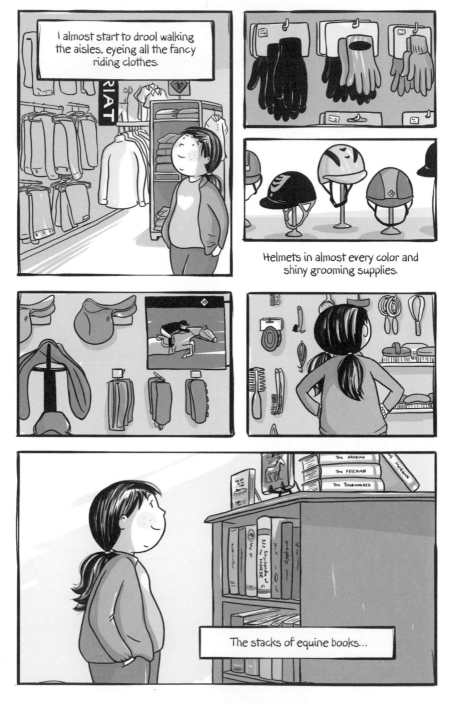

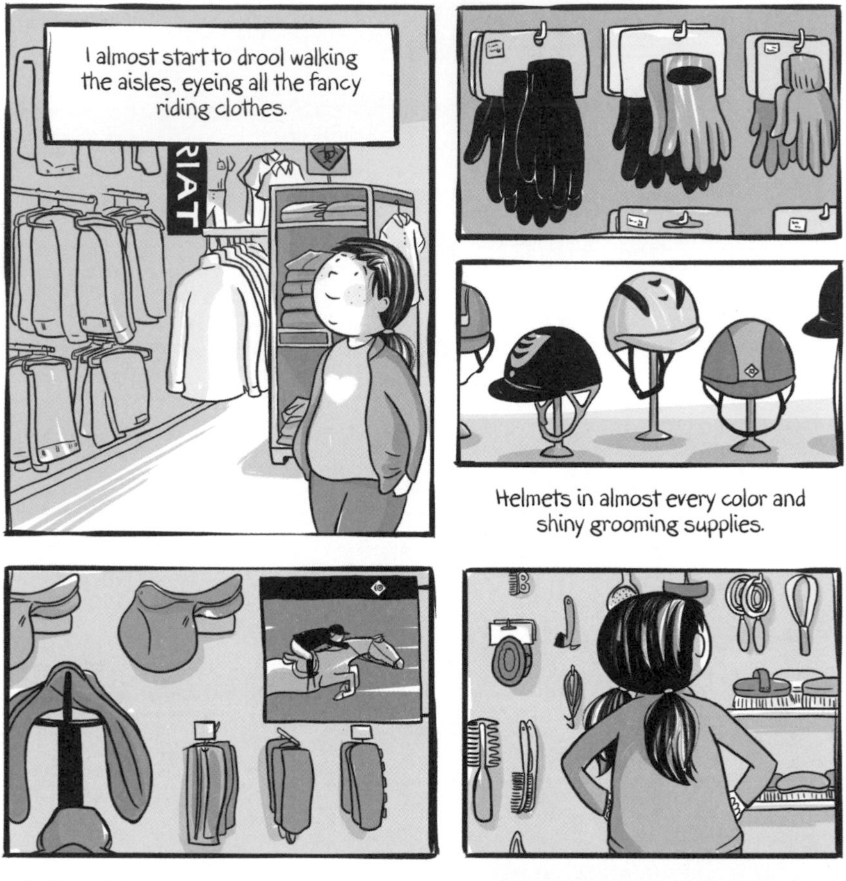
I almost start to drool walking the aisles, eyeing all the fancy riding clothes.
RIAT
Helmets in almost every color and shiny grooming supplies.
The ARABIAN
The FRIESIAN
MORGAN
Encyclopedia of the HORSE
The stacks of equine books...

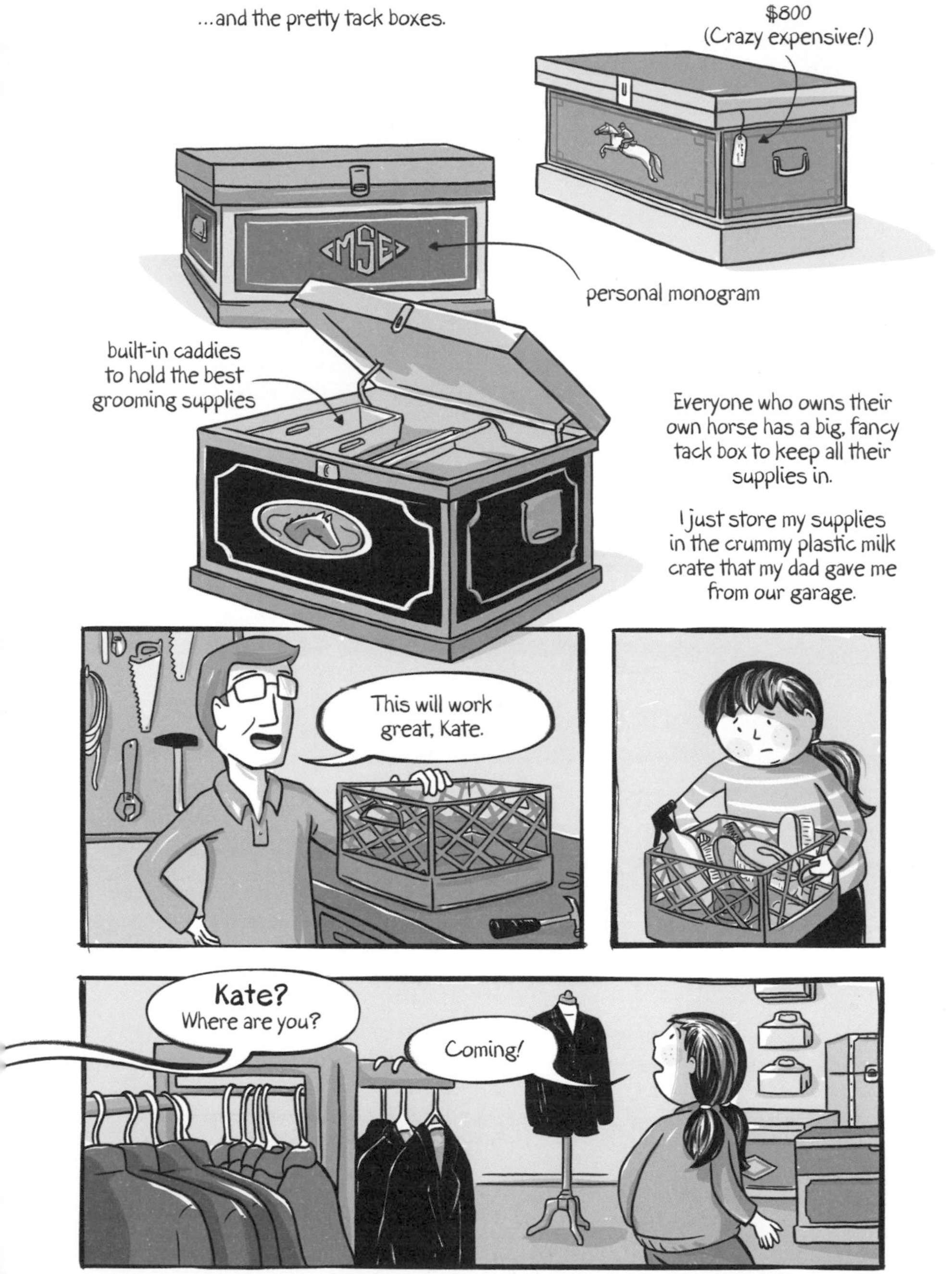
...and the pretty tack boxes.
$800
(Crazy expensive!)
personal monogram
built-in caddies to hold the best grooming supplies
Everyone who owns their own horse has a big, fancy tack box to keep all their supplies in.
I just store my supplies in the crummy plastic milk crate that my dad gave me from our garage.
This will work great, Kate.
Kate? Where are you?
Coming!

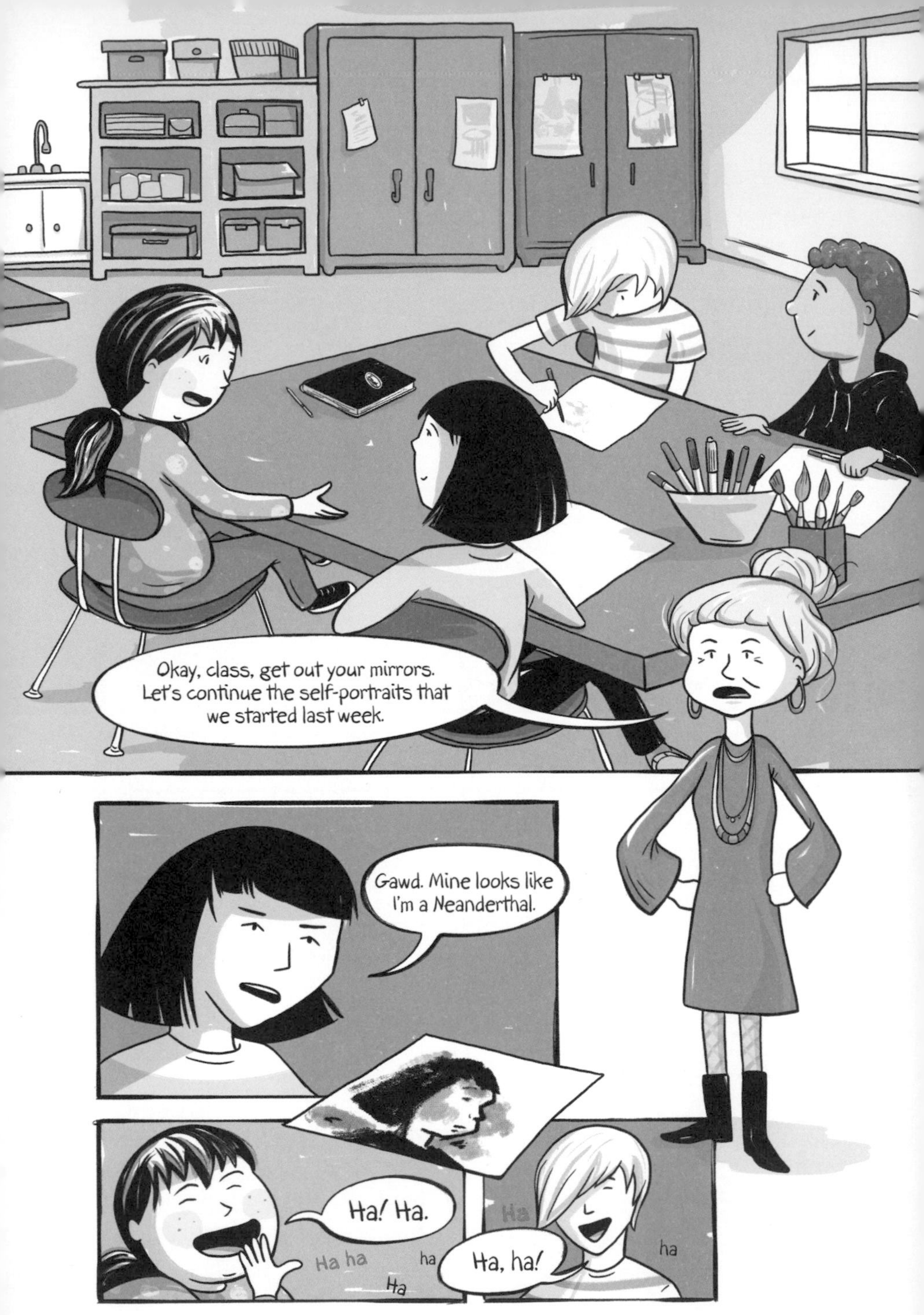
Okay, class, get out your mirrors. Let's continue the self-portraits that we started last week.
Gawd. Mine looks like I'm a Neanderthal.
Ha! Ha.
Ha ha
ha
Ha
Ha
Ha, ha!
ha

My hands are completely sweaty.

I get so nervous sitting across from Grayson. He is so hot. His name even sounds like Hollywood.

shake   shake

Dreaming about Grayson helps ease the sting of Matthew's Becky obsession.

great hair

GRAYSON

AQUARIUS

12 Years

dreamy eyes

styley plaid shirt

Into 👍
Art
French fries
Skateboarding
New sneakers
Video games
Comic books

Not Into 👎
Football
Math class
Drama queens
Baggy pants
K-Pop bands

chips

backpack with patches

sketchbook

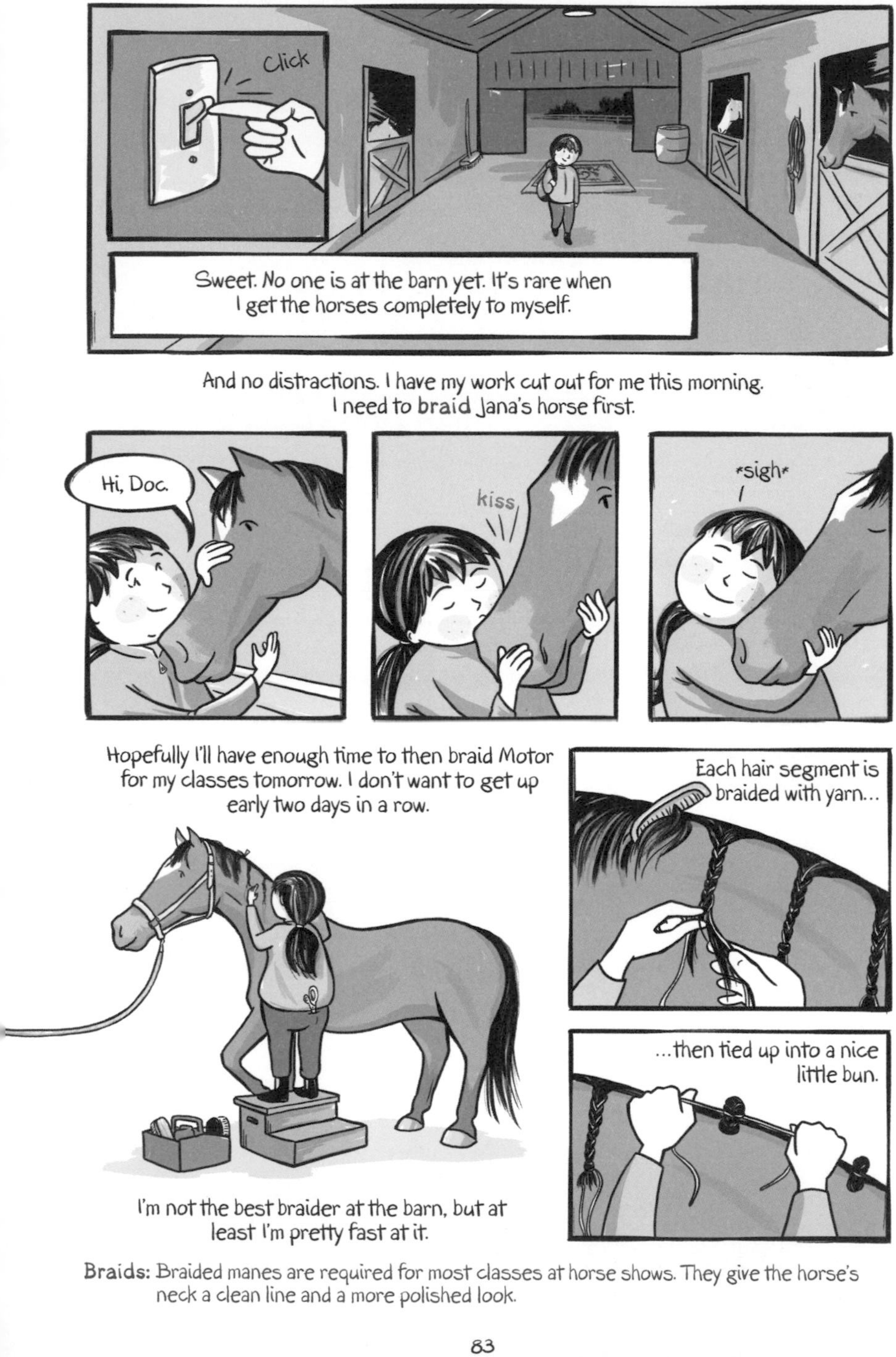
Click
Sweet. No one is at the barn yet. It's rare when I get the horses completely to myself.
And no distractions. I have my work cut out for me this morning. I need to braid Jana's horse first.
Hi, Doc.
kiss
sigh
Hopefully I'll have enough time to then braid Motor for my classes tomorrow. I don't want to get up early two days in a row.
I'm not the best braider at the barn, but at least I'm pretty fast at it.
Each hair segment is braided with yarn...
...then tied up into a nice little bun.

Braids: Braided manes are required for most classes at horse shows. They give the horse's neck a clean line and a more polished look.

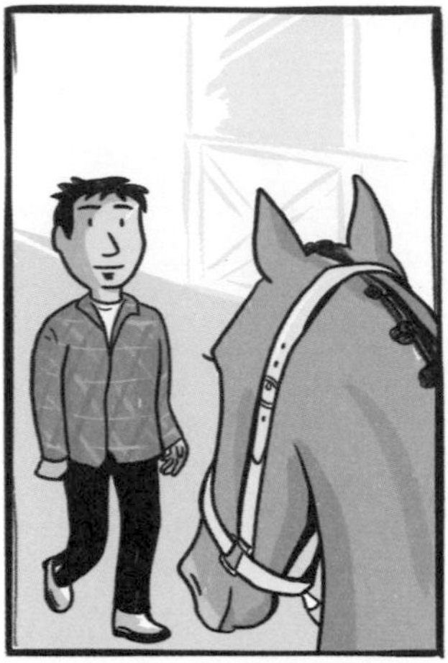

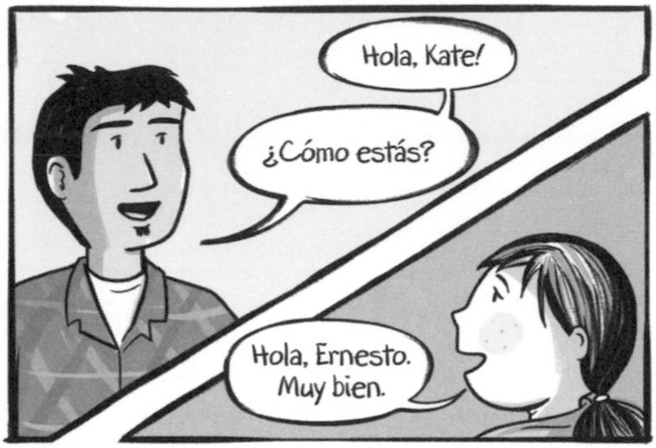
Hola, Kate!
¿Cómo estás?
Hola, Ernesto. Muy bien.

Ernesto works as a barn hand at Millcreek Farm. Barb hired him last year. He lives in a trailer at the far end of the property, all alone.

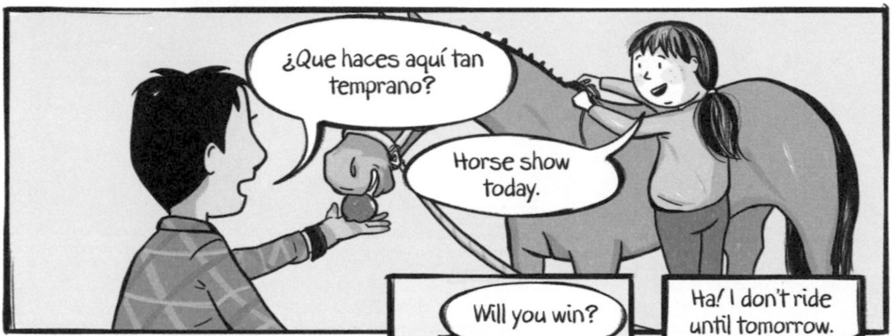
¿Que haces aquí tan temprano?
Horse show today.

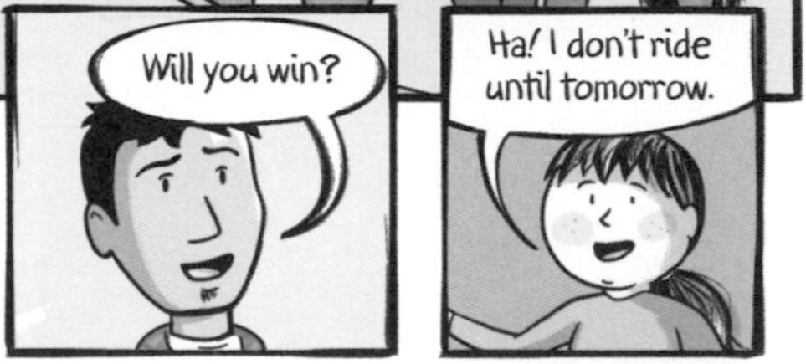
Will you win?
Ha! I don't ride until tomorrow.

Ernesto is great. He loves the horses, too. Something about his smile puts me at ease. I also get to practice my Spanish with him. He thinks it's really cool that I'm learning.

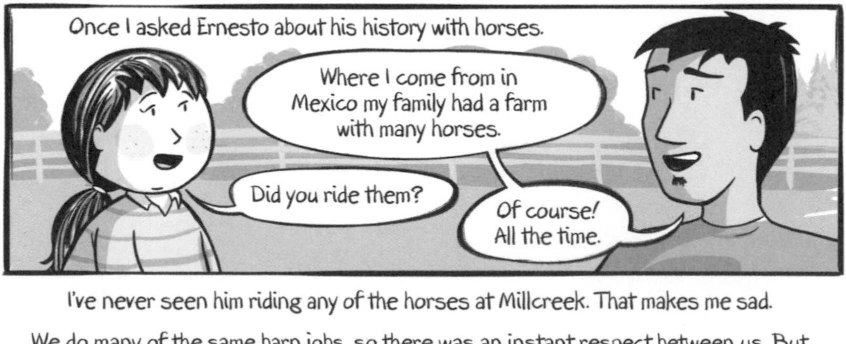
Once I asked Ernesto about his history with horses.
Where I come from in Mexico my family had a farm with many horses.
Did you ride them?
Of course! All the time.

I've never seen him riding any of the horses at Millcreek. That makes me sad.

We do many of the same barn jobs, so there was an instant respect between us. But sometimes I wonder how Ernesto really feels about working here.

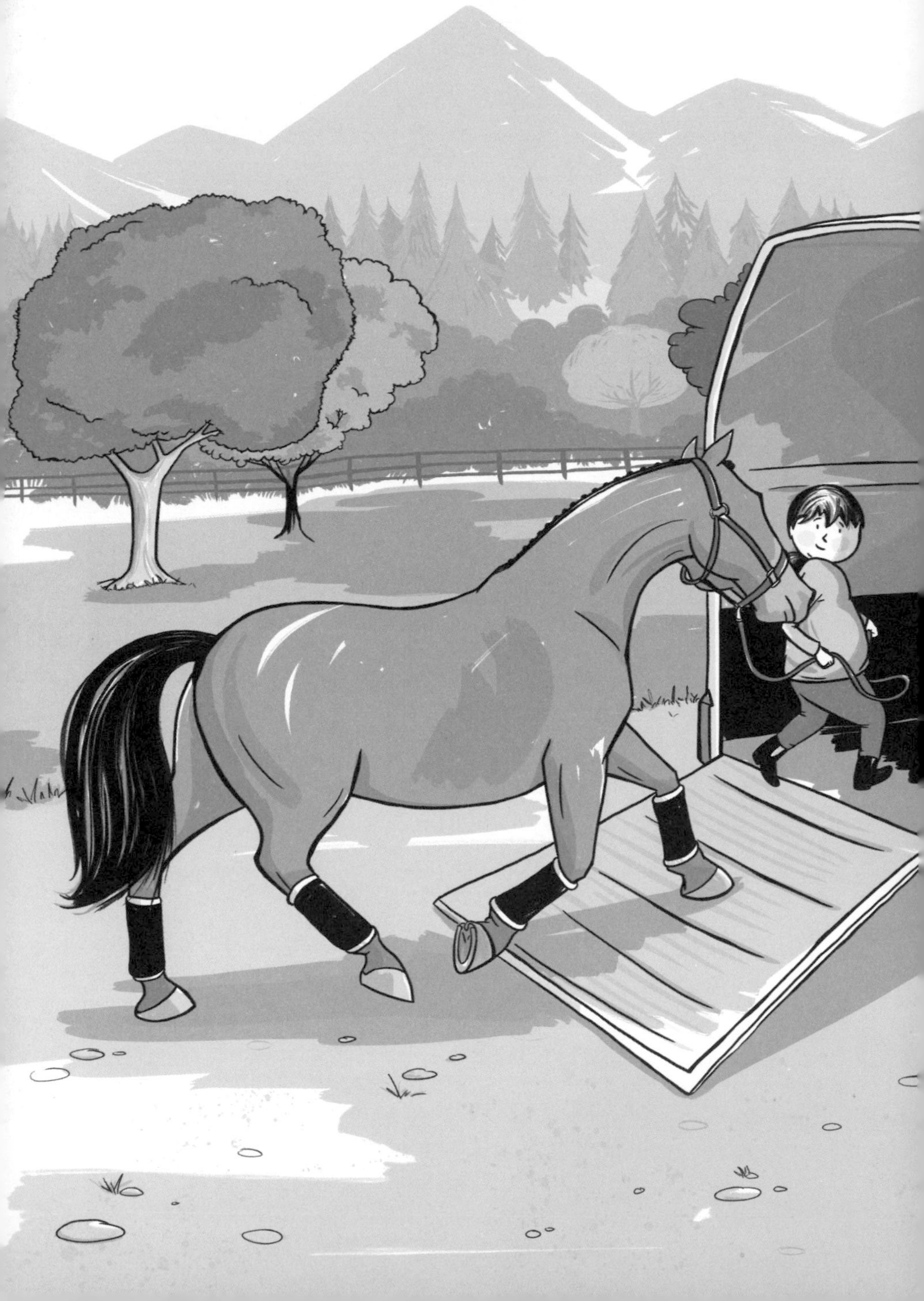

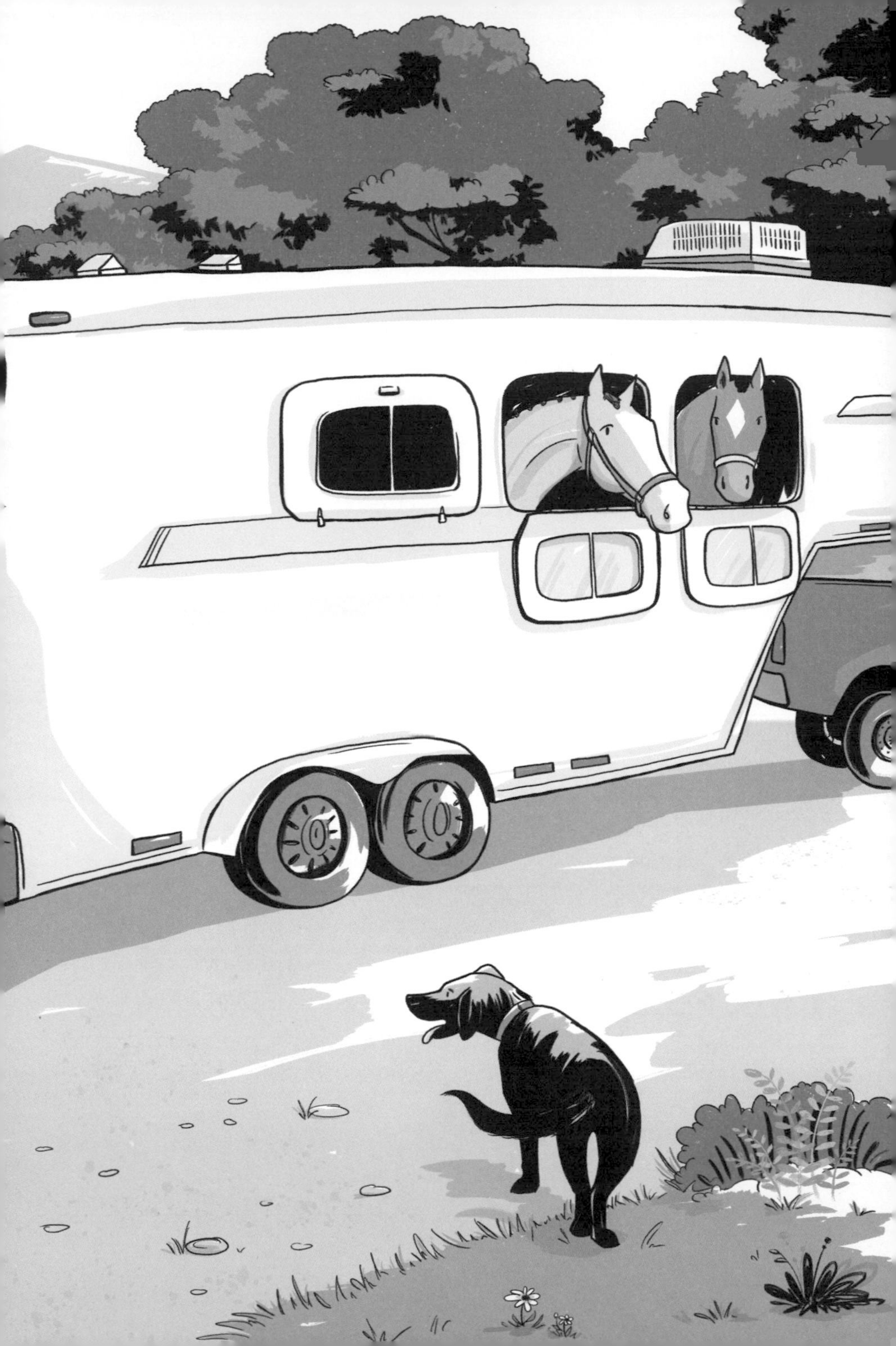

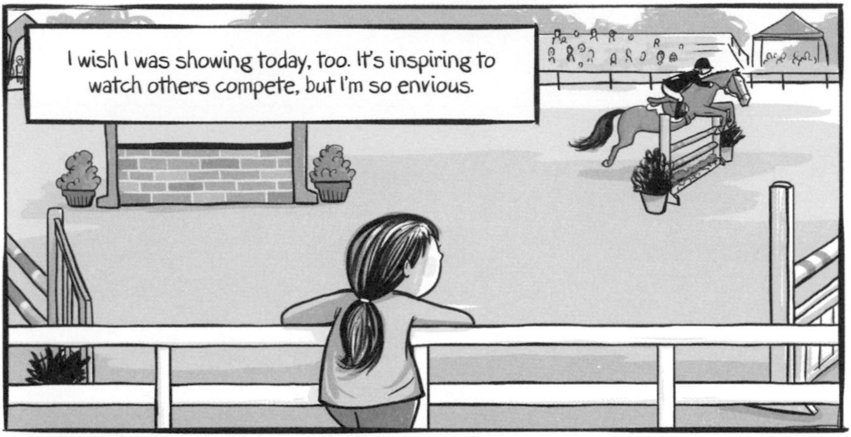
I wish I was showing today, too. It's inspiring to watch others compete, but I'm so envious.

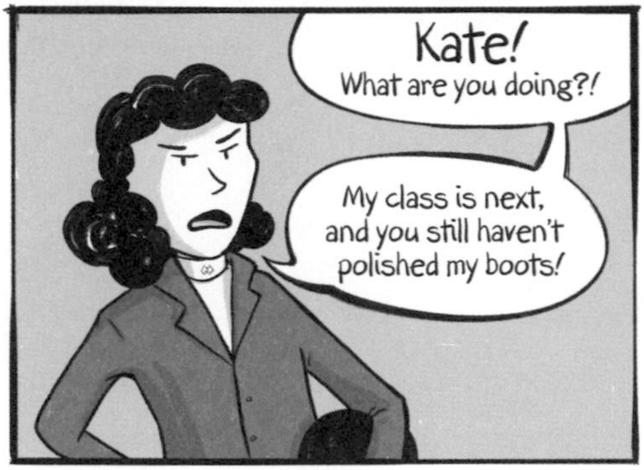
Kate!
What are you doing?!
My class is next, and you still haven't polished my boots!

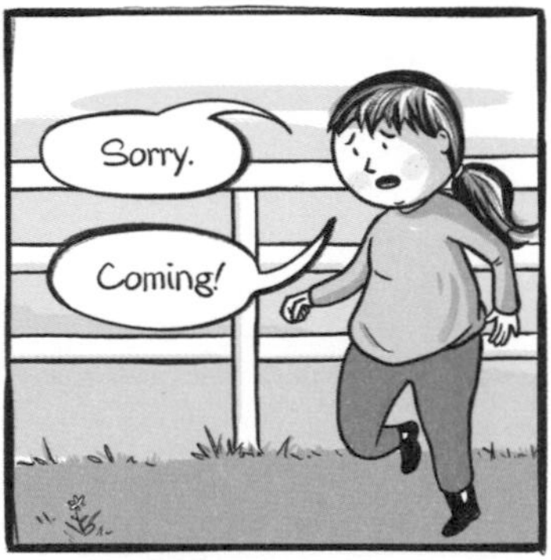
Sorry.
Coming!

Jana keeps me busy the rest of the day.

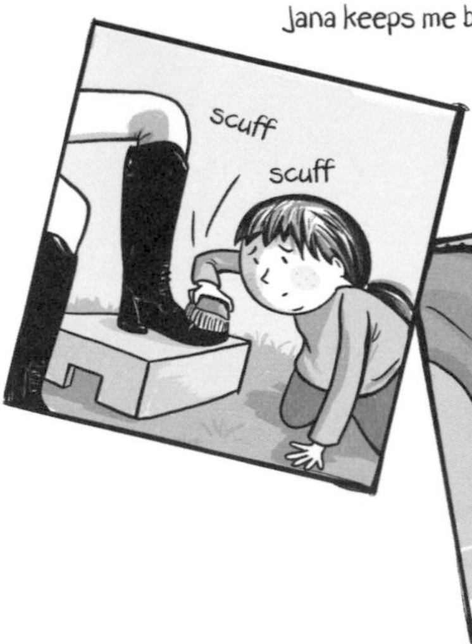
scuff
scuff

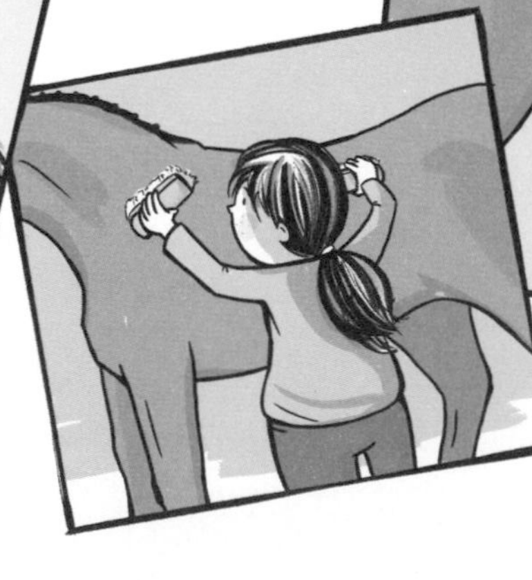

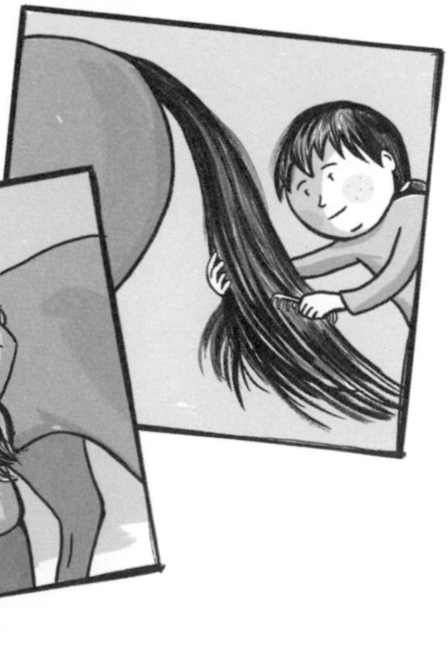

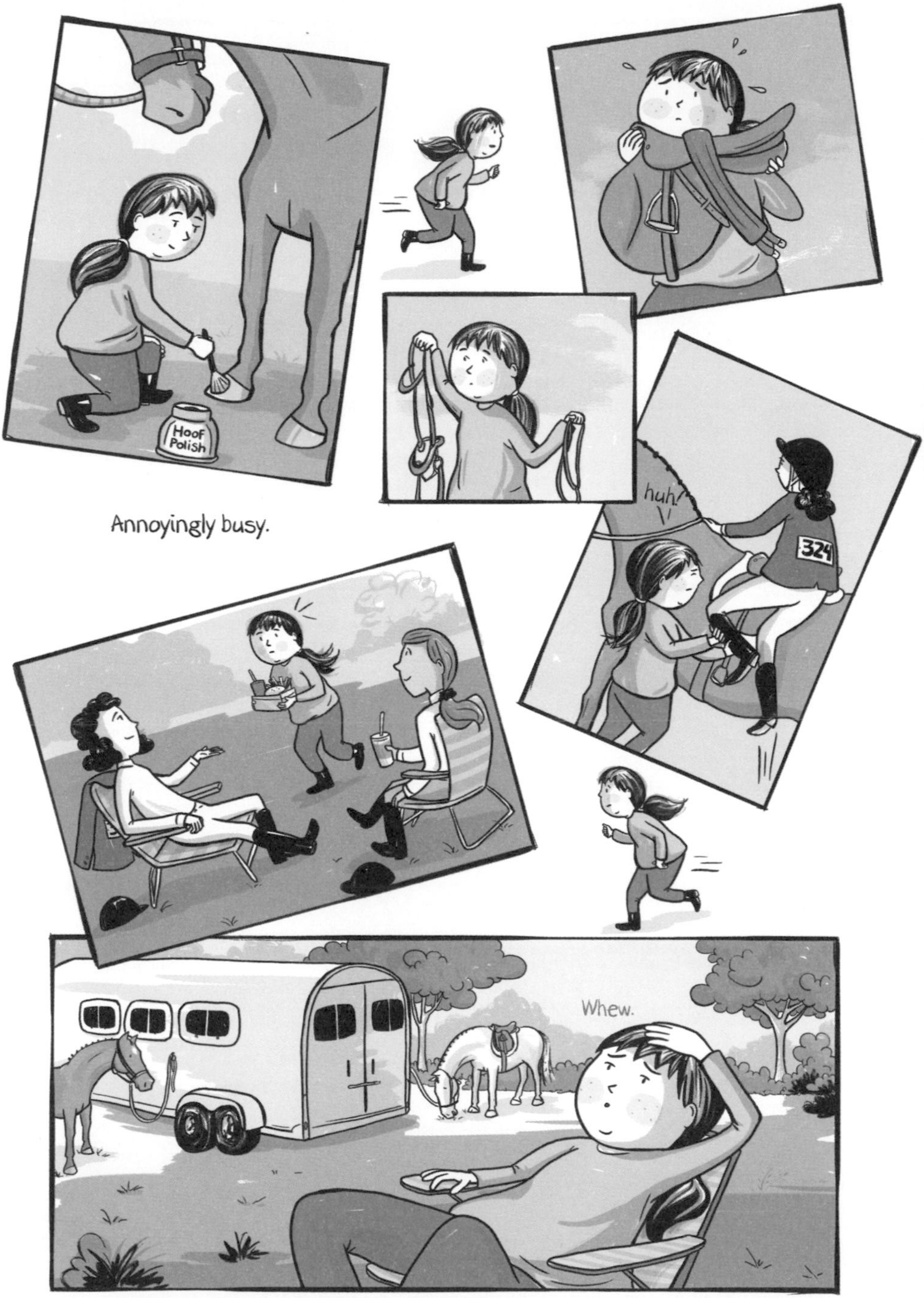
Hoof
Polish
Annoyingly busy.
huh!
324
Whew.

I like to lay out all my clothes the night before a horse show.

Even though I won't actually get dressed in my show clothes until right before my classes start, I like to get a visual of how it all comes together.

hunt coat

freshly polished boots

shiny black helmet

crisply pressed, white show shirt

fancy monogrammed stock pin I got for Christmas last year (goes on the collar)

black leather show gloves

favorite lucky socks

breeches with real suede patches (that I'm only allowed to wear to horse shows)

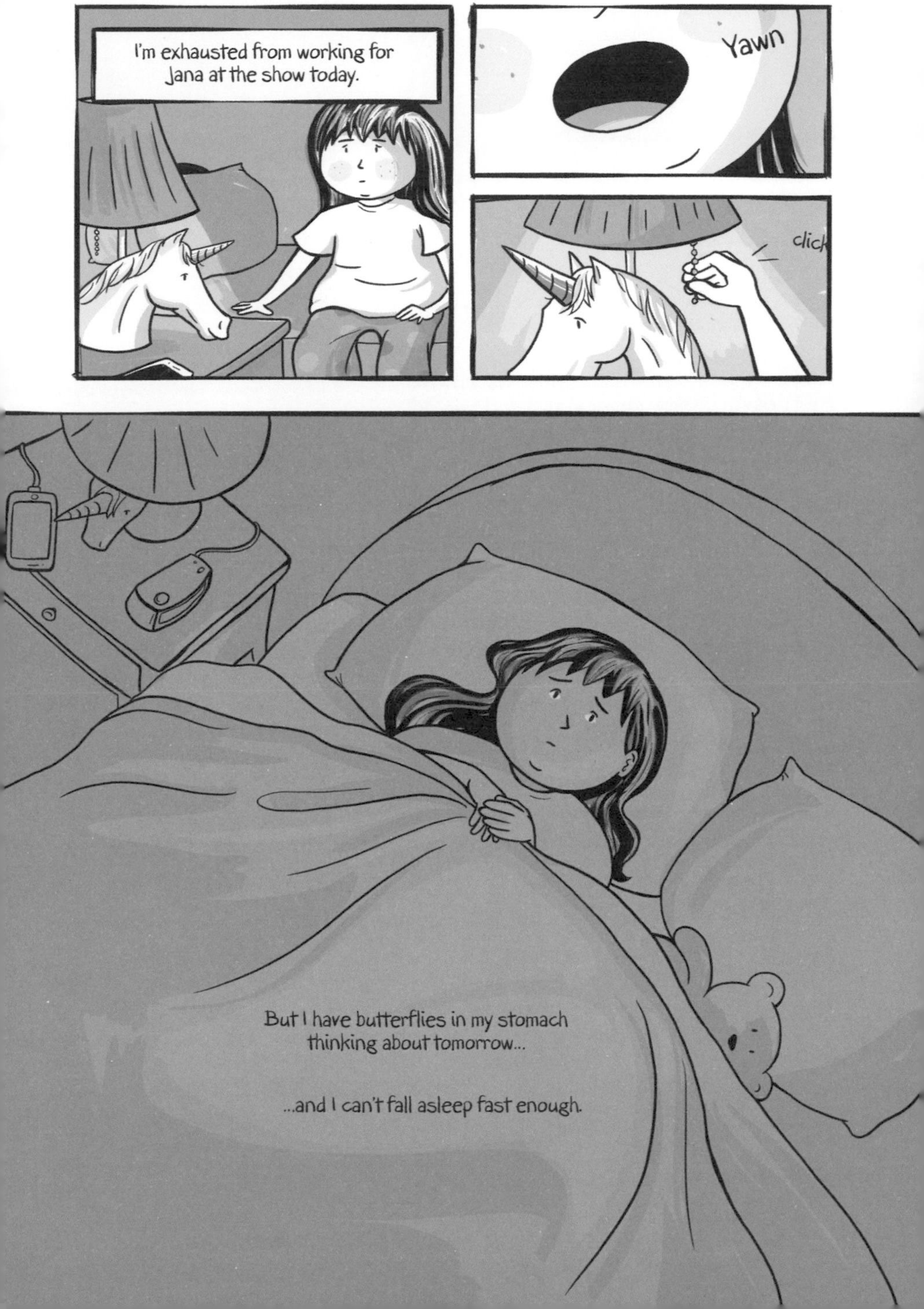
I'm exhausted from working for Jana at the show today.
Yawn
click
But I have butterflies in my stomach thinking about tomorrow...
...and I can't fall asleep fast enough.

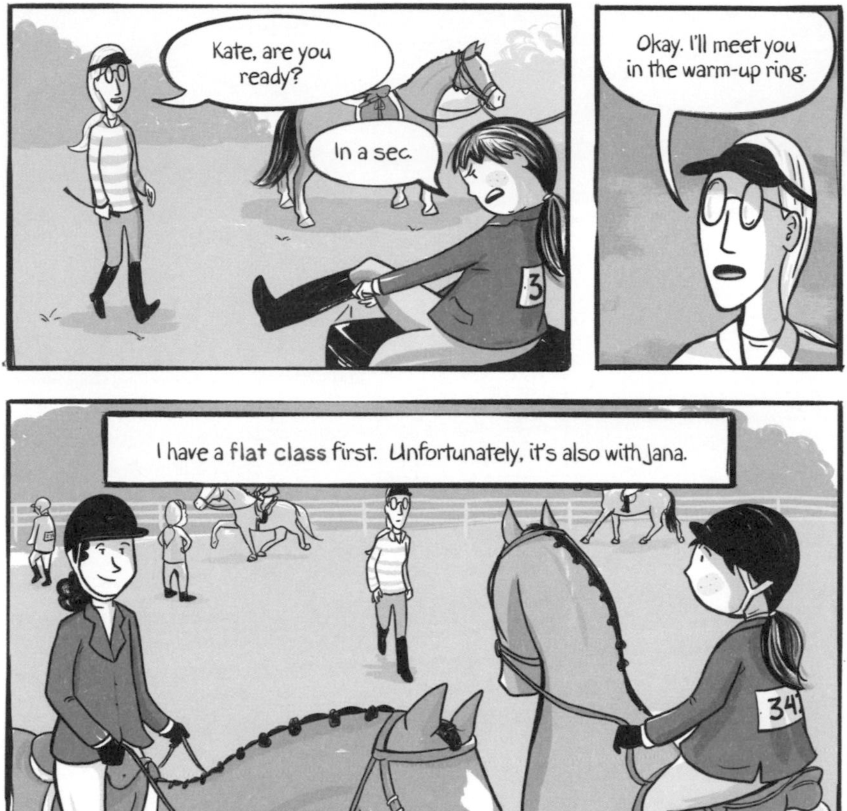
Kate, are you ready?
In a sec.
Okay. I'll meet you in the warm-up ring.
I have a flat class first. Unfortunately, it's also with Jana.
Ladies, you know what to do.
This is an under saddle class so keep your horses nice and collected.
And make sure to leave plenty of space between you and the rider in front of you.

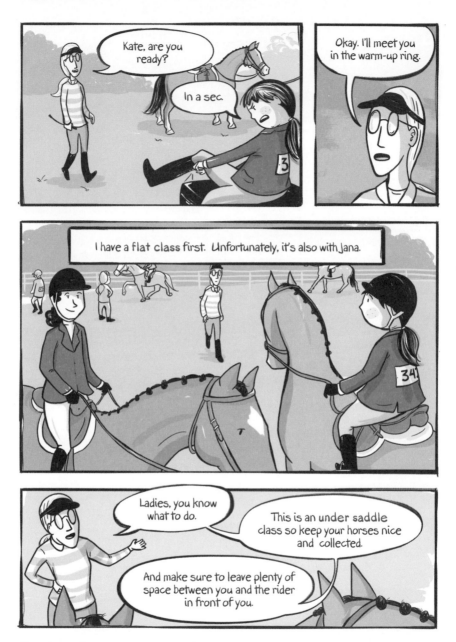

Flat class: All riders are directed by a judge and ride along the outside of the ring at a walk, trot, and canter. There is no jumping and winners are chosen out of a lineup at the class's end.

Under saddle: The class is judged on how well the horse (not the rider) moves and performs.

Canter: A controlled, three-beat gait that is faster than the trot but slower than the gallop. The rider can sit more easily in a canter, whereas the trot is a two-beat gait, and gives the rider a bounce.

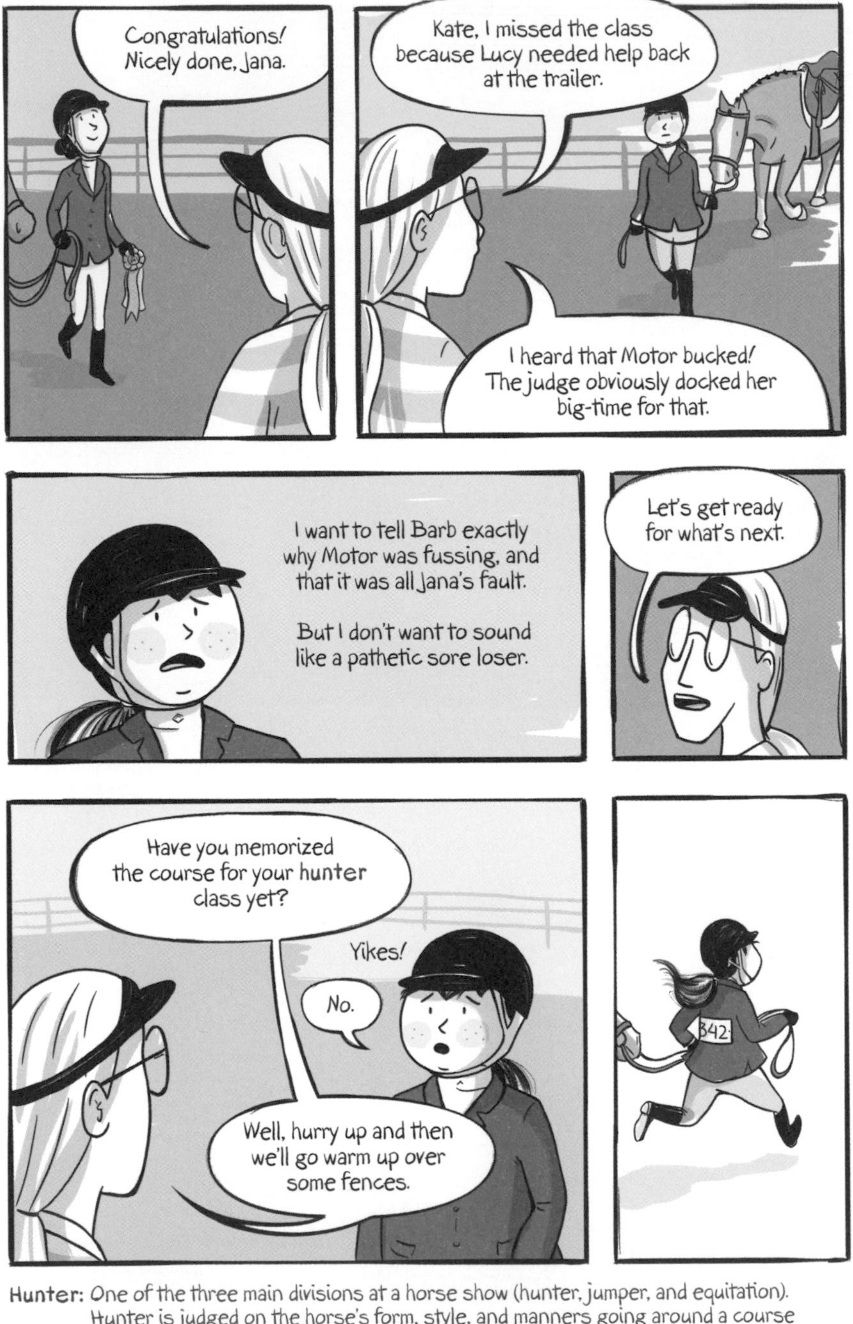
Congratulations! Nicely done, Jana.
Kate, I missed the class because Lucy needed help back at the trailer.
I heard that Motor bucked! The judge obviously docked her big-time for that.
I want to tell Barb exactly why Motor was fussing, and that it was all Jana's fault.
But I don't want to sound like a pathetic sore loser.
Let's get ready for what's next.
Have you memorized the course for your hunter class yet?
Yikes!
No.
Well, hurry up and then we'll go warm up over some fences.
342

Hunter: One of the three main divisions at a horse show (hunter, jumper, and equitation). Hunter is judged on the horse's form, style, and manners going around a course of jumps that are designed to emulate a classic fox hunt.

I quickly forget about Jana and the flat class in a panic to study the jump sequence.

I run it through my head:

- smooth transition in and out of the ring
- always end with a circle
- keep a steady pace, don't rush it!

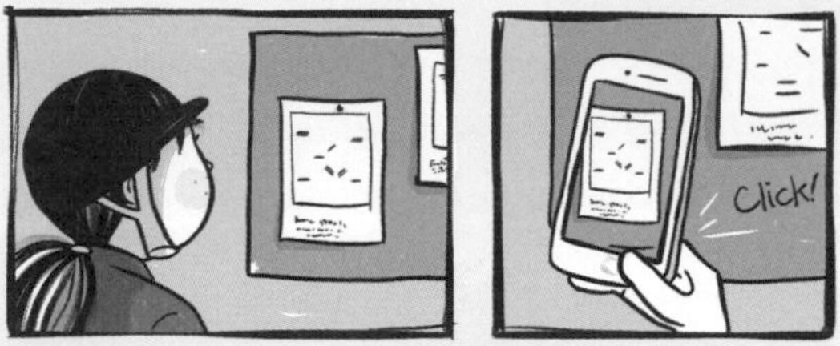
Click!

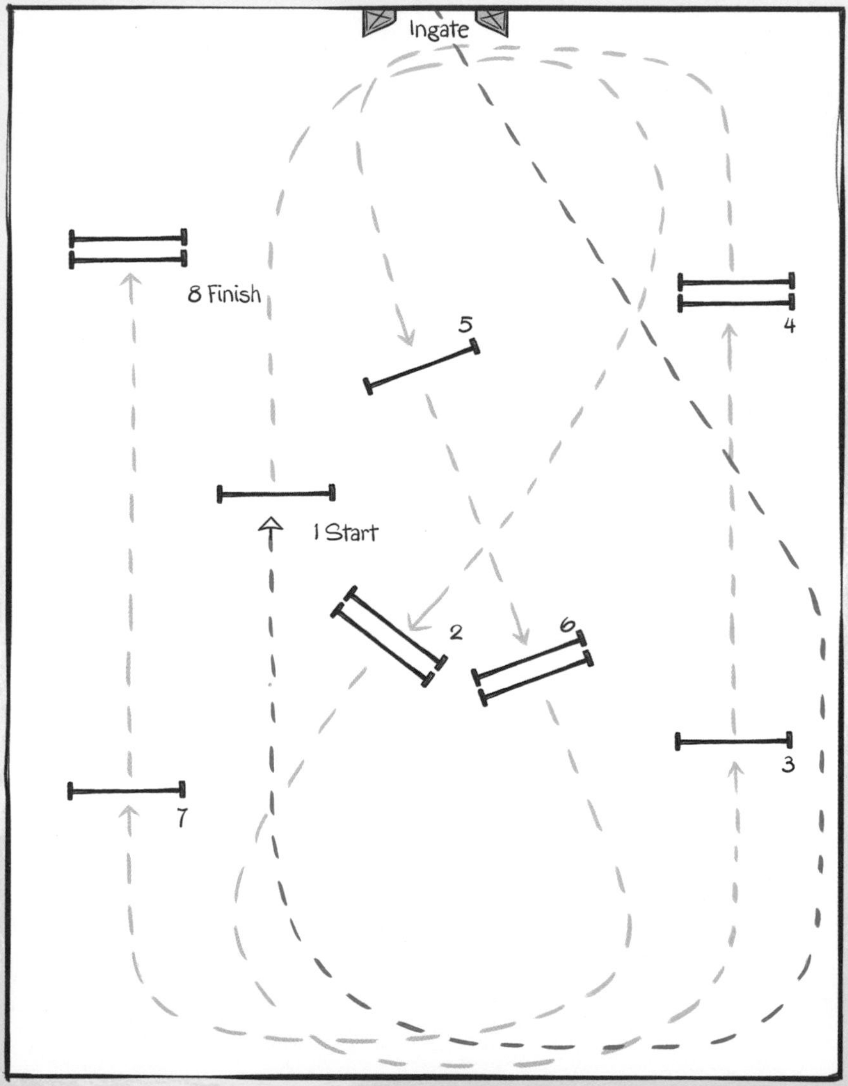
Ingate
8 Finish
5
4
1 Start
2
6
3
7

Entering the ring is always scary. Just you and your horse. Everyone watching.

Show name: Often horses use a different name (usually flashier, longer, or descriptive of their personality or physical traits) when they are competing at a horse show.

I walk Motor around to cool her down and I can fully breathe again. There are five more riders to go in the class.

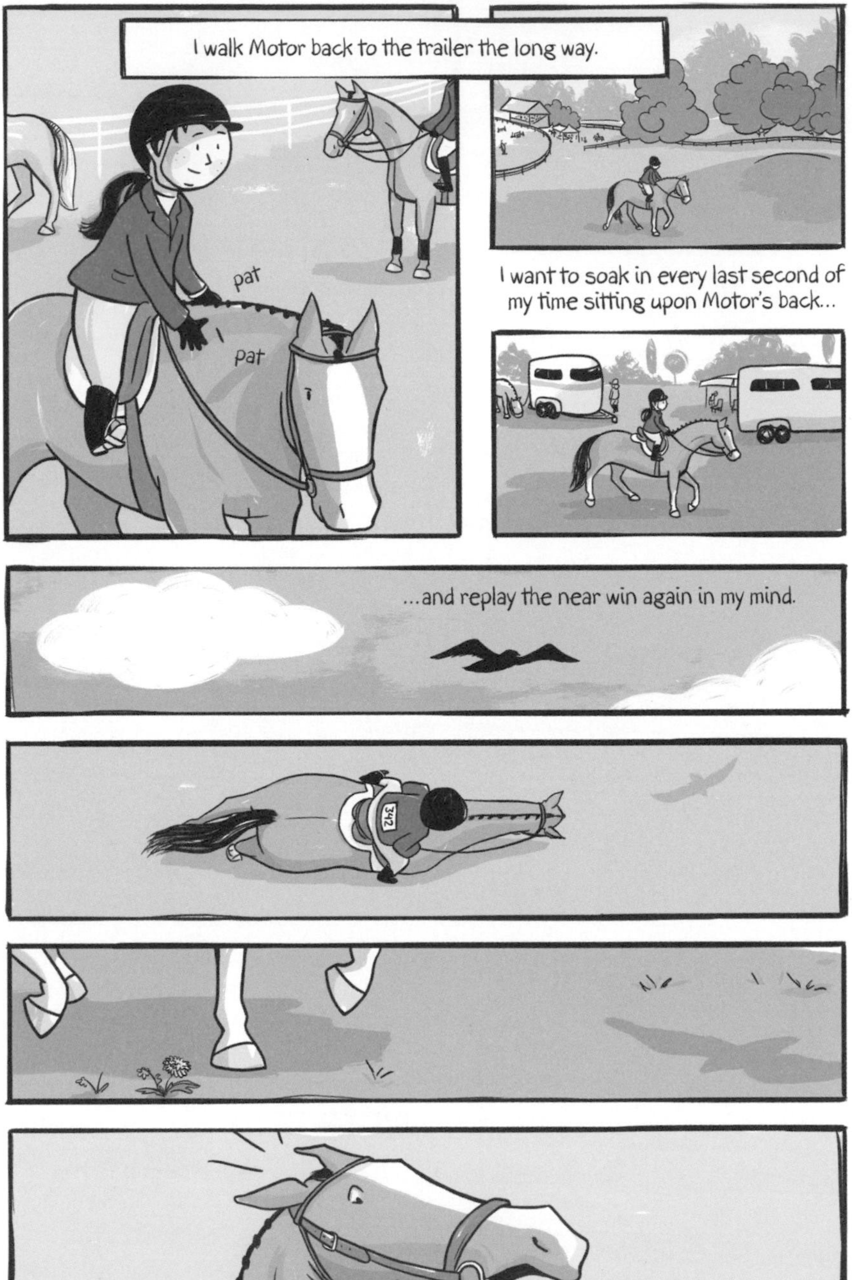
I walk Motor back to the trailer the long way.
pat
pat
I want to soak in every last second of my time sitting upon Motor's back...
...and replay the near win again in my mind.
342

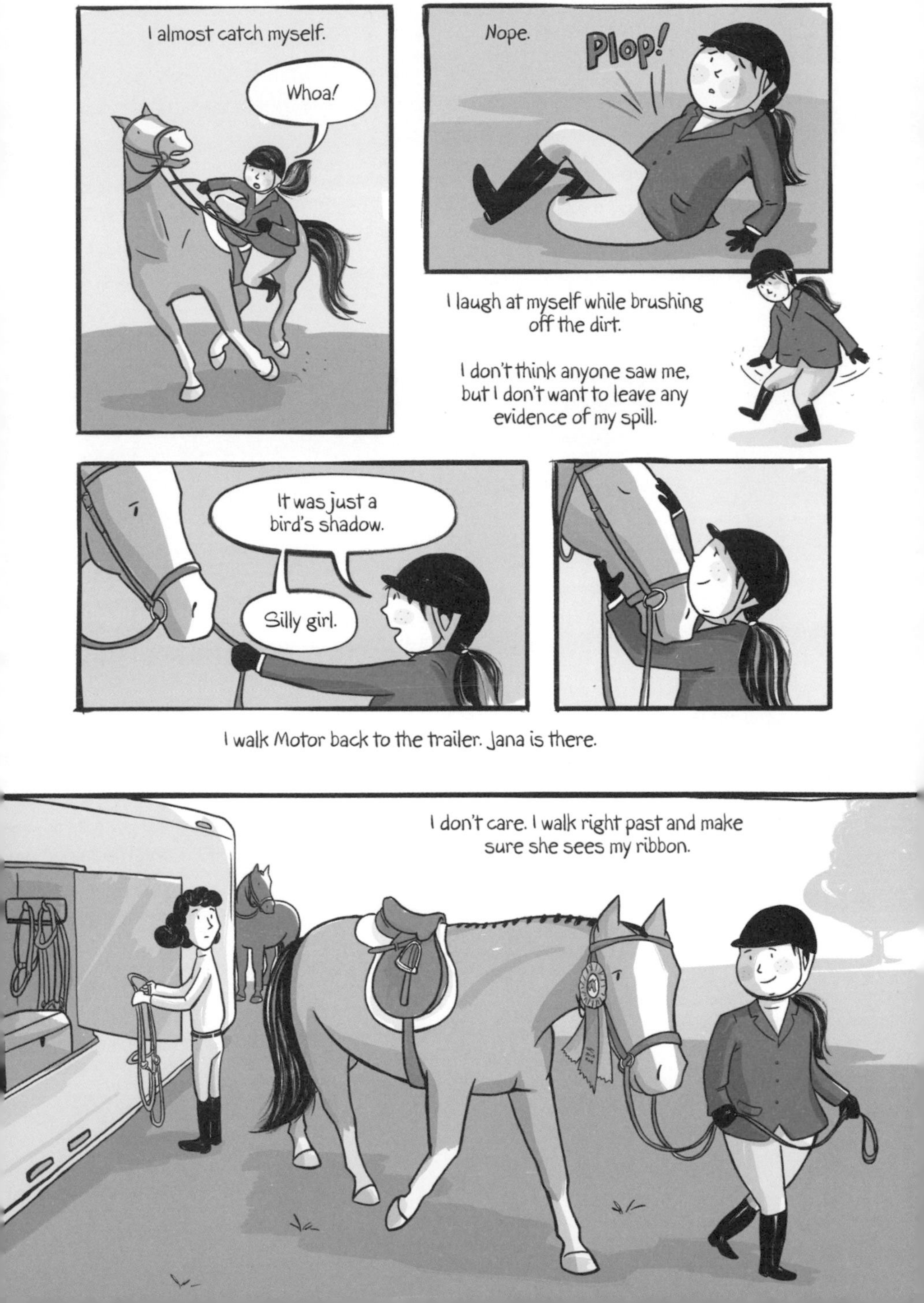
I almost catch myself.
Whoa!
Nope.
Plop!
I laugh at myself while brushing off the dirt.
I don't think anyone saw me, but I don't want to leave any evidence of my spill.
It was just a bird's shadow.
Silly girl.
I walk Motor back to the trailer. Jana is there.
I don't care. I walk right past and make sure she sees my ribbon.

Chapter 5
Stream Dunk

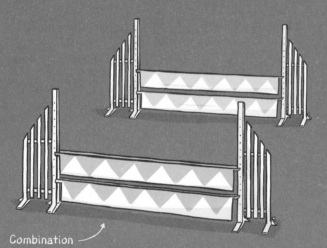

Combination

Two (or three) jumps in succession with no more than two strides between each.

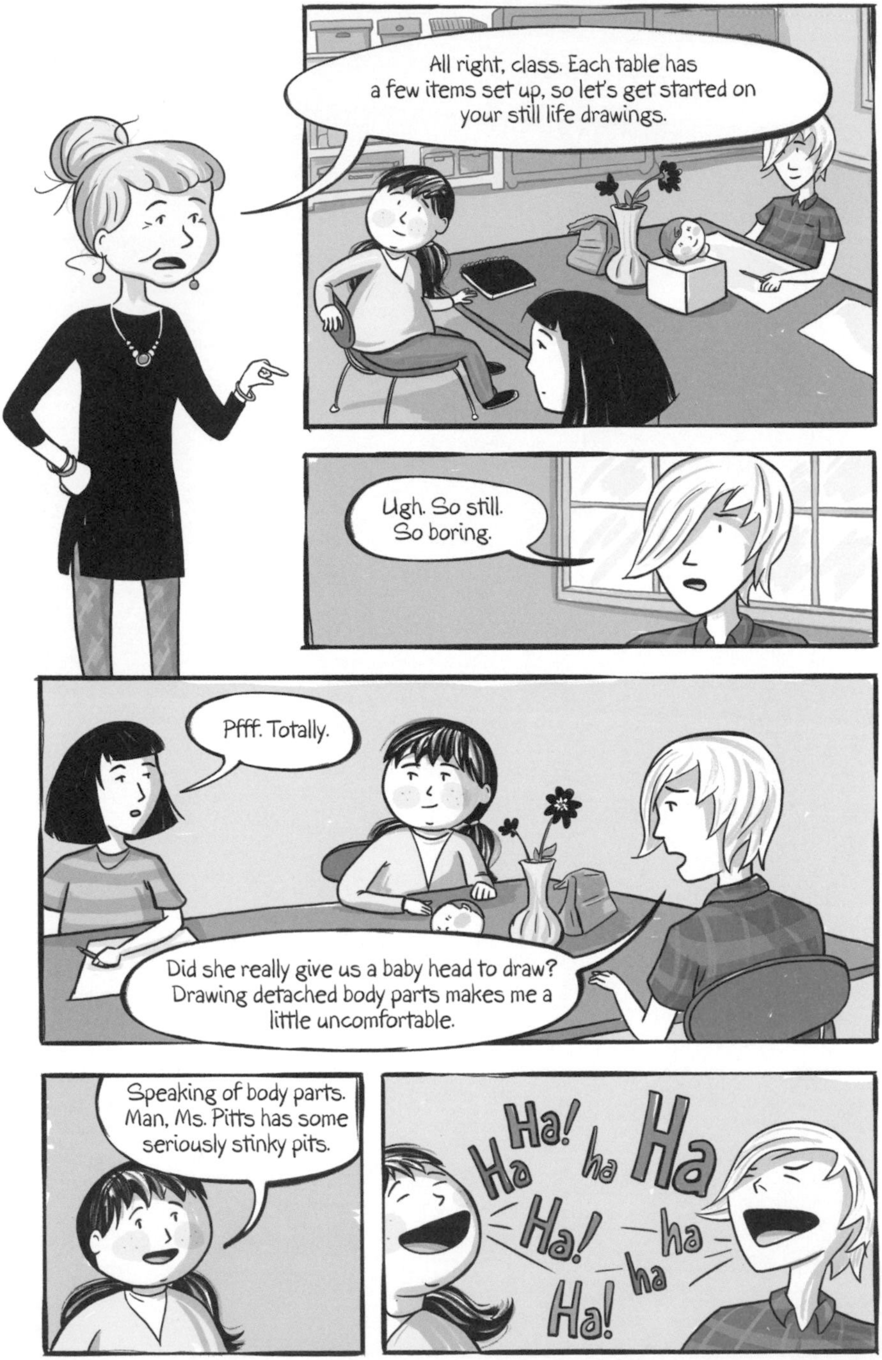
All right, class. Each table has a few items set up, so let's get started on your still life drawings.
Ugh. So still. So boring.
Pfff. Totally.
Did she really give us a baby head to draw? Drawing detached body parts makes me a little uncomfortable.
Speaking of body parts. Man, Ms. Pitts has some seriously stinky pits.
Ha Ha! ha Ha Ha! ha ha Ha!

105

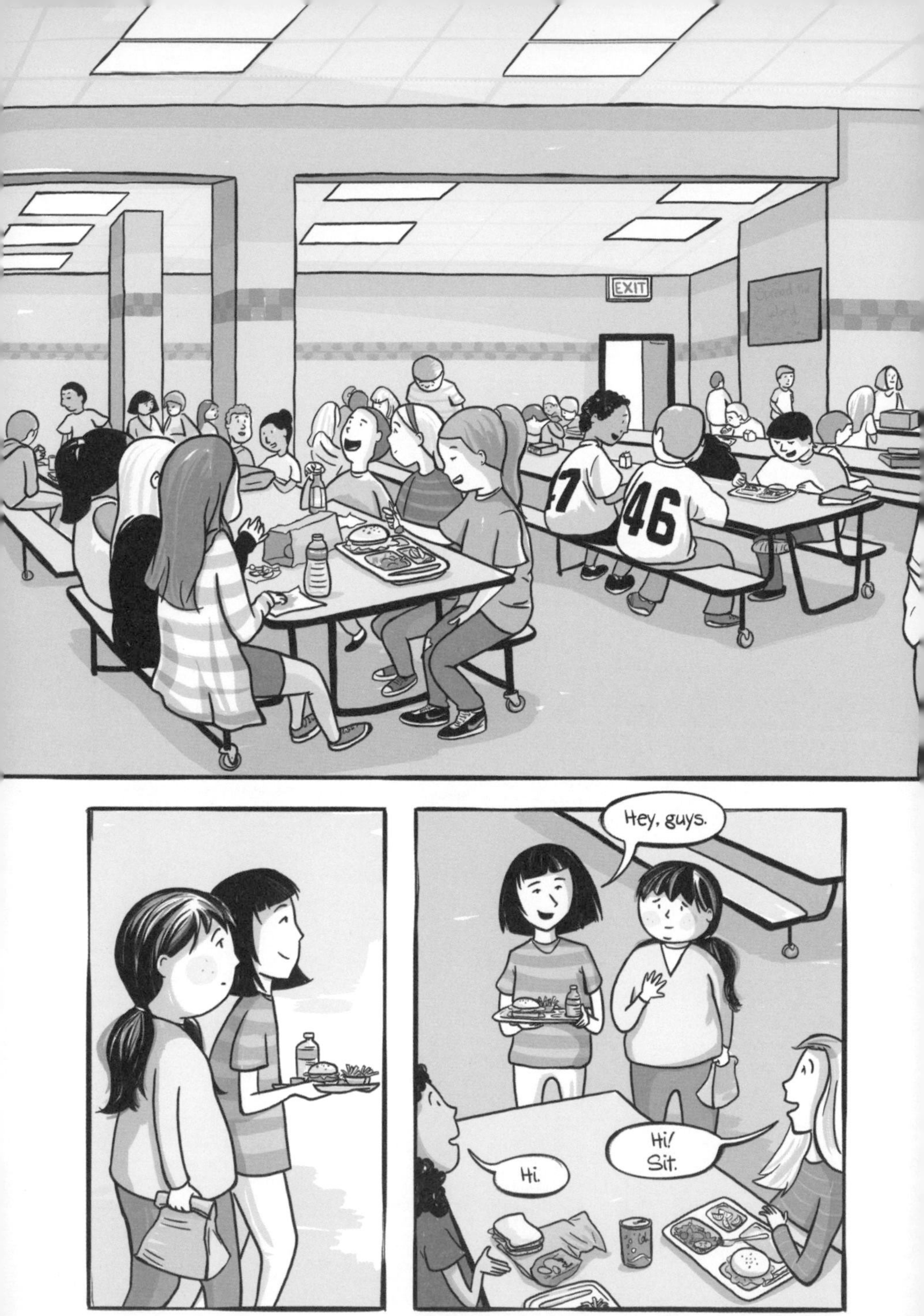
EXIT
Hey, guys.
Hi!
Sit.
Hi.

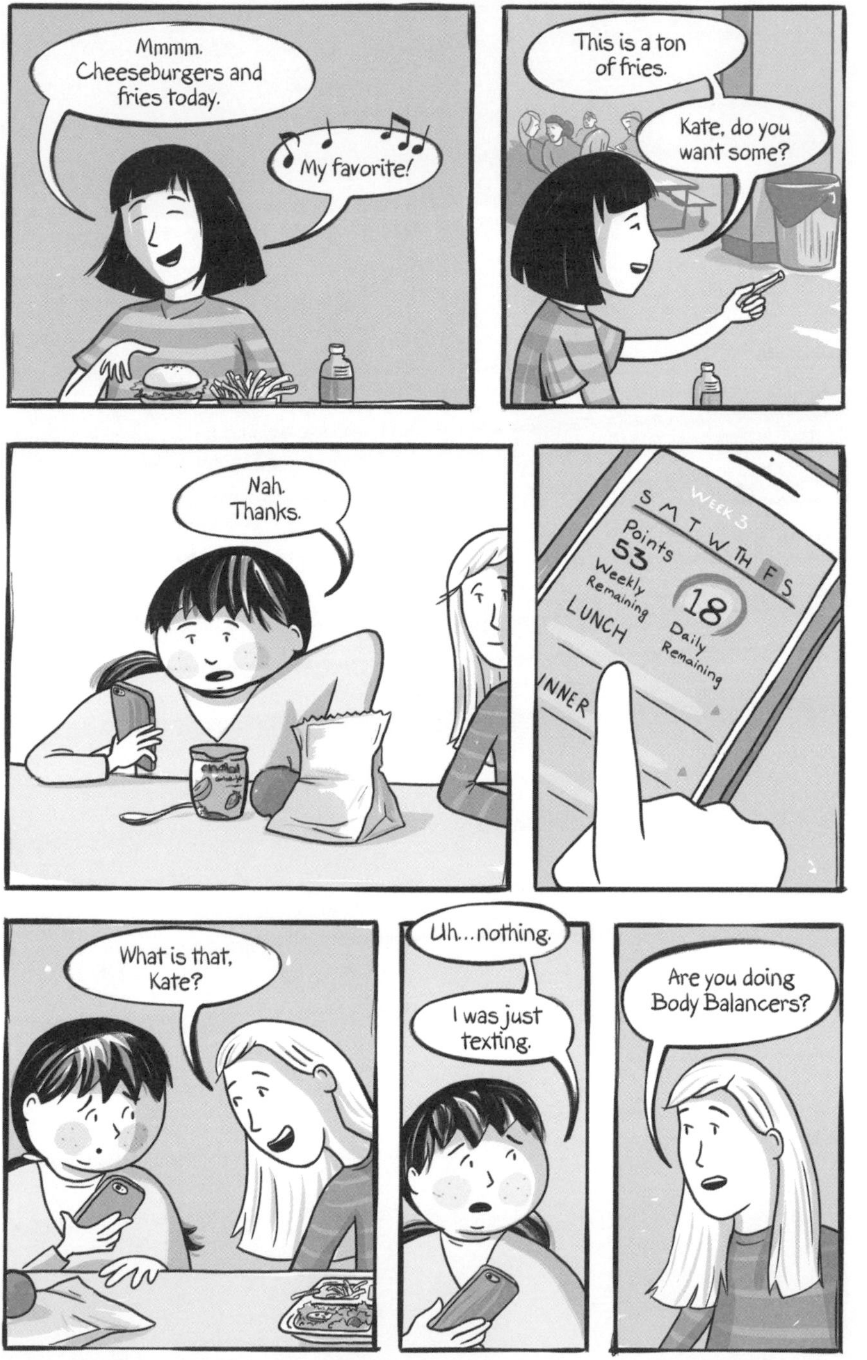
Mmmm. Cheeseburgers and fries today.
My favorite!
This is a ton of fries.
Kate, do you want some?
Nah. Thanks.
WEEK 3
S M T W TH F S
Points
53
Weekly Remaining
18
Daily Remaining
LUNCH
What is that, Kate?
Uh...nothing.
I was just texting.
Are you doing Body Balancers?

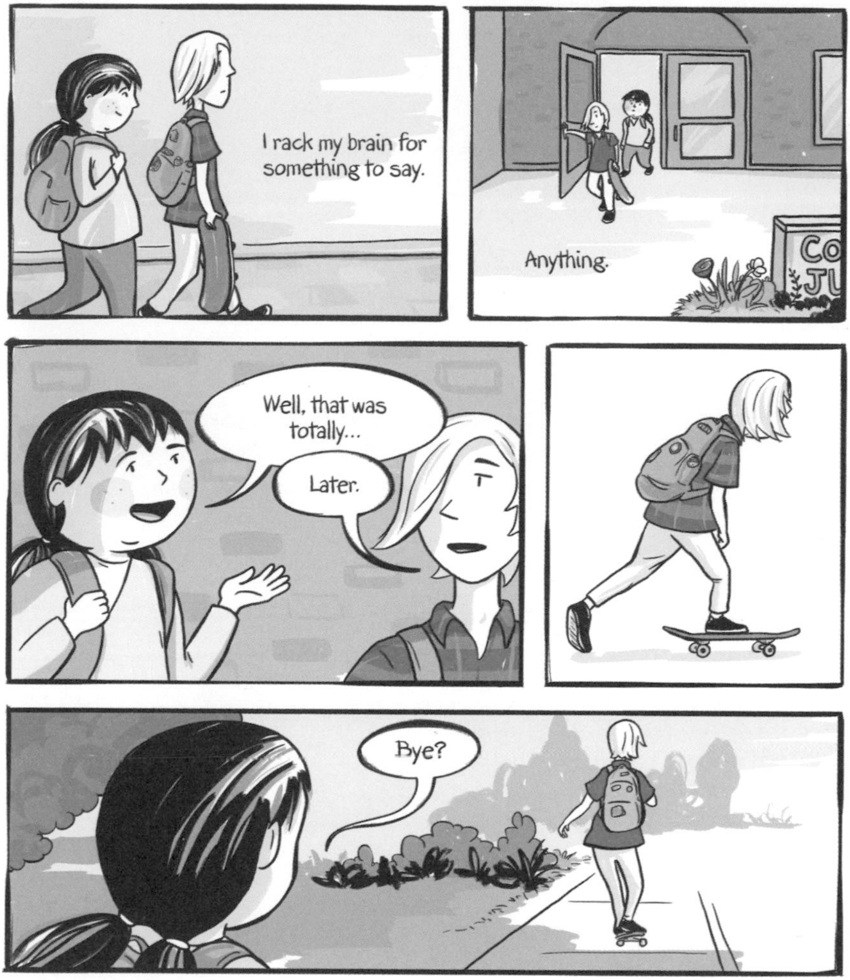
I rack my brain for something to say.
Anything.
Well, that was totally...
Later.
Bye?

I'm starving since I trashed most of my lunch, but I've got some money in my backpack.

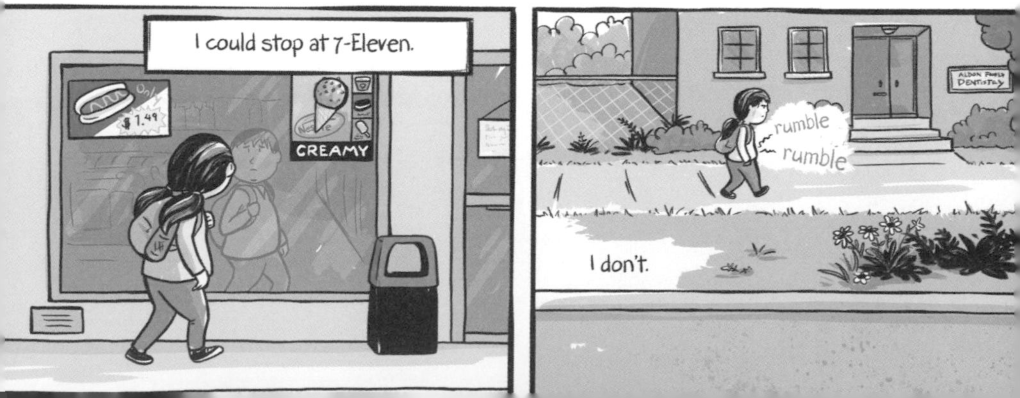
I could stop at 7-Eleven.
Only
$1.49
CREAMY
rumble
rumble
I don't.

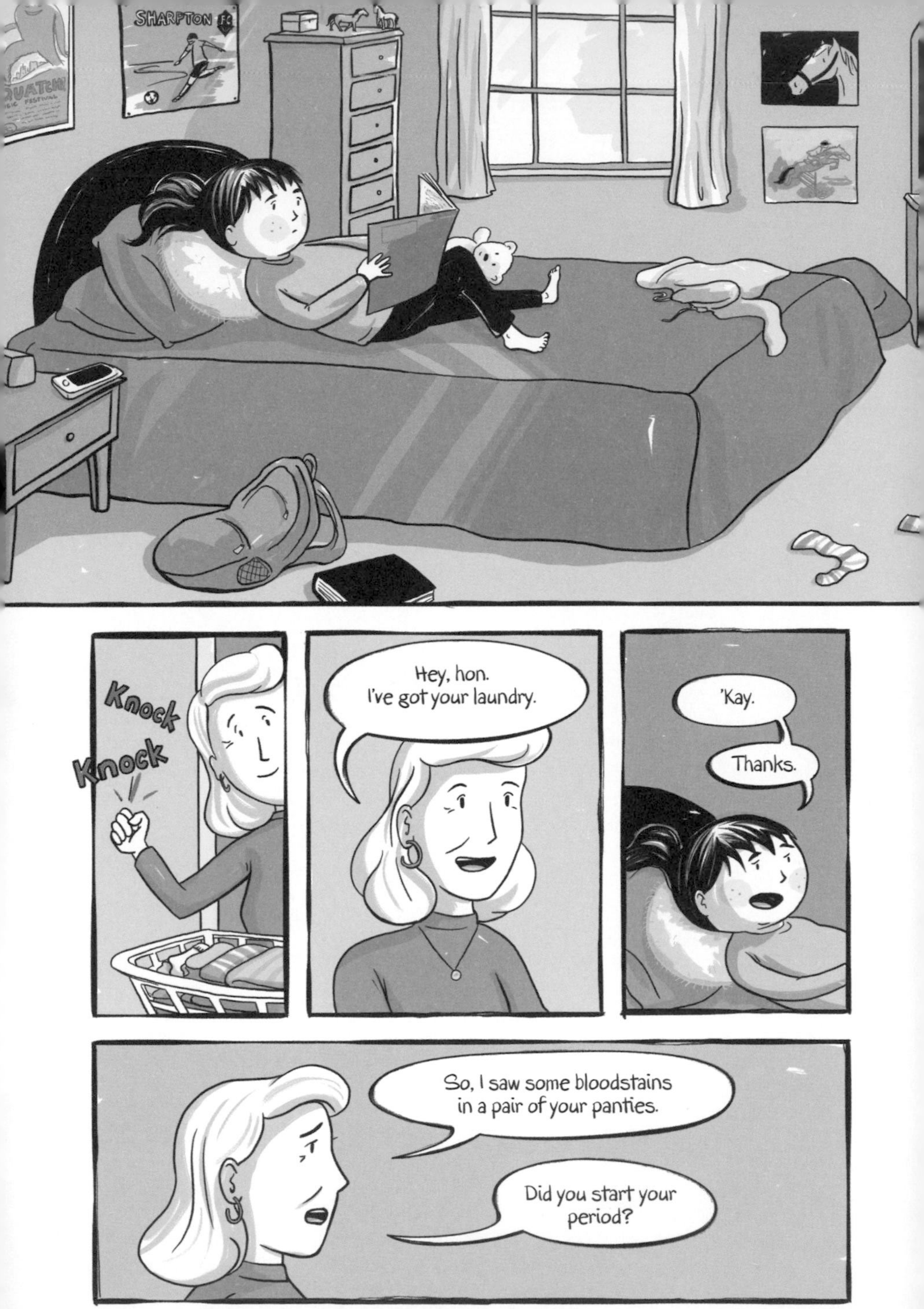
SHARPTON FC
Knock
Knock
Hey, hon.
I've got your laundry.
'Kay.
Thanks.
So, I saw some bloodstains
in a pair of your panties.
Did you start your
period?

115

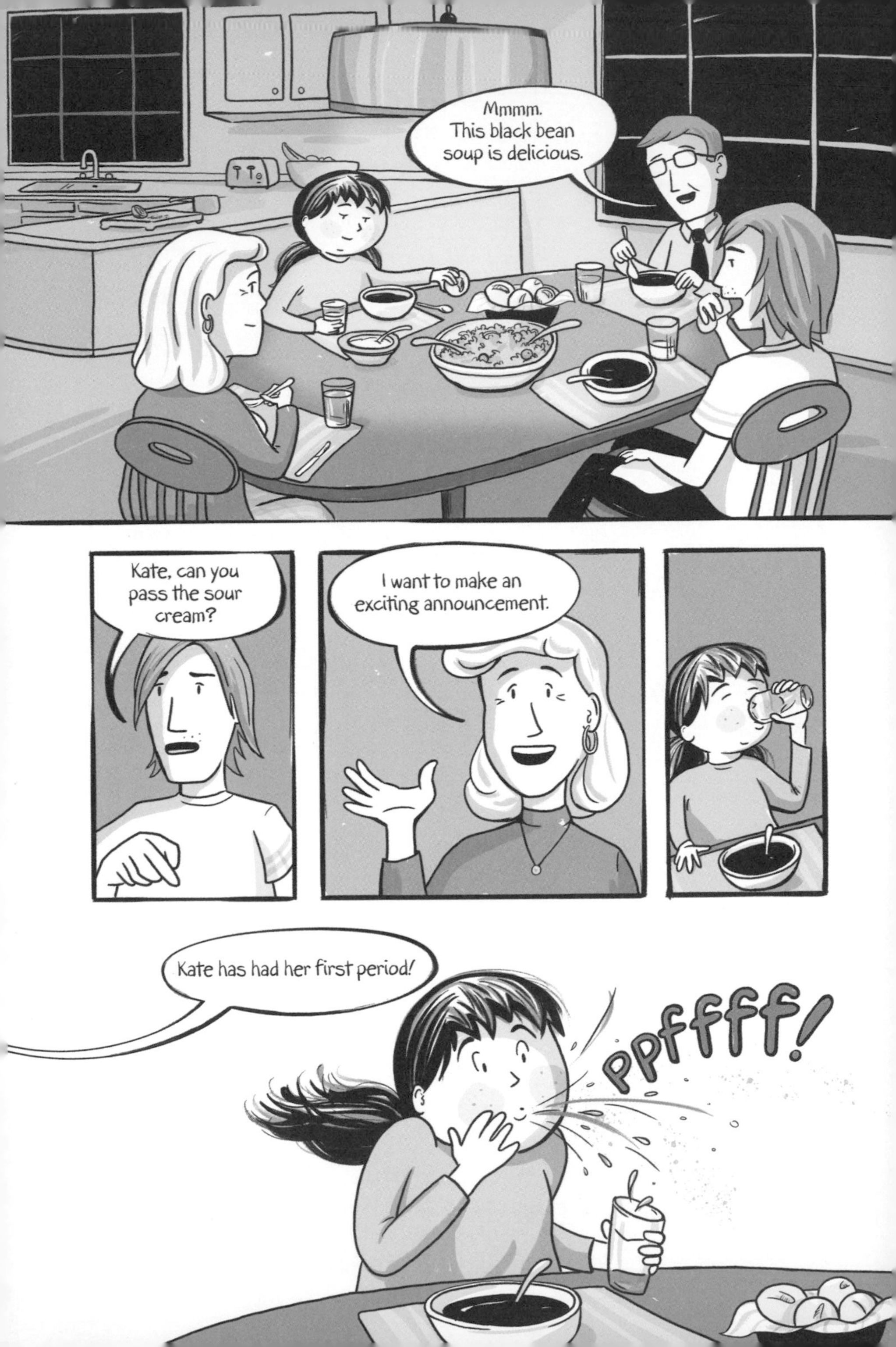
Mmmm.
This black bean
soup is delicious.
Kate, can you
pass the sour
cream?
I want to make an
exciting announcement.
Kate has had her first period!
PPFFFF!

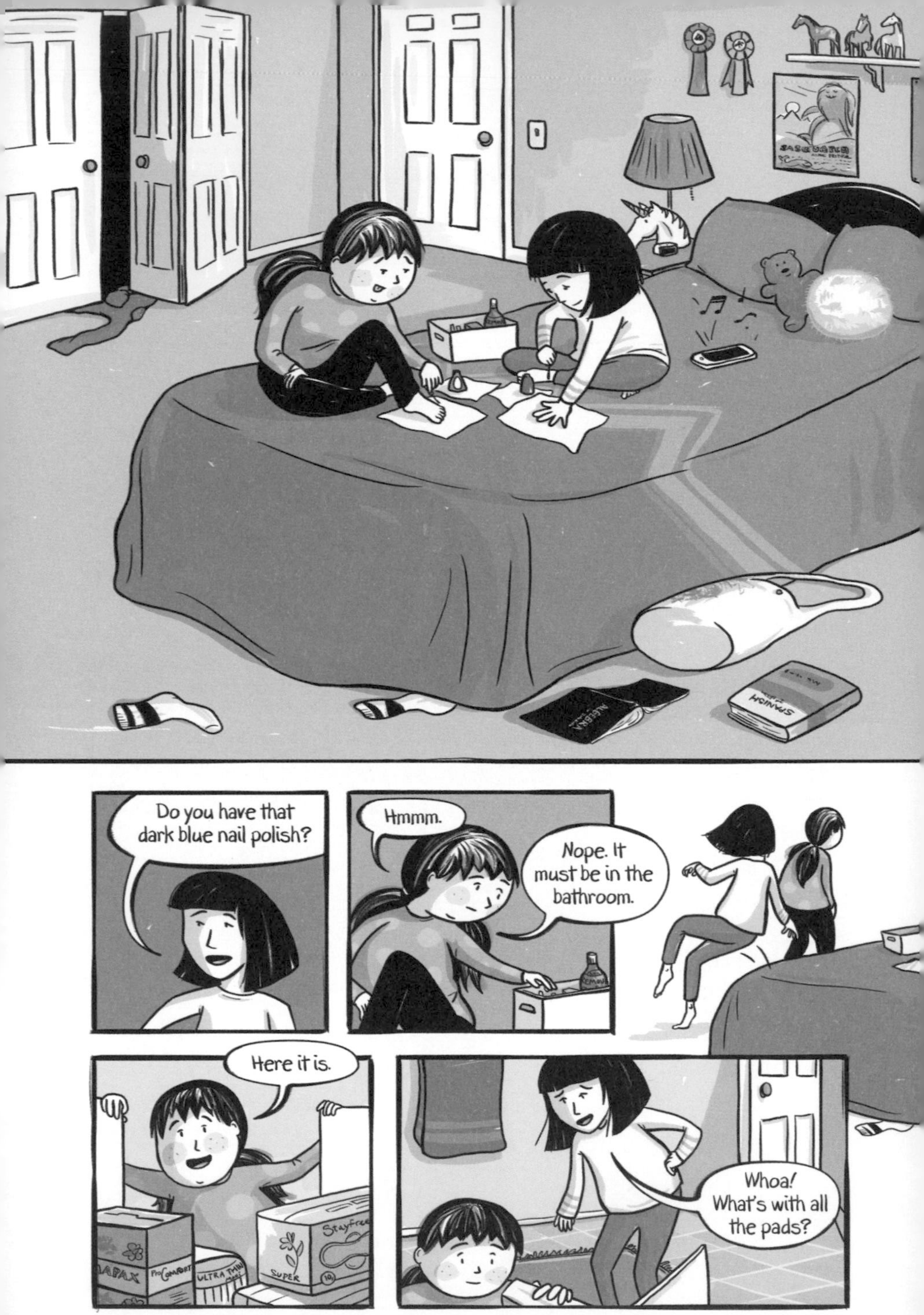
Do you have that dark blue nail polish?
Hmmm.
Nope. It must be in the bathroom.
Here it is.
Stayfree
SUPER
ULTRA THIN
Whoa! What's with all the pads?

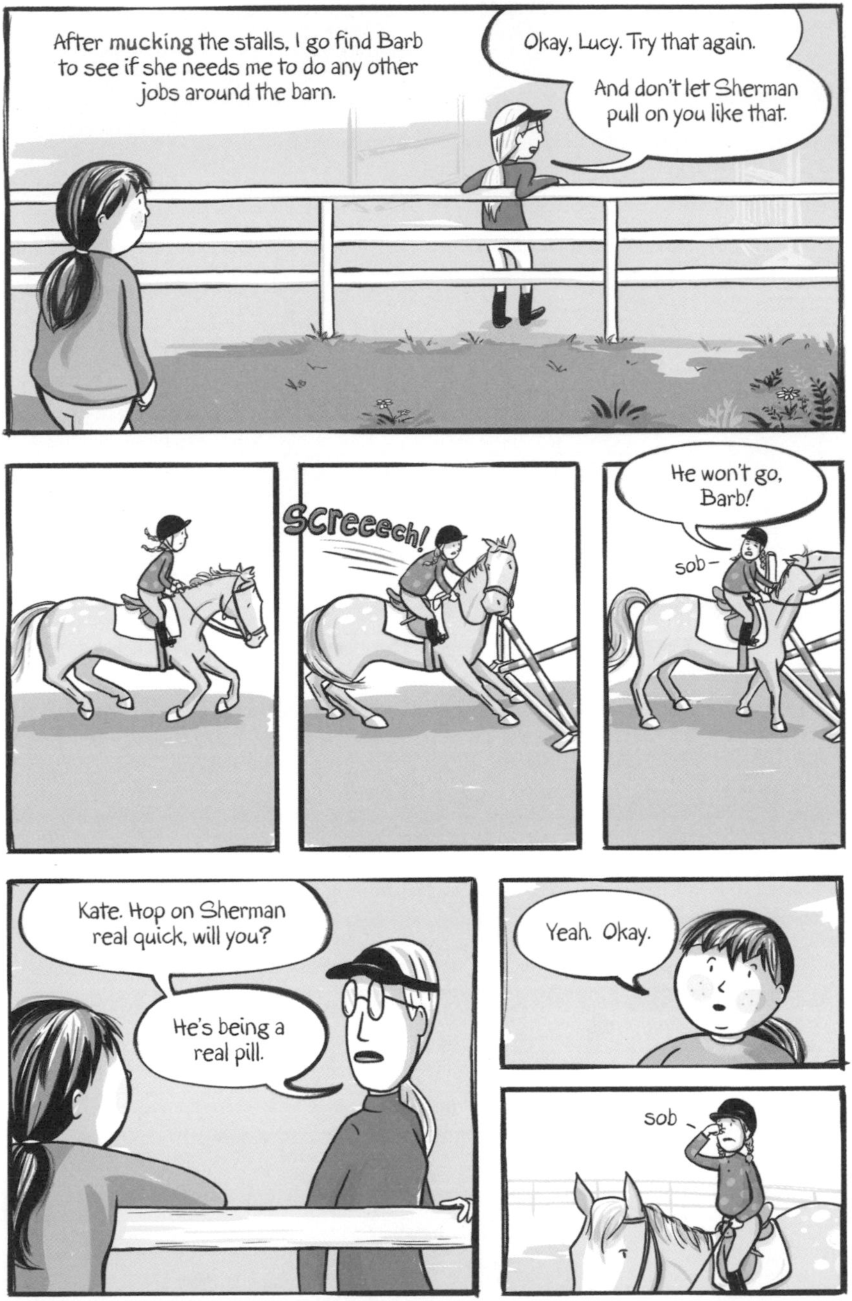
After mucking the stalls, I go find Barb to see if she needs me to do any other jobs around the barn.
Okay, Lucy. Try that again.
And don't let Sherman pull on you like that.
SCREEECH!
He won't go, Barb!
sob-
Kate. Hop on Sherman real quick, will you?
He's being a real pill.
Yeah. Okay.
sob

Mucking: Cleaning a stall by picking through the sawdust or ground bedding and removing the horse poop.

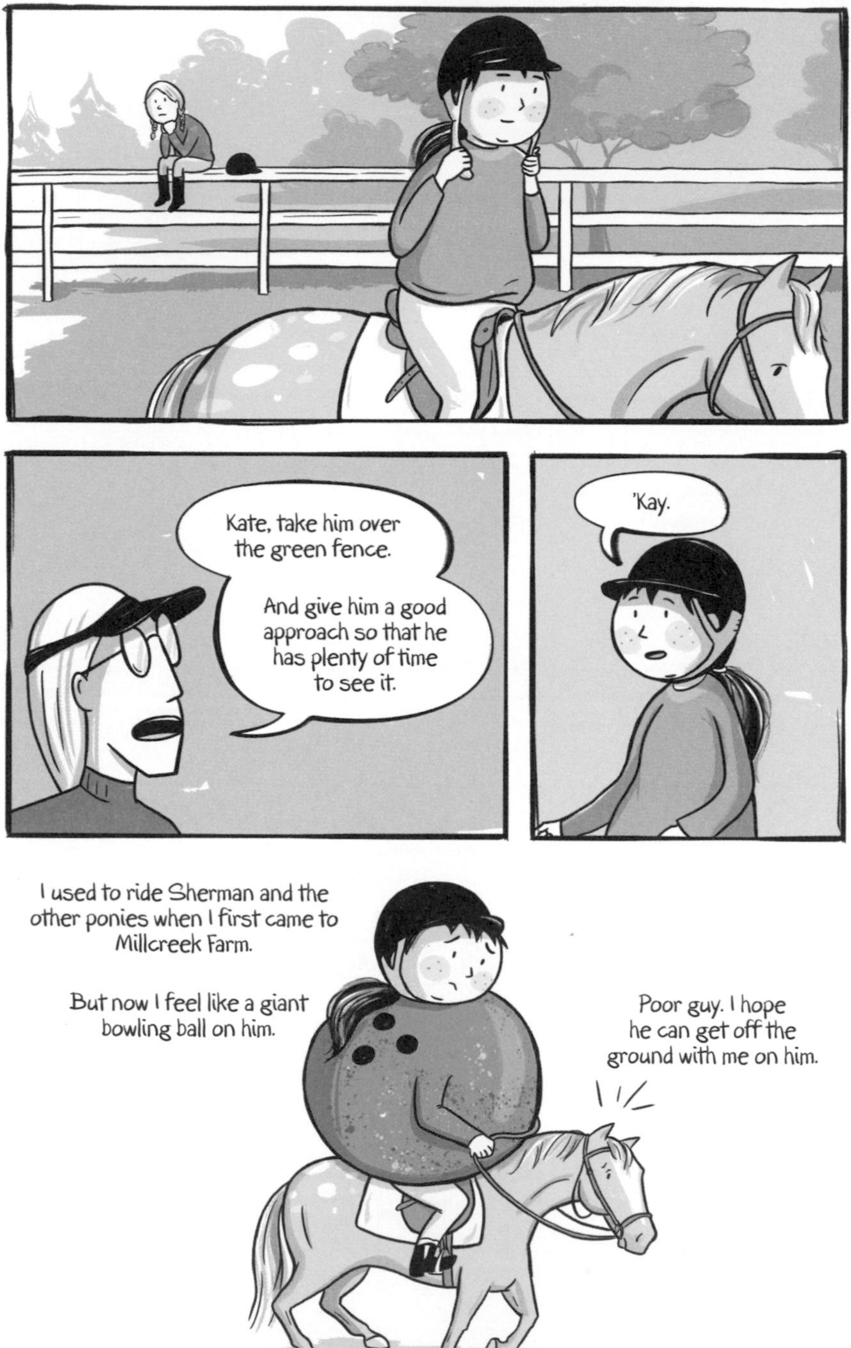
Kate, take him over the green fence.
And give him a good approach so that he has plenty of time to see it.
'Kay.
I used to ride Sherman and the other ponies when I first came to Millcreek Farm.
But now I feel like a giant bowling ball on him.
Poor guy. I hope he can get off the ground with me on him.

In-and-Out: Two jumps that are separated with just enough space for the horse to land from the first jump and take one or two strides before jumping the second fence (also called a combination).

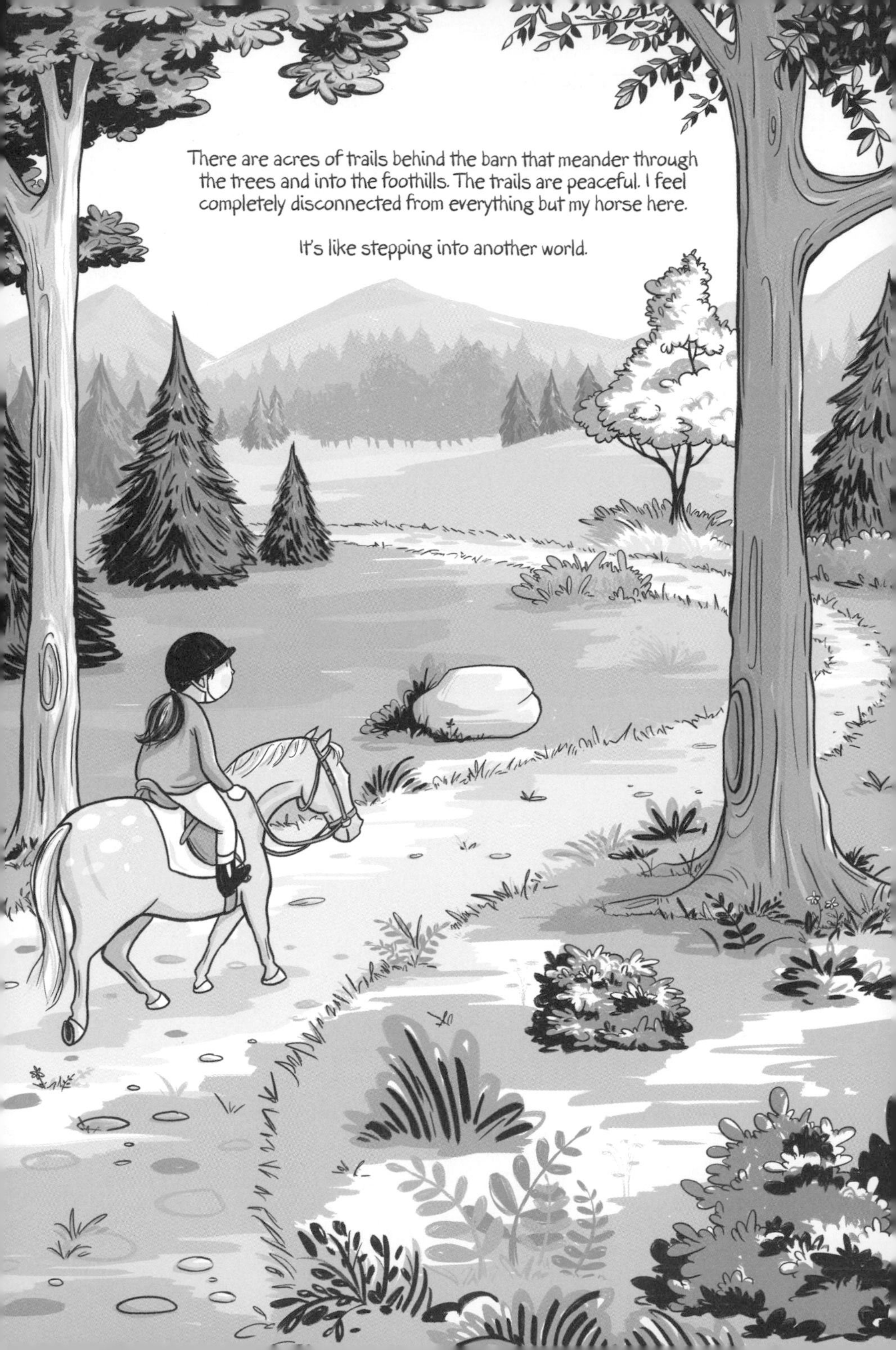
There are acres of trails behind the barn that meander through the trees and into the foothills. The trails are peaceful. I feel completely disconnected from everything but my horse here.
It's like stepping into another world.

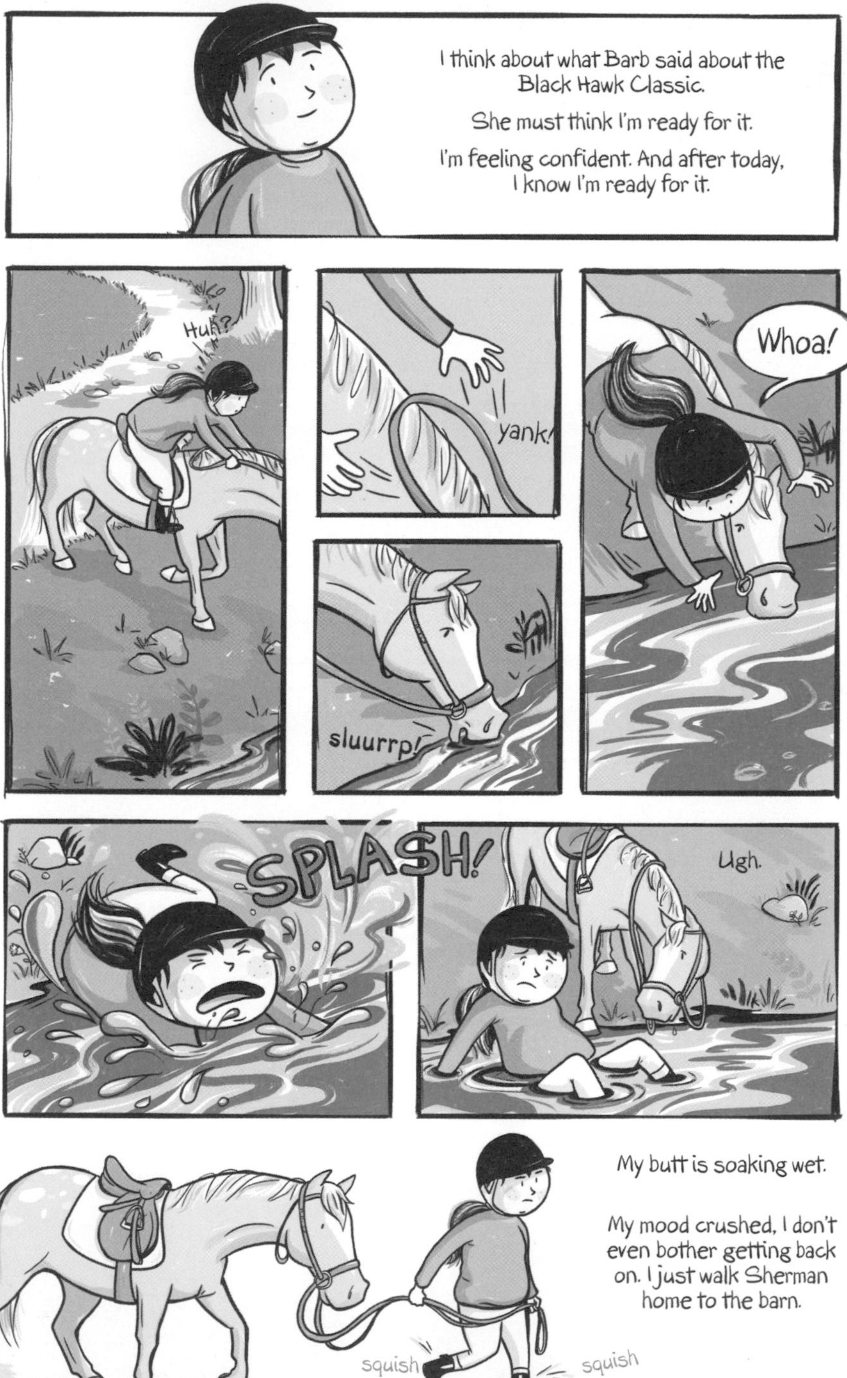
I think about what Barb said about the Black Hawk Classic.
She must think I'm ready for it.
I'm feeling confident. And after today, I know I'm ready for it.
Huh?
yank!
sluurrp!
Whoa!
SPLASH!
Ugh.
My butt is soaking wet.
My mood crushed, I don't even bother getting back on. I just walk Sherman home to the barn.
squish
squish
squish

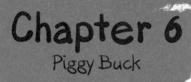

Chapter 6
Piggy Buck

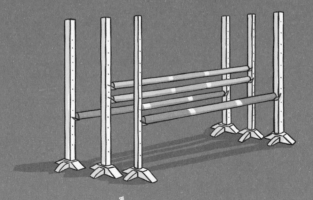

Hogsback

A type of spread (distance) fence with three rails where the tallest
pole is in the center.

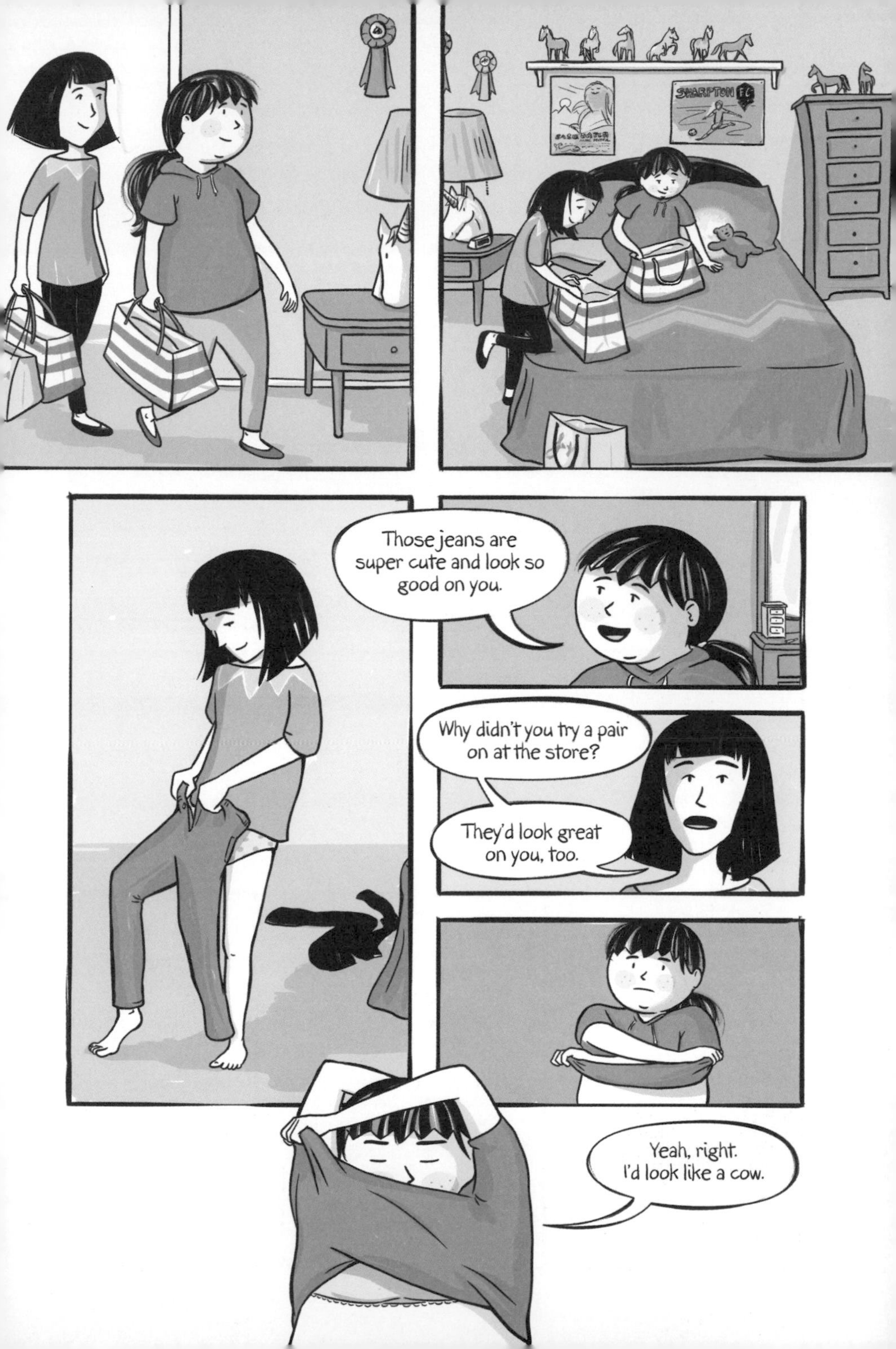
Those jeans are super cute and look so good on you.
Why didn't you try a pair on at the store?
They'd look great on you, too.
Yeah, right. I'd look like a cow.

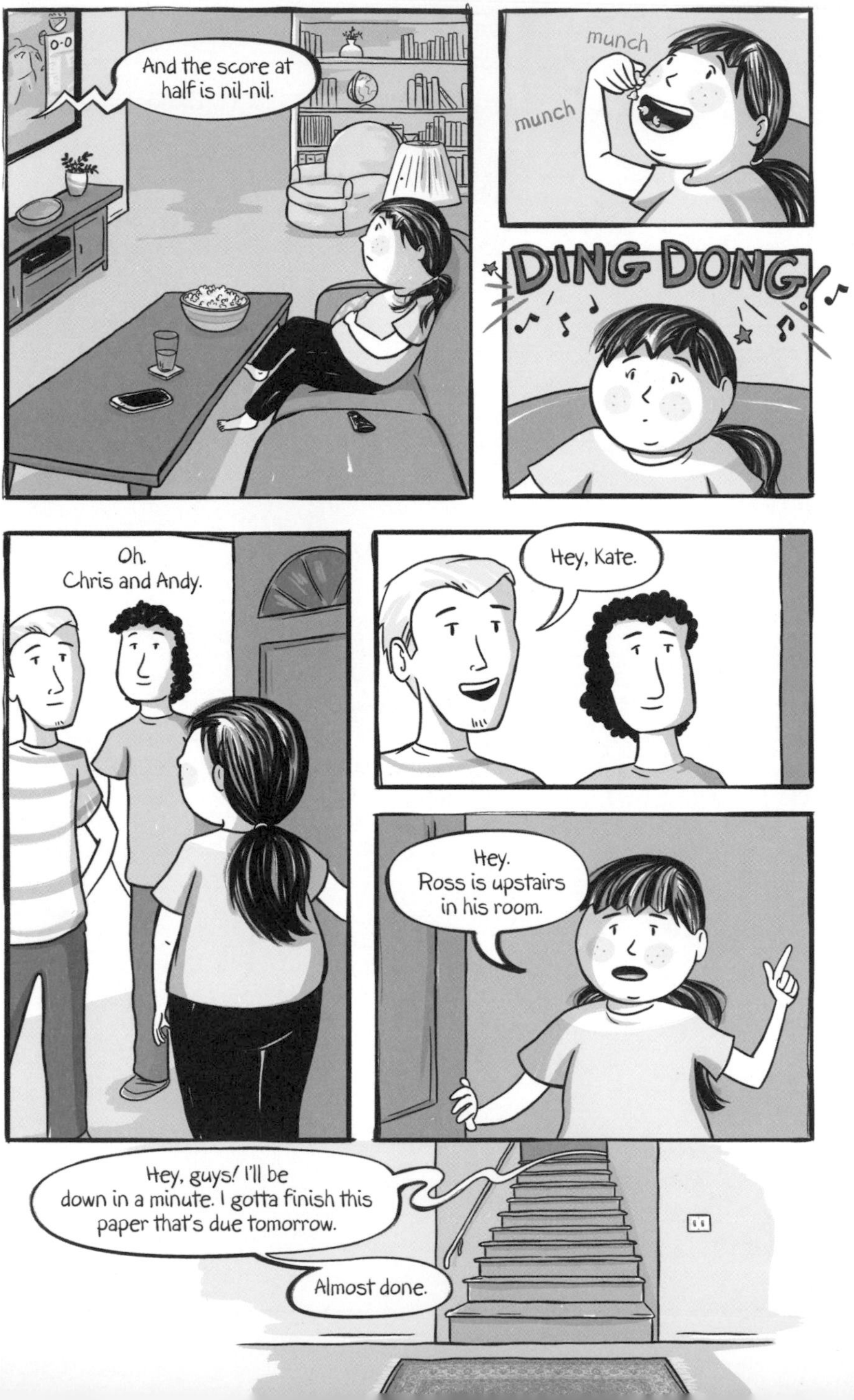
0-0
And the score at half is nil-nil.
munch
munch
DING DONG!
Oh. Chris and Andy.
Hey, Kate.
Hey. Ross is upstairs in his room.
Hey, guys! I'll be down in a minute. I gotta finish this paper that's due tomorrow.
Almost done.

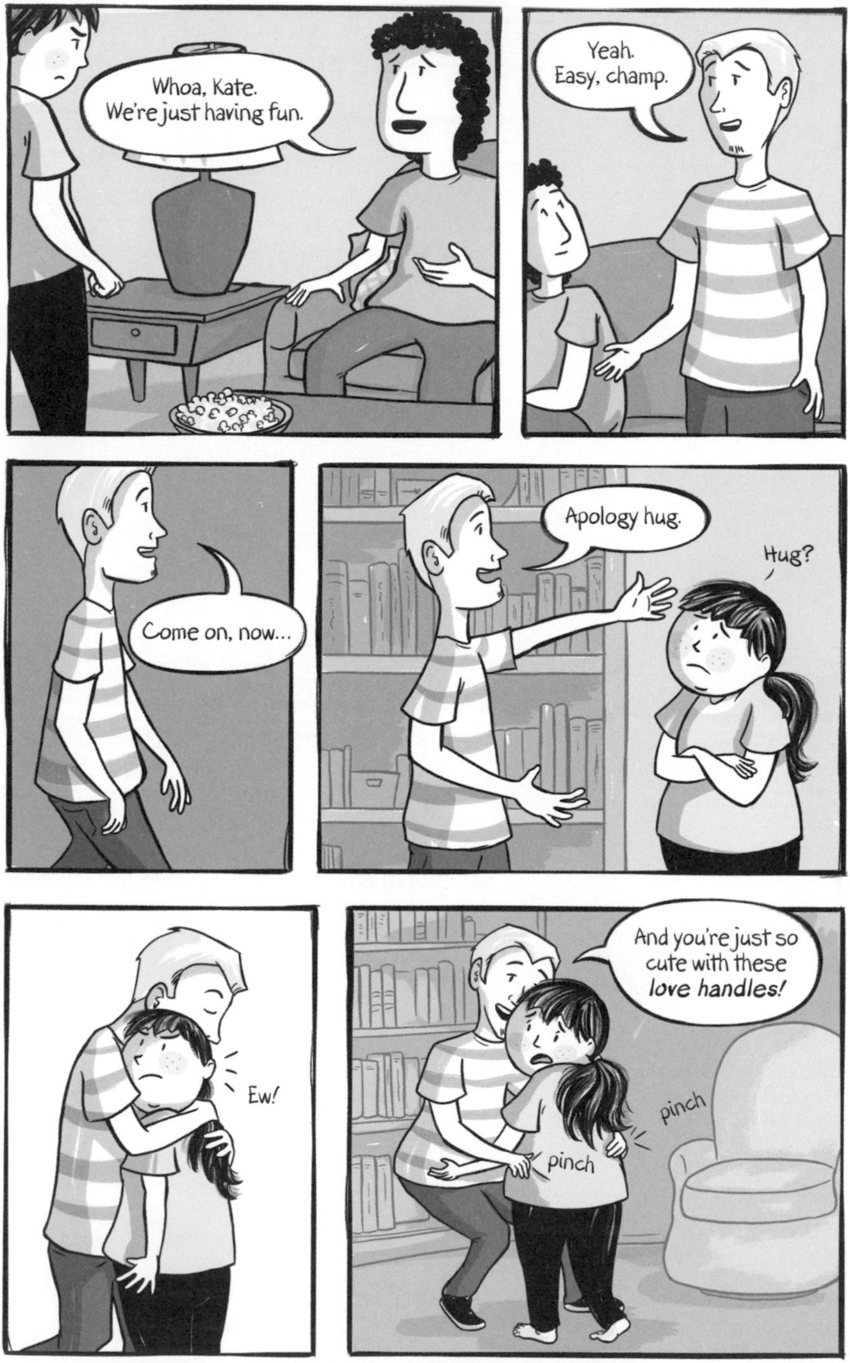
Whoa, Kate.
We're just having fun.
Yeah.
Easy, champ.
Come on, now...
Apology hug.
Hug?
Ew!
And you're just so cute with these *love handles!*
pinch
pinch

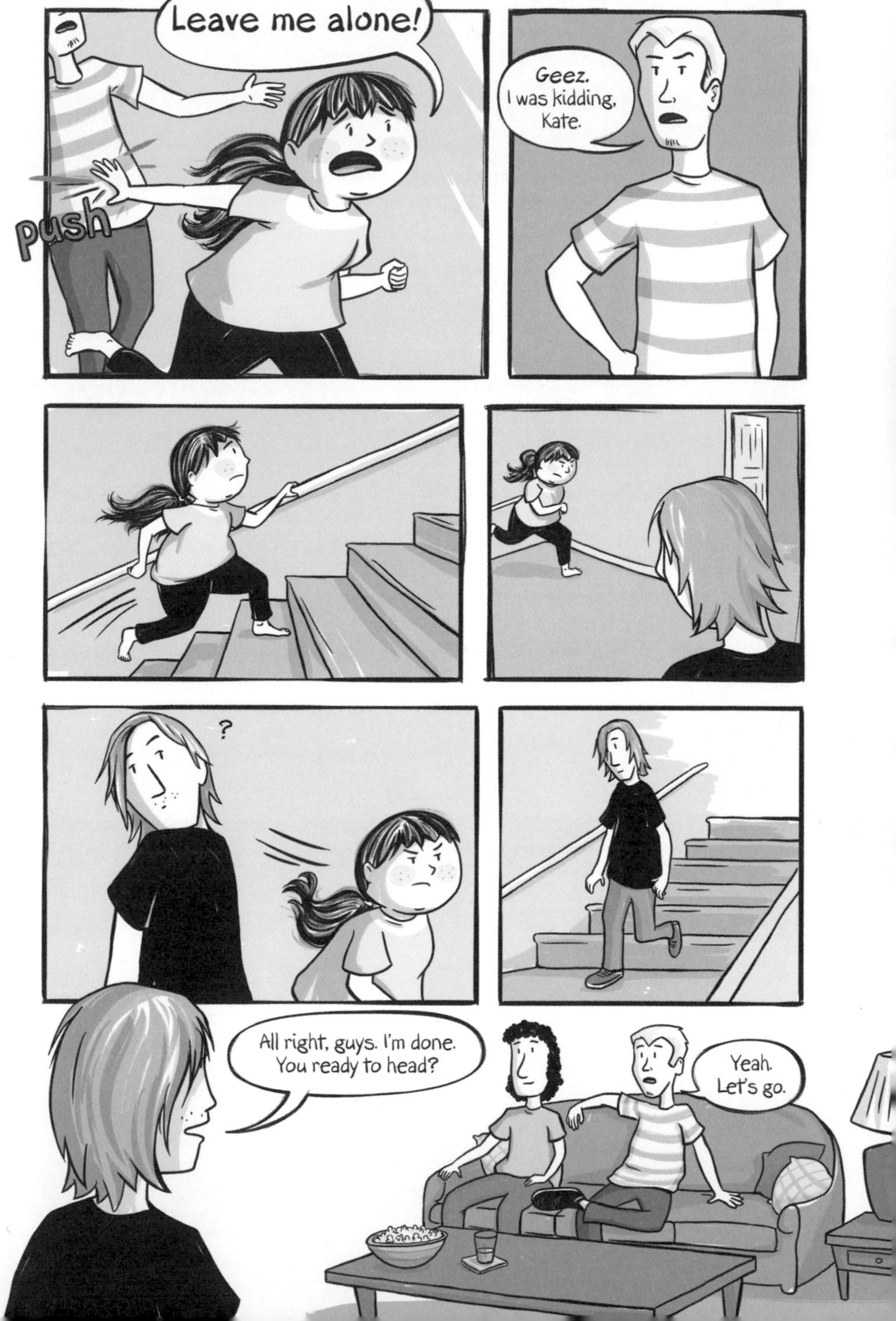
Leave me alone!
push
Geez. I was kidding, Kate.
?
All right, guys. I'm done. You ready to head?
Yeah. Let's go.

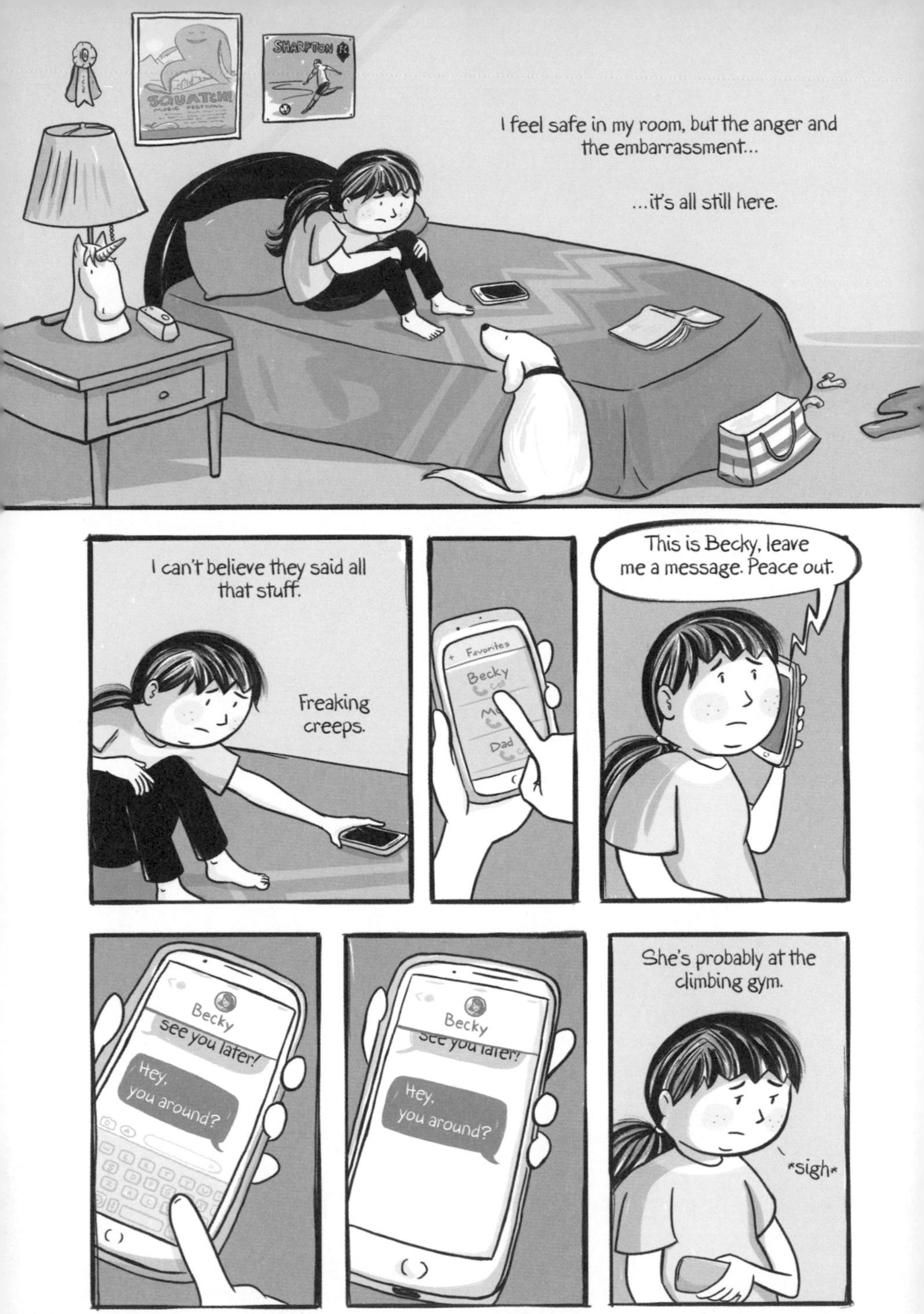
SQUATCH! MUSIC FESTIVAL
SHARPTON FC
I feel safe in my room, but the anger and the embarrassment...
...it's all still here.
I can't believe they said all that stuff.
Freaking creeps.
Favorites
Becky
Dad
This is Becky, leave me a message. Peace out.
Becky
see you later!
Hey, you around?
Becky
see you later!
Hey, you around?
She's probably at the climbing gym.
sigh

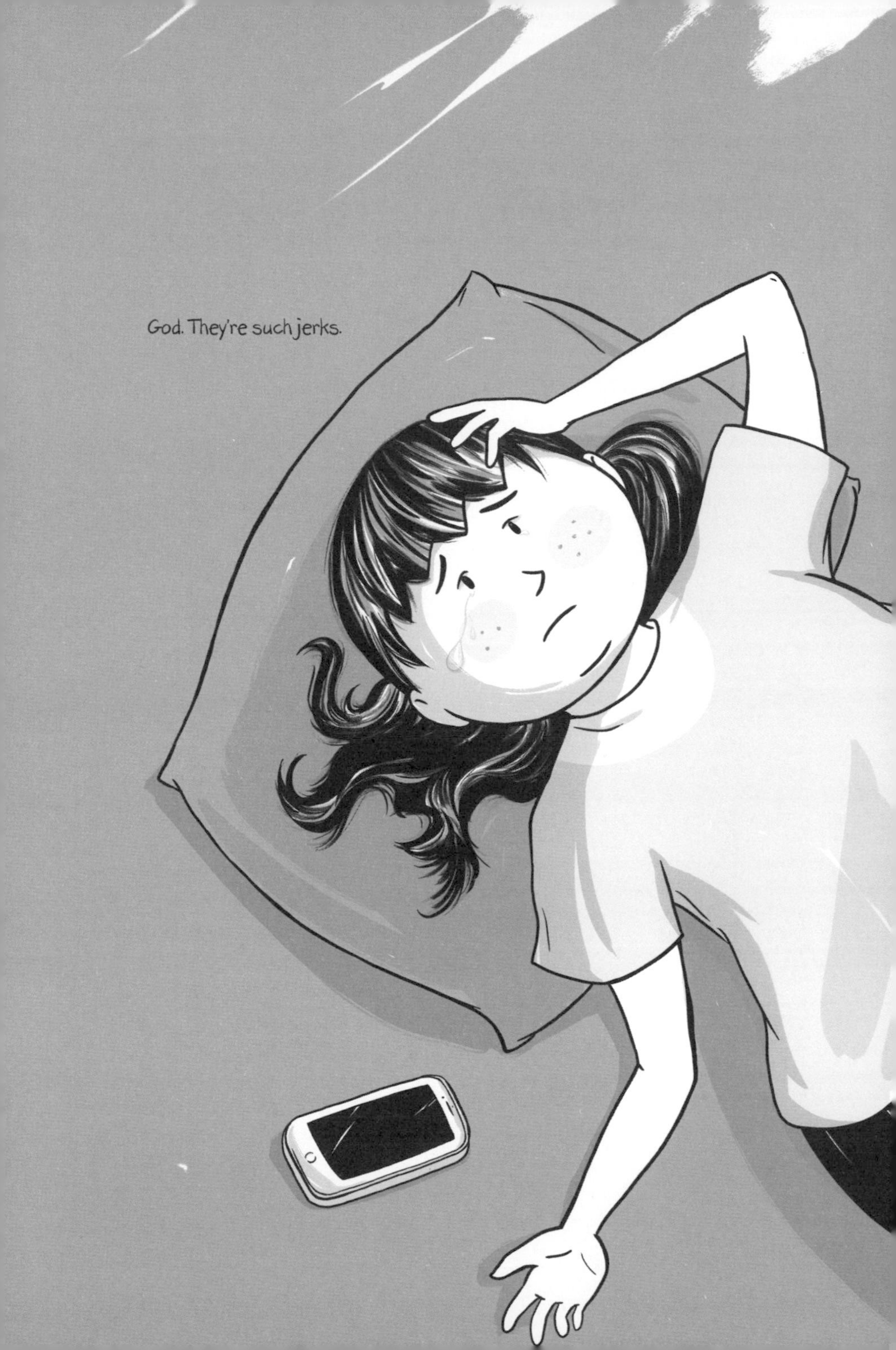
God. They're such jerks.

I should be excited about summer.

But this summer, Becky is going away to climbing camp...

...for two months!

kick

I've never spent a summer without her.

138

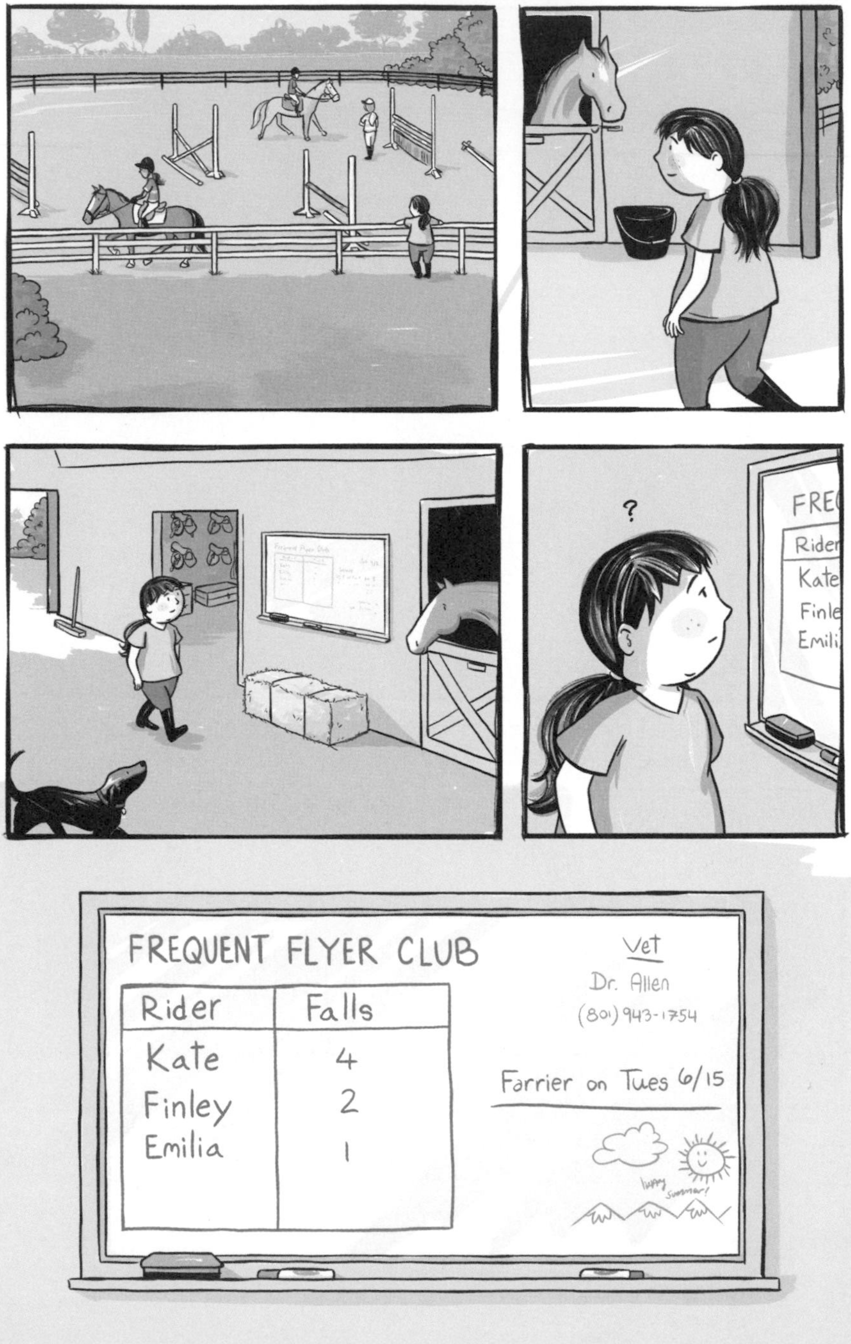
?
FREQUENT FLYER CLUB
Rider
Falls
Kate
4
Finley
2
Emilia
1
Vet
Dr. Allen
(801) 943-1754
Farrier on Tues 6/15
happy summer!

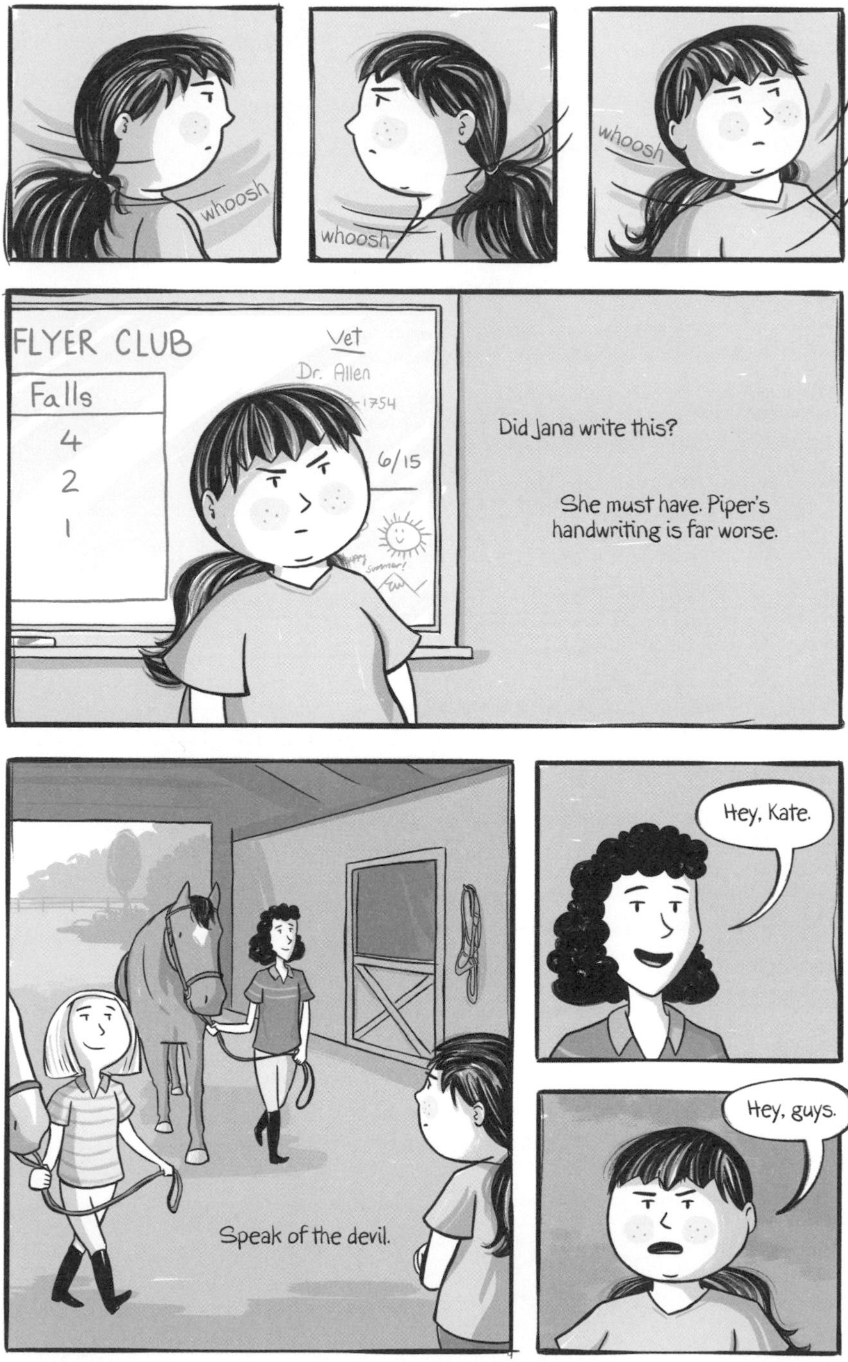
whoosh
whoosh
whoosh
FLYER CLUB
Falls
4
2
1
Vet
Dr. Allen
6/15
Did Jana write this?
She must have. Piper's handwriting is far worse.
Speak of the devil.
Hey, Kate.
Hey, guys.

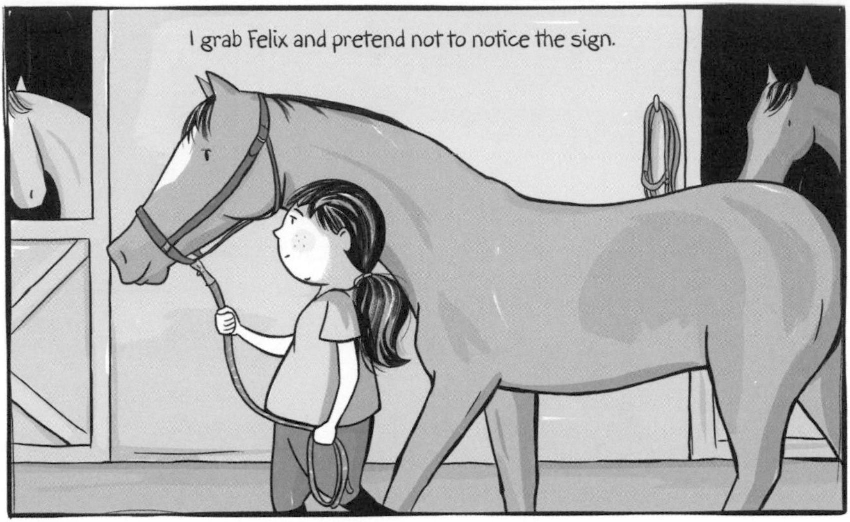
I grab Felix and pretend not to notice the sign.

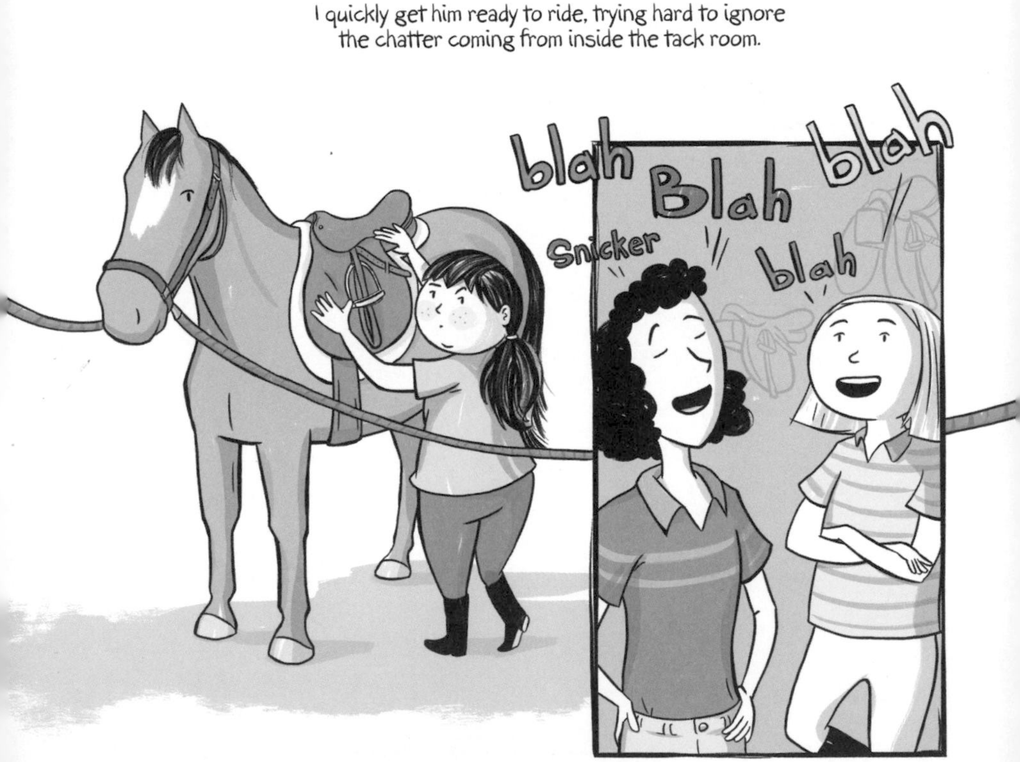
I quickly get him ready to ride, trying hard to ignore
the chatter coming from inside the tack room.
blah
Blah
blah
Snicker
blah

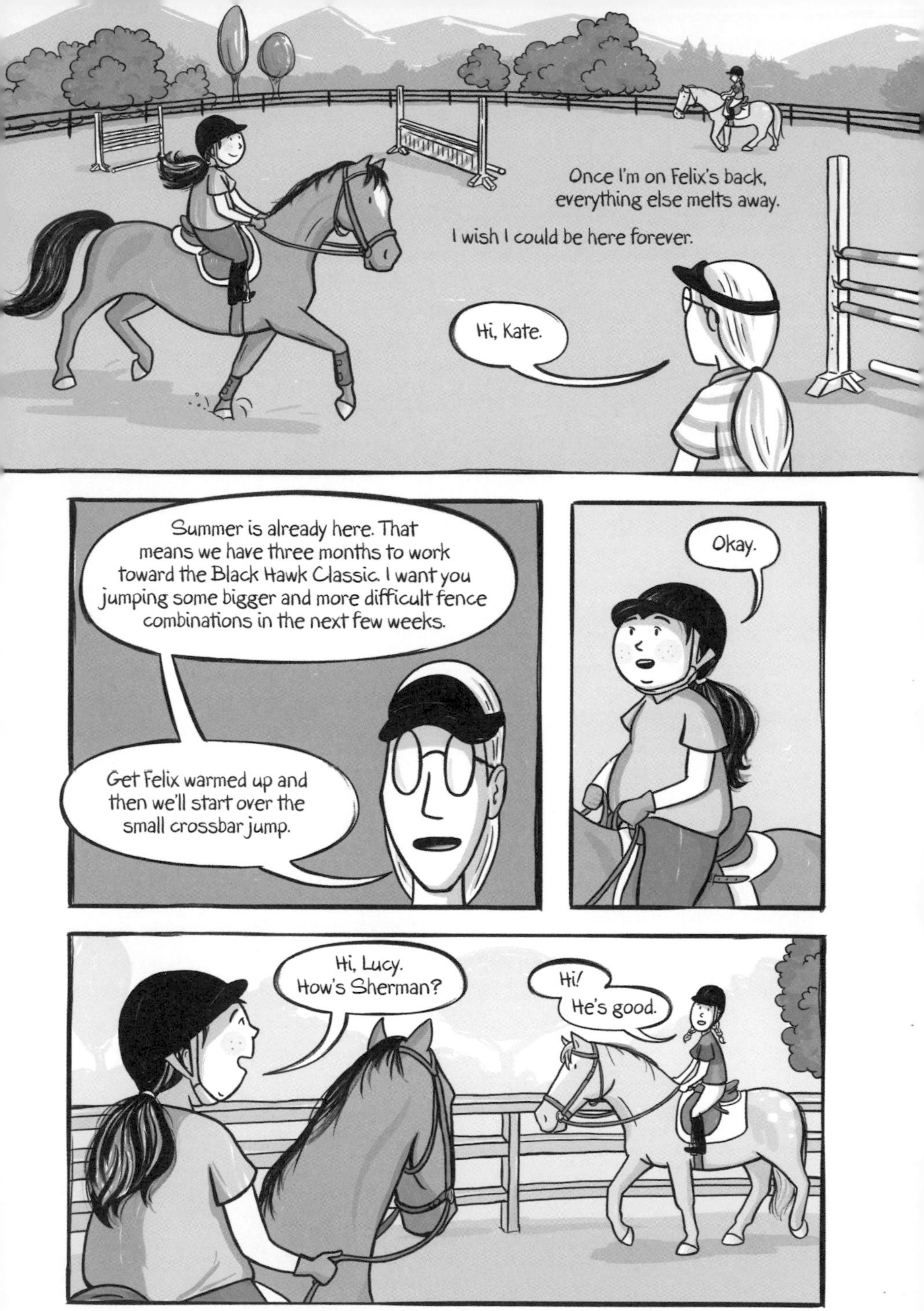

Once I'm on Felix's back, everything else melts away.
I wish I could be here forever.
Hi, Kate.
Summer is already here. That means we have three months to work toward the Black Hawk Classic. I want you jumping some bigger and more difficult fence combinations in the next few weeks.
Get Felix warmed up and then we'll start over the small crossbar jump.
Okay.
Hi, Lucy. How's Sherman?
Hi! He's good.

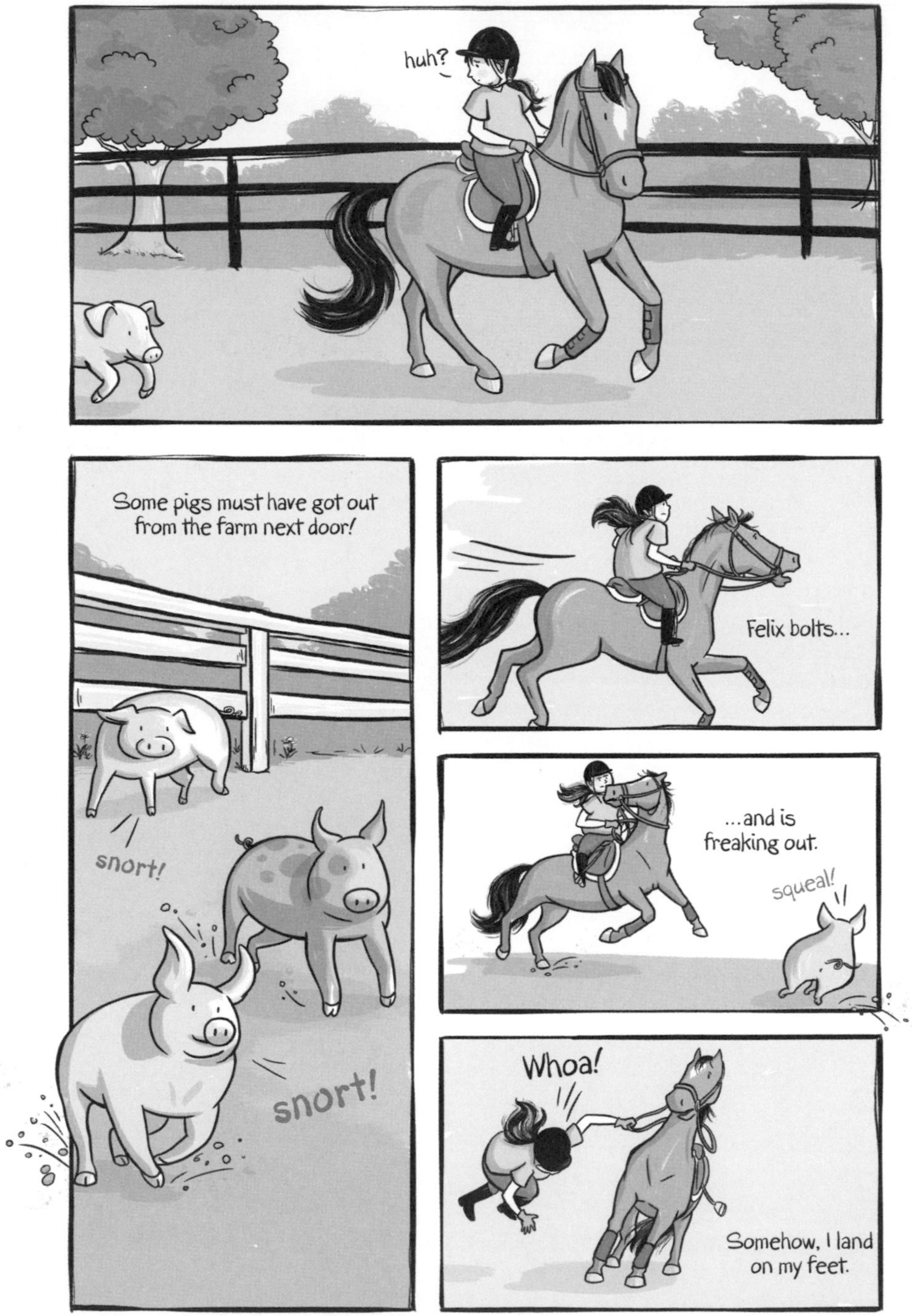
huh?
Some pigs must have got out from the farm next door!
snort!
snort!
Felix bolts...
...and is freaking out.
squeal!
Whoa!
Somehow, I land on my feet.

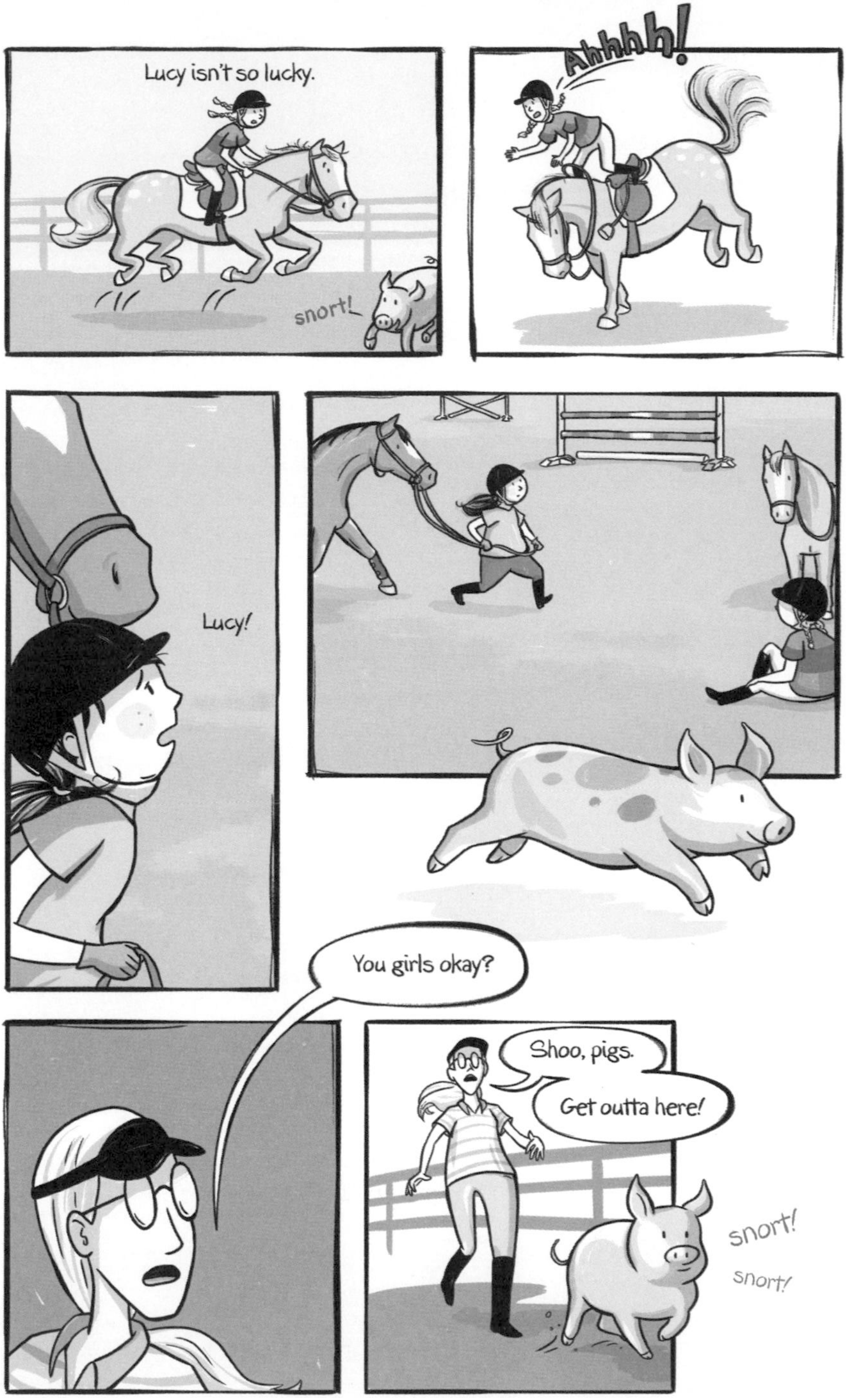
Lucy isn't so lucky.
snort!
Ahhhh!
Lucy!
You girls okay?
Shoo, pigs.
Get outta here!
snort!
snort!

I'm relieved that Lucy's okay. But I also feel some comfort in not being the only one dumped on the ground for a change.

Chapter 7
Bridle Swipe

Liverpool

A ditch or large tray of water placed beneath a vertical fence.

I also ran into her at the grocery store last week and she actually seemed like she wanted to hang out this summer.

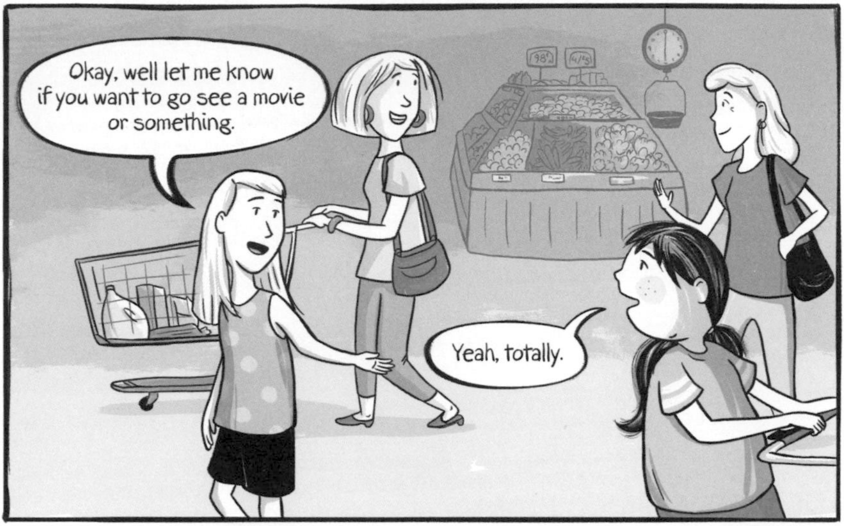
Okay, well let me know if you want to go see a movie or something.
Yeah, totally.

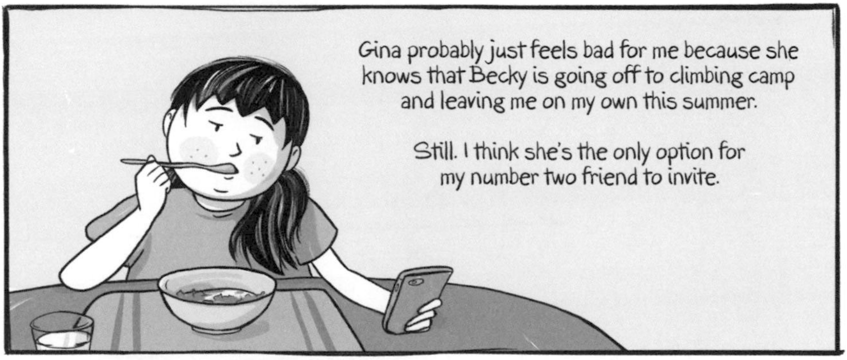
Gina probably just feels bad for me because she knows that Becky is going off to climbing camp and leaving me on my own this summer.
Still, I think she's the only option for my number two friend to invite.

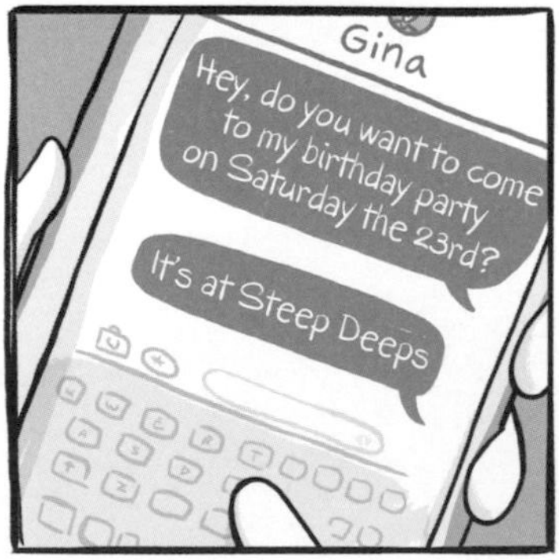
Gina
Hey, do you want to come to my birthday party on Saturday the 23rd?
It's at Steep Deeps

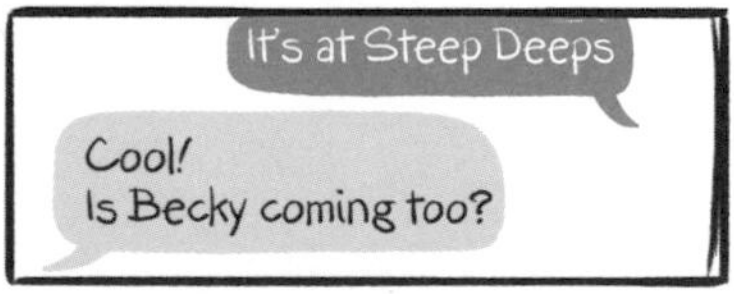
It's at Steep Deeps
Cool!
Is Becky coming too?

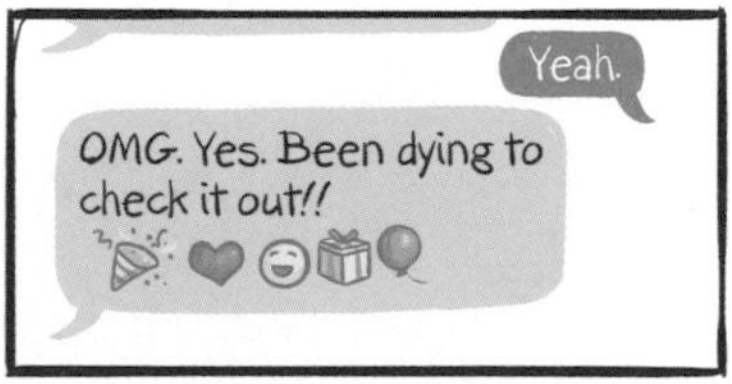
Yeah.
OMG. Yes. Been dying to check it out!!

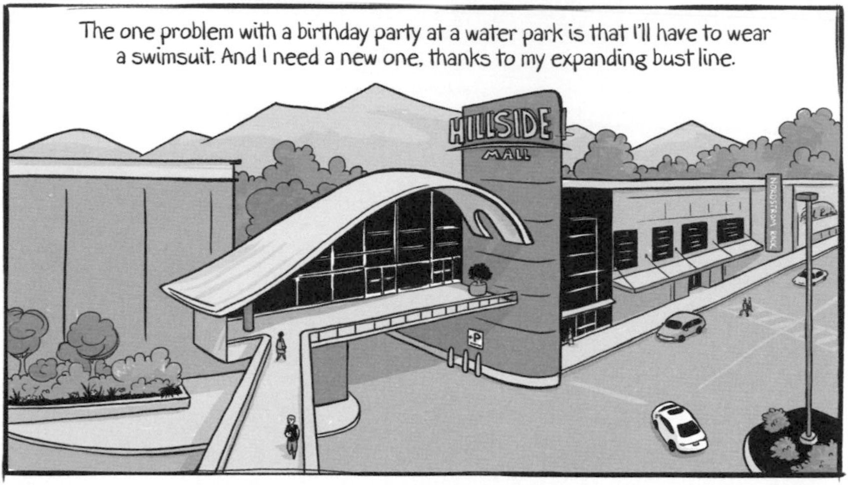
The one problem with a birthday party at a water park is that I'll have to wear a swimsuit. And I need a new one, thanks to my expanding bust line.
HILLSIDE
MALL

There is something really depressing about an indoor shopping mall during summertime.

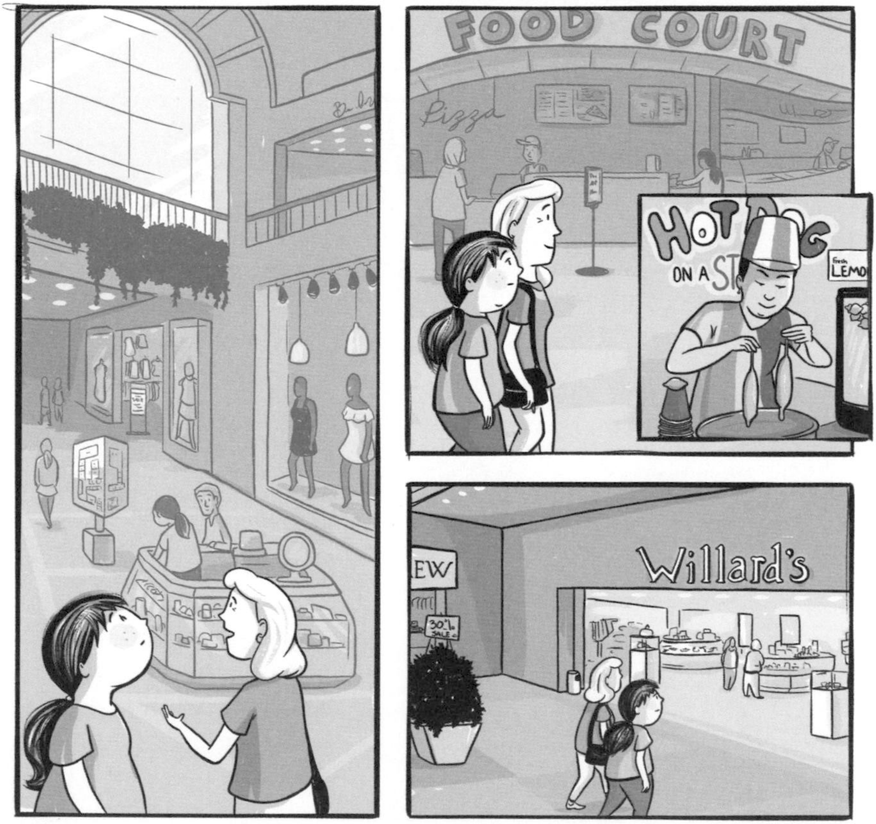
FOOD COURT
Pizza
Willard's

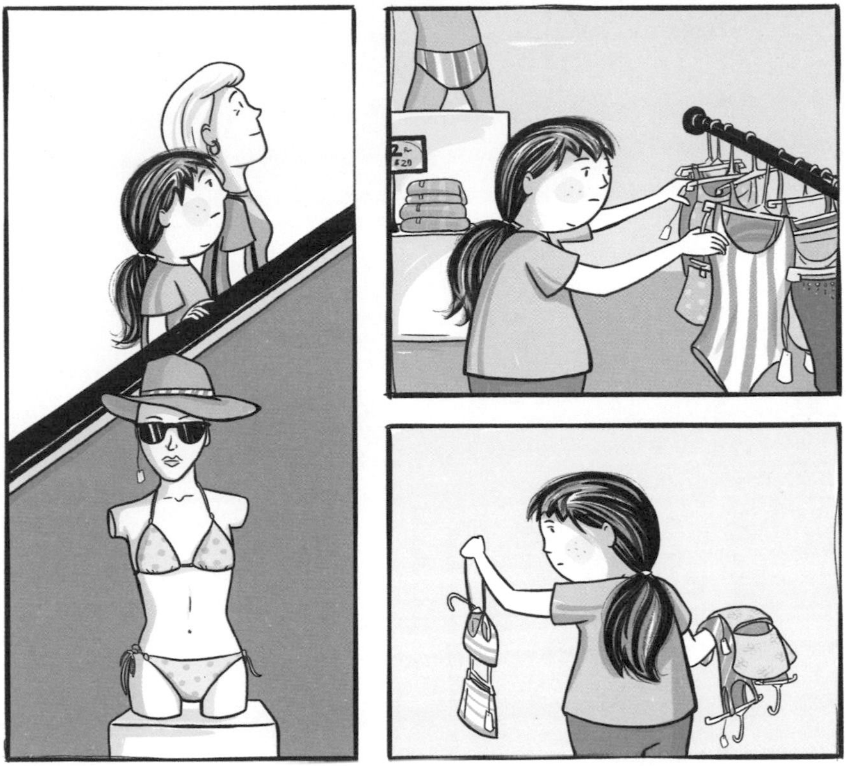

And there's probably nothing more horrible than trying on swimsuits.

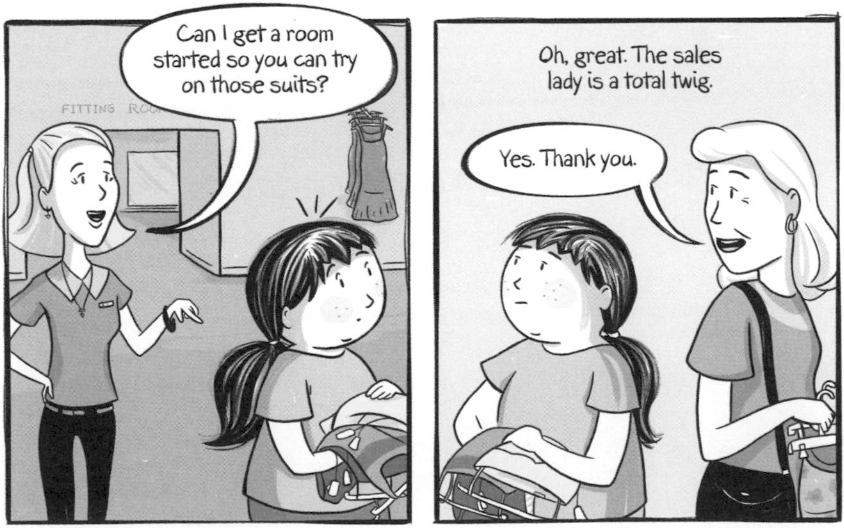
FITTING ROO
Can I get a room started so you can try on those suits?
Oh, great. The sales lady is a total twig.
Yes. Thank you.

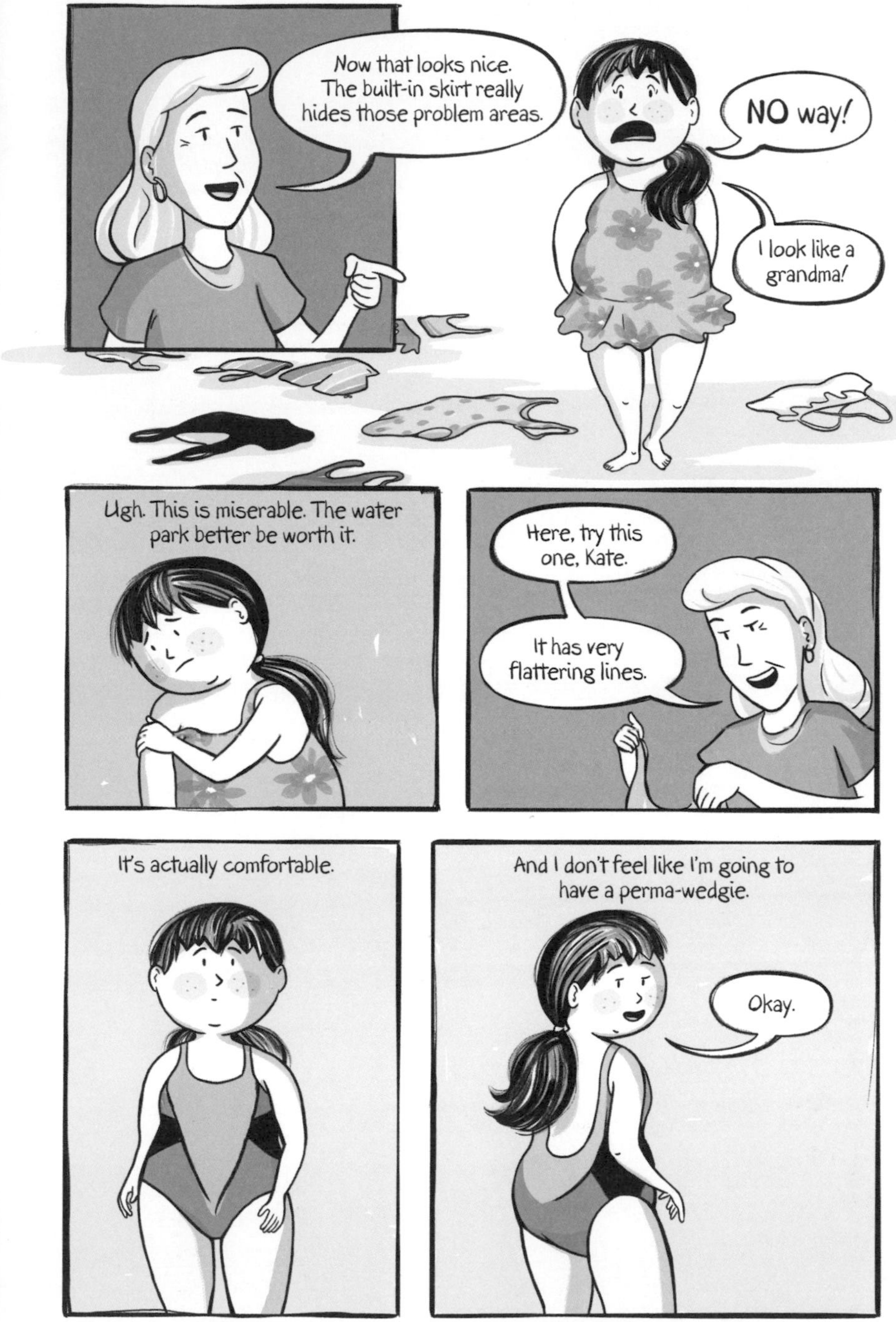
Now that looks nice. The built-in skirt really hides those problem areas.
NO way!
I look like a grandma!
Ugh. This is miserable. The water park better be worth it.
Here, try this one, Kate.
It has very flattering lines.
It's actually comfortable.
And I don't feel like I'm going to have a perma-wedgie.
Okay.

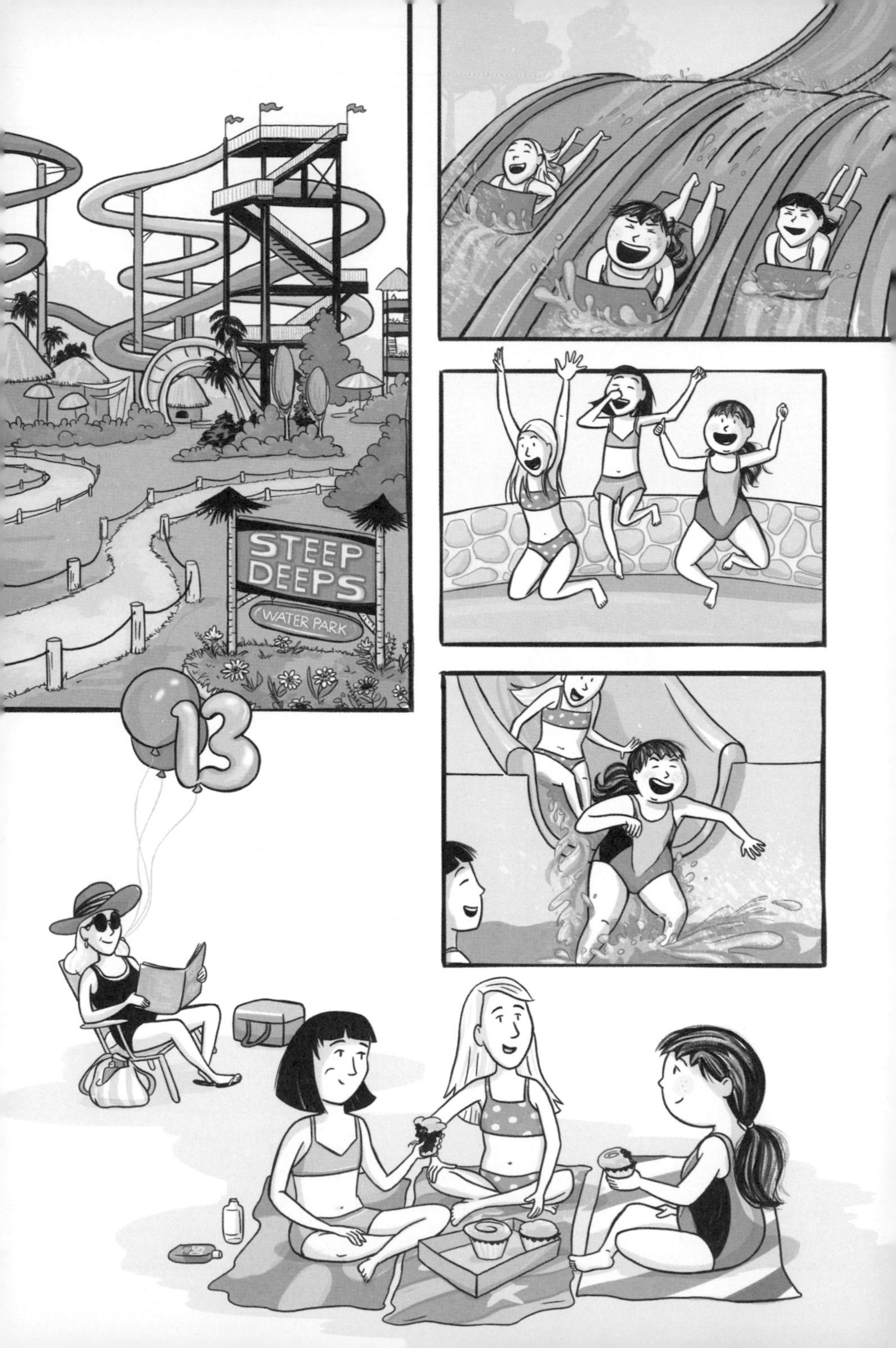
STEEP DEEPS
WATER PARK
13

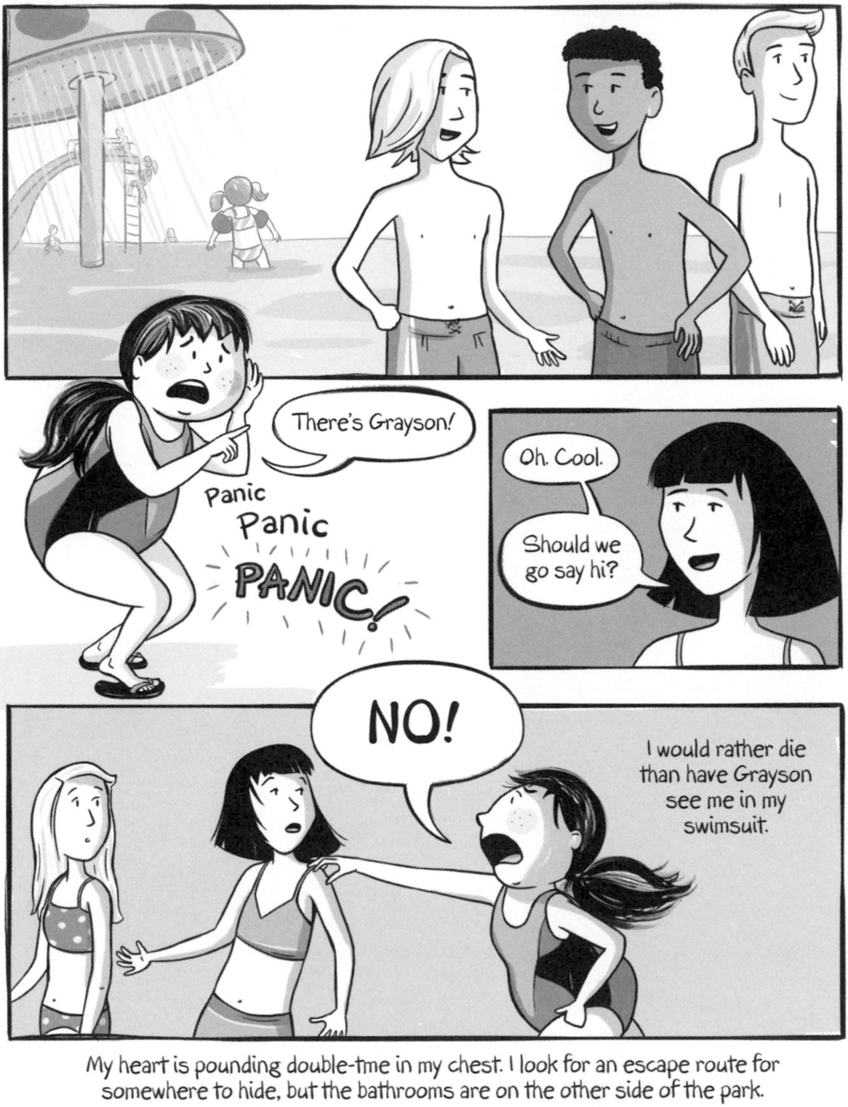

There's Grayson!
Panic
Panic
PANIC!
Oh. Cool.
Should we go say hi?
NO!
I would rather die than have Grayson see me in my swimsuit.
My heart is pounding double-tme in my chest. I look for an escape route for somewhere to hide, but the bathrooms are on the other side of the park.
I freeze.

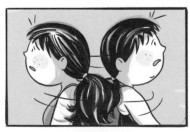

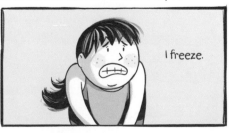

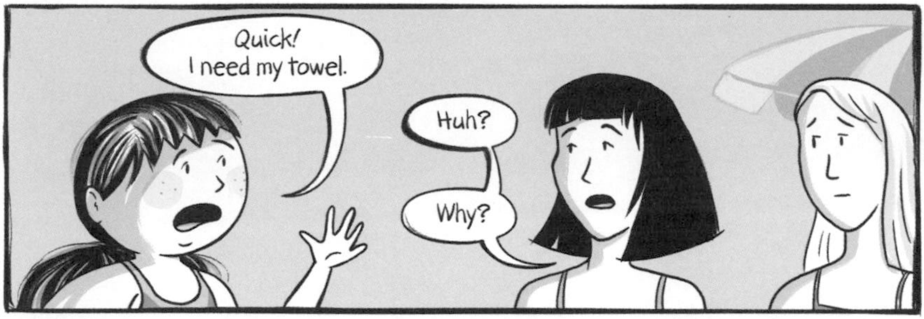
Quick!
I need my towel.
Huh?
Why?

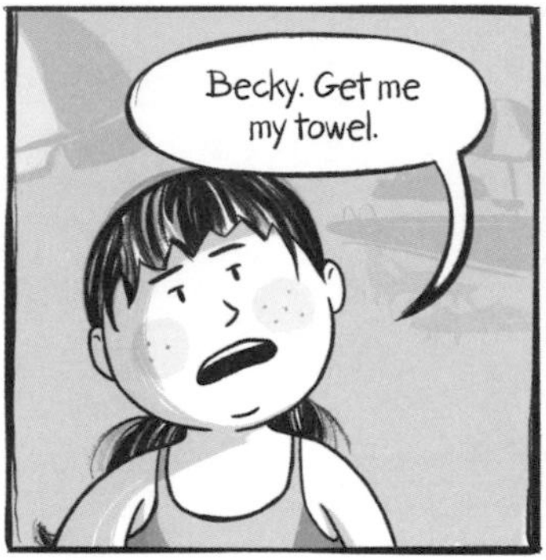
Becky. Get me
my towel.

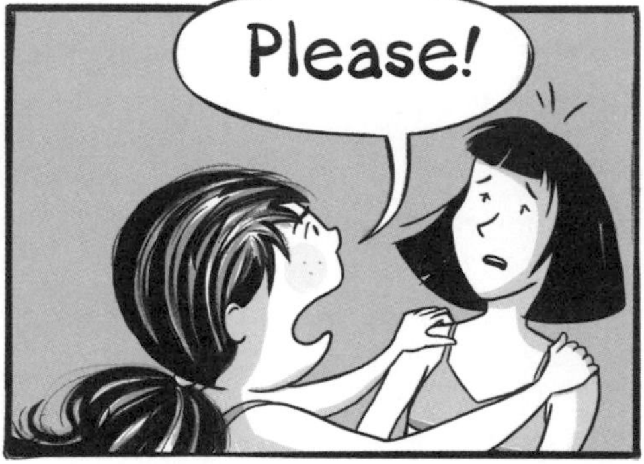
Please!

I feel completely exposed, like I'm stuck in one of those horrible dreams where you're caught in public (worst of all, a crowded school hallway) without your clothes on.

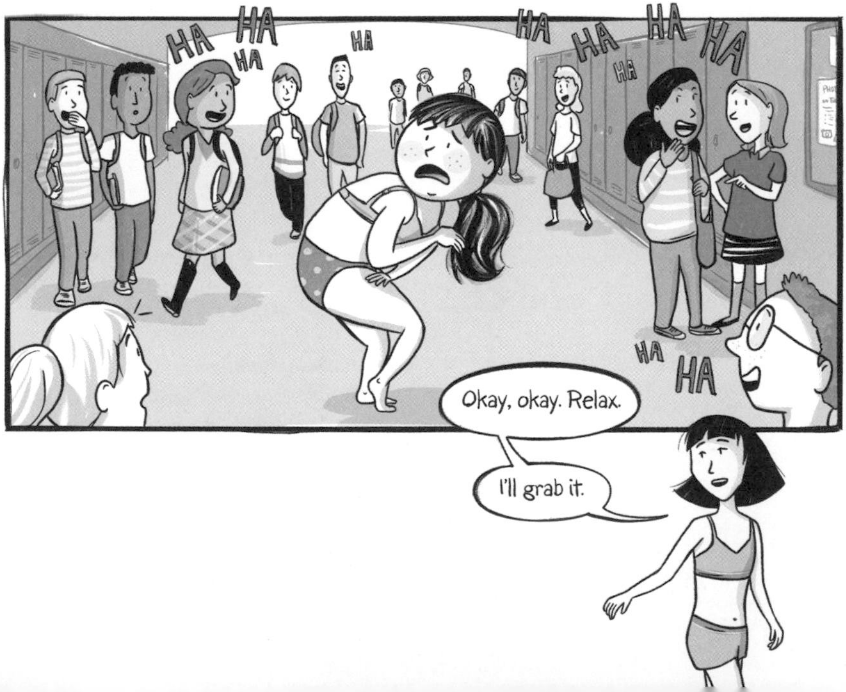
HA HA HA HA
HA HA HA HA HA HA
HA HA
Okay, okay. Relax.
I'll grab it.

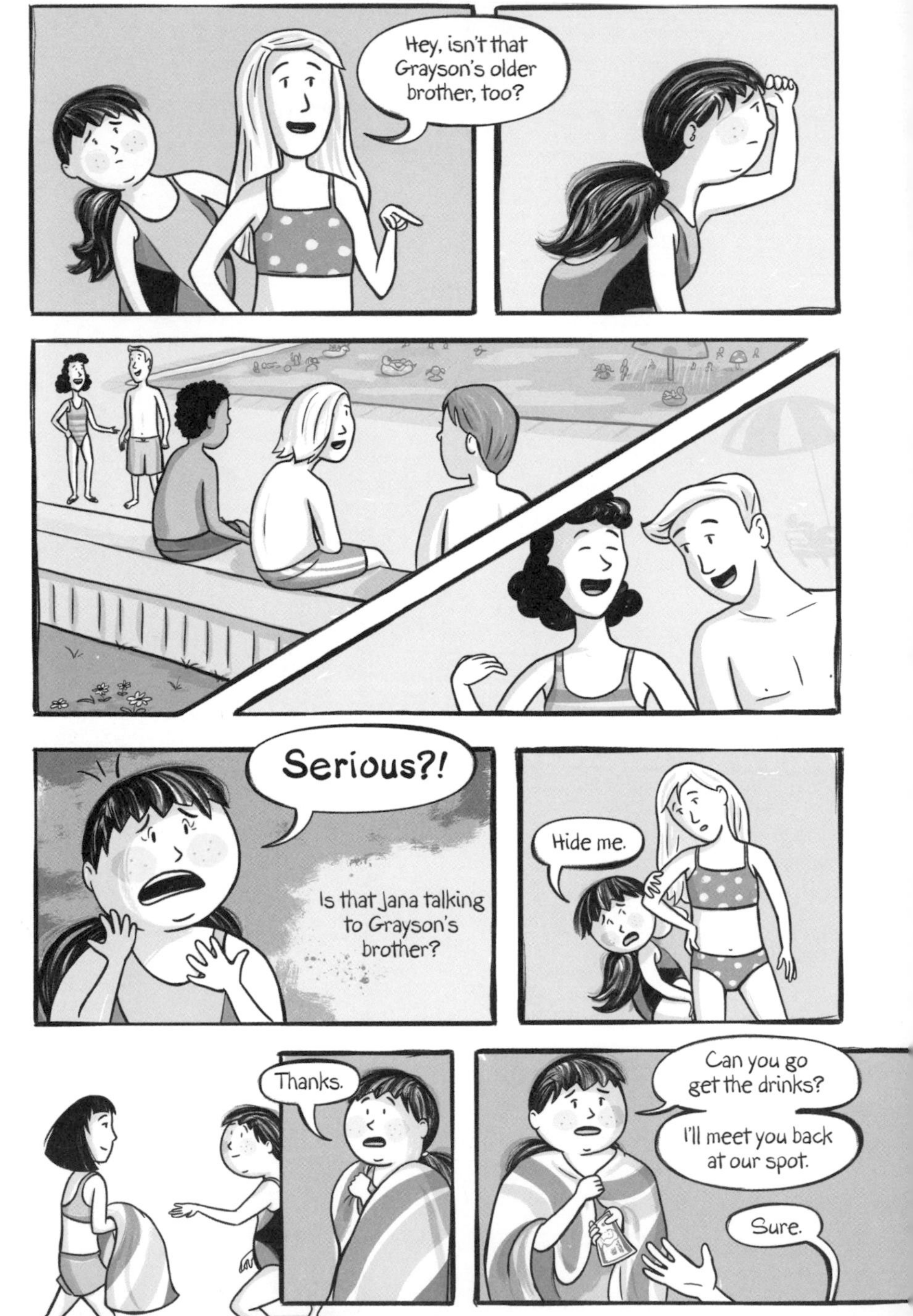
Hey, isn't that Grayson's older brother, too?
Serious?!
Is that Jana talking to Grayson's brother?
Hide me.
Thanks.
Can you go get the drinks?
I'll meet you back at our spot.
Sure.

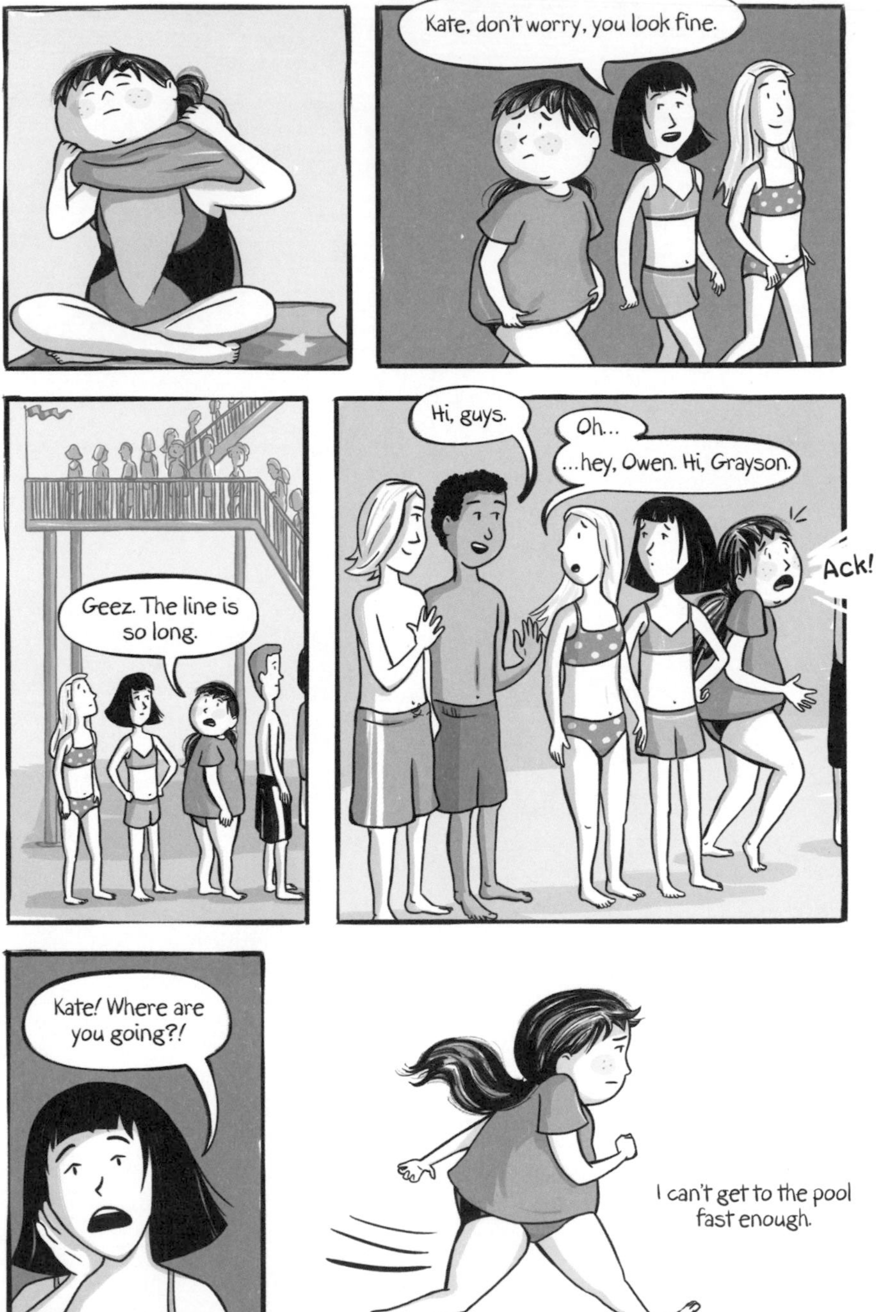
Kate, don't worry, you look fine.
Geez. The line is so long.
Hi, guys.
Oh...
...hey, Owen. Hi, Grayson.
Ack!
Kate! Where are you going?!
I can't get to the pool fast enough.

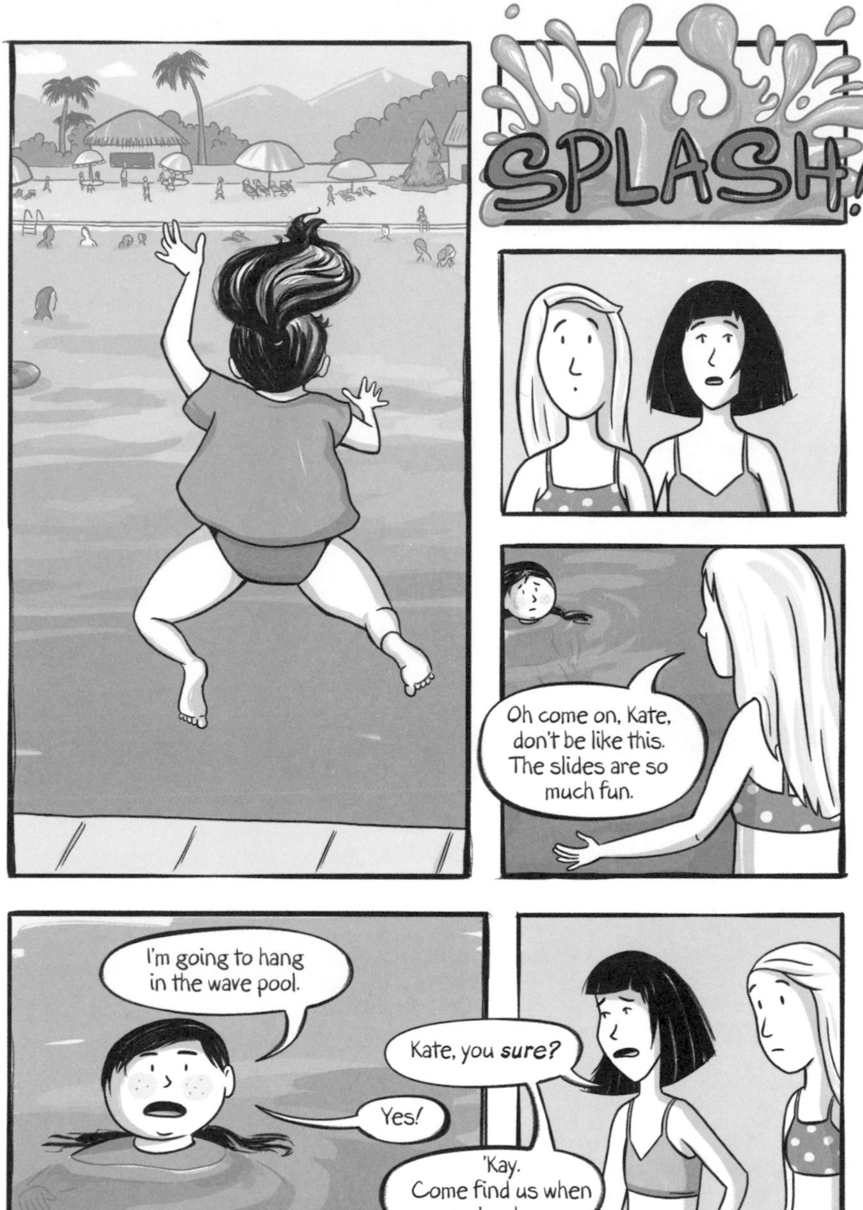
SPLASH!
Oh come on, Kate, don't be like this. The slides are so much fun.
I'm going to hang in the wave pool.
Kate, you *sure?*
Yes!
'Kay. Come find us when you're done.

I don't dare leave the pool. There's no way I'm standing in line for one of the waterslides with my thunder thighs in plain view for Grayson to see.

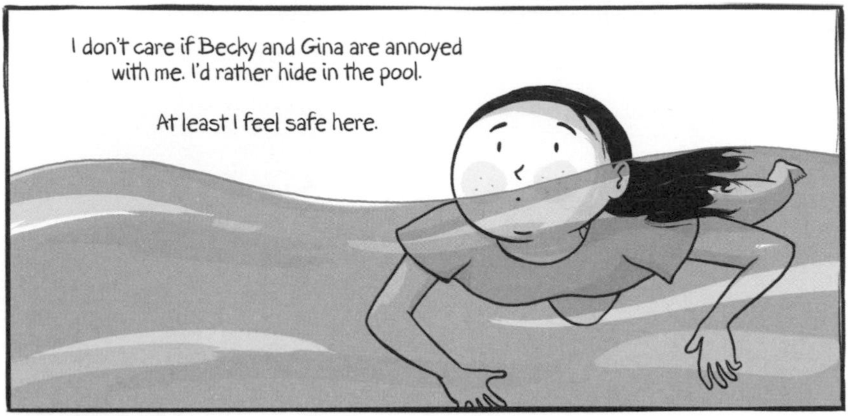
I don't care if Becky and Gina are annoyed with me. I'd rather hide in the pool.
At least I feel safe here.

To keep myself entertained, I try body surfing one of the big waves, but my soaked shirt is heavy and weighs me down, making my swimming clumsy.

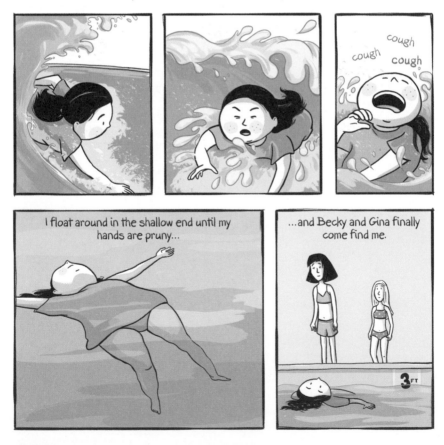

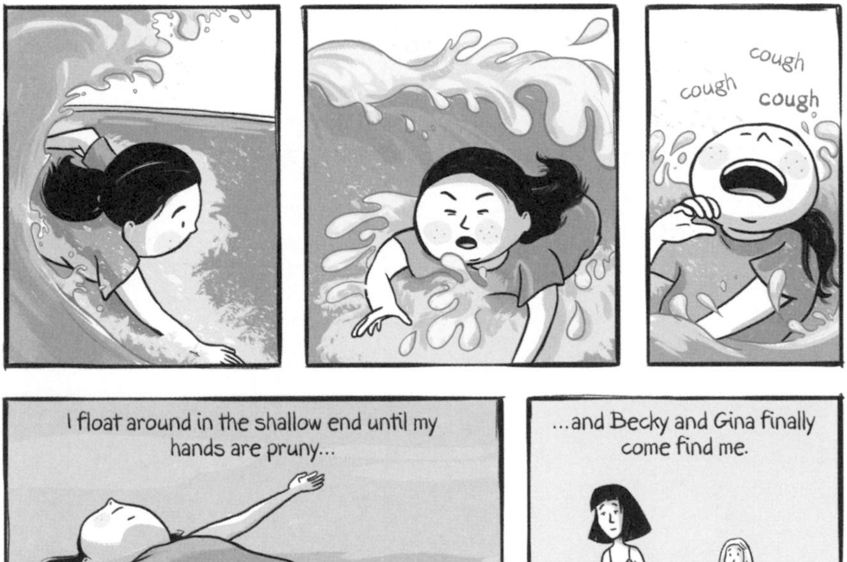
cough
cough
cough
I float around in the shallow end until my hands are pruny...
...and Becky and Gina finally come find me.
3 FT

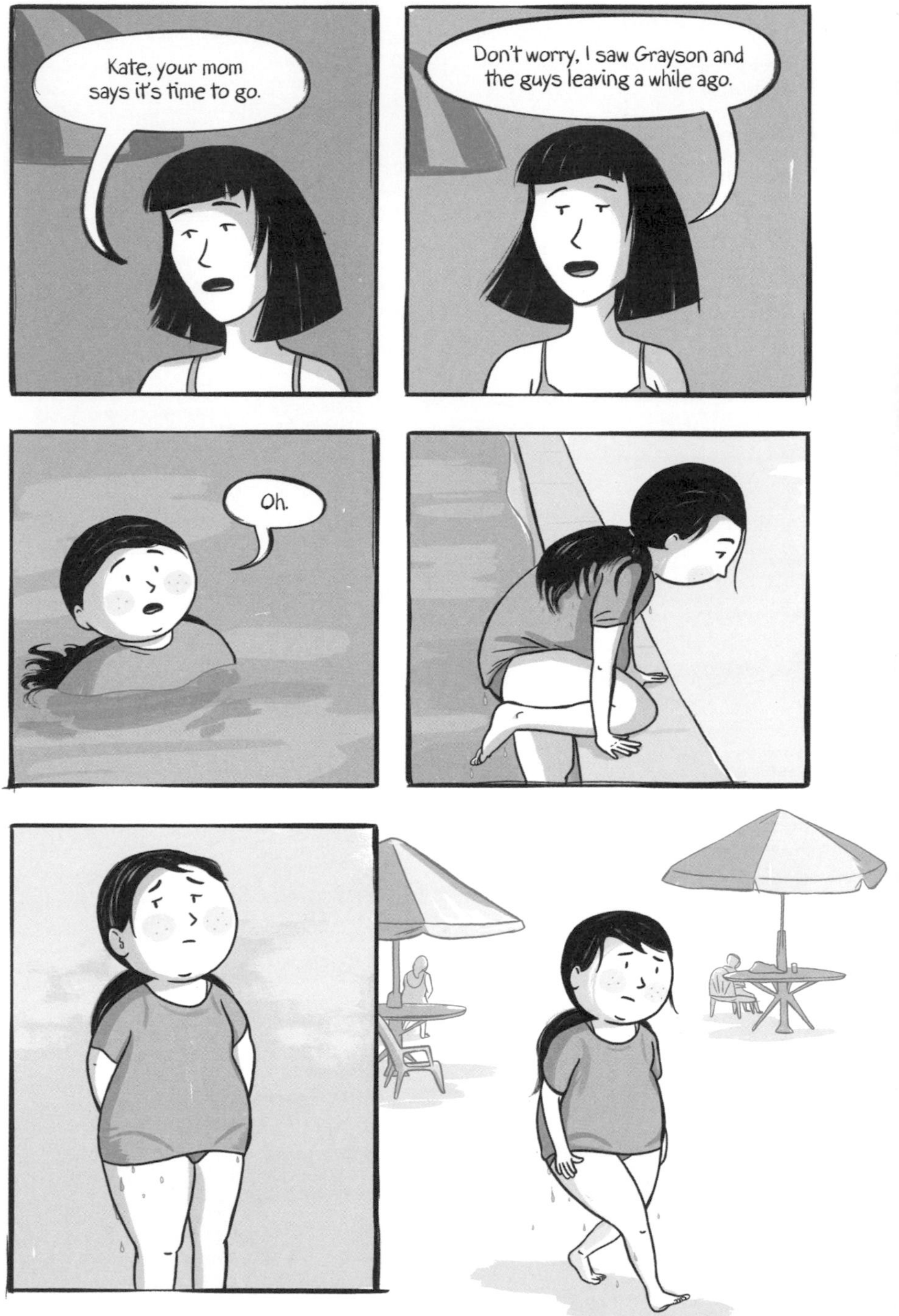
Kate, your mom says it's time to go.
Don't worry, I saw Grayson and the guys leaving a while ago.
Oh.

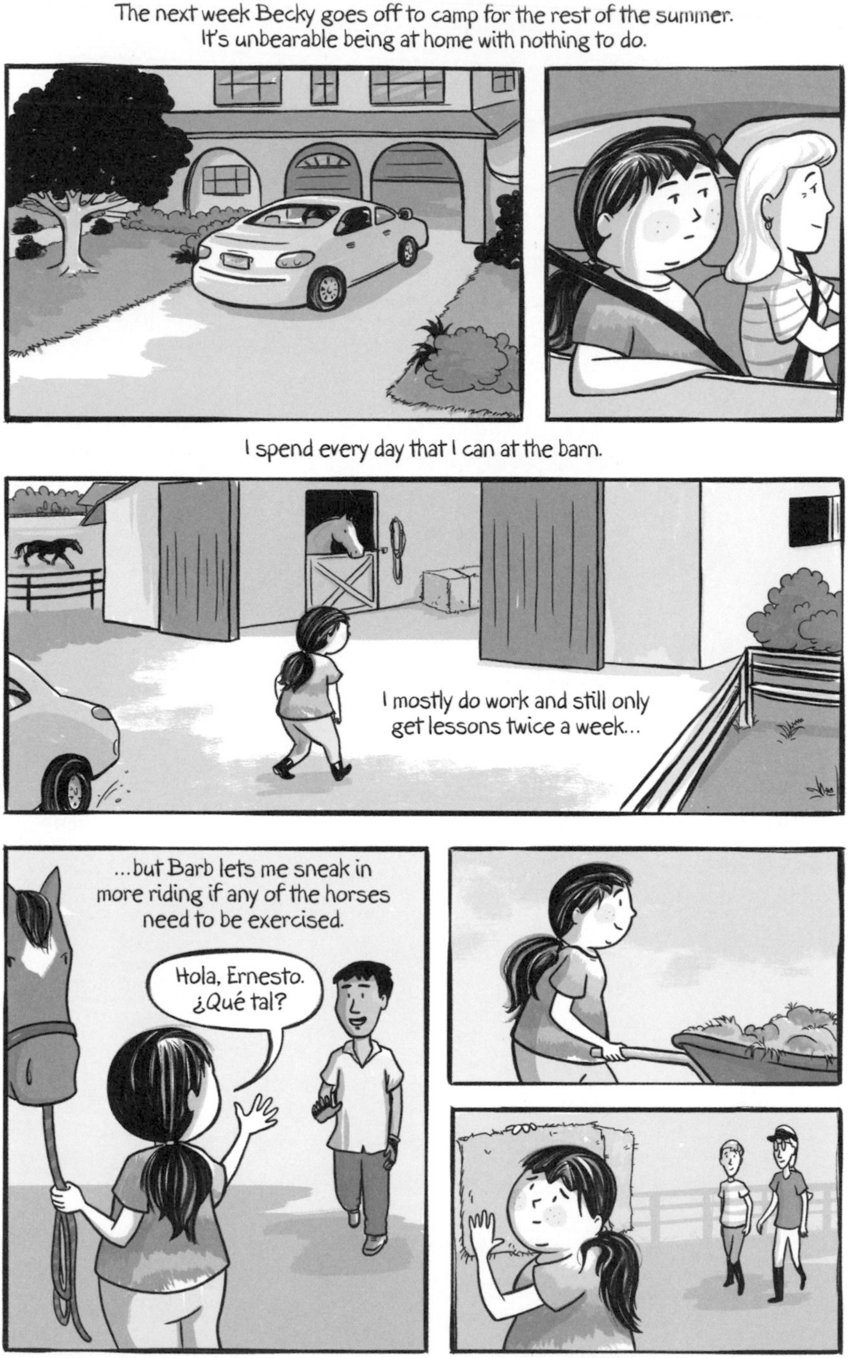
The next week Becky goes off to camp for the rest of the summer.
It's unbearable being at home with nothing to do.
I spend every day that I can at the barn.
I mostly do work and still only get lessons twice a week...
...but Barb lets me sneak in more riding if any of the horses need to be exercised.
Hola, Ernesto. ¿Qué tal?

Despite some of my initial feelings about Valerie, I'm starting to become a big fan.

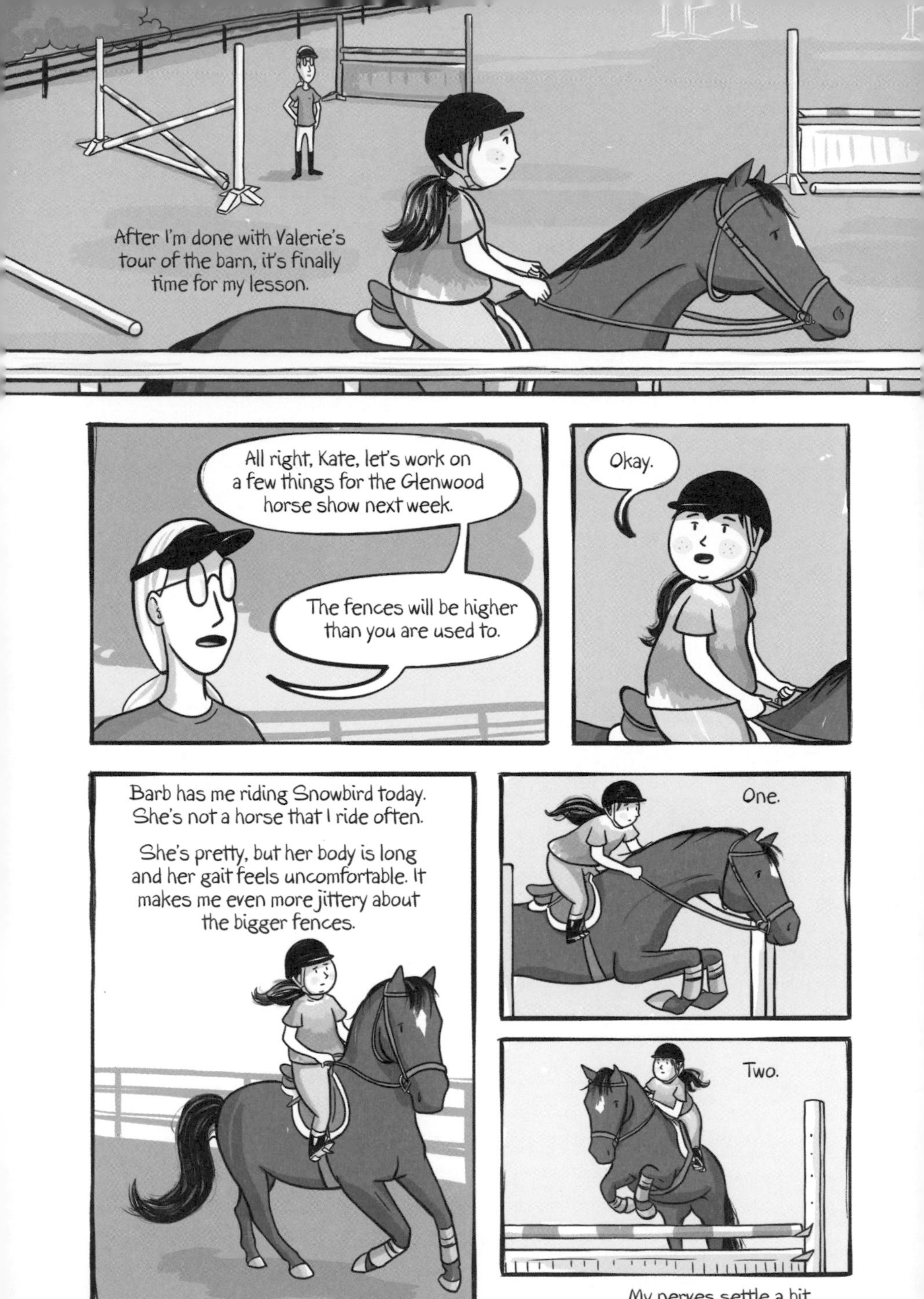
After I'm done with Valerie's tour of the barn, it's finally time for my lesson.
All right, Kate, let's work on a few things for the Glenwood horse show next week.
The fences will be higher than you are used to.
Okay.
Barb has me riding Snowbird today. She's not a horse that I ride often.
She's pretty, but her body is long and her gait feels uncomfortable. It makes me even more jittery about the bigger fences.
One.
Two.
My nerves settle a bit.

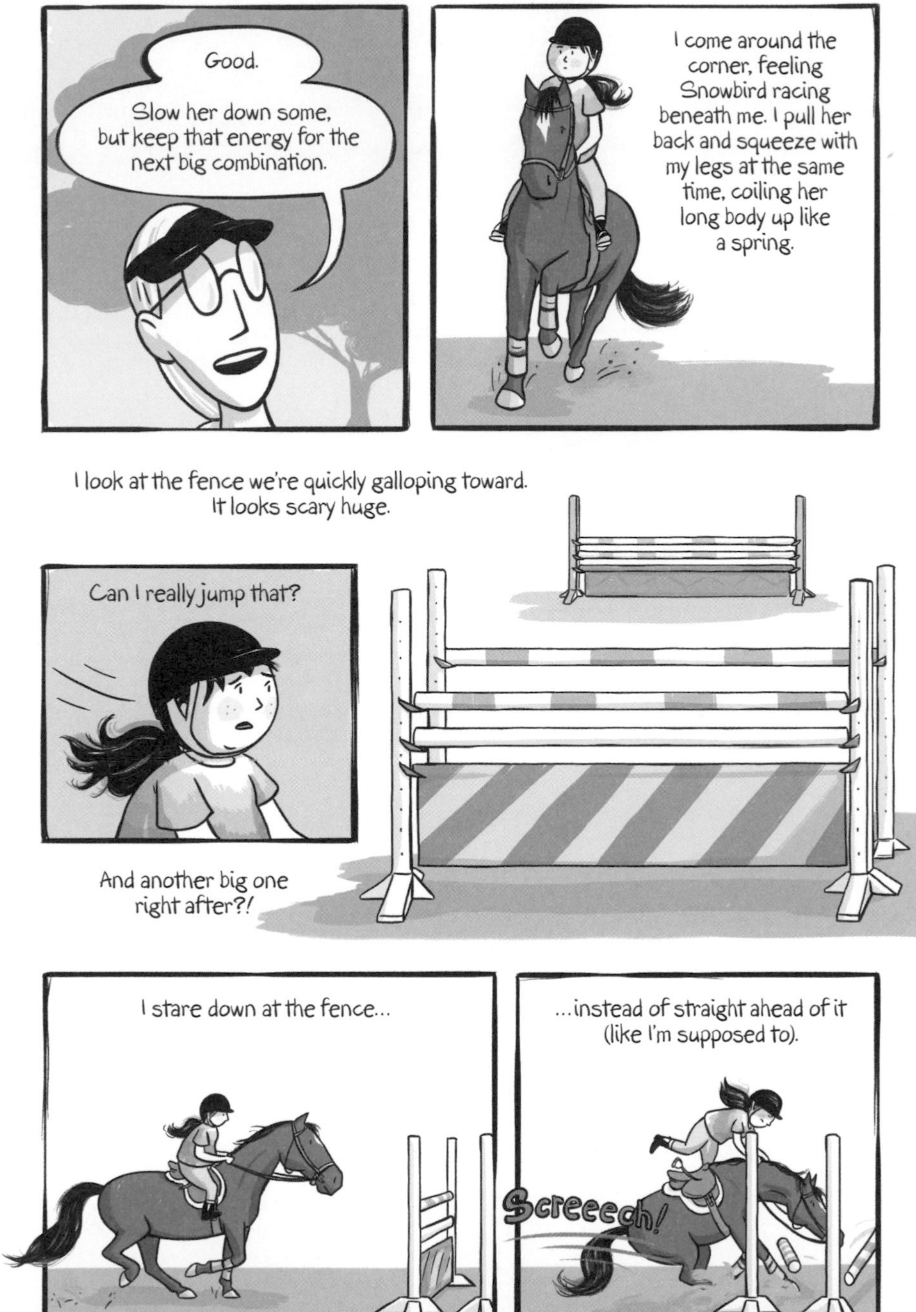
Good.
Slow her down some, but keep that energy for the next big combination.
I come around the corner, feeling Snowbird racing beneath me. I pull her back and squeeze with my legs at the same time, coiling her long body up like a spring.
I look at the fence we're quickly galloping toward. It looks scary huge.
Can I really jump that?
And another big one right after?!
I stare down at the fence...
...instead of straight ahead of it (like I'm supposed to).
Screeech!

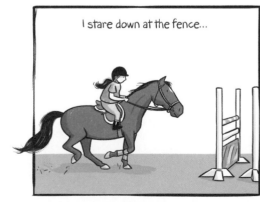

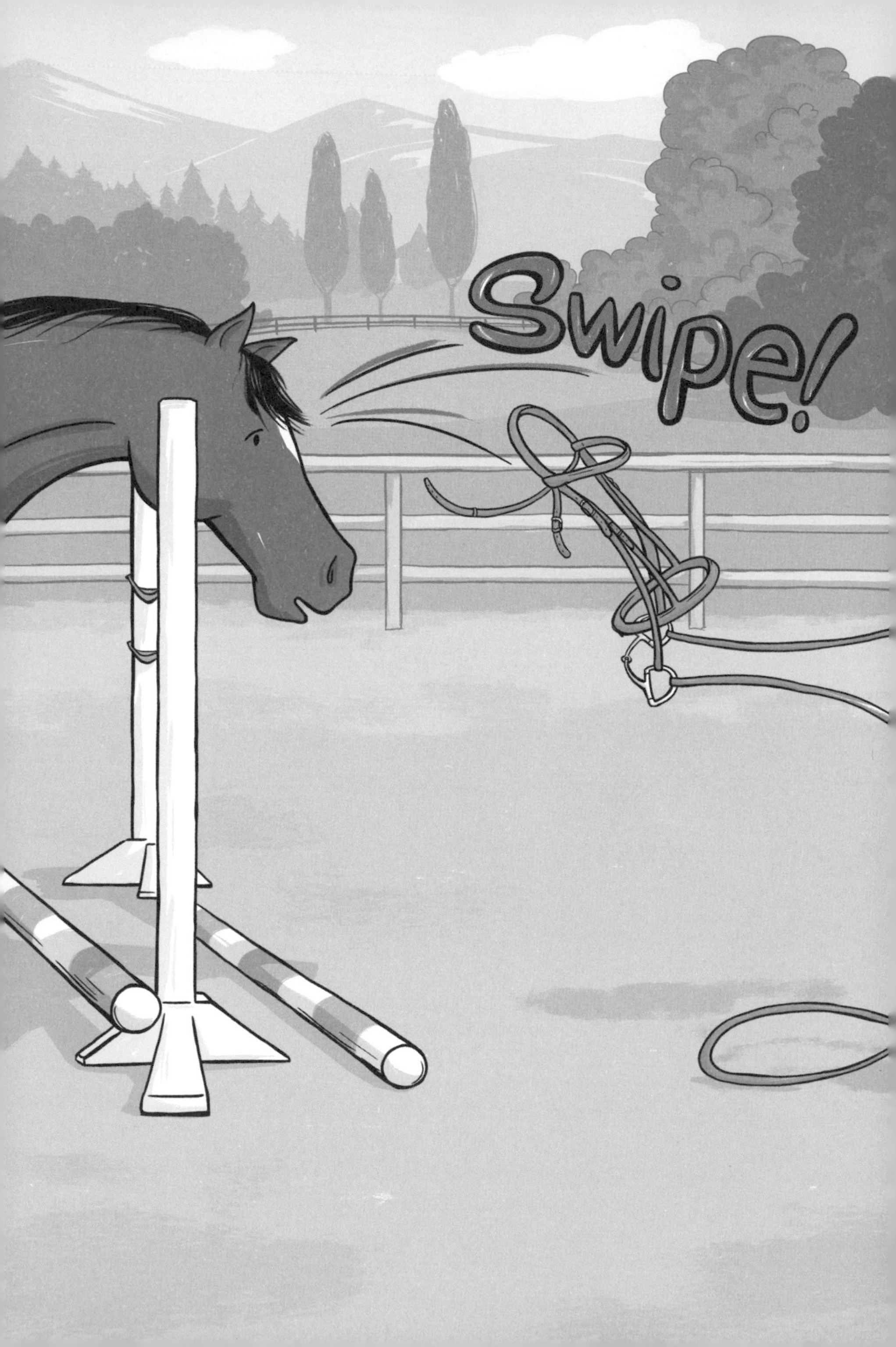
Swipe!

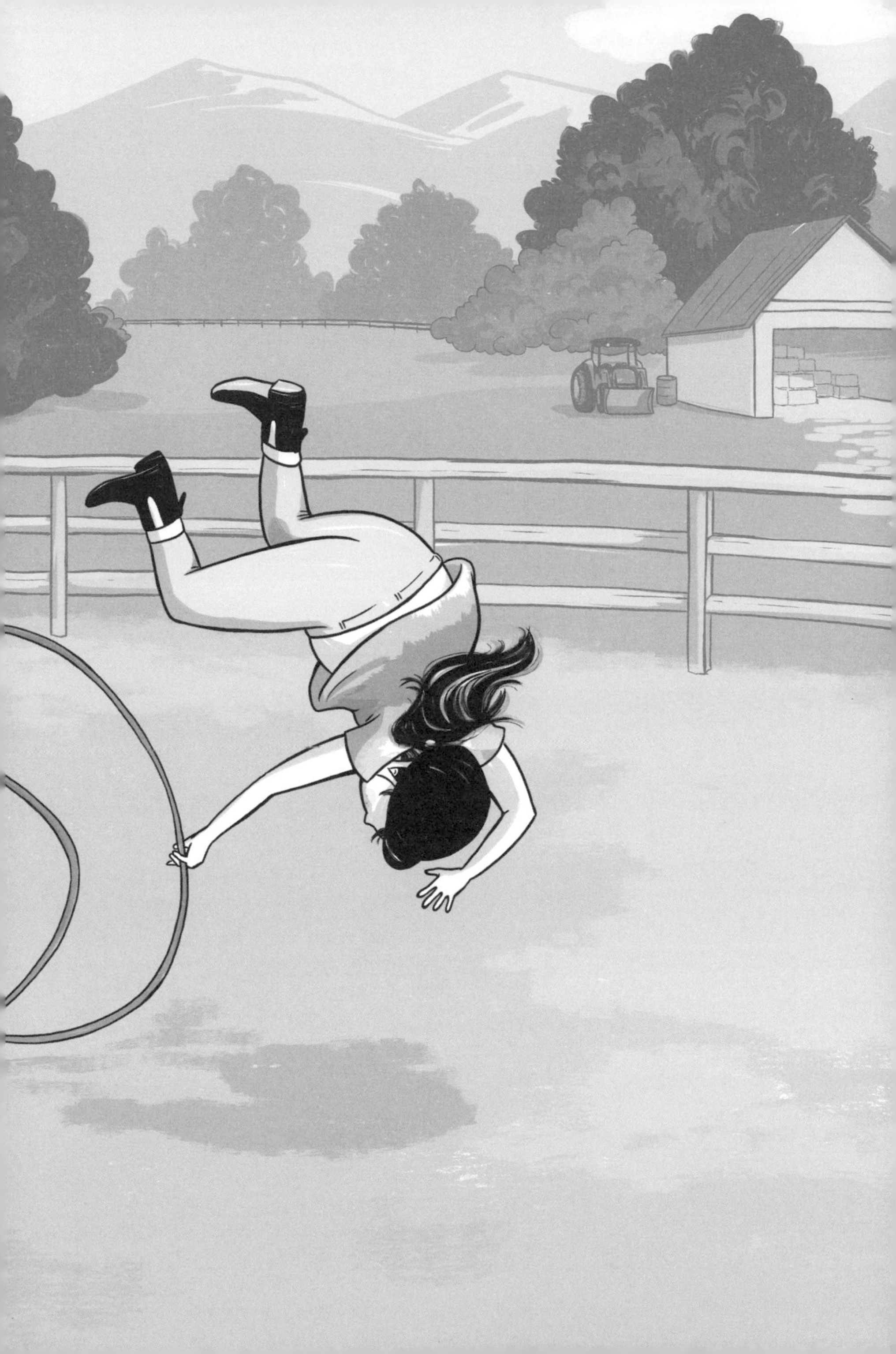

Chapter 8
Dump and Jump

Wall →

A jump that is painted to look like a brick or stone wall, but the "bricks" are made of a lightweight material and fall easily when knocked.

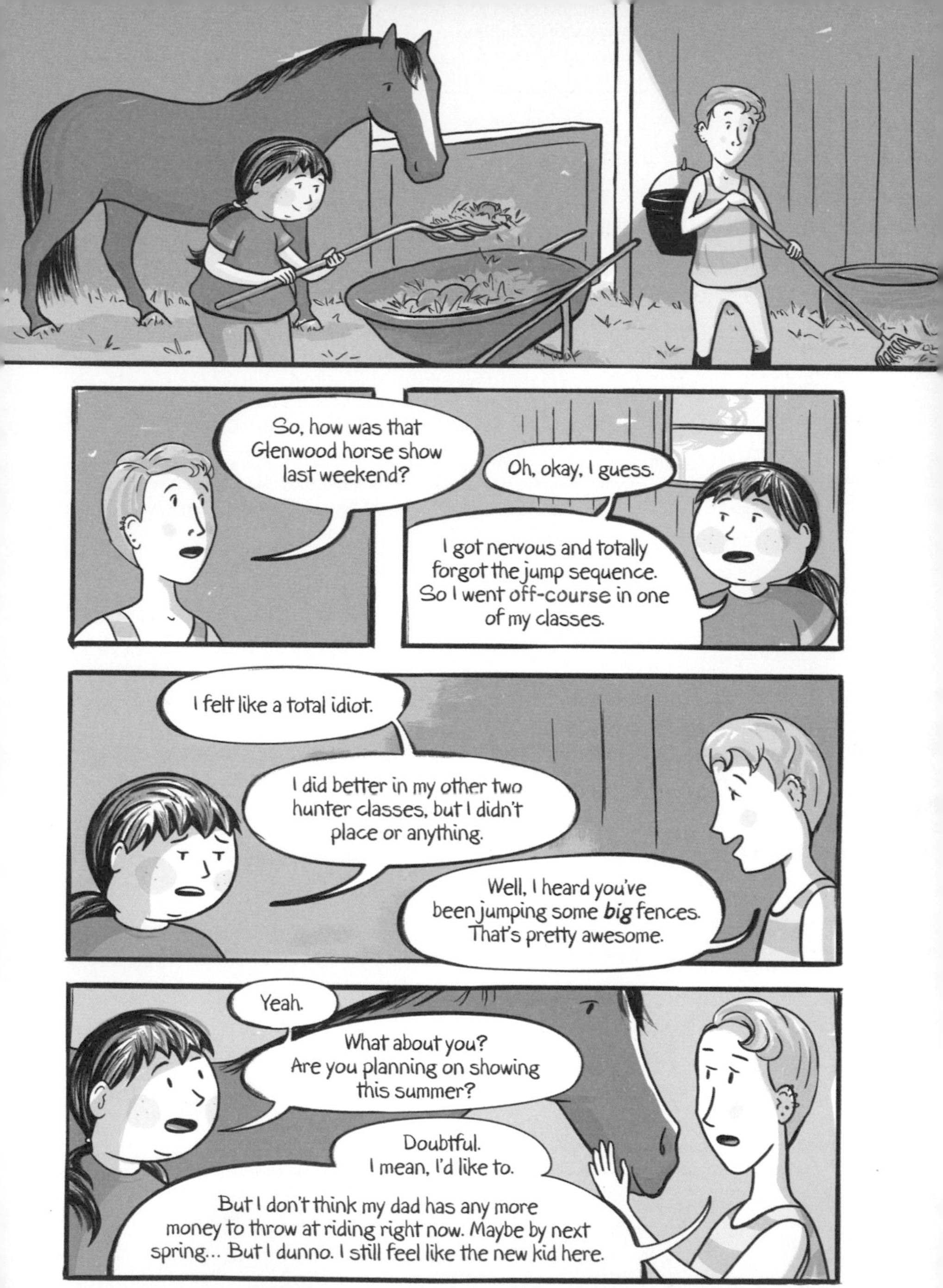

So, how was that Glenwood horse show last weekend?
Oh, okay, I guess.
I got nervous and totally forgot the jump sequence. So I went off-course in one of my classes.
I felt like a total idiot.
I did better in my other two hunter classes, but I didn't place or anything.
Well, I heard you've been jumping some *big* fences. That's pretty awesome.
Yeah.
What about you? Are you planning on showing this summer?
Doubtful. I mean, I'd like to.
But I don't think my dad has any more money to throw at riding right now. Maybe by next spring... But I dunno. I still feel like the new kid here.

Off-course: When a rider jumps fences during a competition in the incorrect order, which results in an immediate disqualification from the class.

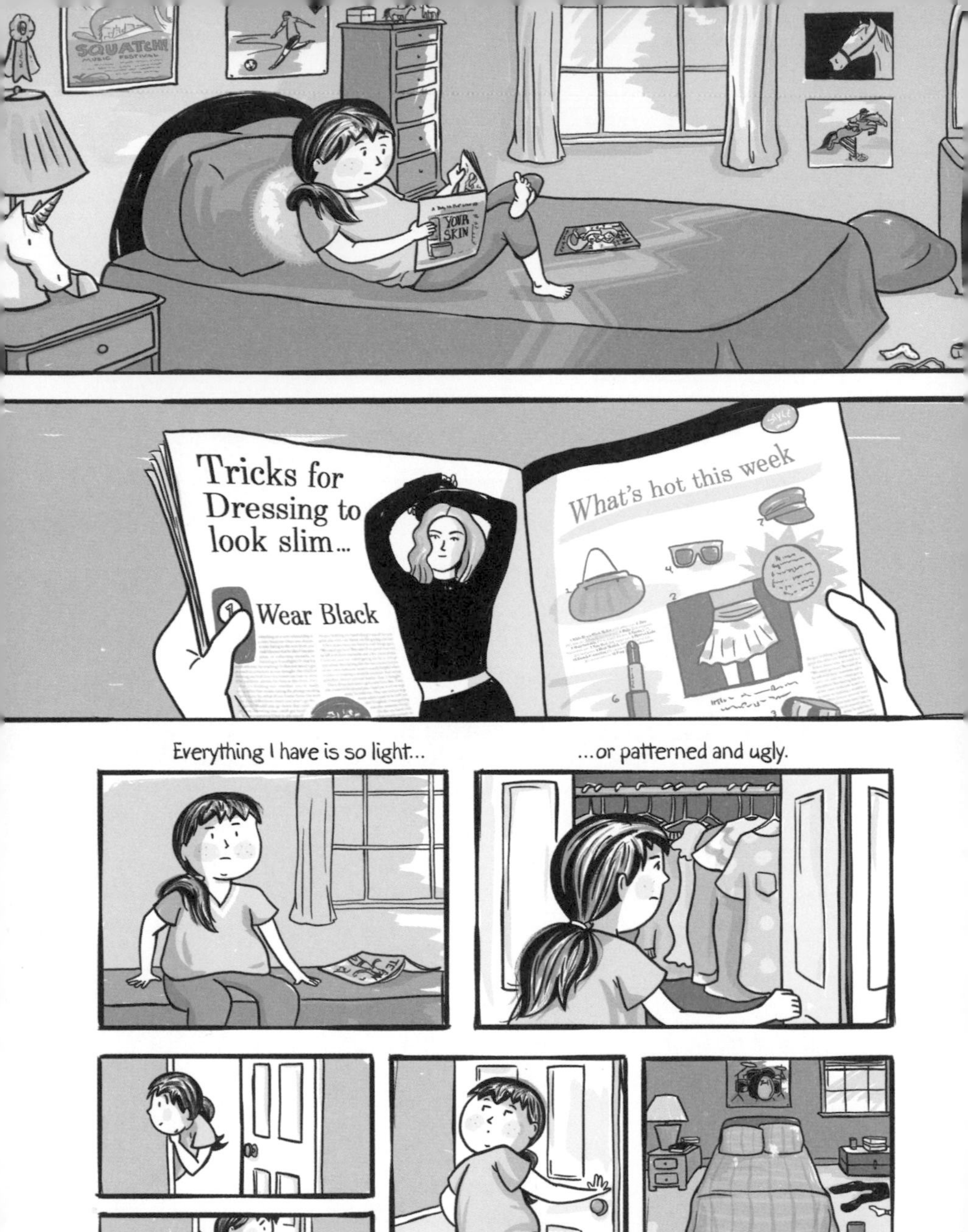
SQUATCH
MUSIC FESTIVAL
YOUR SKIN
Tricks for Dressing to look slim...
1 Wear Black
STYLE
What's hot this week
Everything I have is so light...
...or patterned and ugly.

drumming
Beat!
Thump!
Thump!
Beat!
squeak
Ross!
If I sneak out through the garage, maybe he won't see me wearing his shirt.
click
Hmmm.

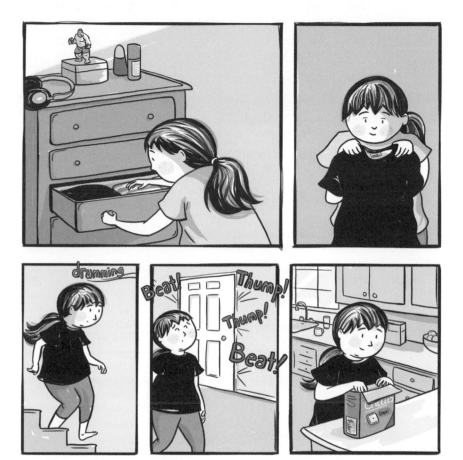

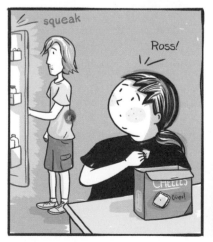

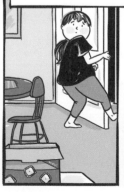

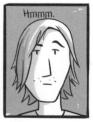

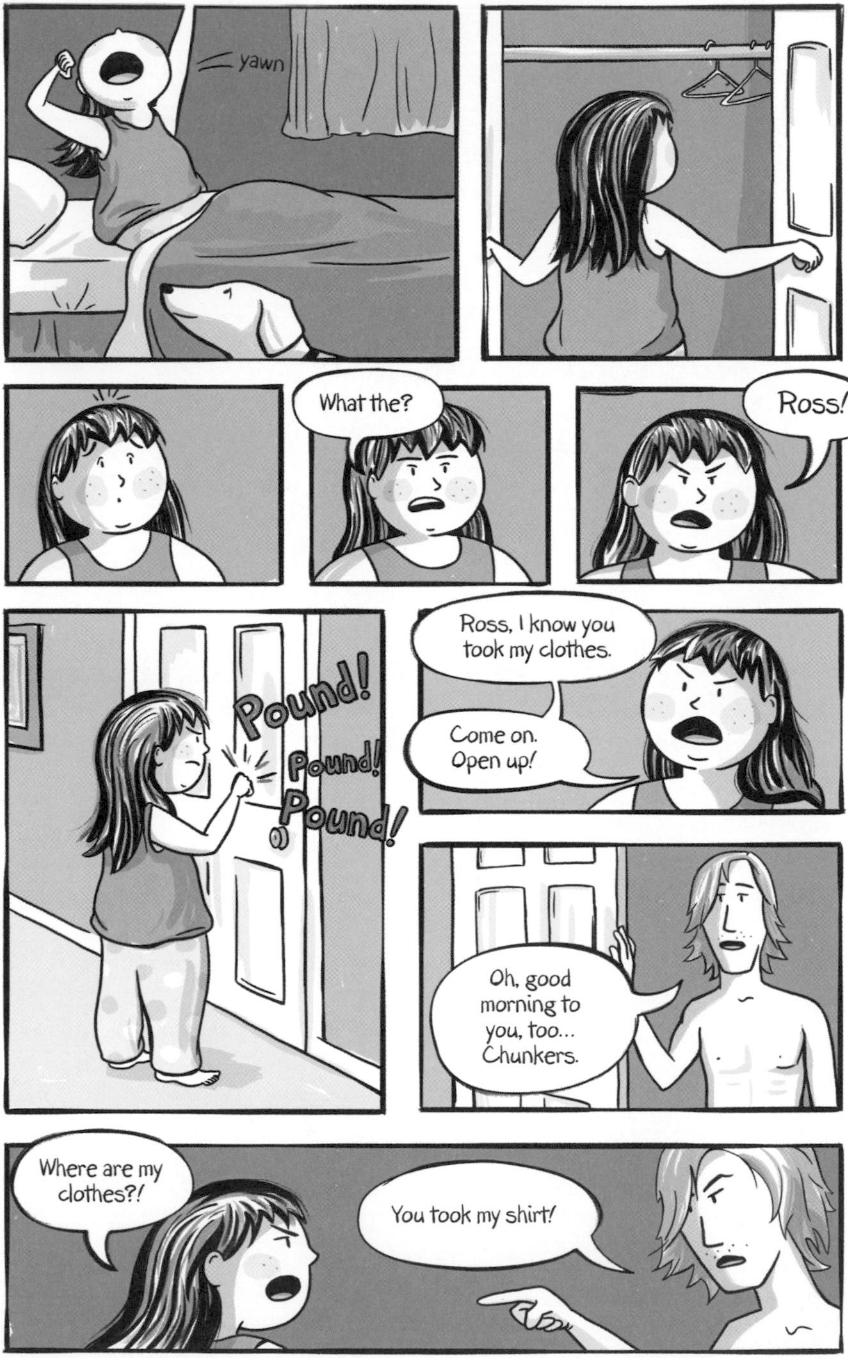

yawn
What the?
Ross!
Pound!
Pound!
Pound!
Ross, I know you took my clothes.
Come on. Open up!
Oh, good morning to you, too... Chunkers.
Where are my clothes?!
You took my shirt!

Valerie and I spend most days together now at the barn. I'm not threatened anymore when we share the barn work. There are still enough horses to ride between the two of us.

¡Que chistoso!

Ha! ha ha ha Ha!

And Barb gives us plenty of chores to keep us busy all summer.

Valerie makes even the boring days (when we don't get to ride) fun.

Hey, Kate, want to come over to my house after we're done at the barn today?

Sure.

I don't have a ride home because my dad is working, but it's only about a twenty-minute walk.

Cool.

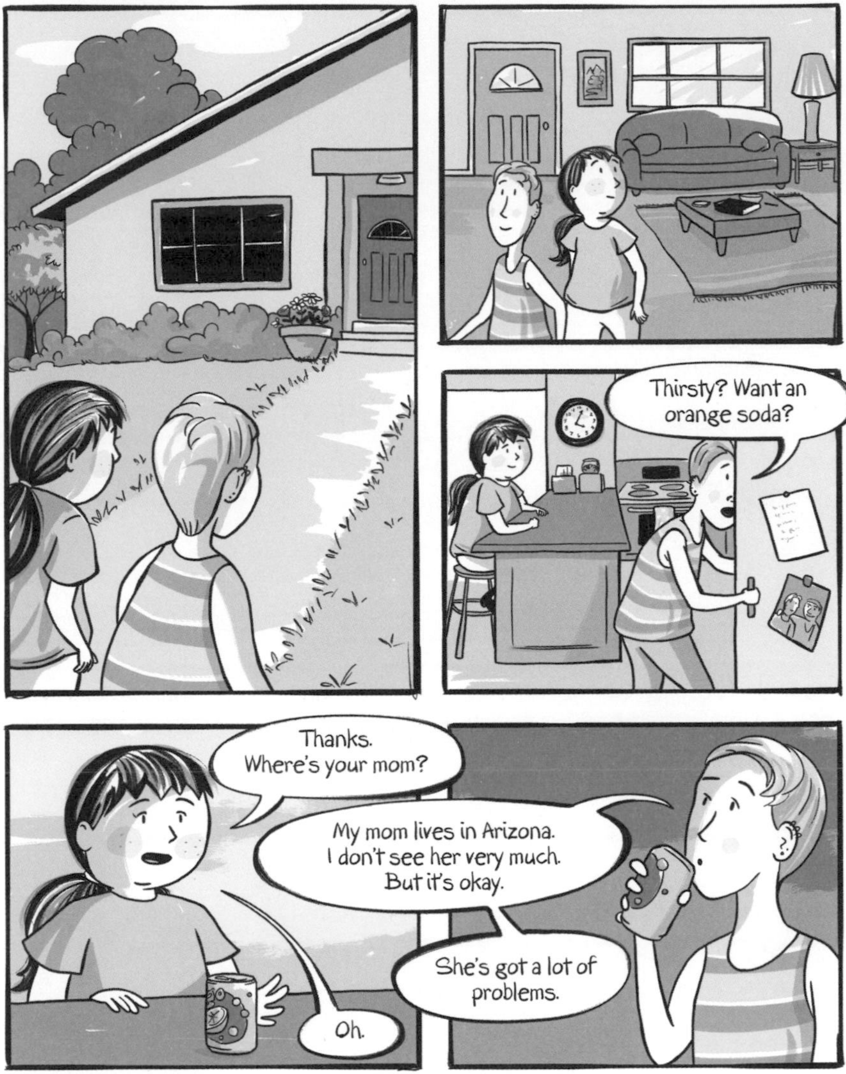
Thirsty? Want an orange soda?
Thanks. Where's your mom?
My mom lives in Arizona. I don't see her very much. But it's okay.
She's got a lot of problems.
Oh.

I don't ask any more questions about Valerie's mom, even though I'm curious.

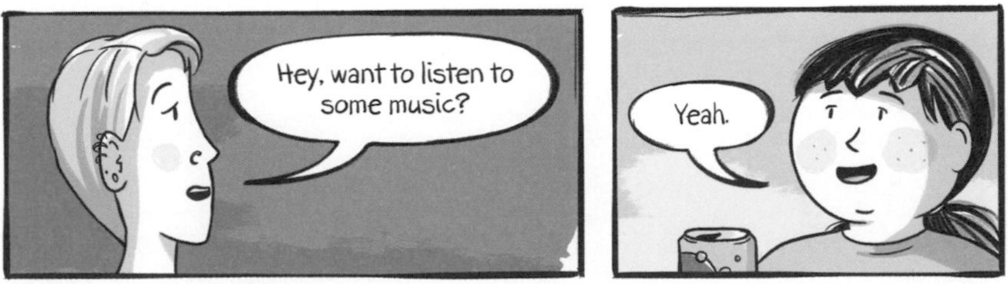
Hey, want to listen to some music?
Yeah.

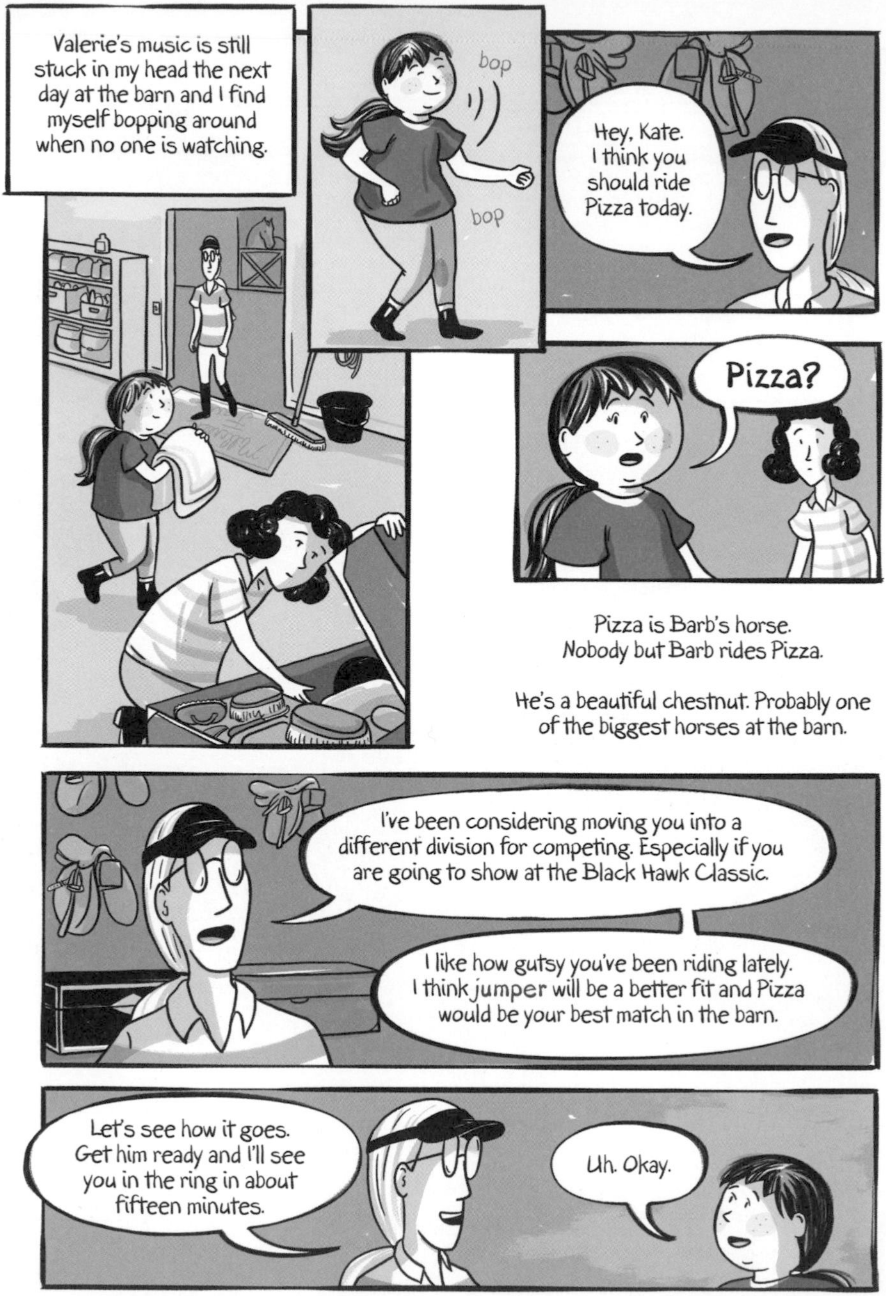

Valerie's music is still stuck in my head the next day at the barn and I find myself bopping around when no one is watching.
bop
bop
Hey, Kate. I think you should ride Pizza today.
Pizza?
Pizza is Barb's horse. Nobody but Barb rides Pizza.
He's a beautiful chestnut. Probably one of the biggest horses at the barn.
I've been considering moving you into a different division for competing. Especially if you are going to show at the Black Hawk Classic.
I like how gutsy you've been riding lately. I think jumper will be a better fit and Pizza would be your best match in the barn.
Let's see how it goes. Get him ready and I'll see you in the ring in about fifteen minutes.
Uh. Okay.

Jumper: One of the three main divisions at a horse show (hunter, jumper, and equitation). Jumper classes are not scored on style, but the speed at which the rider completes the course.

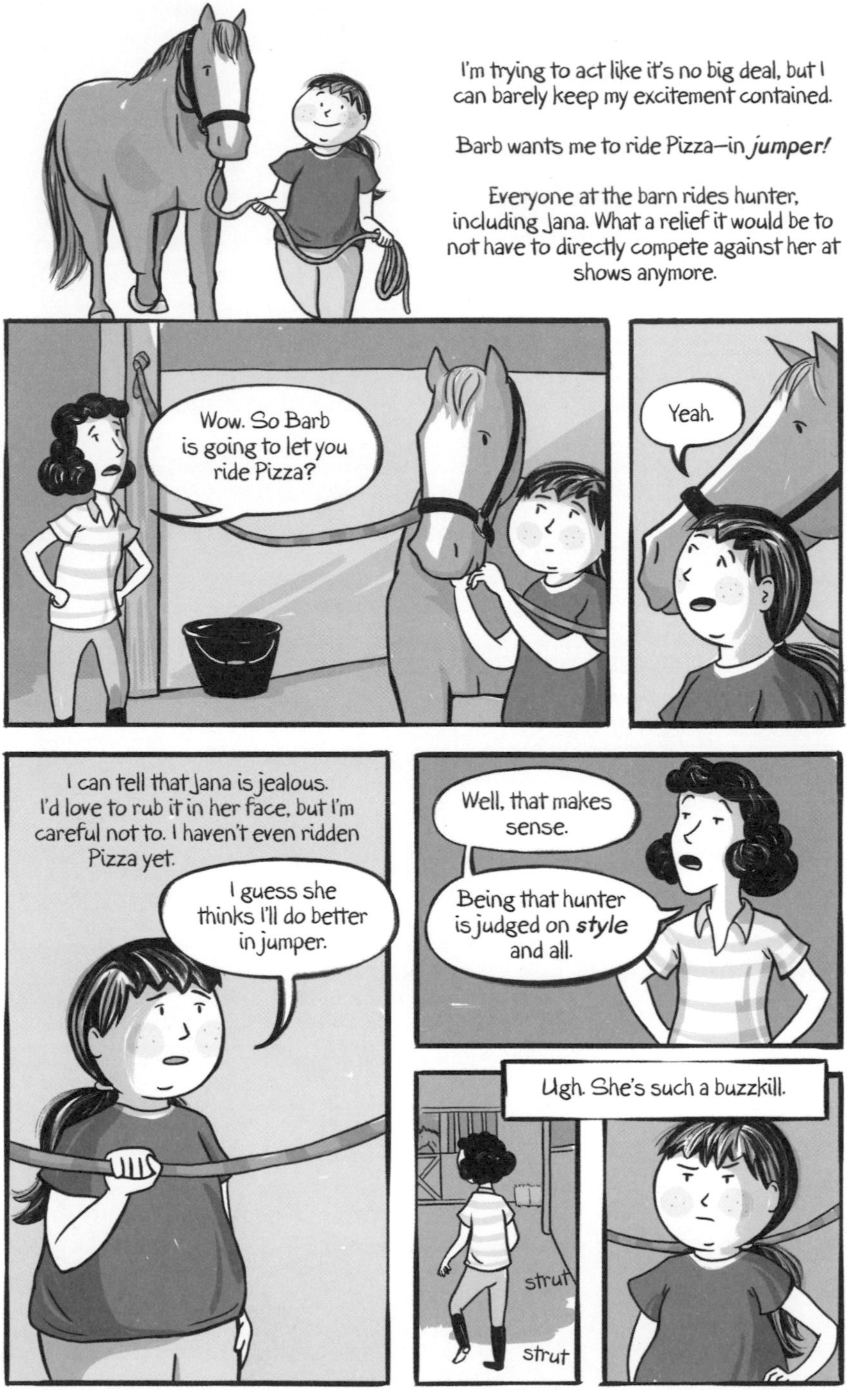
I'm trying to act like it's no big deal, but I can barely keep my excitement contained.
Barb wants me to ride Pizza—in ***jumper!***
Everyone at the barn rides hunter, including Jana. What a relief it would be to not have to directly compete against her at shows anymore.
Wow. So Barb is going to let you ride Pizza?
Yeah.
I can tell that Jana is jealous. I'd love to rub it in her face, but I'm careful not to. I haven't even ridden Pizza yet.
I guess she thinks I'll do better in jumper.
Well, that makes sense.
Being that hunter is judged on ***style*** and all.
Ugh. She's such a buzzkill.
strut
strut

I'm amped up, full of adrenaline, and my head is swirling with emotions.

Jana Go! Jumper!

everyone rides hunter

Bigger fences faster!

Barb's horse

Go! Speed!

Nah naa, na nah naaa! Pizza!

I can't focus on what Barb is saying and I only zone in on... *speed.*

I charge Pizza at the next jump.

Kate! Slow him down!

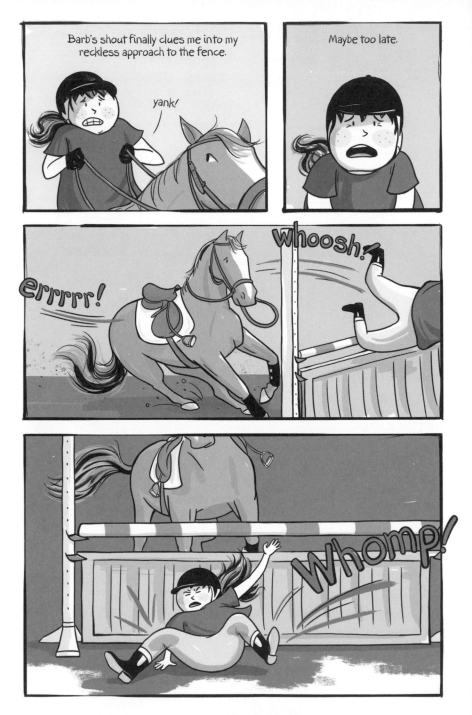

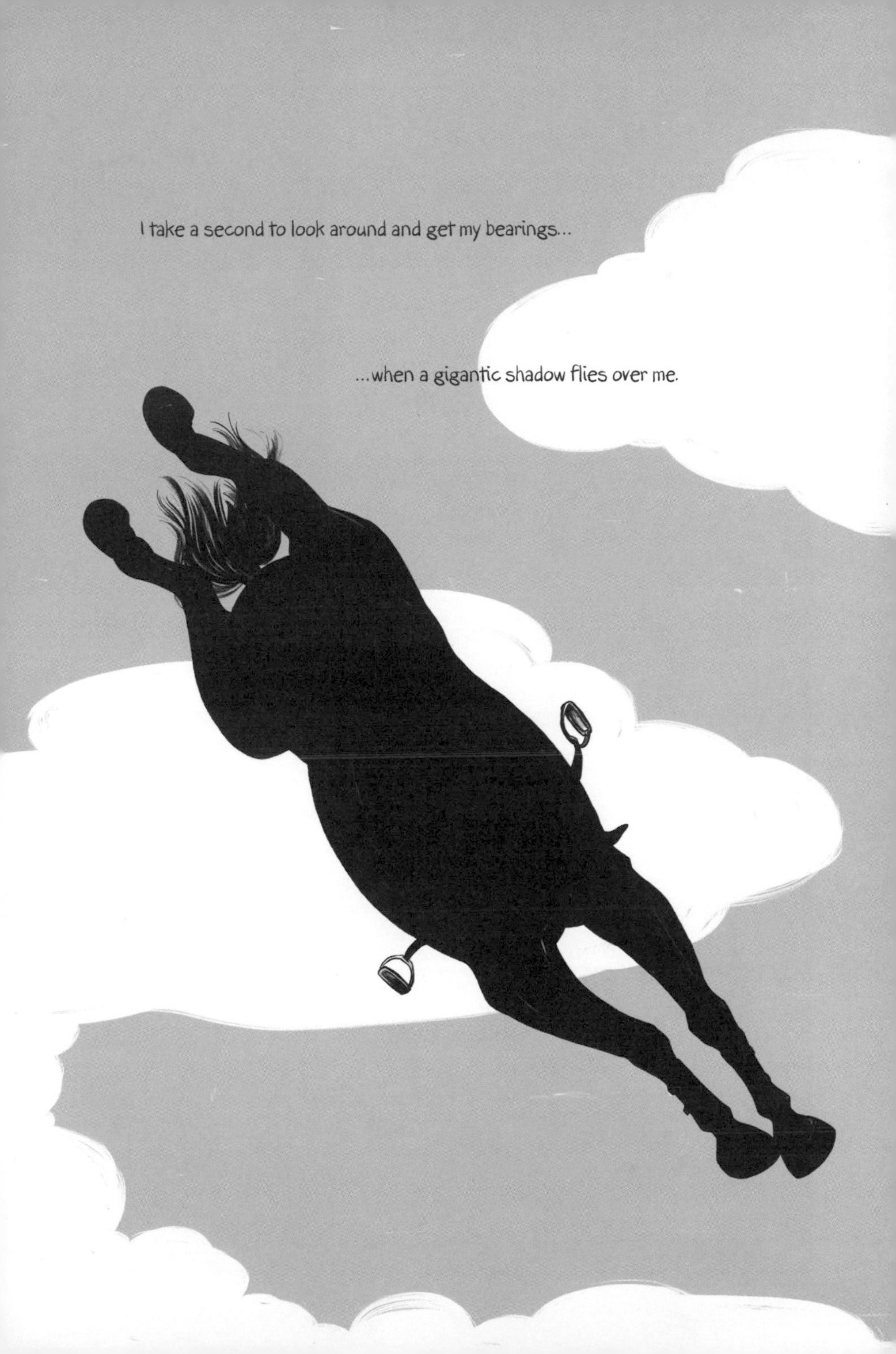
I take a second to look around and get my bearings...
...when a gigantic shadow flies over me.

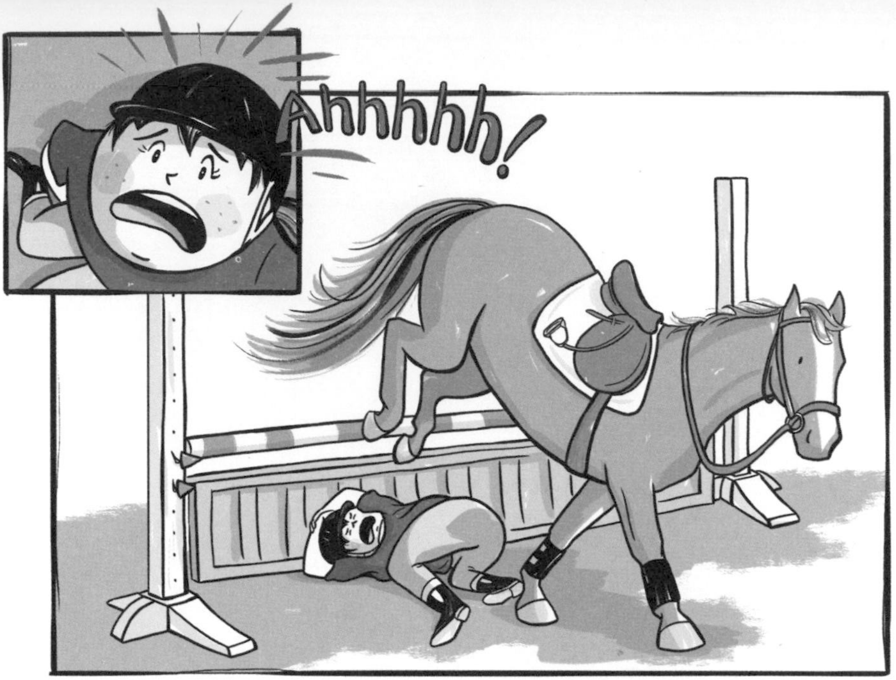
Ahhhhh!

I don't know how Pizza missed landing on me.
Or why he even jumped the fence by himself?!

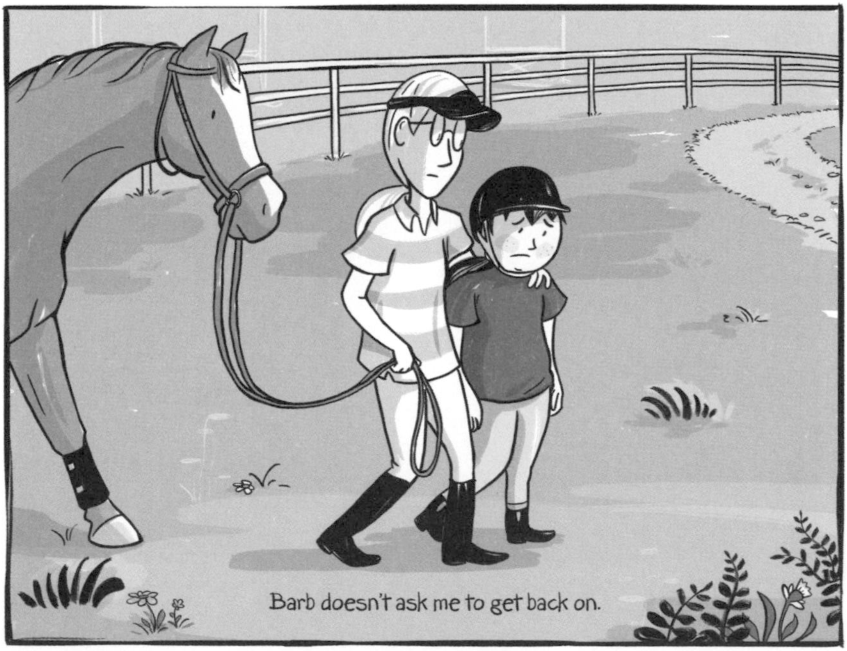
Barb doesn't ask me to get back on.

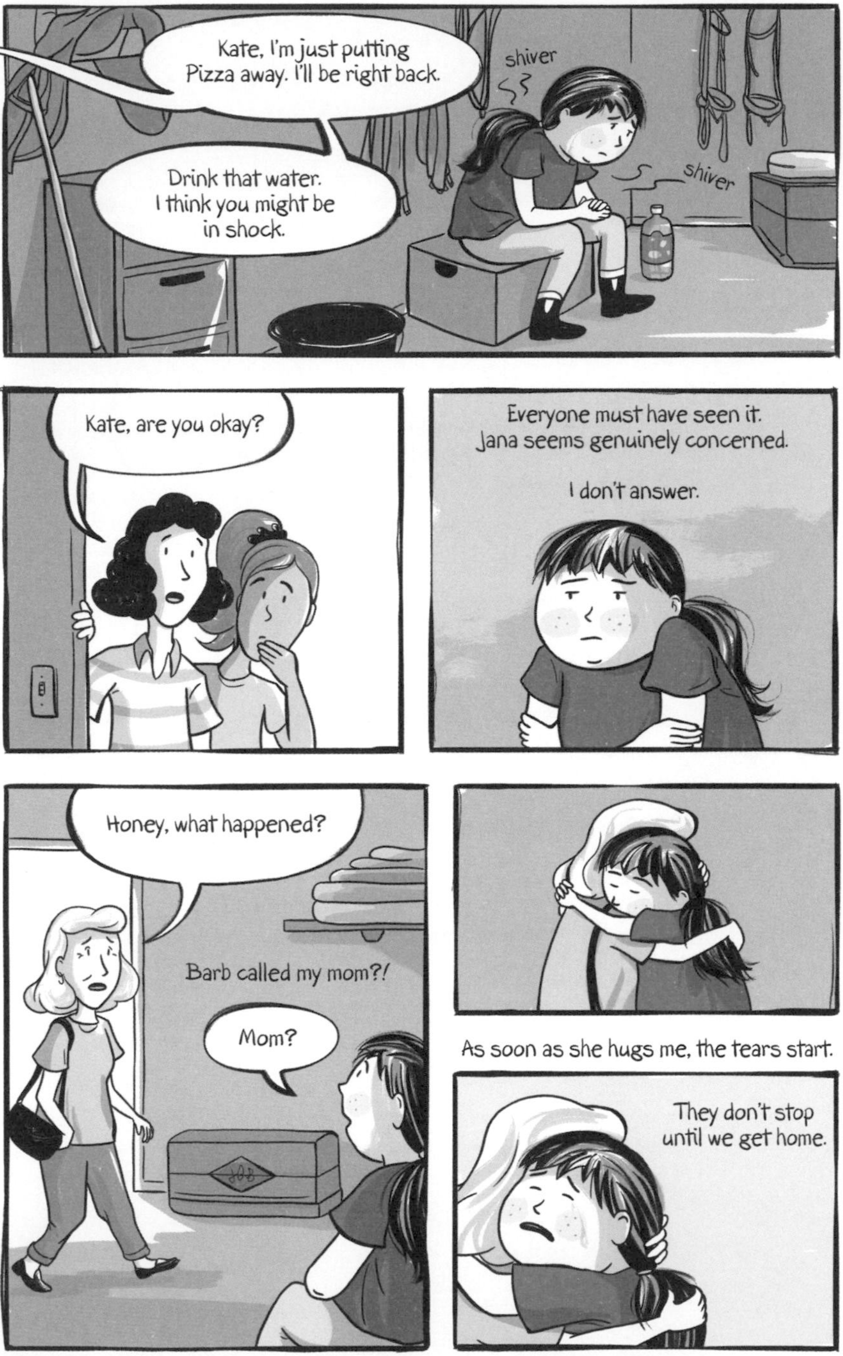
Kate, I'm just putting Pizza away. I'll be right back.
Drink that water. I think you might be in shock.
shiver
shiver
Kate, are you okay?
Everyone must have seen it. Jana seems genuinely concerned.
I don't answer.
Honey, what happened?
Barb called my mom?!
Mom?
As soon as she hugs me, the tears start.
They don't stop until we get home.

Chapter 9
BMX Bounce

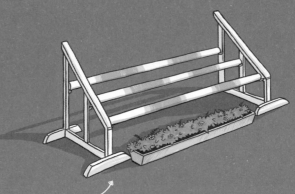

Triple Bar

A spread (distance) fence consisting of three elements at different heights, usually in ascending order.

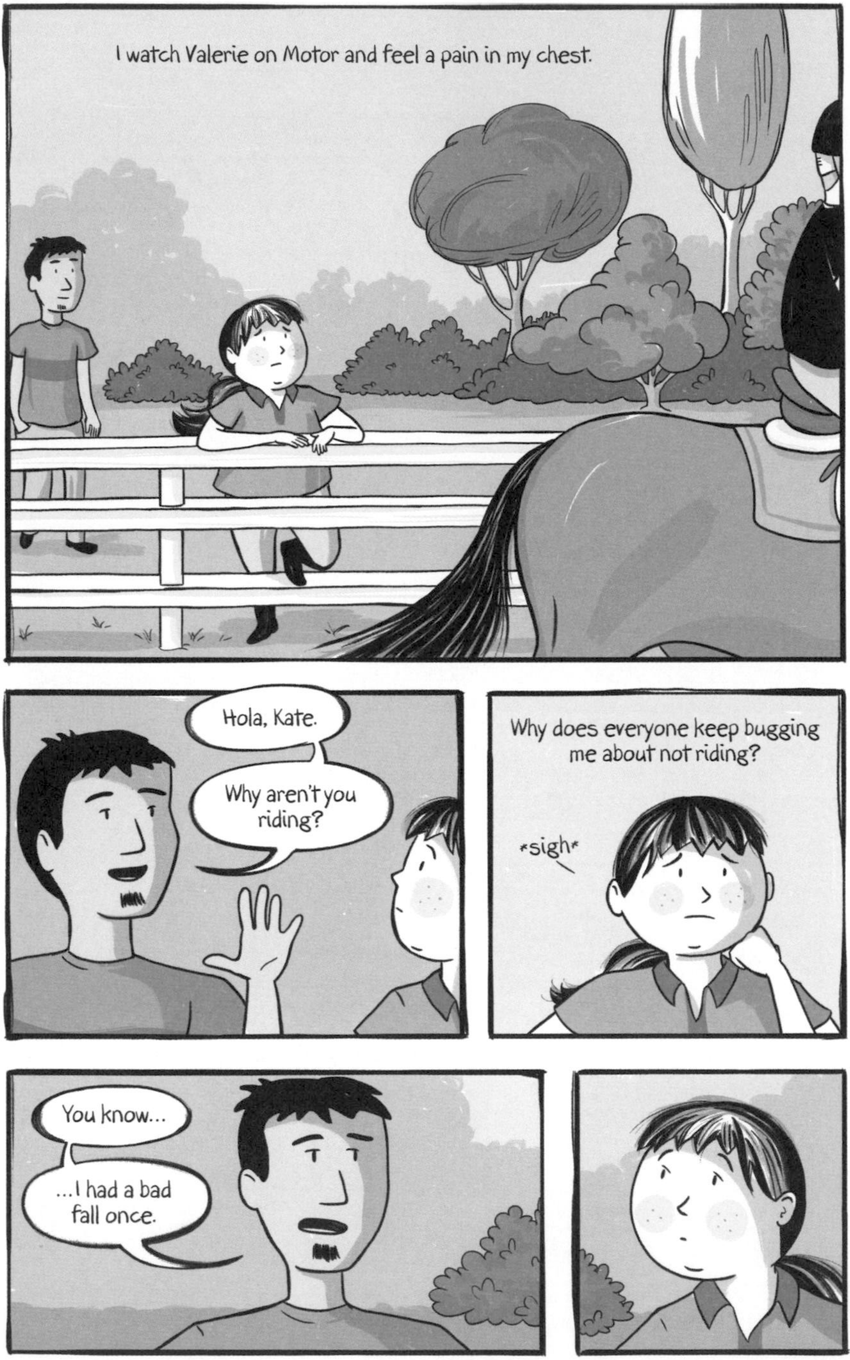
I watch Valerie on Motor and feel a pain in my chest.
Hola, Kate.
Why aren't you riding?
Why does everyone keep bugging me about not riding?
sigh
You know...
...I had a bad fall once.

As I finish the rest of my chores, I think about Ernesto and his whistling. I'm not sure if I buy it, but I'm getting desperate. I have my lesson with Barb today, and the thought of getting back on makes my gut twist in knots.

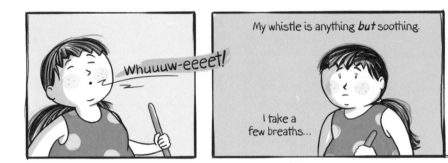

Whuuuw-eeeet!

My whistle is anything *but* soothing.

I take a few breaths...

...and try a soft hum instead.

Hummm mmaaa hoooom

Hummmmmmmm mmaaa hoooomm

I do it again, louder.

Felix's ears prick forward to listen.

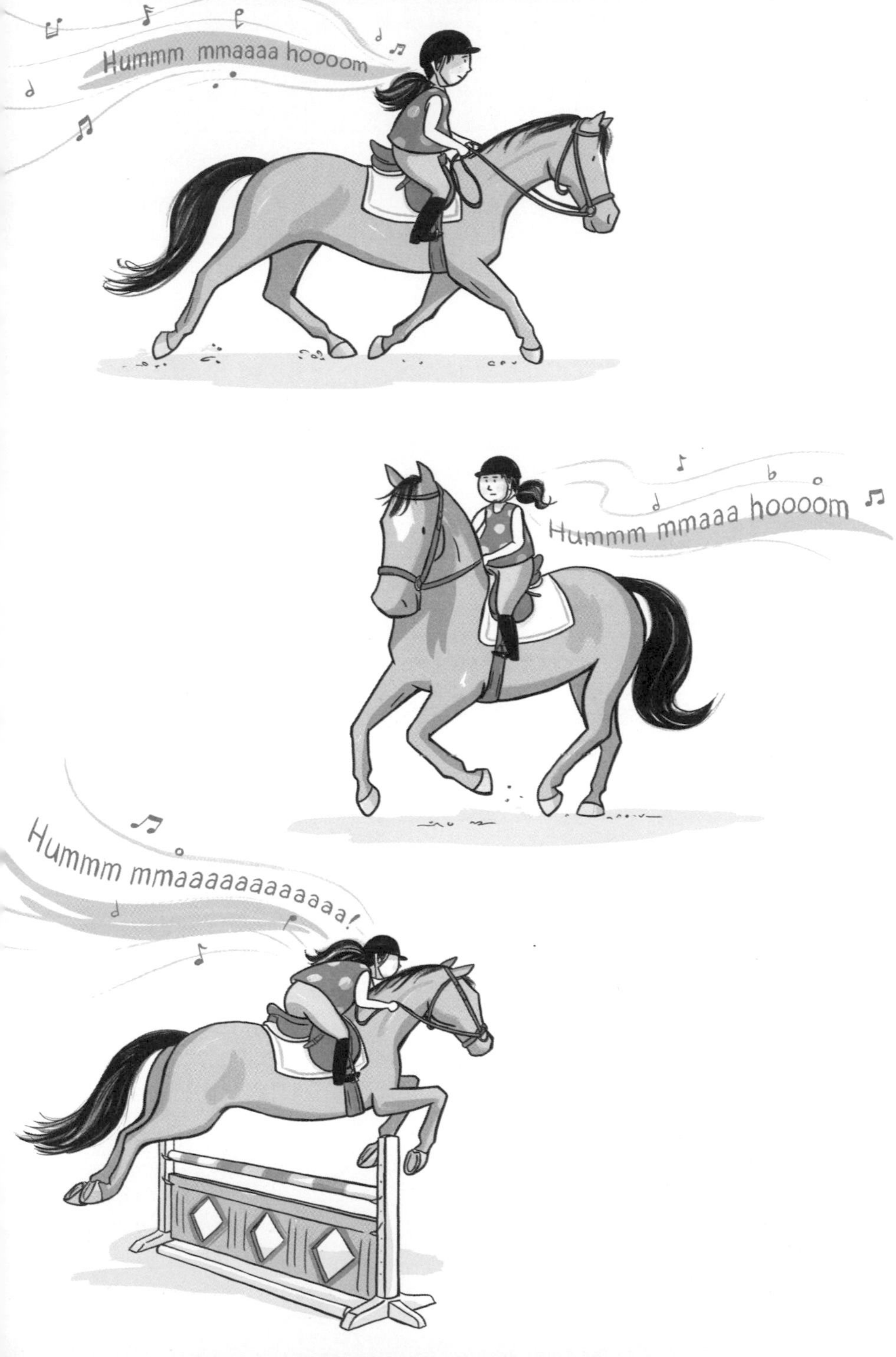
Hummm mmaaaa hoooom
Hummm mmaaa hoooom
Hummm mmaaaaaaaaaaaa!

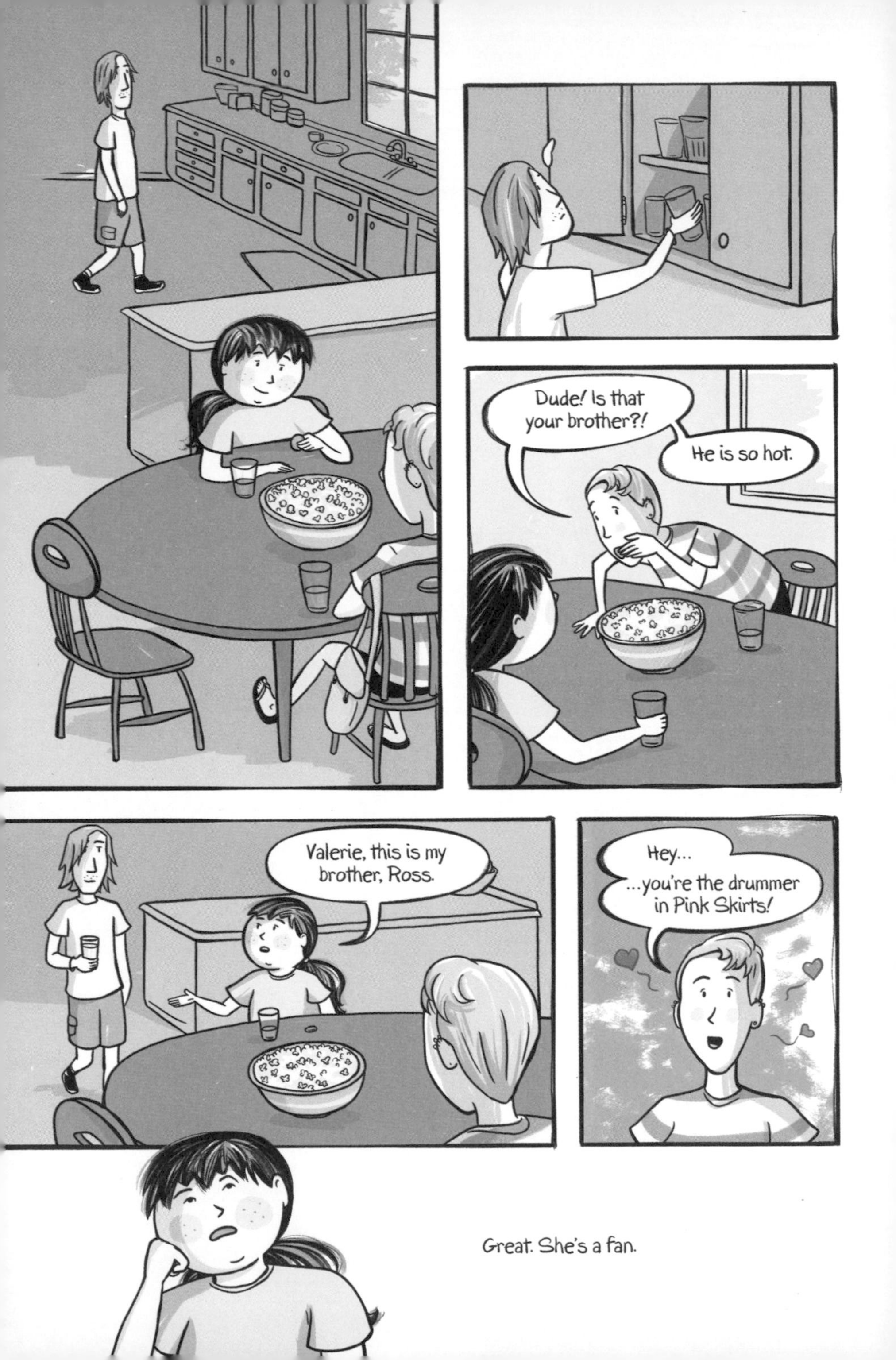
Dude! Is that your brother?!
He is so hot.
Valerie, this is my brother, Ross.
Hey...
...you're the drummer in Pink Skirts!
Great. She's a fan.

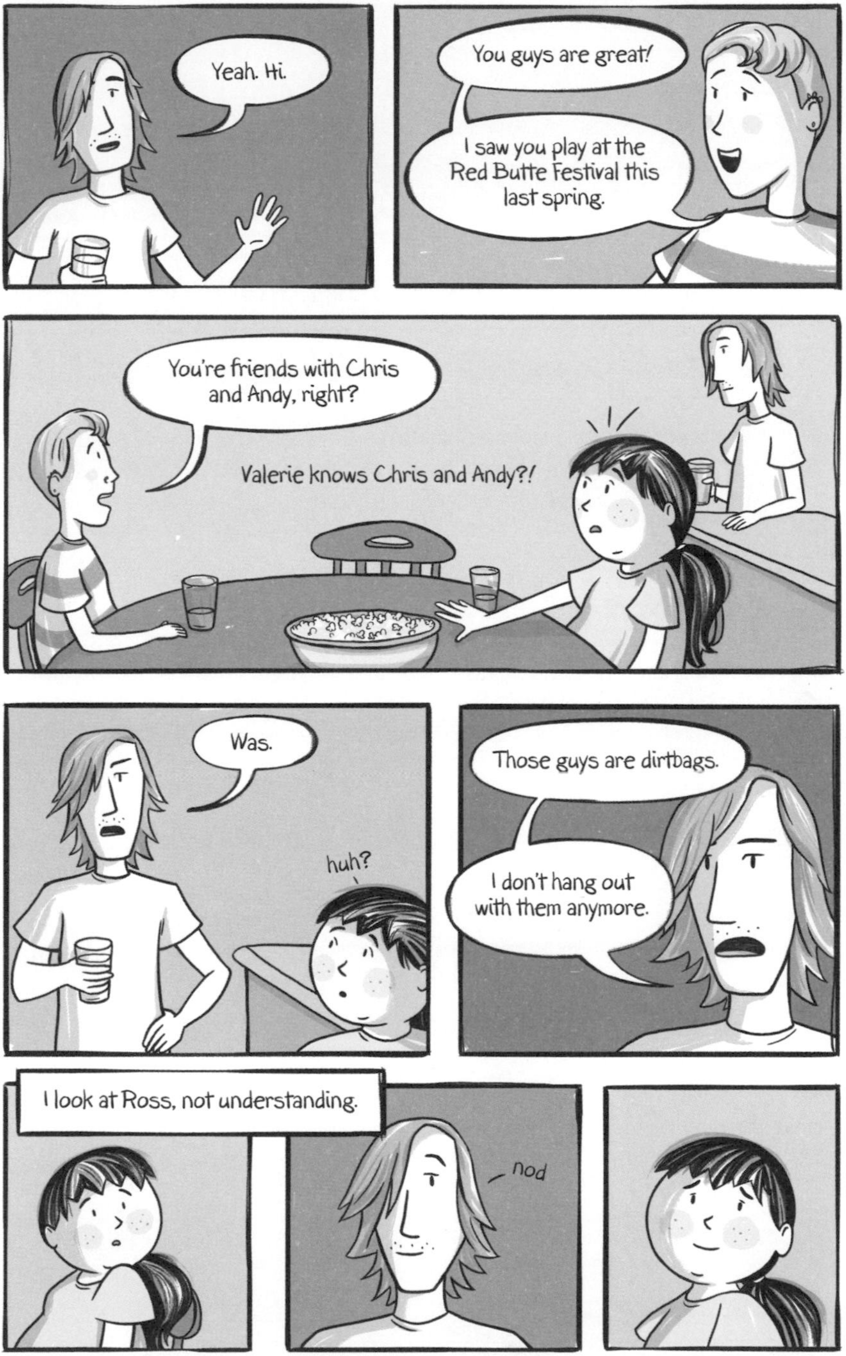
Yeah. Hi.
You guys are great!
I saw you play at the Red Butte Festival this last spring.
You're friends with Chris and Andy, right?
Valerie knows Chris and Andy?!
Was.
huh?
Those guys are dirtbags.
I don't hang out with them anymore.
I look at Ross, not understanding.
nod

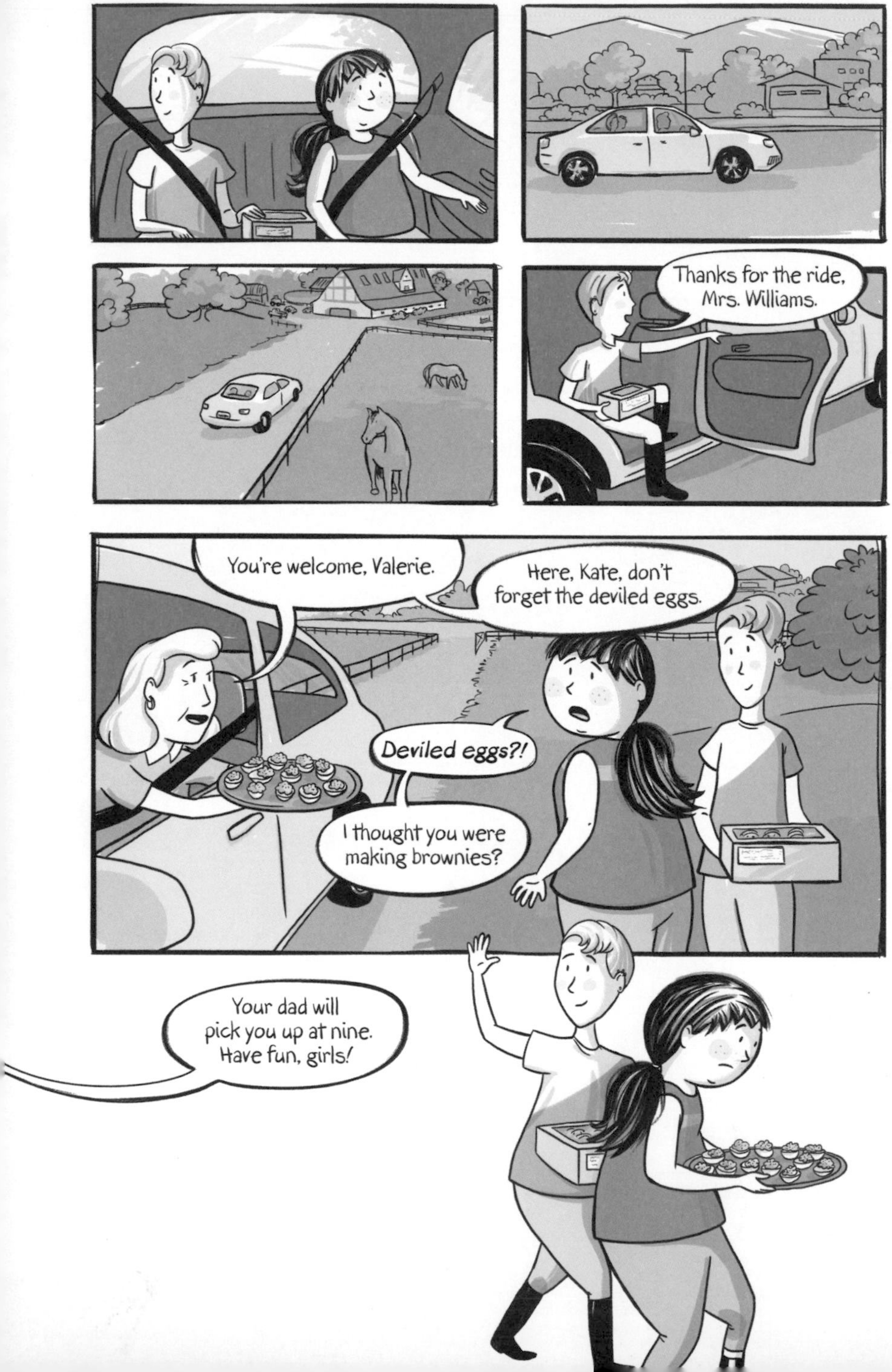
Thanks for the ride, Mrs. Williams.
You're welcome, Valerie.
Here, Kate, don't forget the deviled eggs.
Deviled eggs?!
I thought you were making brownies?
Your dad will pick you up at nine. Have fun, girls!

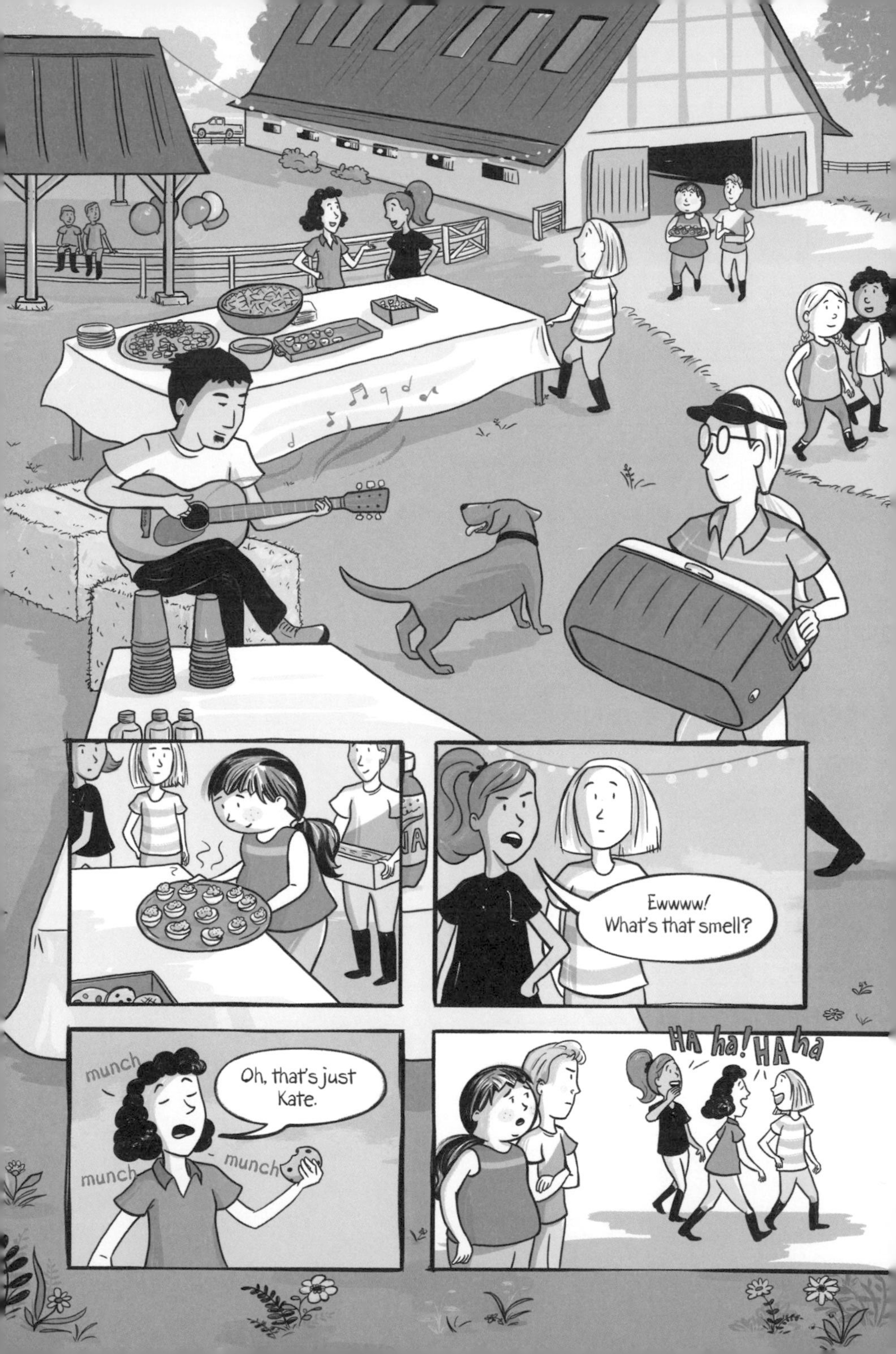

Ewwww! What's that smell?
munch
Oh, that's just Kate.
munch
munch
HA ha! HA ha

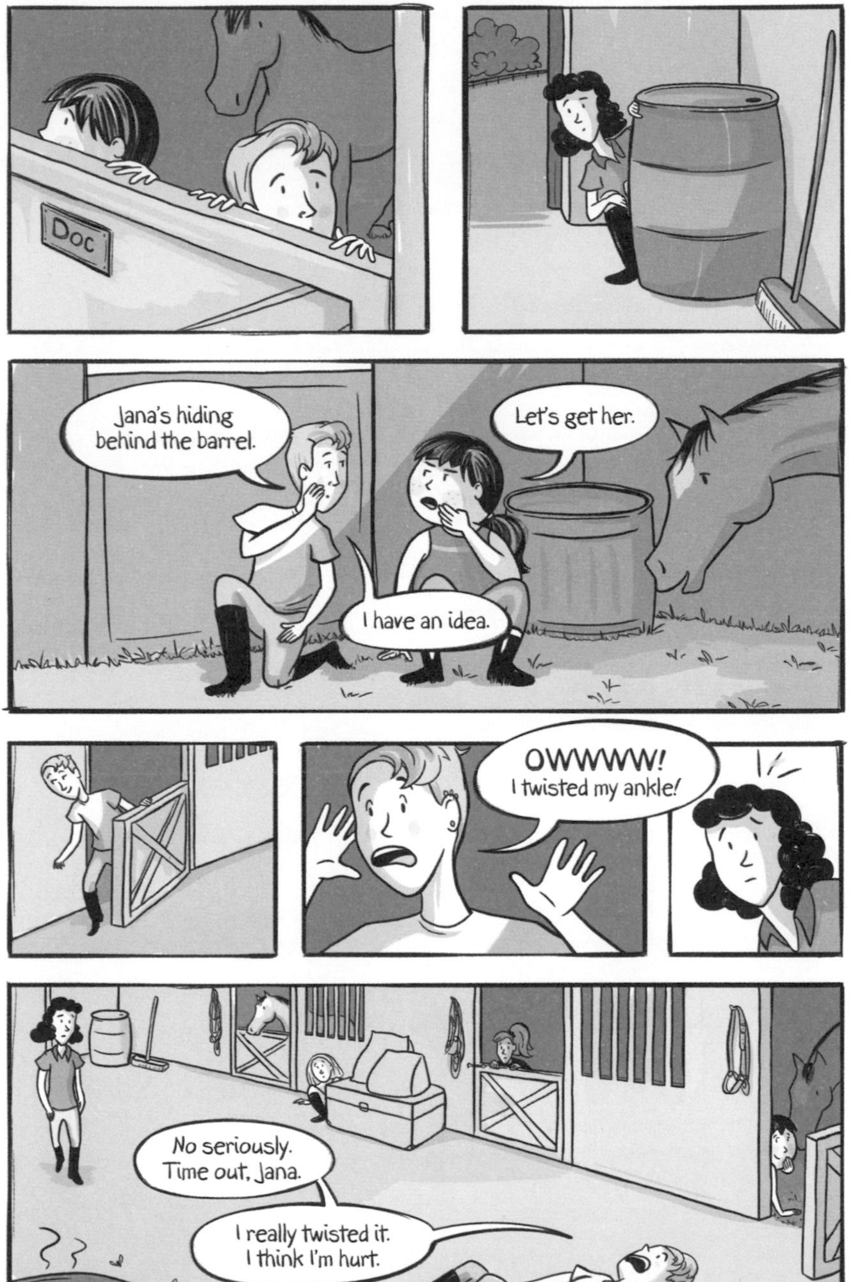
Doc
Jana's hiding behind the barrel.
Let's get her.
I have an idea.
OWWWW!
I twisted my ankle!
No seriously.
Time out, Jana.
I really twisted it.
I think I'm hurt.

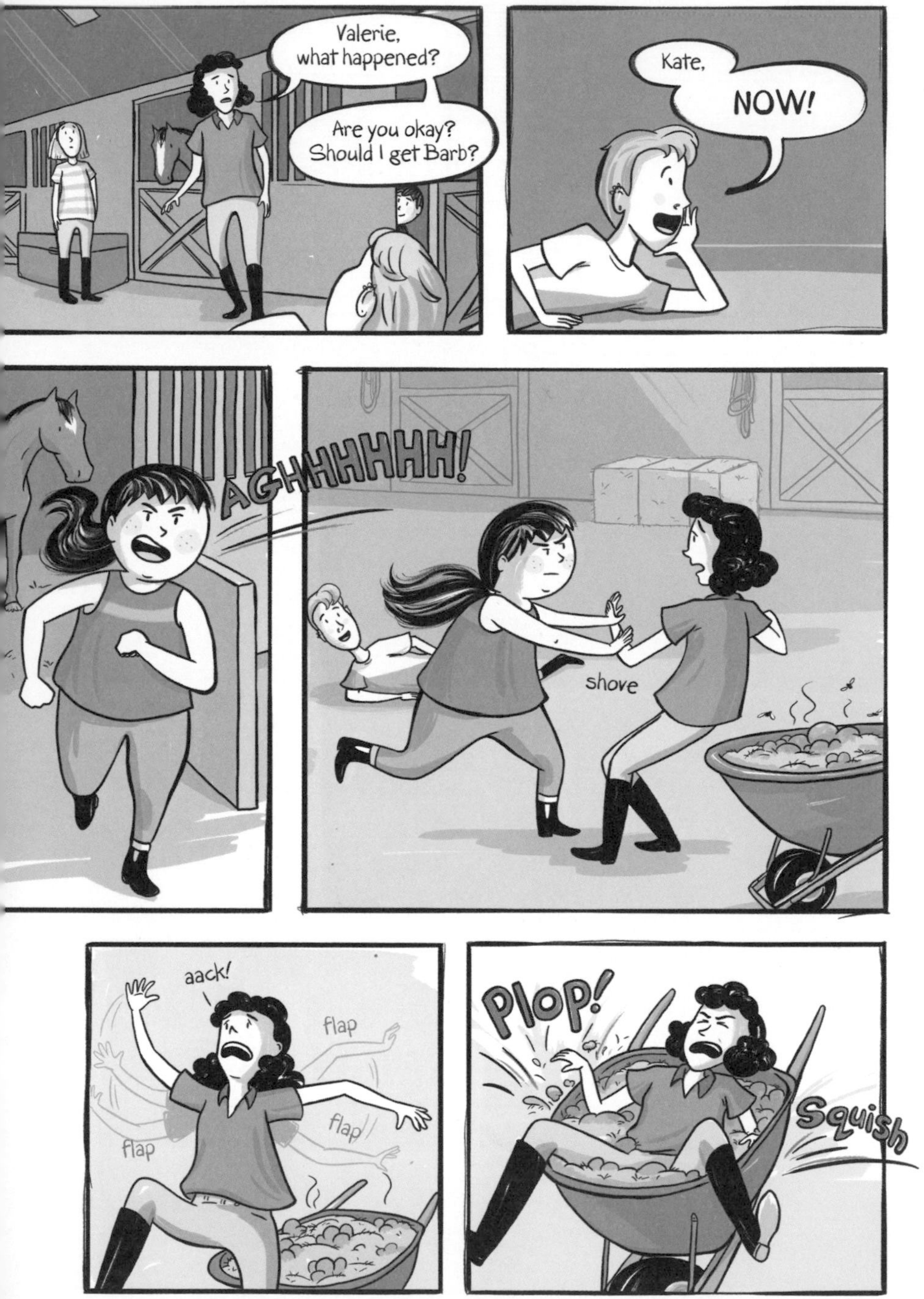
Valerie,
what happened?
Are you okay?
Should I get Barb?
Kate,
NOW!
AGHHHHHH!
shove
aack!
flap
flap
flap
PLOP!
Squish

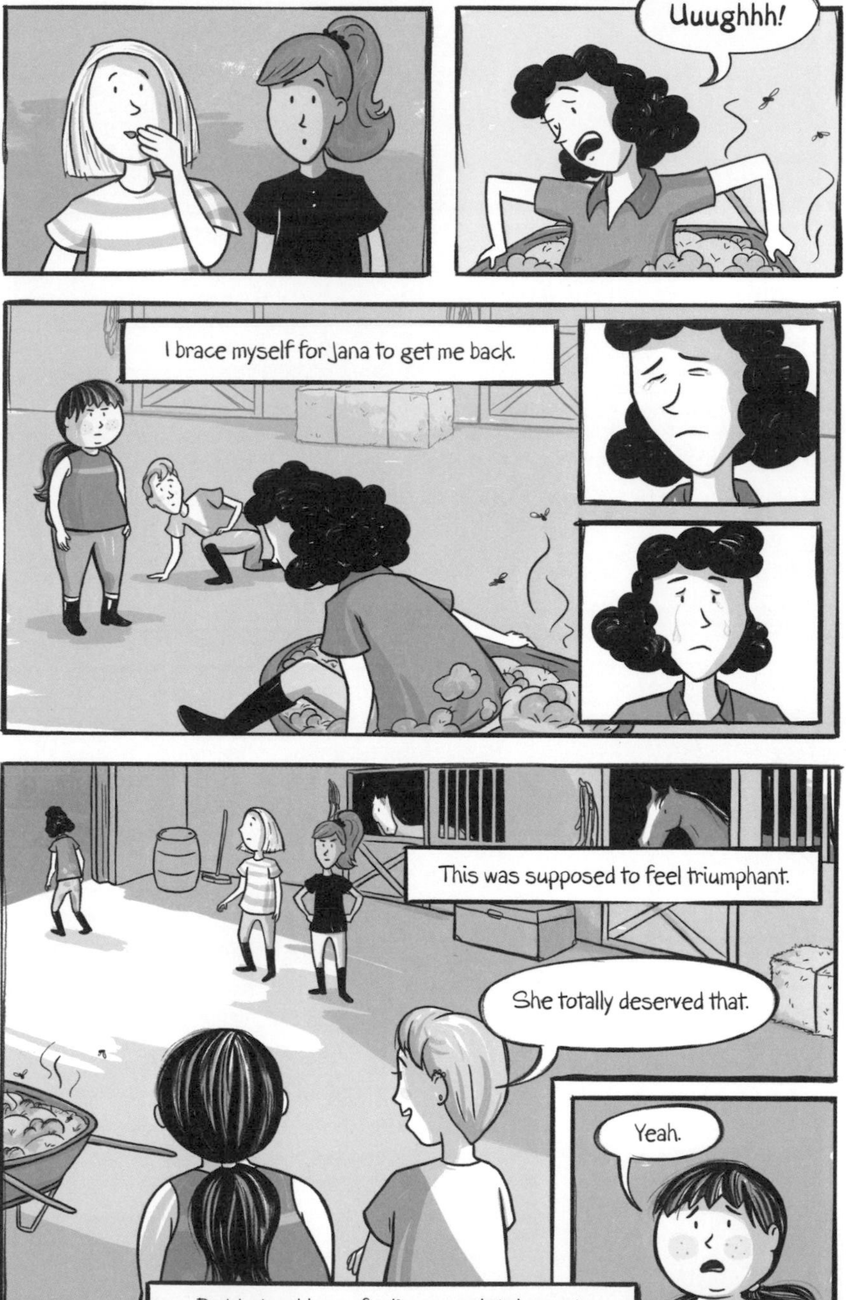
Uuughhh!
I brace myself for Jana to get me back.
This was supposed to feel triumphant.
She totally deserved that.
Yeah.
But I stand here, feeling completely empty.

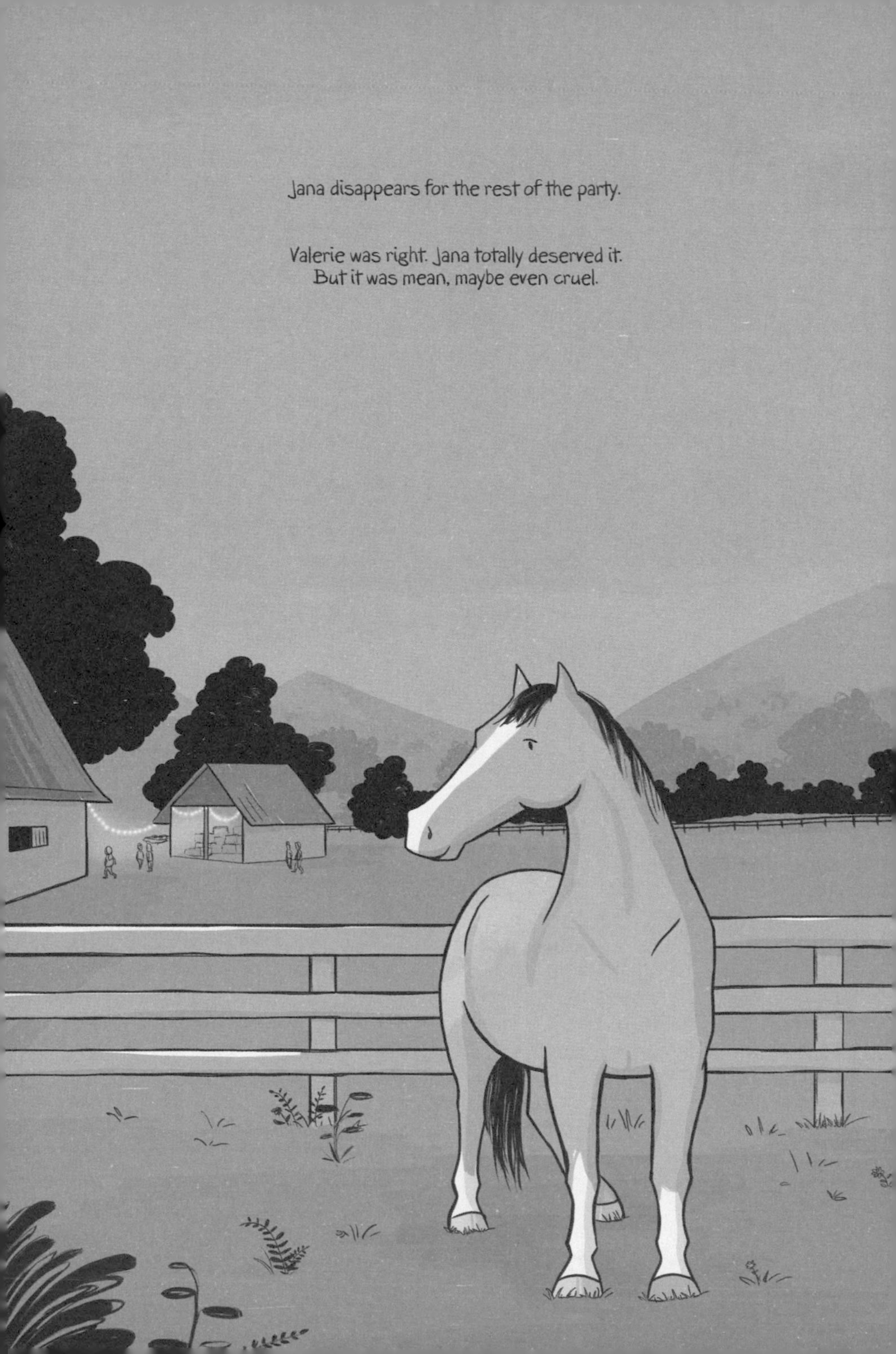
Jana disappears for the rest of the party.
Valerie was right. Jana totally deserved it. But it was mean, maybe even cruel.

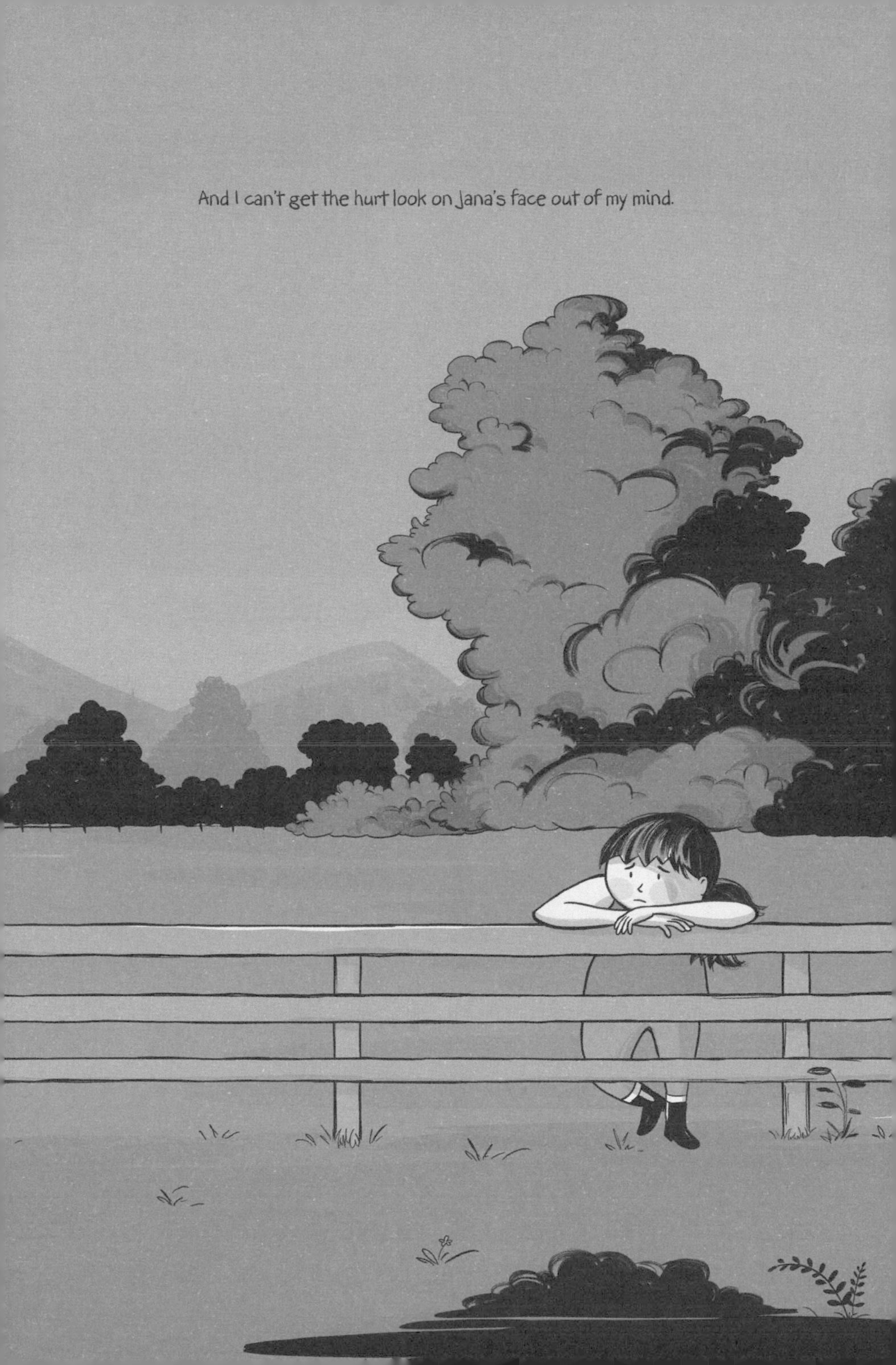
And I can't get the hurt look on Jana's face out of my mind.

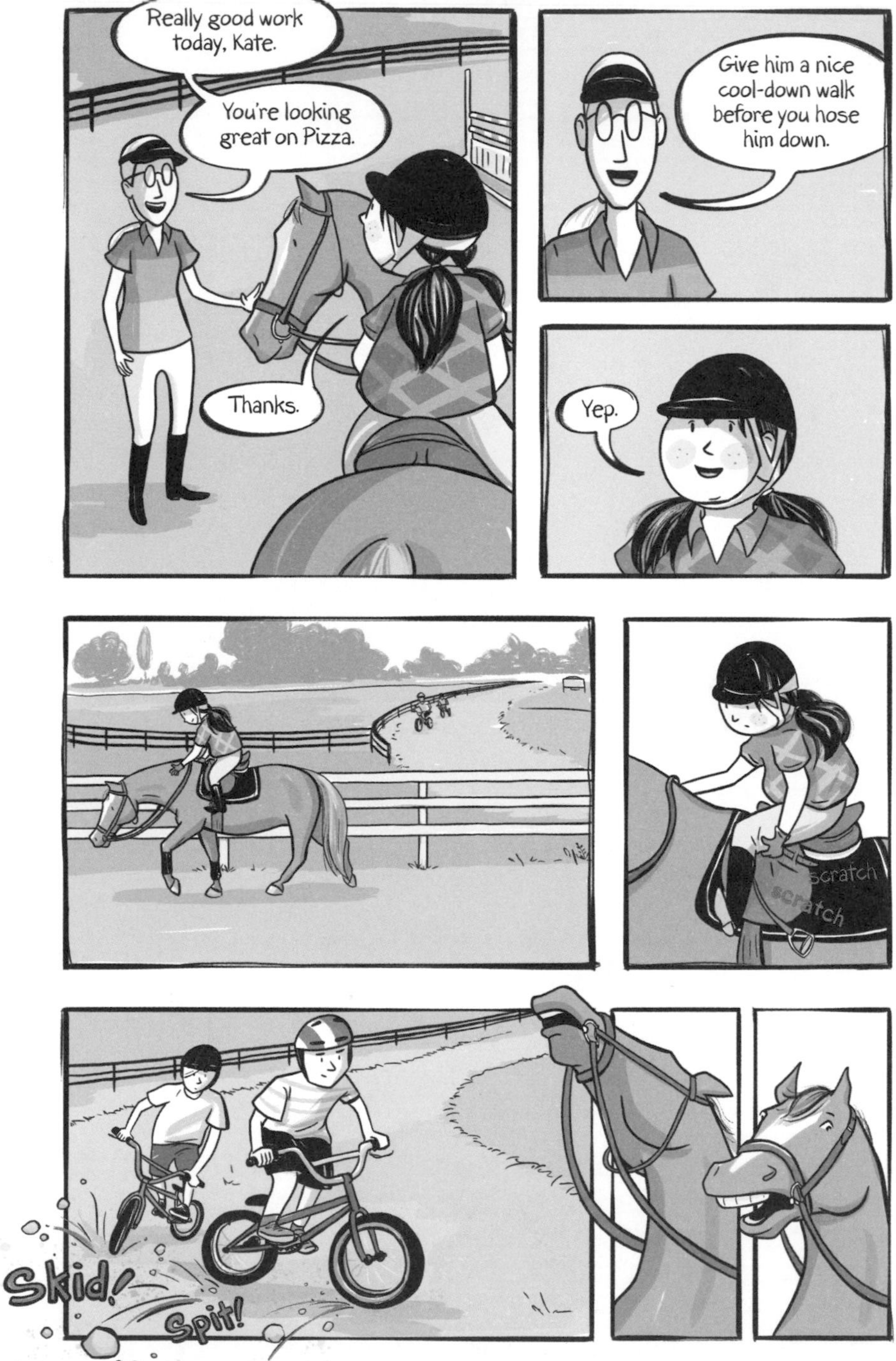
Really good work today, Kate.
You're looking great on Pizza.
Thanks.
Give him a nice cool-down walk before you hose him down.
Yep.
scratch
scratch
Skid!
Spit!

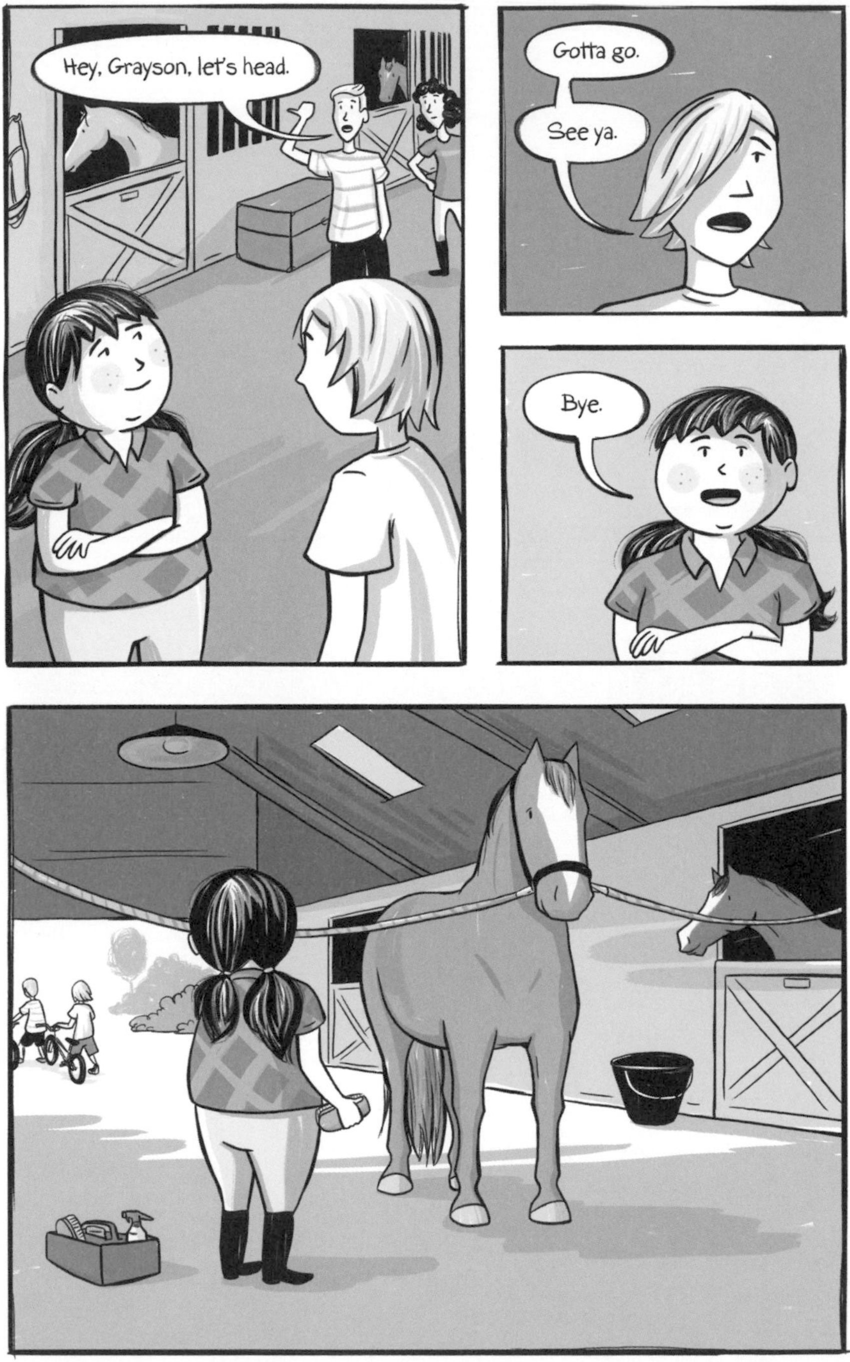
Hey, Grayson, let's head.
Gotta go.
See ya.
Bye.

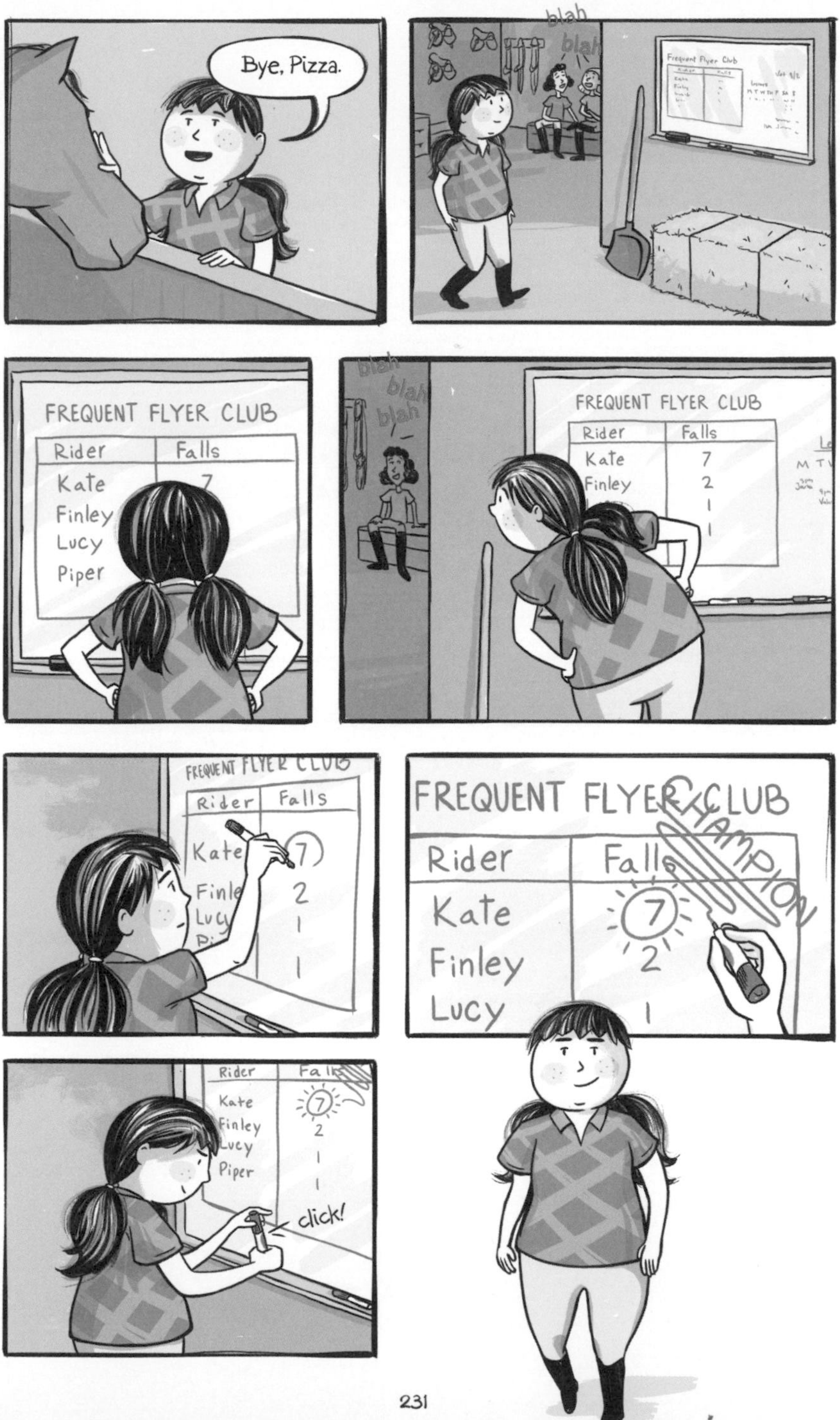
Bye, Pizza.
blah
blah
FREQUENT FLYER CLUB
Rider
Falls
Kate 7
Finley
Lucy
Piper
blah
blah
blah
FREQUENT FLYER CLUB
Rider
Falls
Kate 7
Finley 2
FREQUENT FLYER CLUB
Rider
Falls
Kate 7
2
1
1
FREQUENT FLYER CLUB
CHAMPION
Rider
Falls
Kate 7
Finley 2
Lucy 1
Rider
Kate
Finley
Lucy
Piper
7
2
1
1
click!

Chapter 10
Fly Through

Oxer

Two vertical fences placed near each other to make one single wide jump. Also called a spread.

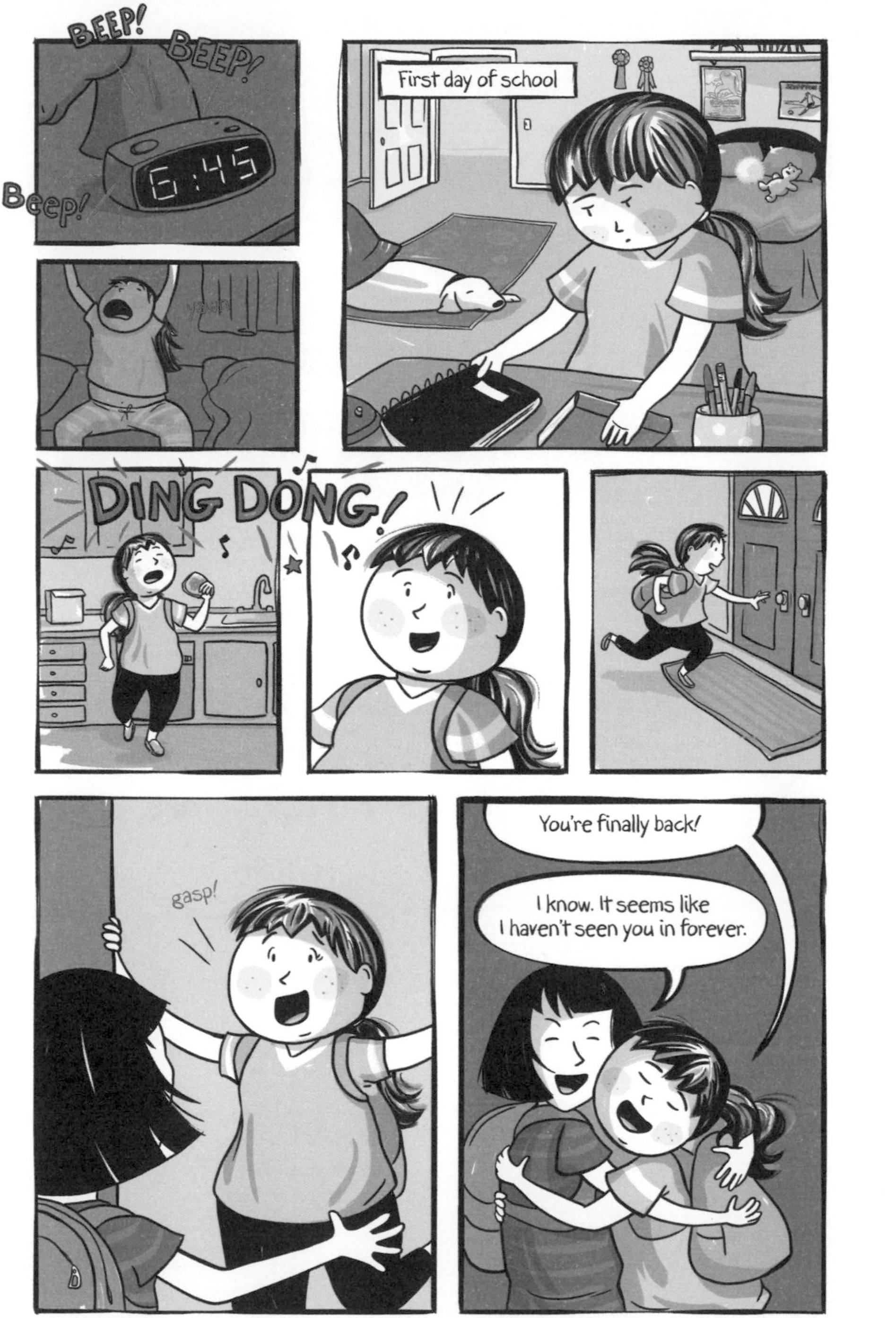
BEEP!
BEEP!
Beep!
First day of school
DING DONG!
gasp!
You're finally back!
I know. It seems like
I haven't seen you in forever.

234

235

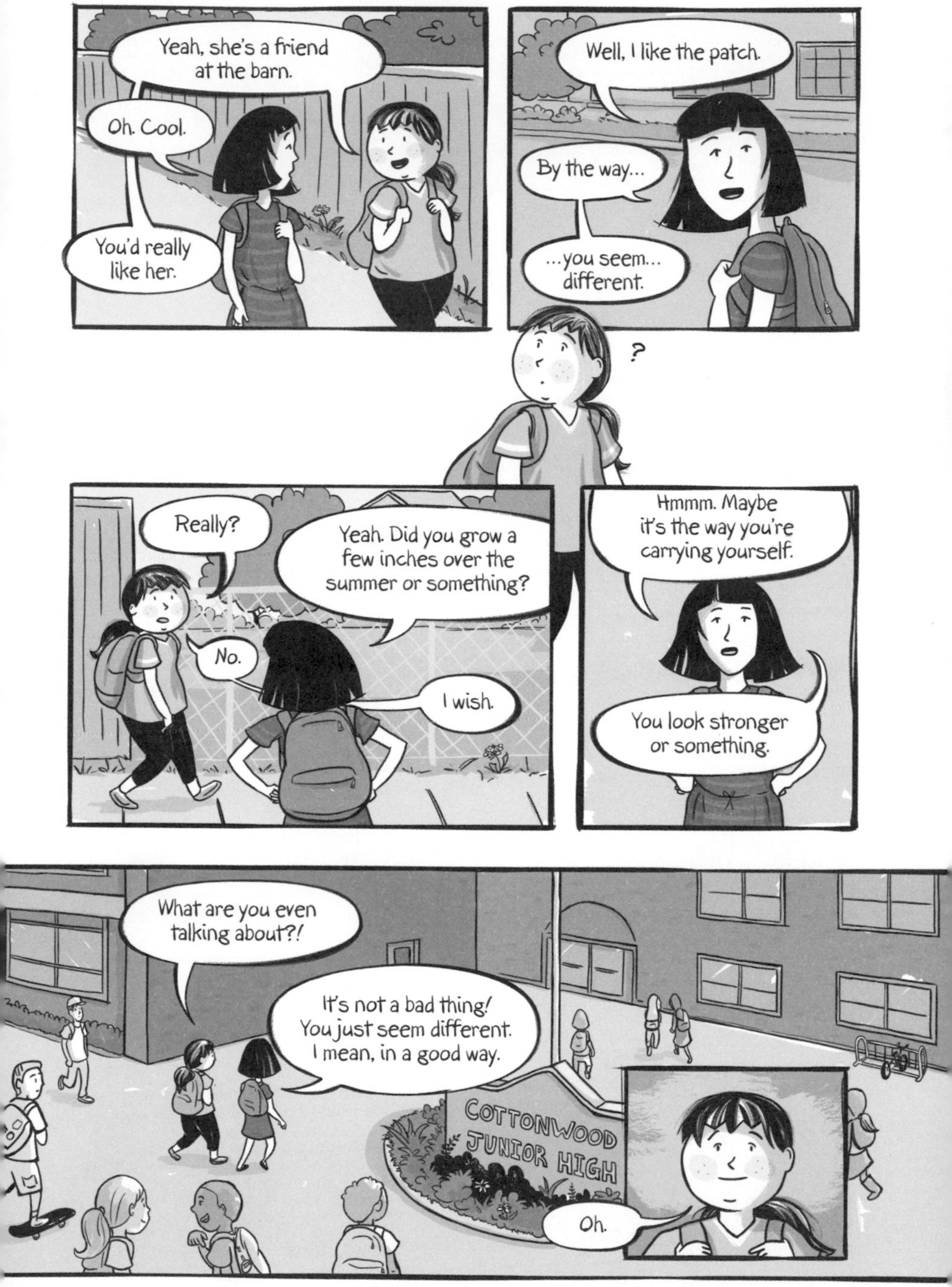
Yeah, she's a friend at the barn.
Oh. Cool.
You'd really like her.
Well, I like the patch.
By the way...
...you seem... different.
?
Really?
Yeah. Did you grow a few inches over the summer or something?
No.
I wish.
Hmmm. Maybe it's the way you're carrying yourself.
You look stronger or something.
What are you even talking about?!
It's not a bad thing! You just seem different. I mean, in a good way.
COTTONWOOD JUNIOR HIGH
Oh.

238

239

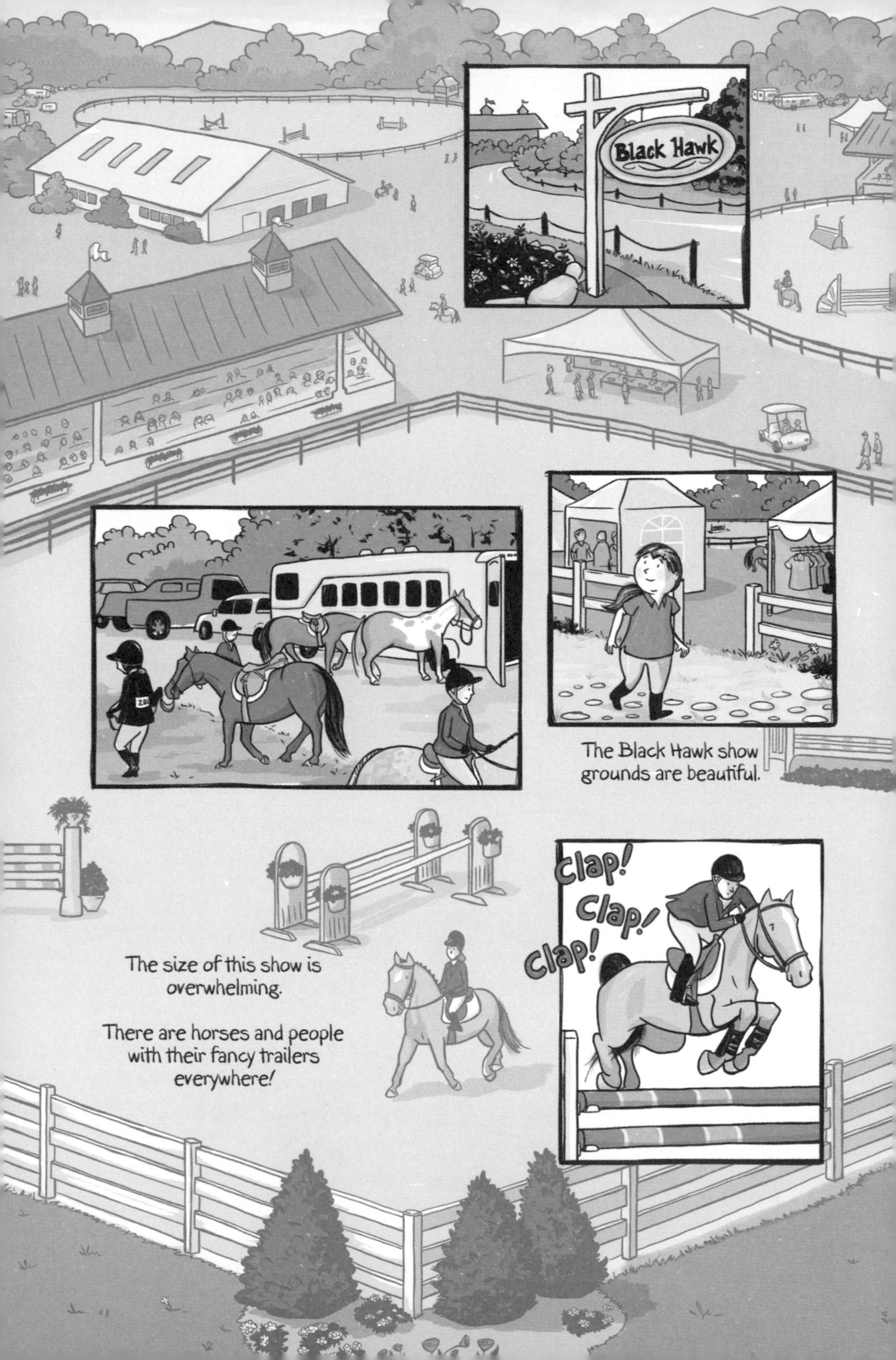
Black Hawk
The Black Hawk show grounds are beautiful.
The size of this show is overwhelming.
There are horses and people with their fancy trailers everywhere!
Clap!
Clap!
Clap!

246

249

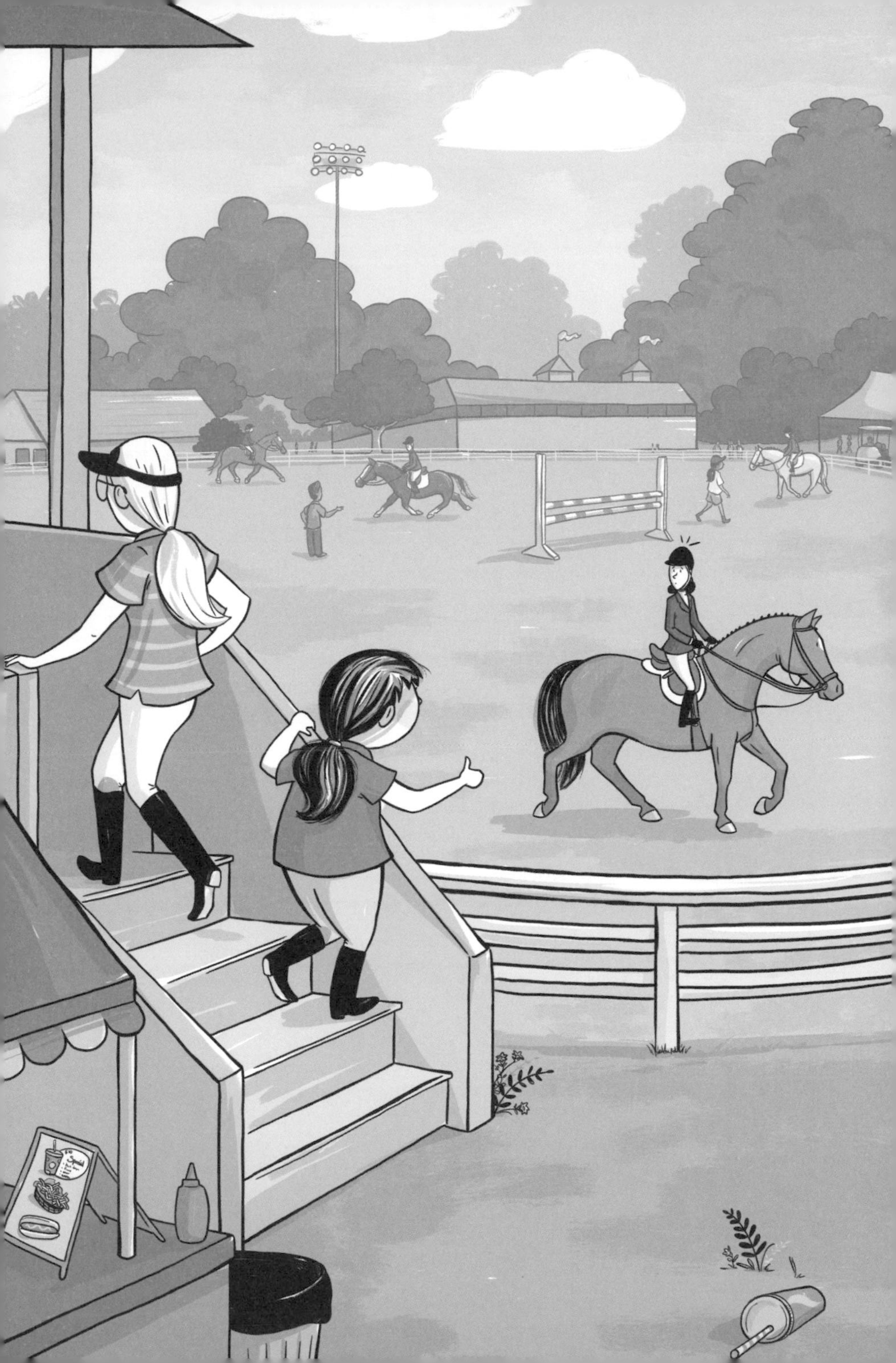

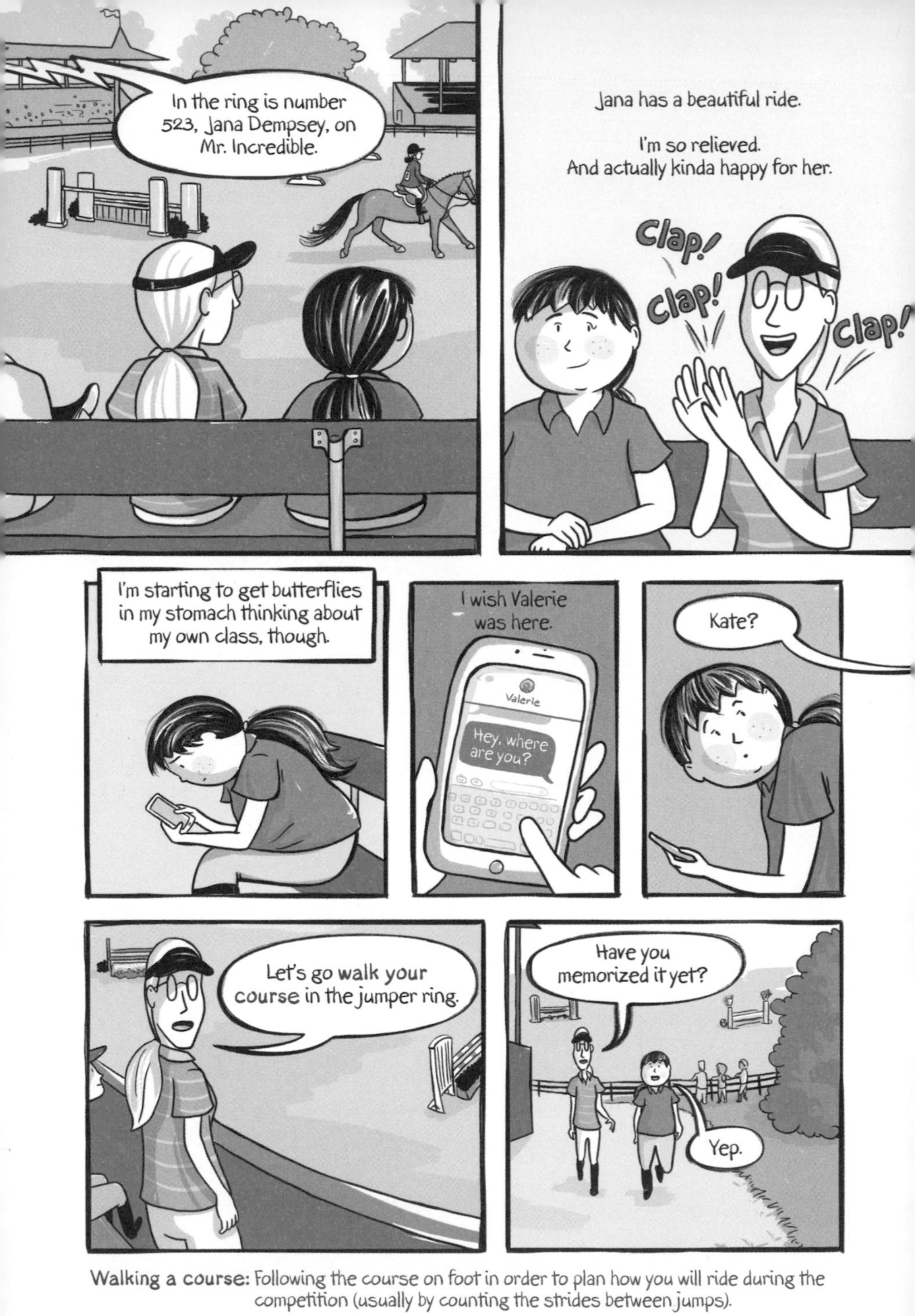
In the ring is number 523, Jana Dempsey, on Mr. Incredible.
Jana has a beautiful ride.
I'm so relieved.
And actually kinda happy for her.
Clap!
Clap!
Clap!
I'm starting to get butterflies in my stomach thinking about my own class, though.
I wish Valerie was here.
Valerie
Hey, where are you?
Kate?
Let's go walk your course in the jumper ring.
Have you memorized it yet?
Yep.

Walking a course: Following the course on foot in order to plan how you will ride during the competition (usually by counting the strides between jumps).

Jump-off: The second round of a jumper class, in which all riders without faults (no rails knocked down or time penalties), advance to ride another shortened version of the course to determine final placement. The rider with the fastest time wins the class.

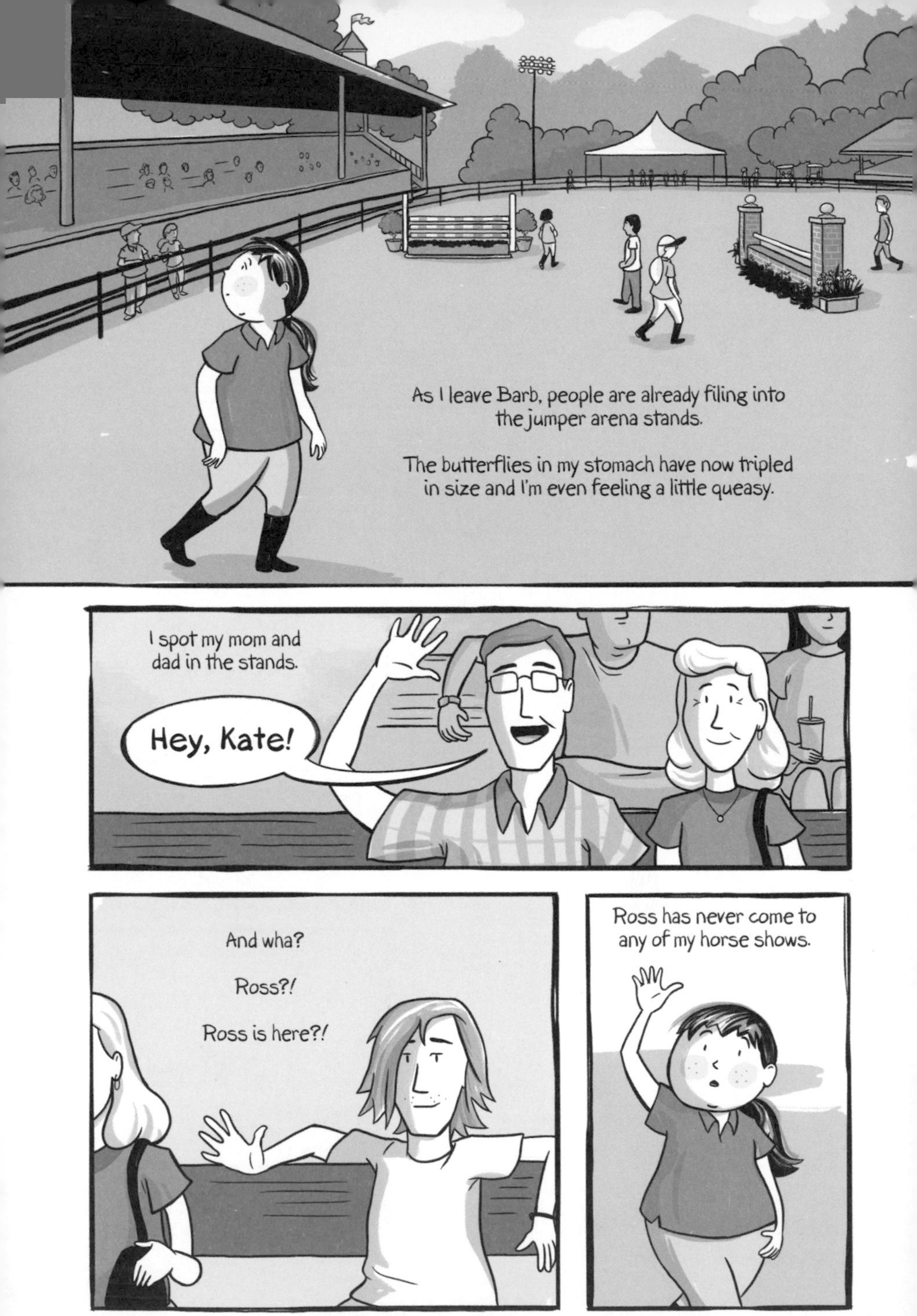
As I leave Barb, people are already filing into the jumper arena stands.
The butterflies in my stomach have now tripled in size and I'm even feeling a little queasy.
I spot my mom and dad in the stands.
Hey, Kate!
And wha?
Ross?!
Ross is here?!
Ross has never come to any of my horse shows.

Thirty minutes later, I've got Pizza ready. I have myself ready.
I do a time check and see a text from Valerie.

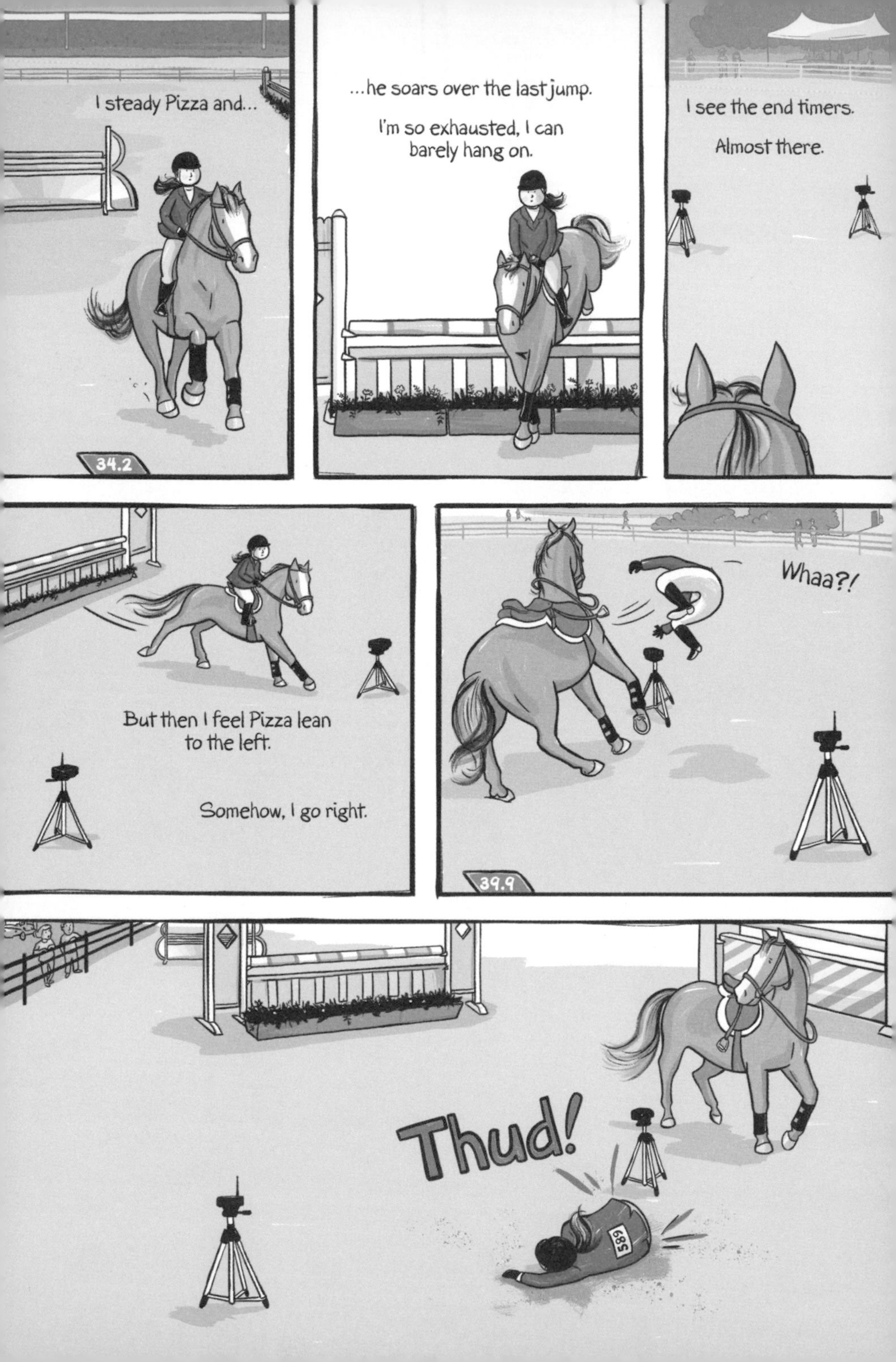
I steady Pizza and...
34.2
...he soars over the last jump.
I'm so exhausted, I can barely hang on.
I see the end timers.
Almost there.
But then I feel Pizza lean to the left.
Somehow, I go right.
Whaa?!
39.9
Thud!
589

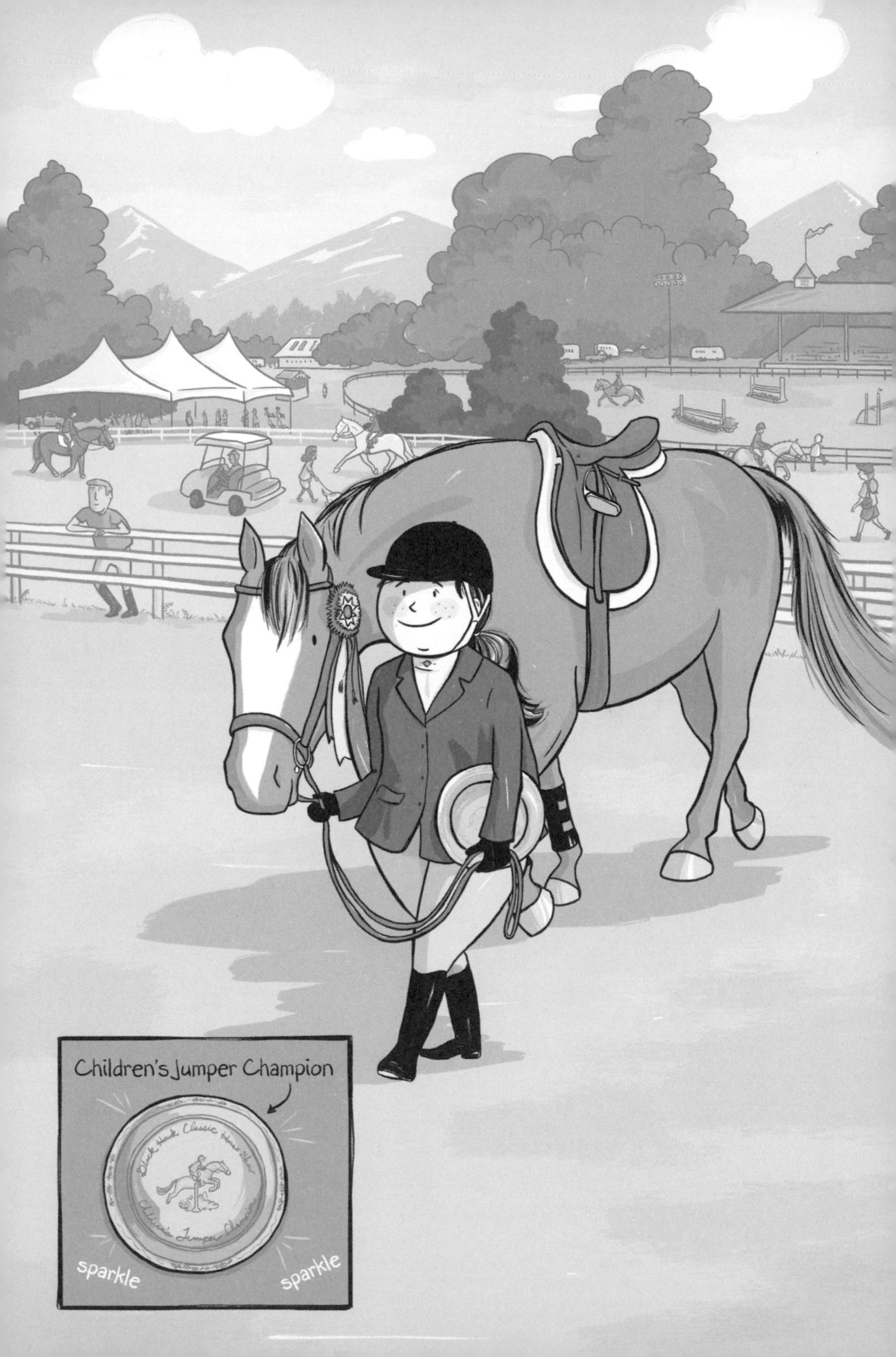
Children's Jumper Champion
Black Hawk Classic Horse Show
Children's Jumper Champion
sparkle
sparkle

264

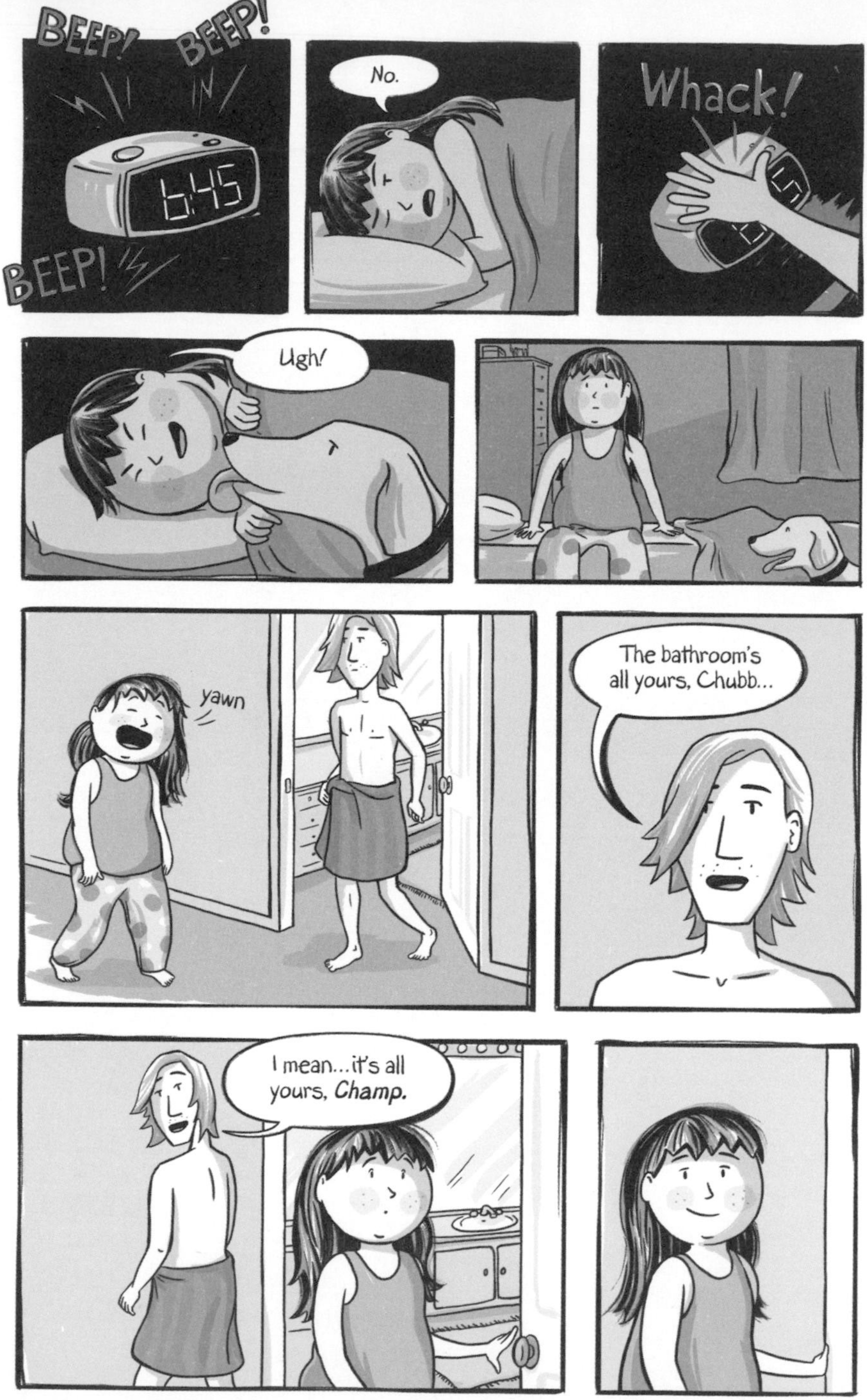
BEEP! BEEP!
6:45
BEEP!
No.
Whack!
Ugh!
yawn
The bathroom's all yours, Chubb...
I mean... it's all yours, *Champ.*

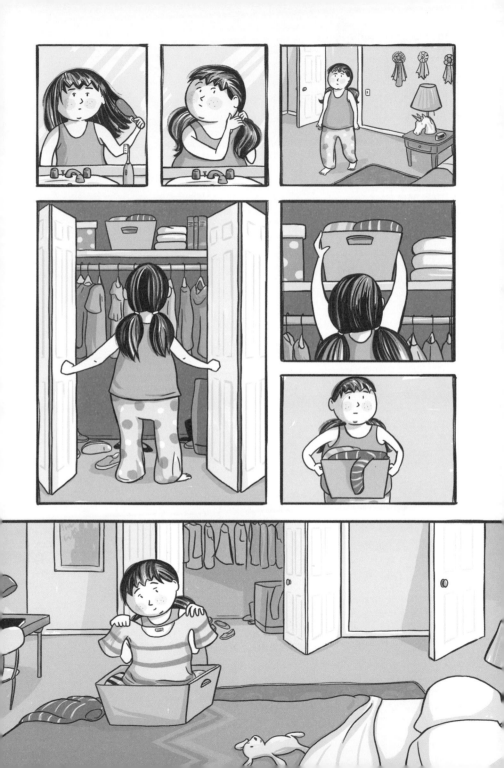

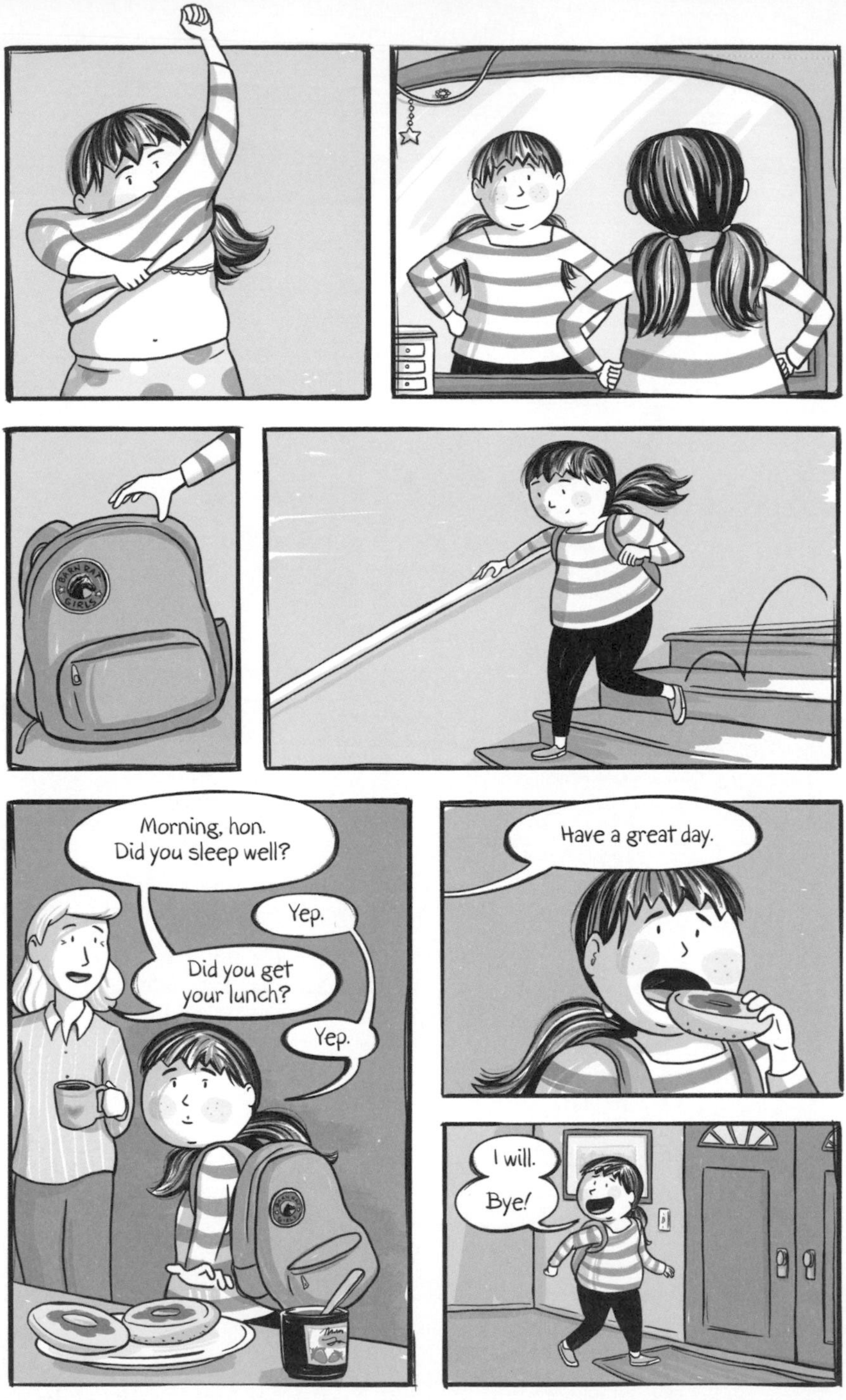

BARN RAT GIRLS
Morning, hon. Did you sleep well?
Yep.
Did you get your lunch?
Yep.
Have a great day.
I will.
Bye!

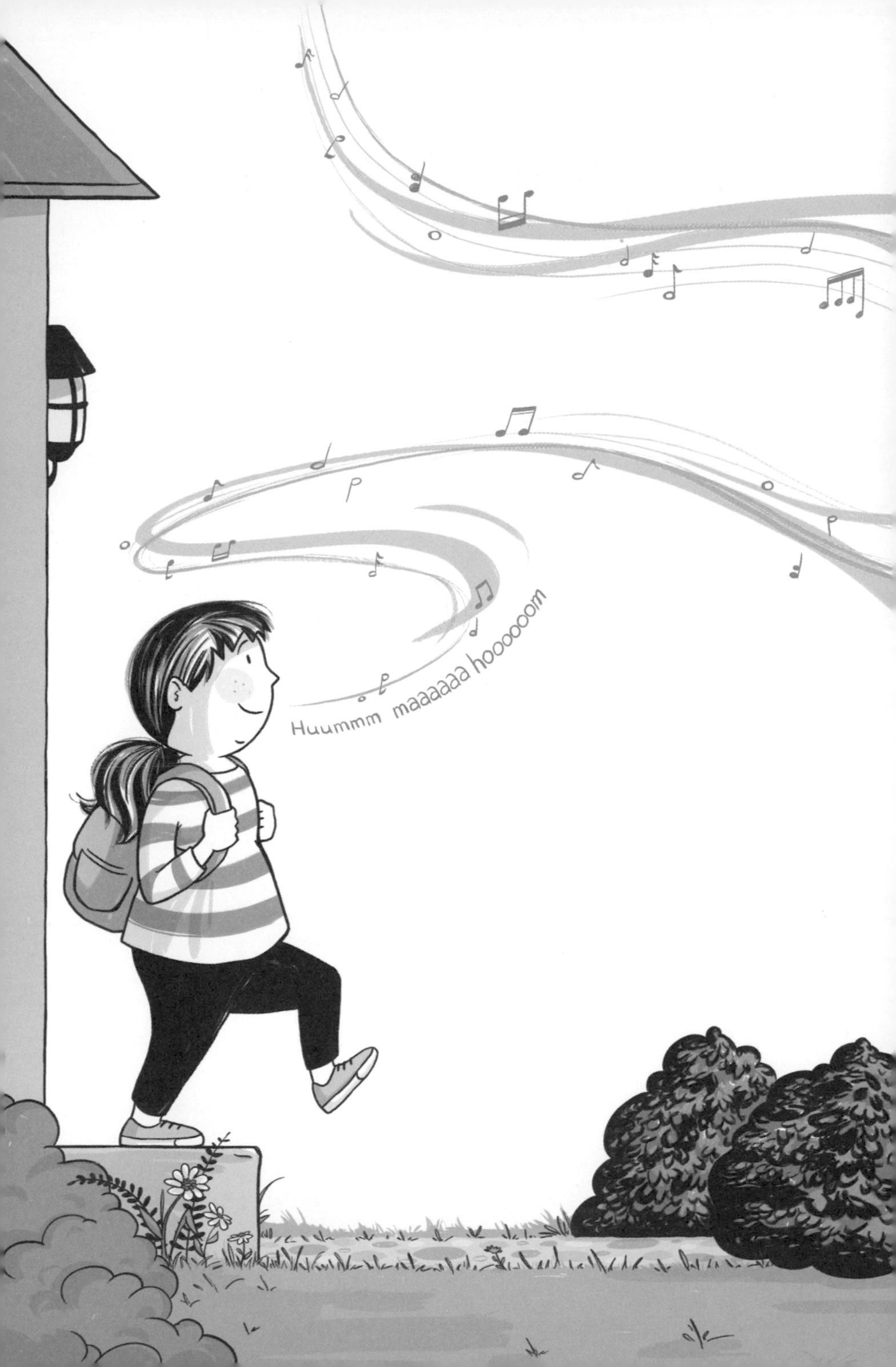
Huummm maaaaaa hoooooom

Author's Note

Although this book is not a memoir, it is inspired by many of my childhood experiences that actually did happen.

It all started at Trefoil Ranch, where I rode horses at camp the summer before starting fourth grade. From then on, I was a bona fide horse nut. I hung horse posters and calendars all over my bedroom walls. I drew endless pictures of them and started collecting models. I devoured horse books and subscribed to riding magazines. Every year I asked Santa for a horse for Christmas. I begged and pleaded for lessons and eventually began riding regularly at various barns. At the age of fourteen, after years of chores, lessons, and showing, I was extremely lucky and finally got my very own horse.

My years spent with horses are some of my most cherished memories. Anyone who shares the passion for these magnificent creatures understands how strong the bond between horse and rider can become. But along with the love and devotion come the hardships, like falling off. There are ten times that Kate falls off her horse in this book. All of those falls are based on true stories. Five of them are my own, and the others I collected from friends. Falling off is hard, and can be terrifying, but getting back on is by far the most difficult part.

The relationships that develop between riders at barns can be hardships, too. The Jana in this book didn't actually exist—not at my barn anyway, where I was fortunate enough to experience a genuine camaraderie and form some lifelong friendships. That's not to say I never encountered any bullying, it just wasn't in the riding arena. I was a chubby kid throughout my childhood—the subject of fat jokes and name-calling that happened at school, dance class, the swimming pool, and all around my neighborhood. I still see myself as "the fat kid," and probably always will. It's an identity that even today as an adult I have found difficult to shed. I know I'm not alone in feeling body insecurities or being called names. My hope in writing *Horse Trouble* is that it might let some kids know that they're not alone, either.

There is no doubt in my mind that riding horses gave me the strength both physically and mentally to persevere through many of my crummiest situations in childhood. I could always escape through horses, but the grit and tenacity I gained from riding them, being thrown off, and climbing back on again...and again, forced me to become confident and trust myself. Horses not only made me strong, but they helped me decide who I should be, giving me a strong sense of self. Maybe this story can help other kids to do the same. At least, I hope that it will be an inspiration to follow your passion through the best and worst moments, whether it be playing sports, performing on stage, creating cool stuff...or even just loving a big, four-legged animal.

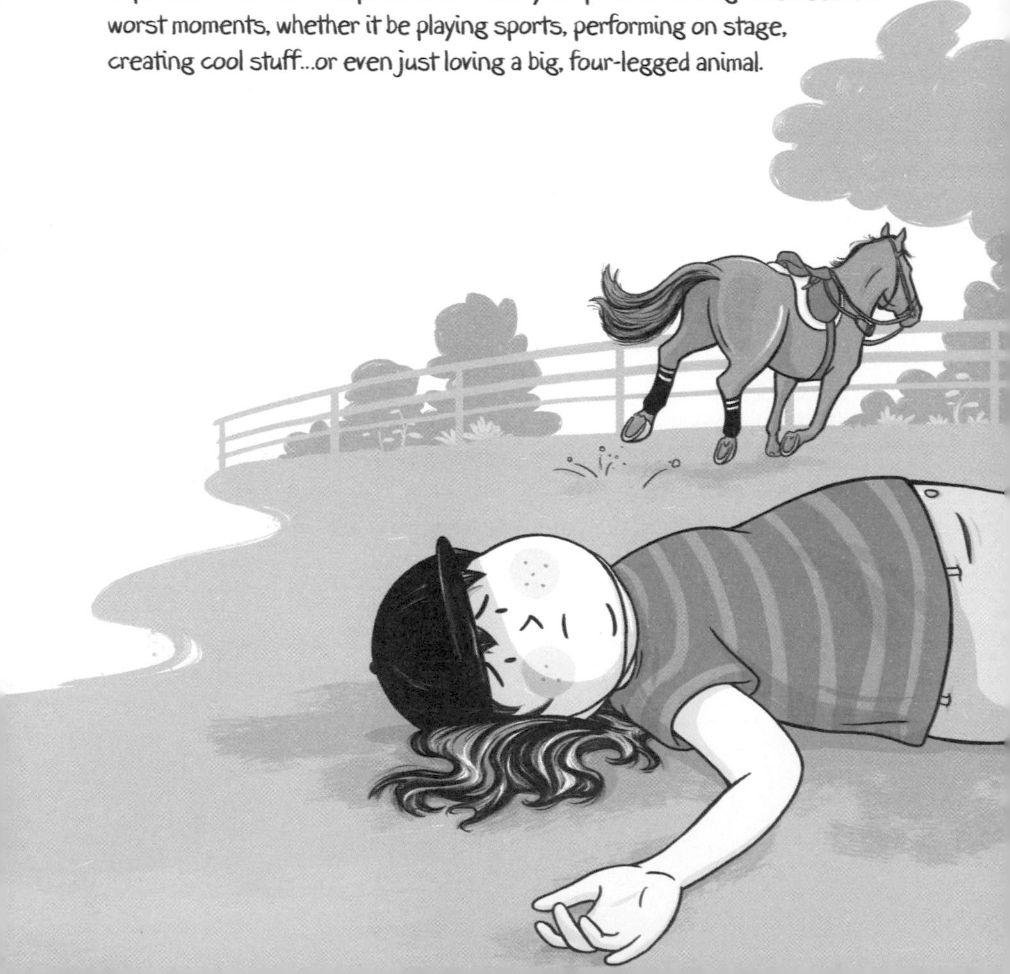

Fourth Grade

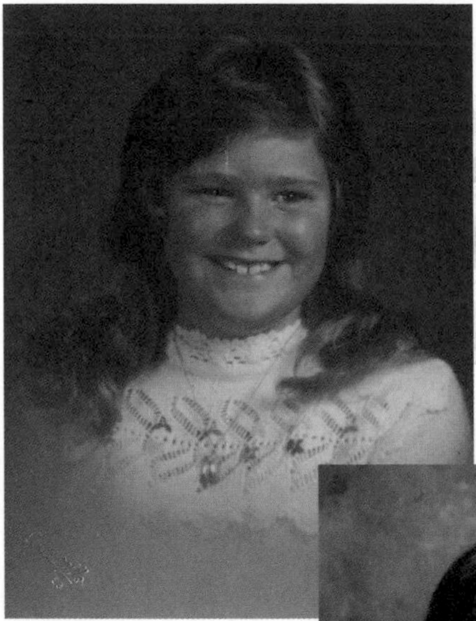

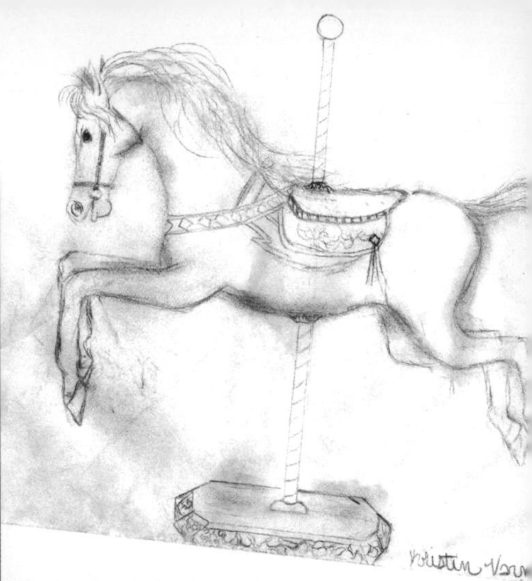

Sixth Grade

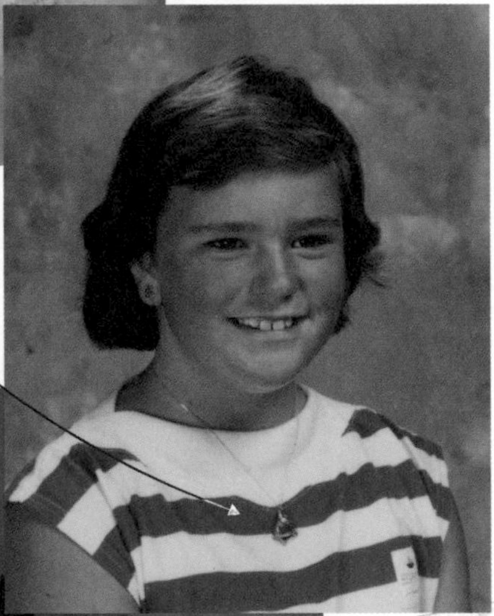

my old drawings

horse necklace!

Seventh Grade

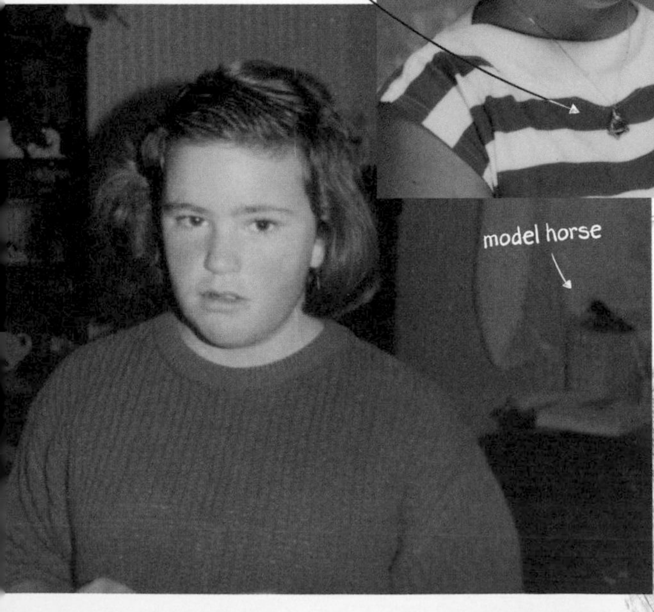
model horse

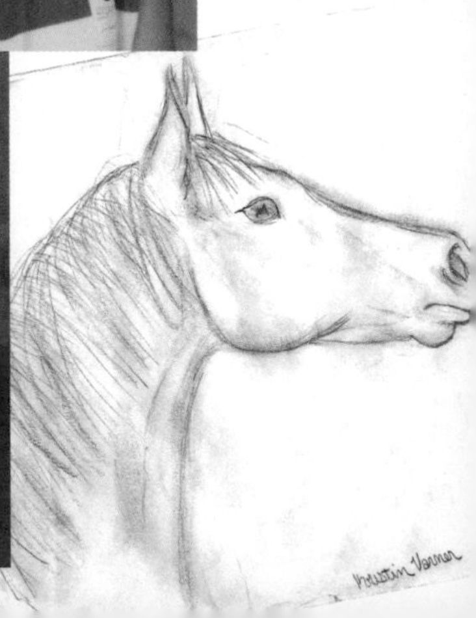

Riding my horse, Doc

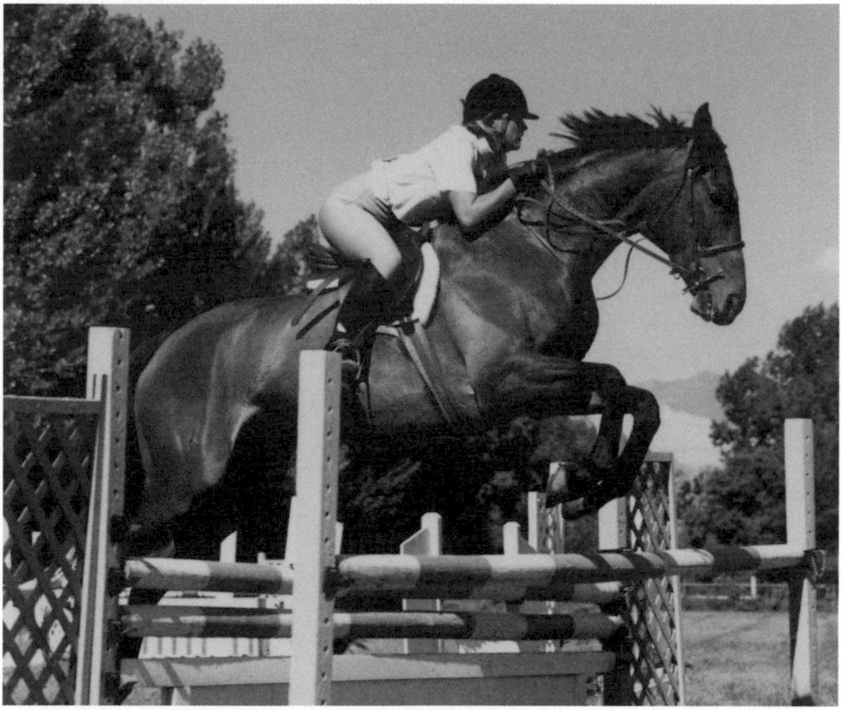

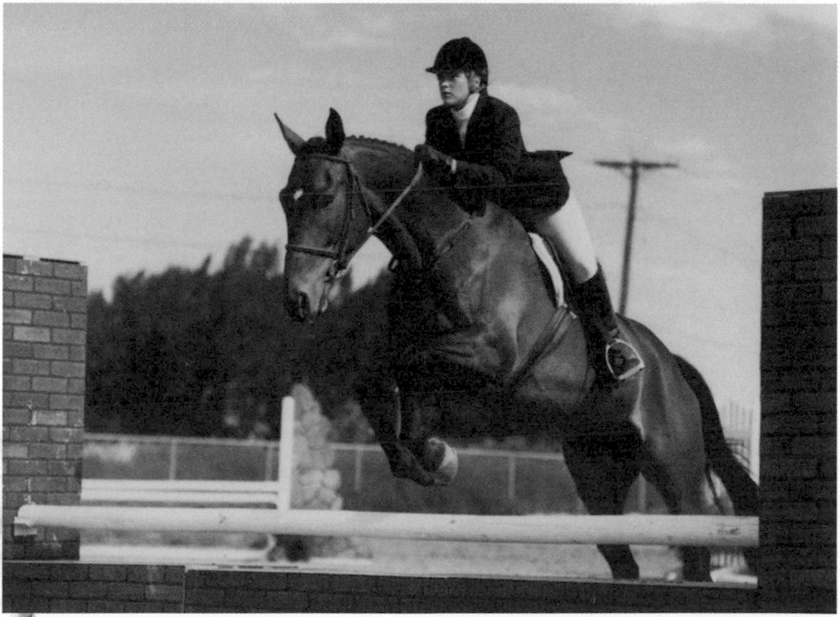

Horse show photos by Pam Olsen of Pro Photo

Early character sketches

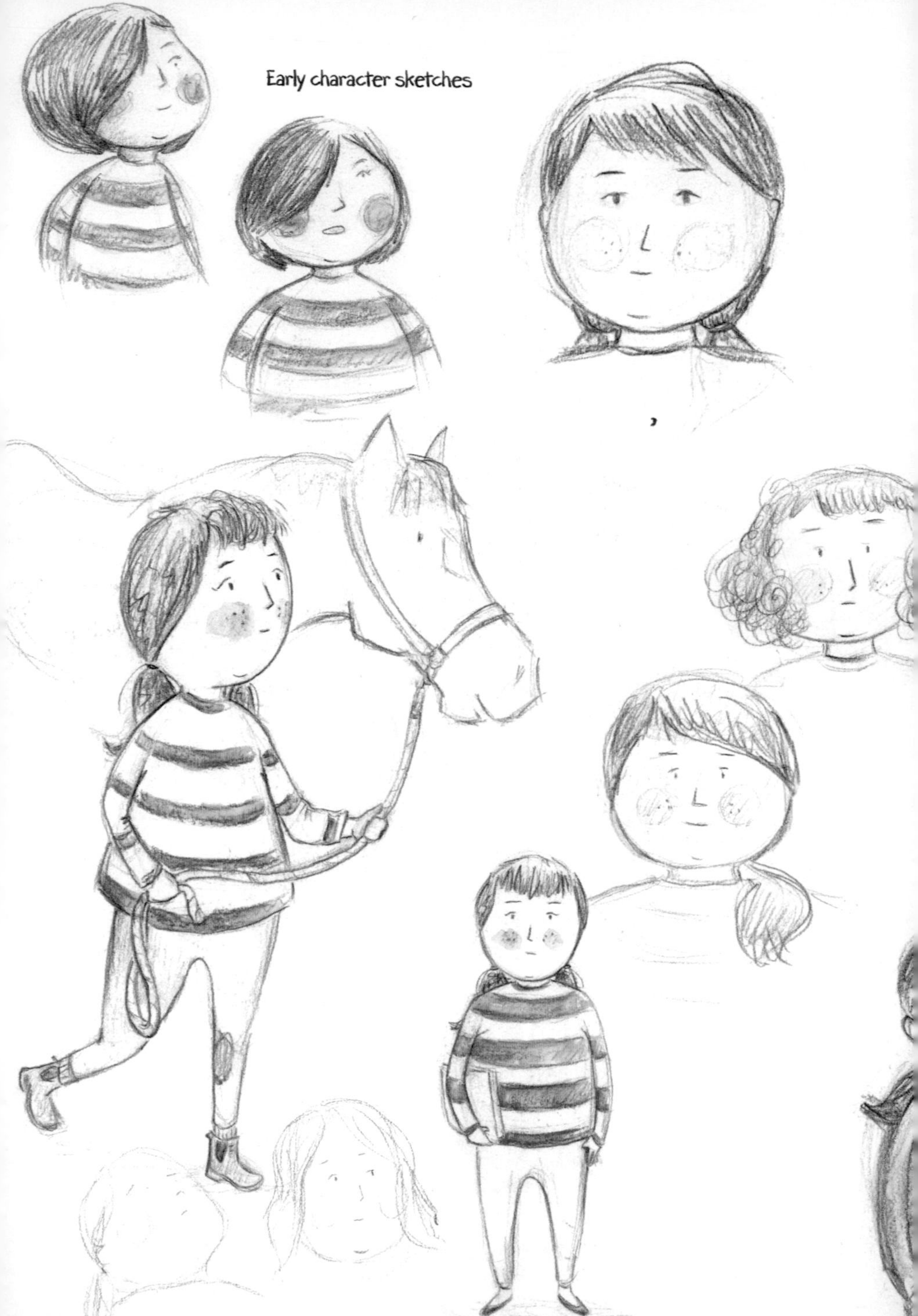

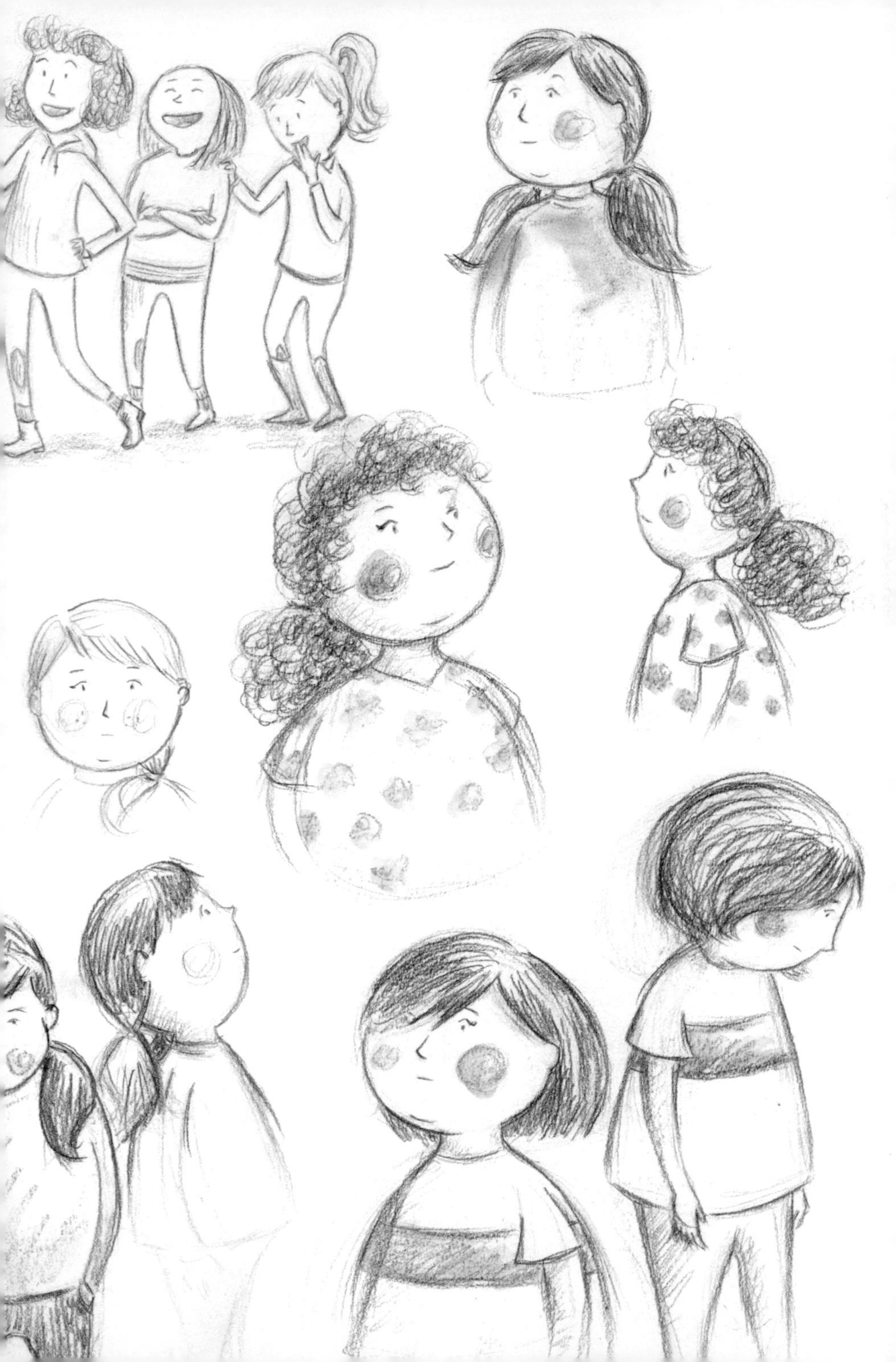

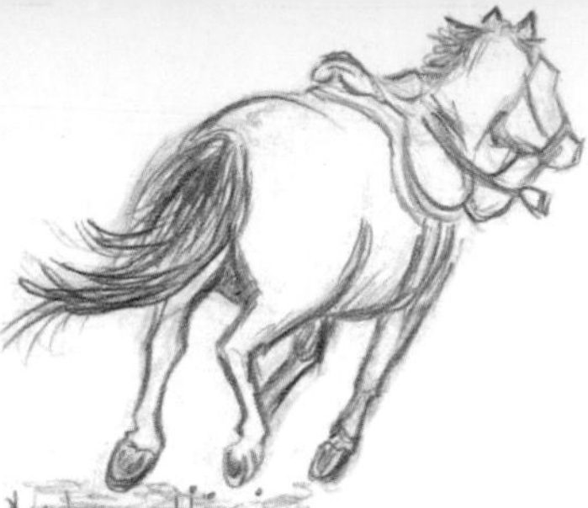

Cover Sketches

A lot of sketches were done for the cover of this book! These are just a few of them.

The original title was *Ten Times I Fell Off My Horse* (*Horse Trouble* is a little shorter).

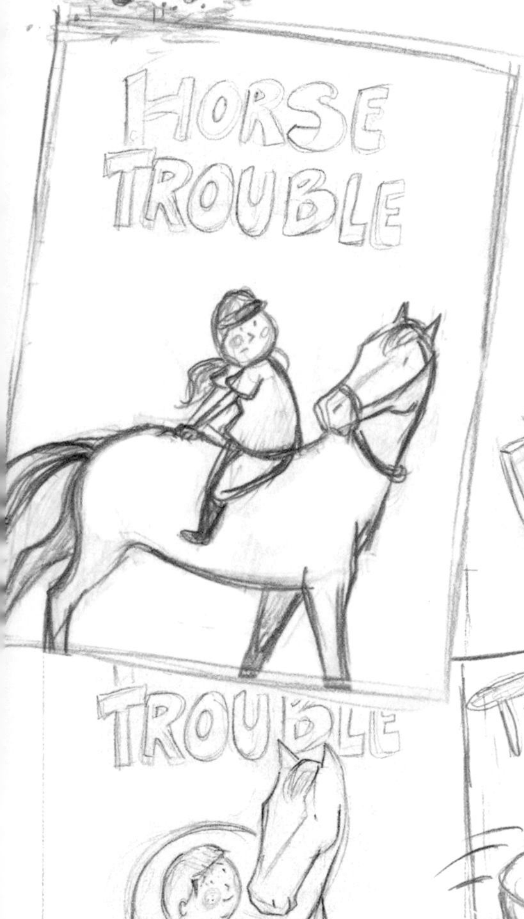
HORSE
TROUBLE

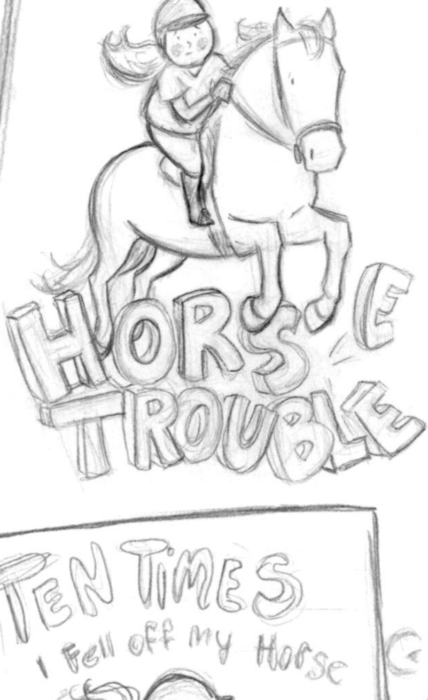
HORSE
TROUBLE

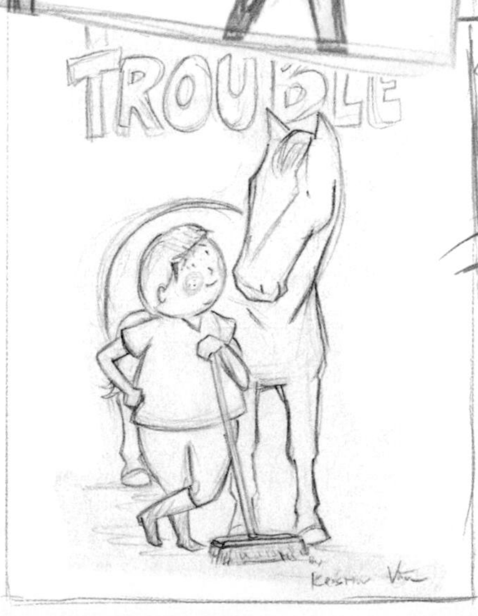
TROUBLE

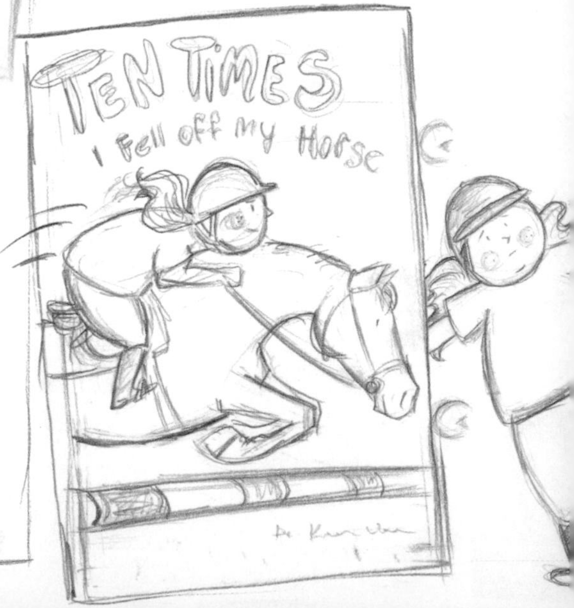
TEN TIMES
I Fell off my Horse

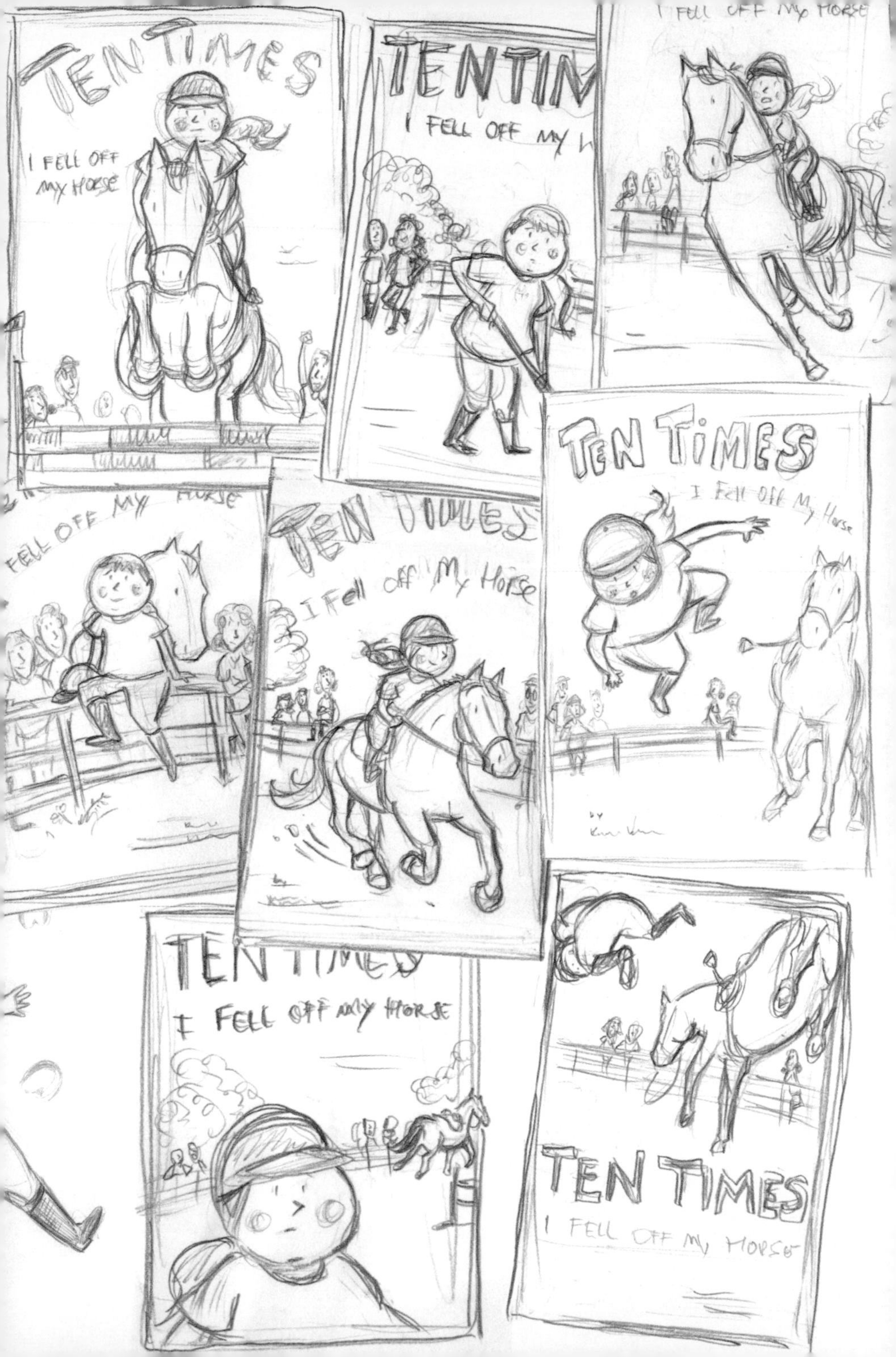
TEN TIMES
I FELL OFF MY HORSE
TENTIM
I FELL OFF MY H
I FELL OFF MY HORSE
FELL OFF MY HORSE
I FELL OFF MY HORSE
TEN TIMES
I FELL OFF MY HORSE
by
TEN TIMES
I FELL OFF MY HORSE
TEN TIMES
I FELL OFF MY HORSE

My Process

① The first stage of the book is the script. I print out each chapter to determine the page turns and story layout. I will often scribble out dialogue or make changes to the text as I go.

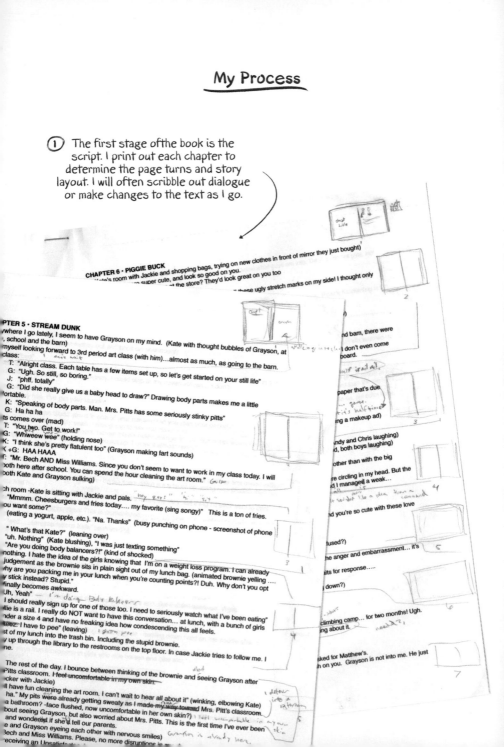

CHAPTER 6 · PIGGIE BUCK
...te's room with Jackie and shopping bags, trying on new clothes in front of mirror they just bought)
...n super cute, and look so good on you.
...n the store? They'd look great on you too
" ...hose ugly stretch marks on my side! I thought only

..PTER 5 · STREAM DUNK
..where I go lately, I seem to have Grayson on my mind. (Kate with thought bubbles of Grayson, at .., school and the barn)
..myself looking forward to 3rd period art class (with him)...almost as much, as going to the barn.
class:
   T: "Alright class. Each table has a few items set up, so let's get started on your still life"
   G: "Ugh. So still, so boring."
   J: "phff. totally"
   G: "Did she really give us a baby head to draw?" Drawing body parts makes me a little ..ortable.
   K: "Speaking of body parts. Man. Mrs. Pitts has some seriously stinky pitts"
   G: Ha ha ha
..ts comes over (mad)
   T: "You two. Get to work!"
   G: "Whweew wee" (holding nose)
   K: "I think she's pretty flatulent too" (Grayson making fart sounds)
   K+G: HAA HAAA
   T: "Mr. Bech AND Miss Williams. Since you don't seem to want to work in my class today. I will ..oth here after school. You can spend the hour cleaning the art room." Gulp.
..ch room -Kate is sitting with Jackie and pals.
"Mmmm. Cheeseburgers and fries today... my favorite (sing songy)" This is a ton of fries.
..ou want some?"
..(eating a yogurt, apple, etc.). "Na. Thanks" (busy punching on phone - screenshot of phone)

" What's that Kate?" (leaning over)
"..uh. Nothing" (Kate blushing), "I was just texting something"
"Are you doing body balancers?!" (kind of shocked)
..nothing. I hate the idea of the girls knowing that I'm on a weight loss program. I can already
..hy are you packing me in your lunch when you're counting points?! Duh. Why don't you opt
..y stick instead? Stupid."
..finally becomes awkward.
..Uh, Yeah"
..I should really sign up for one of those too. I need to seriously watch what I've been eating"
..llie is a rail. I really do NOT want to have this conversation... at lunch, with a bunch of girls
..nder a size 4 and have no freaking idea how condescending this all feels.
..uez. I have to pee" (leaving)
..st of my lunch into the trash bin. Including the stupid brownie.
..y up through the library to the restrooms on the top floor. In case Jackie tries to follow me. I
..ne.

..The rest of the day. I bounce between thinking of the brownie and seeing Grayson after
..Pitts classroom. I feel uncomfortable in my own skin.
..cker with Jackie)
..ha." My pits were already getting sweaty as I made my way toward Mrs. Pitt's classroom.
..a bathroom? -face flushed, now uncomfortable in her own skin?)
..bout seeing Grayson, but also worried about Mrs. Pitts. This is the first time I've ever been
..and wondered if she'd tell our parents.
..e and Grayson eyeing each other with nervous smiles)
..Bech and Miss Williams. Please, no more disruptions in..
..eceiving an Unsatisf..

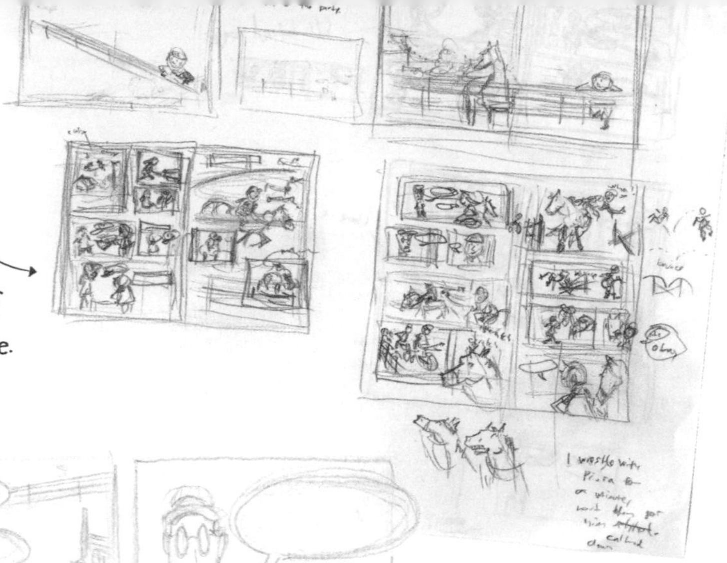

(2) Then I draw quick thumbnail sketches of the pages.

These are super messy and only make sense to me.

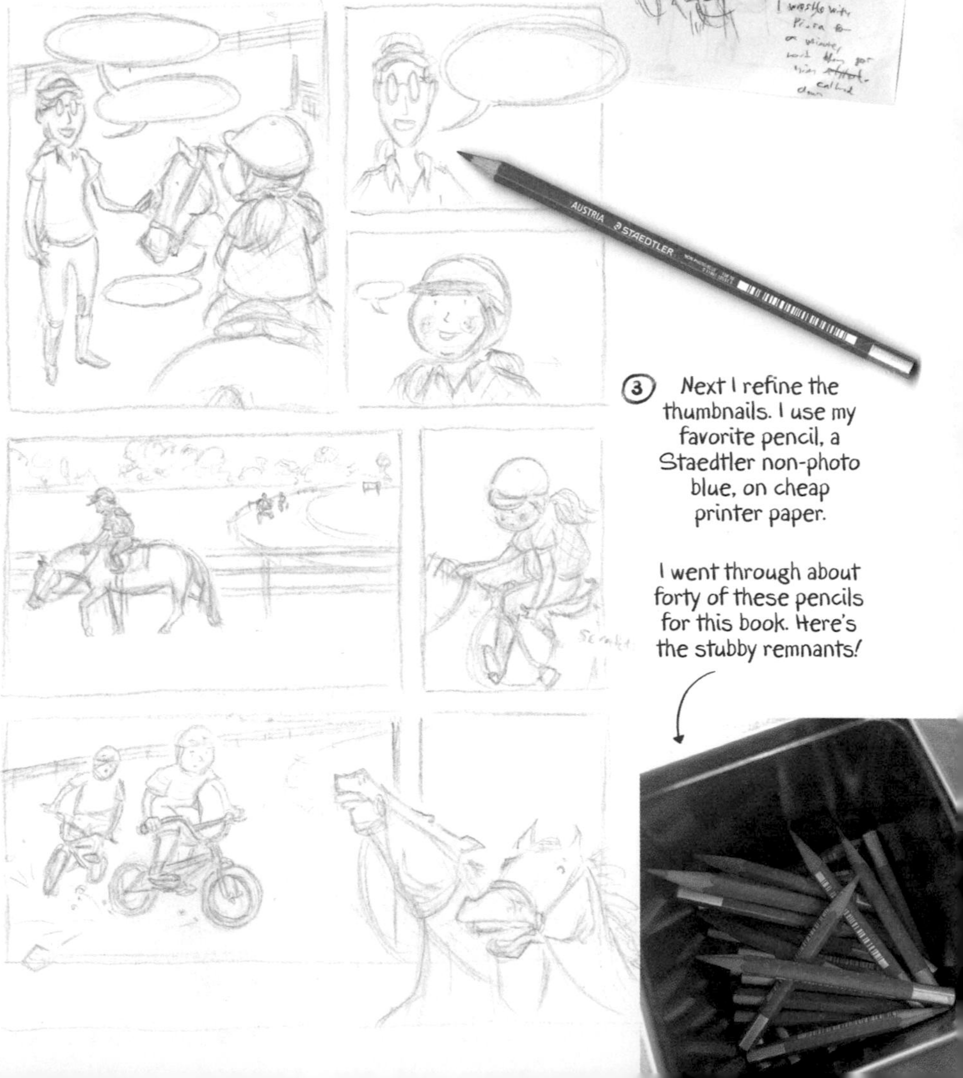

AUSTRIA STAEDTLER

(3) Next I refine the thumbnails. I use my favorite pencil, a Staedtler non-photo blue, on cheap printer paper.

I went through about forty of these pencils for this book. Here's the stubby remnants!

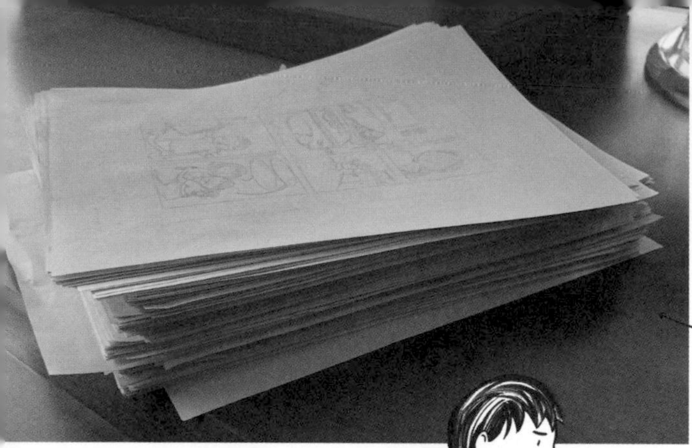

(4) All the sketches are scanned into my computer There are about three hundred pages in this stack.

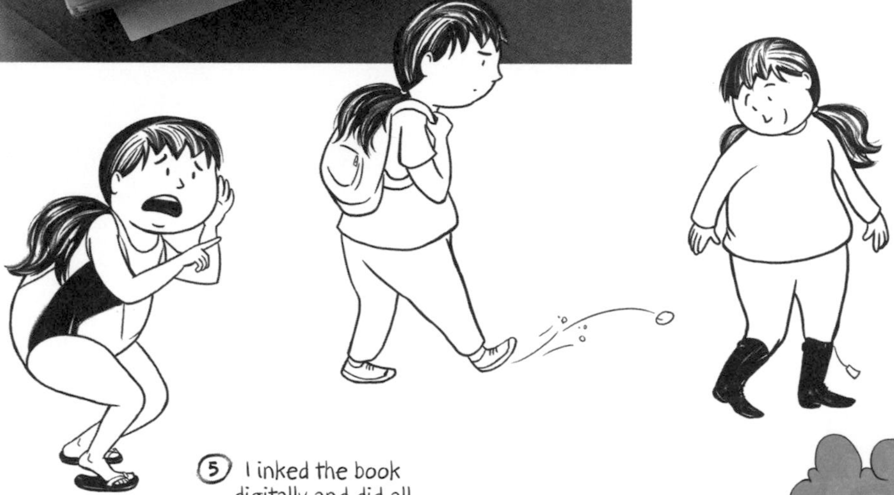

(5) I inked the book digitally and did all the coloring in Photoshop.

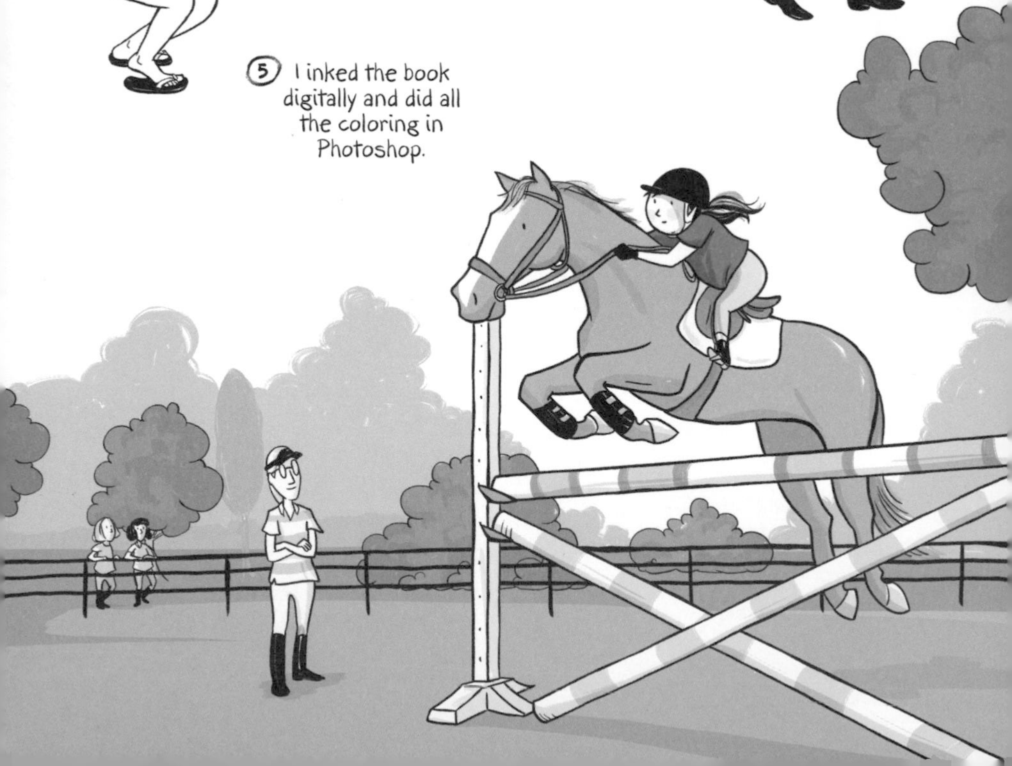

Acknowledgments

There are so many people who have helped make this book possible and I am forever grateful for their support and assistance. Thank you...

- to my amazing agent, Teresa Kietlinski, who not only opened this door for me but also pushed me to write this book. I am still bewildered at her foresight, for realizing this story within me and having absolute confidence and trust that I could execute it.

- to dear friends Laura Cary, Magan Payne, Holly Walker Davis, Vivian Nesbitt, Paula Dare, and Brent Swartz for openly sharing their own stories of riding horses, their experiences of barn life, and their best and worst falls!

- to my wonderful editors (and I was so fortunate to have two of them!), Robyn Chapman and Rachel Stark. Thank you for providing the most excellent guidance and for shaping this story into something that greatly surpassed my initial vision. And, to the entire team at First Second, for making this dream become a reality.

- to Allie Wicks, a partner in crime in some of my favorite riding memories, who was my equestrian expert for this book and fact checker for the current horse show industry. An extra special shout-out to her mother, Barbara Wicks, who was my trainer and the real inspiration behind Barb in the story.

- to all the barns of my past, especially Rose Ranch. May they always be places of magic.

- to Angélica Esquivel for advising and checking all my use of Spanish!

- to Ian Webster for lending a helping hand with his Photoshop wizardry.

- to the Stonich and Triplett families for providing insight with middle-grade lingo.

- to my childhood friends and family, my muses for this story, for patiently standing by my horse obsession over the years.

- and lastly, to Michael for bearing the brunt of this exhausting journey—all the while cheering me on—and to Francis, for being my #1 fan.

FRIENDS! MUSIC! MYSTERY!

These great graphic novels have it all!

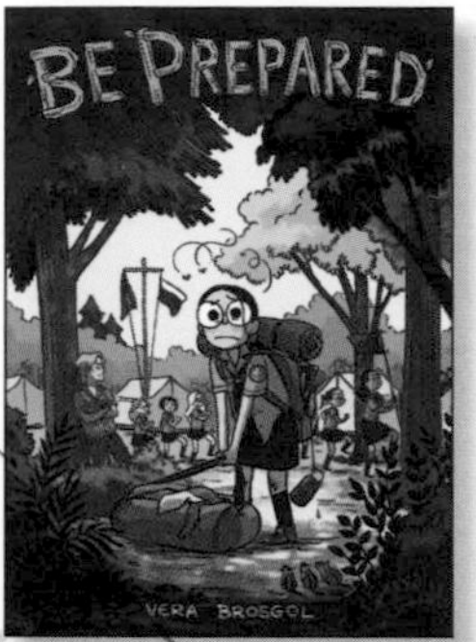
BE PREPARED
VERA BROSGOL

BE PREPARED
by Vera Brosgol

Come along with Vera as she goes to summer camp for the first time ever!

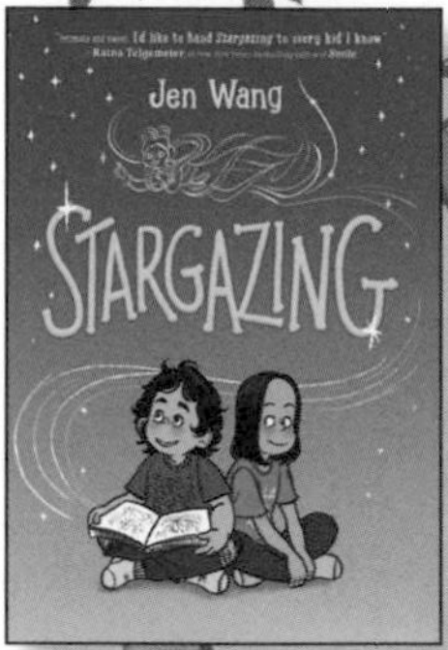
Jen Wang
STARGAZING

STARGAZING
by Jen Wang

Meet Christine and Moon, two friends who have a lot in common, but who couldn't be more different!

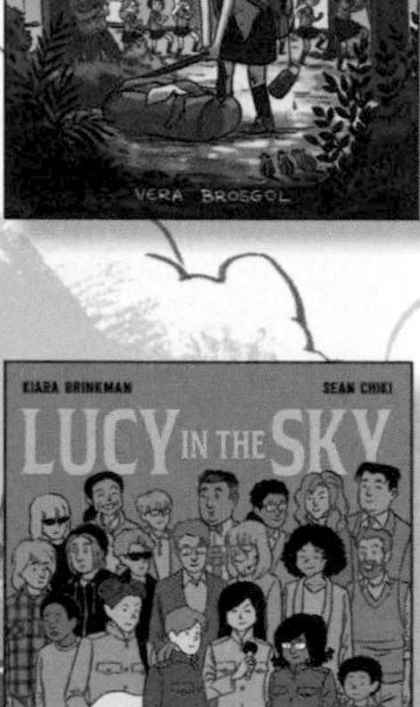
KIARA BRINKMAN
SEAN CHIKI
LUCY IN THE SKY

LUCY IN THE SKY
by Kiara Brinkman and Sean Chiki

Join Lucy as she starts a rock band with her three best friends!

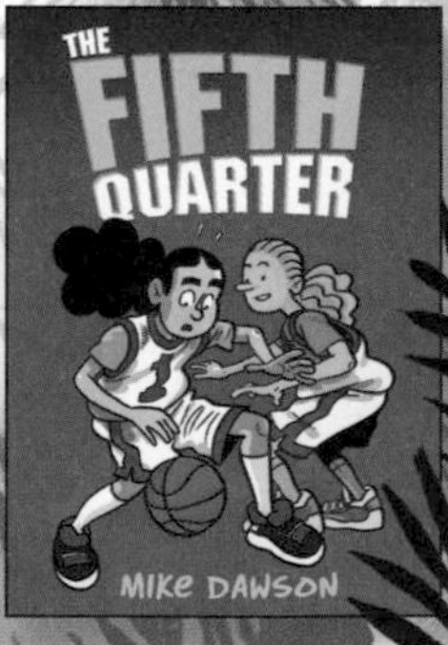
THE FIFTH QUARTER
MIKE DAWSON

THE FIFTH QUARTER
by Mike Dawson

Follow Lori as she tries to gain self-confidence in school, at home, and on the court!

Great graphic novels for every reader